USS Resilience

Honor the Fallen

USS Hamilton Series
Book 11

Mark Wayne McGinnis

Copyright © 2024, by Mark Wayne McGinnis. All rights reserved. No part of this publication may be reproduced, distributed, or transmitted in any form or by any means, including photocopying, recording, or other electronic or mechanical methods, without the prior written permission of the publisher, except in the case of brief quotations embodied in critical reviews and certain other noncommercial uses permitted by copyright law. For permission requests, write to the publisher, addressed "Attention: Permissions Coordinator," to the email address below. This is a work of fiction. Apart from well-known historical figures and actual people, events, and locales that figure in the narrative, all other characters are products of the author's imagination and are not to be construed as real. Any resemblance to persons, living or dead, is entirely coincidental. Where real-life historical persons appear, the situations, incidents, and dialogues concerning those persons are not intended to change the entirely fictional nature of the work.

Published by Avenstar Productions: info@avenstar.net

USS Resilience Paperback

ISBN: 979-8-9894619-9-8

To join Mark's mailing list, jump to:

http://eepurl.com/bs7M9r

Visit Mark Wayne McGinnis at:

http://www.markwaynemcginnis.com

 Created with Vellum

Foreword

By Captain Galvin Quintos

Okay, listen up, space cadets. It's time for a history lesson, and I promise it's more exciting than watching paint dry on a bulkhead.

Picture this: It's 2048, and Earth's just doing its thing, probably arguing about politics or something, when suddenly —WHAM—we get visitors from space. Not just any visitors, mind you, but the Thine. Now, these Thine are a real trip. Imagine super-intelligent worms, about a thousand years ahead of us in the brains department, but with all the physical prowess of a limp noodle.

See, these crafty worms had been spying on us for a while now. They saw how we humans were always ready for a scrap (currently, amongst ourselves) but still had a decent moral compass. In their assessment, that made us prime galactic partner material. Why, you ask? Well, the Thine had a bit of a problem. Some nasty customers called the Grish had been knocking on their door, and the Thine were worried they'd be worm chow if they didn't find some muscle, fast.

Foreword

So, they show up on Earth, basically saying, *Hey, humans! We've got the brains; you've got the brawn. Wanna team up?* Little did we know, we were about to get our own unwelcome visit from the Grish piglets. Talk about a cosmic coincidence, right?

Next thing you know, we're upgrading from fossil fuels to faster-than-light travel quicker than you can say, *beam me up*. Some clever eggheads, probably hopped up on too much coffee and old *Star Trek* reruns, started using the term 'DecaTrek'. It's just a fancy way of saying, *holy cow, that's fast*—ten times the speed of light, to be exact.

On a side note, and to make things even more mind-blowing, the most advanced 22nd-century spacecraft can also call up what is called a 'manufactured wormhole'. Thanks to the Thine again, this technology generates and stabilizes exotic matter to connect a black hole's event horizon to a white hole's, creating a spacetime shortcut for rapid travel. The real magic? Preventing the wormhole from collapsing mid-journey. So, not only can we zip around the galaxy faster than light, but we can also take advantage of interstellar shortcuts.

Suddenly, we're zipping around the galaxy like we own the place. Trips that would've taken generations now take days. The DecaTrek became our new yardstick for space travel, a constant reminder of how far we'd come—and how much farther we could still go.

The Thine shared their tech, we flexed our muscles, and together we showed the Grish they'd picked the wrong solar system to mess with. It was a win-win; the Thine got their bodyguards, and we got a crash course in advanced alien tech.

Around that time, things took an unexpected turn. During an encounter with Princess Shawlee Tee, Pleidian Weonans made their entrance and changed the game. I had freed her from Ironhold Station and a cruel pirate named Cardinal Thun-

Foreword

derballs. From that moment, everything shifted. The sophisticated Pleidian tech and formidable warships turned that grim encounter into another fortuitous partnership.

So now, we've got this fancy thing called the Alliance of the Thine, Humans, and Pleidians. Sounds impressive, doesn't it? It's like we've gone from the local little league to the galactic major leagues. The Thine bring the brains, we humans bring the brawn, and the Pleidians? Well, let's just say they know how to make an entrance.

By this time the new Alliance had other bad actors to deal with, namely the Varapin... think skeletal-robed ghouls who not only fly but thrive off sucking the life-force energy from their victims.

It's taken over a decade but the Grish and the Varapin aren't looking so tough anymore, and we were just starting to make some real noise in the cosmic neighborhood. Enter the Krygian, the seven-foot-tall Praying-Mantis-looking insectile race. They'd entered their breeding period—*and what is needed when trillions of eggs start to hatch?* Real estate... a whole lot of real estate.

And here we are, 137 years after the Thine showed up at our doorstep. The year is 2198 and we're still dealing with the fallout.

Now, if you'll excuse me, I've got a brand-smacking new omninought to skipper, an Alliance to maintain, and a new mission that's starting out inauspicious at best...

Prologue

Frontier Space—Syrin Planetary System
Feron World, Lorynthia
Security Command Center

Defense Minister Eliros Tremain

Tremain, a burly Hybalin with dark, brick-red skin and large brown eyes, epitomized Feron's peace-loving ideals. Despite his imposing stature, he had a gentle demeanor, and his usually calm presence soothed rather than intimidated. Feron, located in Frontier Space, orbited the giant red star Syrin alongside its sister worlds—Ardentis, Thalor, Elyria, Vexalon, and Nyxara.

The capital city, Lorynthia, was now under threat. Despite its lush green landscapes and crystal-blue rivers, a sense of dread loomed as the alarms blared throughout the cramped, outdated, and totally ill-prepared ship's Command Center—mocking him with flickering lights and harsh reminders of recent losses. Tremain's heart sank; fate had been cruel lately, and today seemed determined to twist the knife even further.

Tremain stood frozen, his large hands balled into fists at his sides. The confidence that usually radiated from him had vanished, replaced by a palpable sense of dread that filled the air.

He took a shaky breath, trying to steady himself. The command center, usually a hub of controlled chaos, now felt stagnant and suffocating. The dim, unstable glow of the displays cast an eerie light on the faces of his staff, their eyes silently pleading for reassurance he couldn't give.

Tremain's mind drifted to his grandson, Macky, still waiting by the lake with his little fishing rod. The image made his heart clench. He'd promised to take the boy fishing for his birthday. Just yesterday, Macky had been bouncing with excitement, declaring, "Gonna catch the biggest mongrel-eel in the lake, Grandpa!" The thought of those bright, hopeful eyes waiting in vain by the shore twisted yet another a knife in his gut.

But duty had called, as it always did. The life of a defense minister was never his own, especially not now, with doom descending upon Feron. Five years had passed since his wife, Lira, died in that tragic transport accident. The memory of that dark day weighed heavily on him, especially today, the anniversary of her death.

Tremain had a knack for cutting through tension with humor. Days earlier, when they detected alien scout ships in high orbit, a jittery private had anxiously asked about their safety. Tremain had shot back, "Safer than my arteries after eating a dozen deep-fried Feronian doughnuts. Now get back to work." Chuckles had rippled through the crew, easing the tension, if only briefly.

Today, though, the jokes wouldn't come. The weight of responsibility pressed down on him, made heavier by the day's

USS Resilience

cruel irony. It was little Macky's birthday, but it was also the anniversary of the day Lira had died.

As if personal torment wasn't enough, Feron itself was under threat. The relentless alarms seemed to mock him, a harsh reminder that duty always came first, no matter the cost.

Tremain's hands trembled slightly as he issued orders. "Keep the defensive batteries online for as long as possible," he commanded, his voice tinged with rare vulnerability. Somewhere out there, little Macky was probably still clutching his fishing rod, waiting for a grandfather who wouldn't come.

His fingers tightened around the edge of the control panel, forcing his emotions down. He had to draw on inner reserves of strength he wasn't sure he possessed.

"There's no doubt, Defense Minister... they're the same," the young corporal said. "Same propulsion signatures as the three scout frigates we tracked four cycles past."

Tremain nodded, a grim frown pulling at the corners of his lips. He could not imagine a worse calamity to strike Feron. In its quest for harmony, Feron had focused on diplomacy and avoided military escalation. It was believed Krygian expansion into Frontier Space had been moving away from Feron, leaving this small corner of the galaxy safe from the Krygian scourge. Clearly, his intelligence had been wrong—deadly wrong.

Swallowing hard, he forced himself to keep breathing. The Krygian destroyer, a massive, grotesque shadow, now loomed over the peaceful capital city of Lorynthia. The ship's dark, spindly form blotted out their system's red giant, Syrin, casting a pall over the city's spires and domes. Tremain, eyes wide with rising dread, witnessed nightmarish ships converging into formation. Above, the sky darkened like an imminent storm, each vessel a stark harbinger of the crushing might of the Krygian fleet.

"Minister Tremain, we're detecting smaller enemy vessels

inbound," a voice crackled over the comms, strained with barely contained panic.

"I see them," Tremain replied, his voice was slightly more than a whisper. His hands moved with jerky, uncertain motions over the control panel, desperate to activate the city's defensive batteries. The antiquated systems sputtered and failed, mocking his efforts.

On the displays, the Krygian drop-ships had begun their descent. Each one was a terrifying spectacle, a grotesque fusion of organic and mechanical, bristling with weaponry. The drop-ships' hulls were covered in chitinous armor, their forms reminiscent of those nightmarish insects that had wreaked so much havoc in the not-too-distant past. As they descended, their engines emitted a bone-chilling whine.

"Defense systems are down, Minister," the comms operator reported, his voice tinged with despair.

"Keep trying! We must hold them off!" Tremain barked, his voice cracking under the strain. But deep down, he knew it was futile.

The first drop-ship landed with a thunderous crash, its gangways slamming to the ground. The sound reverberated through the city, a harbinger of the atrocities to come. Tremain's eyes widened in horror as the hatch doors opened, releasing a flood of Krygian warriors. The insects stormed out in a chaotic wave, their mandibles clacking with anticipation. Thousands of hungry, glittering eyes scanned the surroundings, their bodies shimmering with malevolent energy.

"Stay indoors! Hide! Protect your families!" PA warnings echoed through Lorynthia, each plea more frantic than the last. The streets echoed with the cries of terrified civilians. Some stood frozen in fear, faces pale, realizing there was nowhere to hide. Others pushed through the throngs, searching for an escape.

Live feeds broadcast the nightmarish scene unfolding across the surface—swarms of insectoid attackers overwhelming defenseless Hybalin civilians, ripping into them with cold, calculated brutality. The air filled with a cacophony of screams and the sickening sounds of alien predators feasting on their prey.

Tremain's hands shook uncontrollably as he watched the carnage unfold. His staff audibly wept at their stations—helpless against such an overwhelming onslaught. They were being torn apart, devoured by the praying-mantis-like aliens. He saw families trying to flee, only to be cut down by swaths of the relentless insects. A mother shielded her child with her body, only for both to be eviscerated within scissoring mandibles. An elderly Hybalin was being dragged into an alleyway, his cries for mercy cut short by the sound of powerful jaws crunching bone.

Desperate to do something, anything, Tremain turned his attention to the planet's small space fleet. A ragtag group of outdated, barely spaceworthy craft, their only hope lay in numbers and determination. He issued the command, his voice a hollow echo in the vastness of space.

"All ships, engage the Krygian vessels. Do what you can... We must protect Feron."

They swarmed the lone Krygian destroyer high in the sky of Lorynthia, their weapons firing in a desperate bid to cause damage—to slow the unprovoked attack. For a brief moment, it seemed as if they might succeed. But the destroyer's vastly superior firepower obliterated each of them, their fiery deaths painting the sky.

Tremain's horror grew as he watched helplessly. More Krygian drop-ships were descending, each one bringing more and more death and carnage.

"Civilian ships are mobilizing!" came the corporal's excited voice.

But the defense minister had already been tracking the frenetically launched batch of small aircraft—now scrambling to join the havoc within Lorynthia's airspace. He covered his mouth with one hand as their small craft targeted the countless enemy drop-ships the only way they could—by crashing into them kamikaze-style. They burst into desperate, fiery explosions, barely denting the well-armored enemy warships.

Defense Minister Eliros Tremain blinked away tears as realization set in. All was lost. He fumbled his way to his seat, dropping into it with the finality of a corpse. He stared blankly at the feeds—arachnid forms—the Krygian conquerors were attempting to breach the command bunker's outer defenses. Soldiers were trying to hold the line, only to be overwhelmed by the sheer numbers of the invaders. On one feed he saw a young female soldier probably fresh out of boot camp—her face a mask of fear and determination, there with her squad making a final stand. Tremain had to look away as she and the others were suddenly swarmed—torn apart.

He looked up, listened… the sound of thousands of hungry insects as they clamored over each other, their need to feed, all-consuming. Tremain could now feel the building shake with the force of their movement, the vibrations reaching within the once thought-to-be-safe confines of the command center.

The monitors flickered as the Krygian forces breached the last line of defense. The feeds showed the invaders moving with military precision, their grotesque forms a nightmarish blur. Tremain watched in mute horror as they stormed the city's central square, their mandibles clicking, always fucking clicking. They toppled statues and monuments like bowling pins in a perfect strike. Symbols of Feron's proud history and pride—reduced to rubble in moments.

Tremain's eyes filled with tears as he watched the destruction of his home. He had dedicated his life to protecting Feron, and now he could do nothing but watch as it was being systematically demolished. His mind flashed back to the day he took his oath of office, promising to defend his people with every fiber of his being. That promise now felt like a cruel joke. "What world could endure this kind of devastation... eradication? In a week, perhaps two, he pictured the Hybalin race to be completely wiped out—what was happening here was an extinction-class event—no one would survive.

The final blow came as the Krygian conquerors breached the command bunker's heavy outer doors, once thought impenetrable—now crumbling under the relentless assault. The menacing silhouettes of the Krygian warriors filled the doorway, their mandibles snapping with malicious glee. Tremain turned in his chair to look at them straight on, his eyes vacant, his spirit broken.

Krygian warriors swarmed in, sharp appendages slicing through the air, blades glinting under the overhead lights. Tremain's thoughts turned to the weight of the moment... the unimaginable loss of so many... and, of course, his family. He pictured his grandson, Macky. They'd never have an opportunity to try out that new rod of his. He pictured Lira's gentle eyes, a grin tugging at his lips. "I'm coming home..."

Krygian warriors continued to swarm, a relentless tide of destruction, as if hell itself had opened its gates.

Chapter 1

Solar System
Halibart Station

Captain Galvin Quintos

Much of the time I get my marching orders at the same time as the rest of the crew—a message pops up on my TAC-Band with the day, time, and location to check-in.

Three hours ago, I received seven *Priority One* notifications. I was to report to Halibart Station—not in a week or even in a few days but pretty much right f_ing now. All I'd been told... *my next deployment was imminent*. That, and my new ship, described as a Decimation-Class Omninought, was ready to board.

Twenty-eight days had passed since my return to Earth from my last deployment onboard *USS IKE*, a swift Corvette-Class warship I'd grown to admire. My admiration didn't extend to the Krygians—an insectile alien force spreading through the Orpheus Rift like a rampant plague. Our ops mission had brought us to Krygian Hegemony, a span of over a dozen worlds orbiting Hekaton's binary stars. To say we'd been successful would be a bit of a stretch. Sure, we'd destroyed *Oblivion*—the Krygians' latest purchase—but the insectile race was still free to flourish, to propagate. *Oblivion* was a dreadnought I knew well—had once commanded—a lethal warship that the U.S. Space Navy muckety-mucks insisted be eliminated at any cost.

The Krygian race possessed a ravenous hunger and an insatiable drive for new breeding grounds, making them a threat unlike any we had ever faced—and possibly unstoppable.

With the fall of both the Varapin and Grish Empires over the past few months, there were now plenty of U.S. Space Navy captains chafing at the bit to get back into the fight—to throw caution to the wind and hit the enemy with the unbridled military power of the Thine/Pleidian/Human Alliance—led primarily by Earth's United Nations Forces, *EUNF,* along with its primary military arm—the U.S. Space Navy.

As far as I was concerned, let them have at it. I would be just fine never having to set eyes on one of those praying-mantis-looking bugs ever again. They scared the crap out of me—and since we were not officially at war with the alien super-power, I'm good with being deployed out to sectors within Andromeda, Ursa Major, or even Orion. But please, not out to Frontier Space, specifically the Syrin Planetary System where the Krygians rule unopposed.

Returning from 28 days of leave, I felt centered again and ready to dive back into my military duties. Where had I spent my time away, you may be asking?

Well, I'd received an interesting invitation from my longtime friend, Chief Craig Porter. He needed a new bird, namely, an Amazonian Blue-Crested Macaw. Apparently, it's a big, super-rare, and super-smart parrot you can only find within the jungles of the Amazon. With its flashy blue crest and vibrant feathers, this macaw is famous for being surprisingly intelligent—adept at noodling out various problems. The bird also has some pretty cool social skills. When I asked Craig what happened to his last parrot, all he would say was that she—Lucy—had turned traitorous... that, and the bird was now living with the recently promoted from Ensign to Lieutenant Junior Grade, Roisin Blunderton.

Anyway, together, we'd embarked on an adventurous excursion deep into the wilds of South America's Amazonian jungle. While I enjoy a good wilderness adventure, the Amazon wouldn't have been my first choice—too many bugs, and I'd had more than my fill of those recently. Plus, I wasn't particularly fond of reptiles either.

Despite my reservations, I needed a change of scenery, something to lower my stress levels and distract me from the tangled mess of my feelings for Gail Pristy. I know, pathetic... I'd been moping about like a heartbroken teenager—struggling with unrequited love. I needed a serious diversion, and Porter was offering just that.

I'd stowed my TAC-Band deep within my backpack and only checked it every few days, if that. I knew that my niece, Sonya, was in good hands, spending part of her time living with Pristy, and the other part with Empress Shawlee Tee working on some hush-hush, top-secret Symbio project.

Porter's infectious enthusiasm kept us going, regaling me with tales of past adventures and survival tips that were both practical and hilarious. His stories ranged from encounters with elusive wildlife to narrowly escaping treacherous quicksand, each one more captivating than the last. The combination of his wisdom and humor was a welcome distraction from the insect bites and the ever-present humidity.

One particularly funny moment happened during our trek through the jungle. Porter, having spotted the parrot he was most interested in, climbed a tree with incredible urgency... only to realize he was on the tree adjacent to the one he needed to be on. Determined not to lose sight of his quarry, he attempted an ambitious jump from one tree to the other, but the strap of his pack got snagged on a branch, leaving him hanging like a flailing marionette. His predicament had us both laughing for hours, a perfect example of how his adventurous spirit and humor turned even the most frustrating situations into a memorable experience.

Each night, we'd set up our camp tent beneath the dense canopy, the jungle's sounds a natural lullaby. Surprisingly, I found a sense of peace in the wild, untamed surroundings. It took Porter three weeks to find the 'perfect' parrot, one he believed would become a lifelong companion, or whatever that BFF bond is called between man and bird. Oh, and he'd named the bird 'Leal'—the Brazilian Portuguese word for loyal.

Admiral Xavier Gomez dispatched a Craven-Class 550 Off-Worlder to retrieve Porter and me from the heart of the jungle. Apparently, Craig Porter was on my crew roster. As the flight crew secured our gear, including the caged 'Leal', Porter and I were given a wide berth. Three weeks in the steaming jungle had left us both more than a little ripe. No time for a shower or to collect personal items—we were on a tight, zero-tolerance timeline.

Approaching Halibart Station, just a stone's throw from Earth's Moon, ship traffic buzzed in organized chaos. Every berth was occupied, with ships in holding patterns, lined up, awaiting clearance from Station Control as departing vessels navigated their way out.

"Looks like parking is going to be problematic," I said to the young pilot at the controls.

"No Sir," the pilot said. "We've been cleared right into *Roosevelt's* flight bay."

I eyed the young man at the controls, Lieutenant Don Perry. His buzzed hair formed a high-and-tight crew cut, complemented by ears jutting out like radar dishes. He looked fresh from the academy. Beside him stood Lieutenant Glover, equally green but quieter.

Porter and I exchanged a shrug. *"Roosevelt?"* I asked the Off-Worlder's co-pilot. "I'm not familiar—"

"Yes, Captain," Perry said. "She's about as new as a ship can be. One of the new Decimation-Class Omninoughts being built here at Halibart." He gestured, chinning toward a colossal warship just now coming in to view through the diamond glass viewport. Smiling, he said, "I'm envious, would give my right nut to have an assignment on a ship like that."

"Maybe I can put in a good word for you, Lieutenant," I said. "This certainly looks like quite that warship—"

The pilot's eyes gleamed with excitement. "Oh man... I mean, Sir, you have to hear about the upgrades they've made to Decimation-Class Omninoughts like *USS Roosevelt*! The propulsion and weapons systems are off the charts—light years ahead of anything we've seen before!"

I nodded. But that small gesture had unlocked a torrent from the young pilot.

"Sure, we all know these ships come equipped with jump springs and wormhole generators, but this latest generation takes it to a whole new level. The jump drive tech has been supercharged, allowing for lightning-fast spatial jumps that are nearly instantaneous. We're talking about unparalleled in-battle maneuverability that's going to make these ships impossible to pin down."

Porter and I exchanged a glance.

"And wormhole manufacturing? Forget about those clunky, power-hungry systems of the past. *Roosevelt* can create stable, artificially generated wormholes with unprecedented efficiency —much faster generation... no more waiting twenty minutes for full stabilization. Ten minutes max, and you're crossing into the maw of the wormhole. It's a level of strategic mobility that's going to rewrite the rules of engagement.

But the real showstopper is the omninought's firepower. These ships pack the latest in railgun technology - rail spike projectiles traveling at a sizable fraction of light speed, capable of punching straight through enemy shields and hulls. Combine that with the devastation of the broadside cannons' fusion bowlers, smart-missiles that anticipate enemy countermeasures... and, of course, there's the precision of the Phazon Pulsar energy weapons... yup, you've got a ship that can lay waste to just about anything in its path."

Porter rolled his eyes, while I let out an audible breath.

"And let's not forget the advanced stealth systems - this Decimation-Class Omninought can practically disappear off sensors when it needs to! Spanning a hundred decks, not including those within the Circadian Platform, Roosevelt is an engineering marvel through and through. The top three decks are dedicated to the Symbio tech, where the crew can enjoy mind-bending R&R reality environments utilizing cutting-edge Symbio-Poth 3.0 technology. *And* the ship comes equipped with the latest quantum teleportation... having multiple Quansporter compartments. So getting from point A to point B on a six-mile-long vessel takes only seconds with those DeckPorts scattered throughout the ship.

At the heart of it all is that Circadian Platform—a command center that puts the captain—you, Sir, in total control. With the Gravity Well's 3D navigational display and the bridge's dynamic halo interfaces, they can coordinate this ship's systems with pinpoint precision.

I'm telling you, this Decimation-Class is a game-changer. With this kind of speed, firepower, and technological edge, the Alliance will be taking the fight to the enemy, any enemy, and do it on our terms."

I held up a palm, letting him know that would be more than enough. "Thank you, Lieutenant Perry. By any chance do you know an Ensign Blair Paxton?"

"Um... no, I don't think so. Why, Sir?"

"No reason," I said, giving the pilot a pat on his shoulder. "Let's just say she possesses the same gift of gab that you seem to have."

Chapter 2

Orpheus Rift
Krygian Hive Ship, *Vingron-Palsh*

Queen Slith

Three weeks prior...

Deep within the bowels of the Krygian dreadnought, shadows clung to every corner. The vessel loomed in the void—a nightmarish fusion of metal and pulsating organic matter. A chill drifted through the narrow passages, heavy with the stench of decay and something far more primal.

Queen Slith, six times the size of her milling vassals, perched atop her twisted throne, an unsettling vision of beauty and terror. Bioluminescent growths cast ghastly shadows across her segmented body, highlighting a shimmering exoskeleton that rippled with every subtle movement. Her four compound eyes, each moving independently, scanned the chaotic hive with cold calculation.

Queen Slith continued to emit pheromones, specifically citronellol acetate, attracting vassals. Mating remained her primary activity during the season, her eyes always assessing potential suitors. Unabashedly this Queen wanted—and needed—to be laid... and laid often.

The Hive writhed like a living entity, pulsing with energy and raw hunger. Consort vassals scuttled across the slick, slime-coated floors, their movements oscillating between focused purpose and a jittery fear that coiled tighter with each passing moment. They were the lifeblood of her empire, yet her thoughts danced to darker rhythms. Each moment spent here, each taste of flesh consumed, fed a more primitive instinct that clawed at the edges of her consciousness.

She sometimes allowed herself to think of home—the Krygian Hegemony spanning over a dozen worlds orbiting the binary star system of Hekaton in the Orpheus Rift. Her home planet of Krygora was an unforgiving sphere, its surface dominated by spired hive-cities of blackened metal and grinding machine foundries belching toxins into the hazy atmosphere.

As the oppressive gloom settled, a consort vassal approached, its gait unnaturally precise. It bowed low before Slith. Anticipation hummed in the air. The Queen's subtle smile hinted at her pleasure, picturing the vassal's heart racing under her scrutiny.

"Your sample awaits, My Queen," it murmured, offering up the fleshy, decomposition-darkened morsel. Clutched in its clawed appendage was a meaty upper thigh, flesh glistening... oozing pus.

"Remnants of a fray from the Nylor-5 Shipyards, as requested."

The aroma wafted toward her, a heady blend of iron and decay, filling her senses with a thrill beyond mere appetite. Yet, as she reached for the offering, an unfamiliar sensation crackled along her nerve clusters, setting her on edge. Was this... doubt? No. Queens did not doubt. They consumed, expanded, bred. It was the way of things.

Slith's mandibles clicked softly, a sound that might have been mistaken for amusement in a human. "Ah, the sweet bouquet of failure," she mused, her voice a dissonant harmony of tones. "Tell me, little consort vassal, do you think this morsel will taste of their defeat or their victory?"

The consort vassal quivered, uncertain how to respond. Slith's fore-claw shot out, lightning-quick, impaling the creature through its thorax. Green ichor sprayed across her mandibles as she brought the twitching form to her mouthparts.

"No matter," she continued, her tone conversational as she began to consume the still-living consort vassal. "Sometimes the most exquisite flavors are born of adversity."

As she devoured her subordinate, Slith's mind raced with alien calculations. Strategy was not the Krygian way. They were conquerors, swarmers, driven by instinct and hunger. Yet the humans had proven... problematic. Intriguing even.

She paused, mandibles poised over the torn flesh of the human thigh. "Power?" she echoed, a cold smile spreading across her features. "Or merely a distraction?"

As she consumed the remnants, thoughts twisted through her mind—a sense of urgency clawed at her insides. Territory loomed large in her vision, the warm, rich soil of distant worlds calling out to her hunger. She needed to expand, conquer vast swathes of territory to disperse her millions of eggs, to secure the Hive's future in the cold expanse of space.

"Bring me the reports from our ghost droids," Slith commanded, her voice a symphony of conflicting tones that would drive any human mad.

A new consort vassal scurried forward, offering up a pulsating, organic data node. Slith's four eyes focused independently on the holographic images that sprang to life before her. Earth, in all its blue and green splendor, rotated slowly. Cities sprawled across continents, teeming with life. Oceans teemed with potential hosts for her brood.

Ropes of saliva secreted from Slith's mouthparts dripped onto the throne below. The sight of such abundance triggered a primal response, a hunger that went beyond mere sustenance. Earth represented not just food, but the future—a vast incubator for her species.

"Fascinating," she murmured, manipulating the image with her fore-claws. "Such diversity. Such... potential." Her mandibles clicked rapidly, an expression of excitement. "And they defend it so fiercely. One almost admires their tenacity."

The defeated consort vassal at her feet twitched its last, and Slith absently crushed its head beneath her leg. "Almost," she added dryly.

As she studied the images, a new plan began to form in her consciousness, one that defied the instinctual drive to simply overwhelm and devour. It was... unsettling. Unnatural. But so too was defeat.

"We've underestimated them," Slith mused aloud, her voice carrying an edge of curiosity rather than anger. "Their adaptability, their resourcefulness. It's... refreshing." She paused, considering. "Perhaps we should send them a gift. Something to express our... appreciation."

The surrounding consort vassals shifted nervously, unsure of their Queen's meaning.

Slith's eyes refocused on her minions. "Prepare a specialized brood. Something... tailored for our human friends. Let's see how they handle a more... personalized approach."

Rising from her throne with unsettling grace, Slith moved through her obscured corridors, the dim light casting foreboding shadows upon her path. The whispers of a forgotten past trailed her—a reminder of lost territories now kept by the defiant humans.

"Evolution is such a fascinating process, don't you think?" she asked a passing consort vassal, who froze in terror at being addressed. "To adapt or to die. I wonder which path our species will choose."

As she stepped into the heart of her dreadnought, Slith inhaled deeply, tasting the metallic tang of ambition mingled with decay. Her ranks would be bolstered; consort vassals would rise, and she would release her eggs into worlds anew. Each campaign strengthened her—her body, her Hive, her legacy.

"Bring me our most cunning strategists," she commanded. "And our most innovative breeders. It's time we evolved our approach."

The hive burst into frenzied activity at her words. Slith watched with cold amusement, her four eyes tracking multiple scenes at once.

"Oh, and one more thing," she added, almost as an afterthought. "Find me more of those delightful human morsels. I find myself developing quite the taste for them. Perhaps we should start a farm."

As she moved through the darkened corridors, the whisper of uncertainty trailed behind her, but she silenced it with a burst of pheromones that sent nearby consort vassals into another frenzy of activity. Fear would reign—it was their time to conquer. But conquest, Slith was beginning to realize, could take many forms.

The Krygian legacy would thrum through her veins, the taste of flesh an omen of what was to come. But for the first time in her long existence, Queen Slith found herself anticipating not just the hunt but the game itself. The humans had proven themselves worthy adversaries. How delightful it would be to watch them squirm.

Chapter 3

**Solar System
Halibart Station**

Captain Galvin Quintos

Present day...

As Lieutenant Don Perry touched down within *Roosevelt's* main flight bay, I had already moved toward the hatch. Giving Porter a quick, informal salute, I hurried down the gangway and jogged toward the nearest DeckPort. The din of a bustling bay was something I'd come to love—maintenance crews darting about, overhead announcements from the Bay Chief barely audible above the roar of spacecraft engines, and row upon row of bright red Arrow Fighters lined up, ready for action. Two distinct vessels sat askew, as if their pilots had landed in a hurry. One marked a dark maroon Craven-Class 550 Off-Worlder, signaling a high-ranking military officer's transport. Nearby, the official Pleidian

Weonan Royal Schooner awaited, unmistakably Empress Shawlee Tee's ship.

The overhead PA came alive with a familiar, ultra-calm, female voice. NELLA. Apparently, this omninought was utilizing the same ship's AI technology as that of USS *Ike*—the same AI that almost self-destructed the ship. But I couldn't deal with that right now.

**Captain Quintos, your presence
is required within the Gravity Well...**

**Captain Quintos, your presence
is required within the Gravity Well...**

"My presence is going to have to wait a few minutes!" I yelled back to no one in particular.

After Lieutenant Don Perry's detailed rundown, I learned *Roosevelt* shared the same basic layout as its predecessors, *USS Franklin* and *USS Washington*. Prior to entering the DeckPort, I called out, "Circadian Platform Deck F!"

I exited, still running, made a quick right, and made a mad dash toward my captain's quarters—or what I thought were my captain's quarters. On approach, the auto-hatch didn't open. Annoyed, I said, "Captain's override, open the damn hatch, NELLA!"

The auto-hatch swished open, and I darted inside and came to an immediate, wide-eyed stop.

Steam still billowing out from the adjacent bathroom, Gail Pristy stood momentarily paralyzed in the process of wrapping a bath towel around herself. This hesitation granted me an unimpeded view of my XO's completely naked body, every detail stark against the misty backdrop. Her skin glistened with moisture, each curve and contour accentuated by the soft light filtering through the steam. Beads of water clung to her like tiny diamonds, tracing delicate paths down her body. For a fleeting moment, time seemed to stand still, the silence only broken by the distant hum of the ship's systems. The scene was so intimate, so raw, that it felt almost surreal, as if the boundaries of duty and decorum had momentarily dissolved into the swirling mist.

"Uh... I thought this... um, was my..."

She continued to wrap the towel around herself as if my intrusion had been little more than a glimpse of her own reflection in a mirror.

"Nope, the layout's been changed. Didn't you read the *Welcome Aboard Orientation* notes?" She untied the towel wrapped around her head, shaking out her straight, shoulder-length blonde hair. As if seeing me for the first time, her eyes gave me a head-to-toe once over.

"You're looking tan... not sure I ever saw you sporting a beard before. Rustic. I like it. So, where've you been... let me guess. Vacationing on some exotic island with a supermodel? The dashing and famous Captain Galvin Quintos with all the media attention you're getting of late I'm sure you have your pick of the ladies these days."

Flustered, I managed, "Uh... Media attention? Supermodel?"

She waved away my mumblings, swirling the mist still coming off her body. "I sent you several messages."

She gestured to her TAC-Band—so she hadn't been totally naked after all.

"I get it, you were... busy." Her lips formed a smile, yet her eyes stayed distant.

"I was in South America, and I wasn't checking my messages. What is it you... wanted or needed? Is everything okay with Sonya? I should have been checking..." I inwardly chastised myself—I was the closest thing to a father figure she had. Yes, she'll be eighteen soon, an adult... but I had dropped the ball. I knew she was still fragile after being abducted by the Briggans, even though she would never admit it. How could I have let three weeks go by without checking in on her?

"Sonya's fine," she said. "I don't think I've ever met anyone her age so self-reliant."

"So... your messages? What was it you needed from me?"

She opened her mouth to speak.

**Captain Quintos, your presence
is required within the Gravity Well...**

**Captain Quintos, your presence
is required within the Gravity Well...**

Pristy gestured to the auto-hatch. "Your quarters are now two doors down."

"Yeah, best I get cleaned up and throw on a uniform. I'll, uh, see you at the briefing then?"

She nodded, pivoted on her heel, and vanished into the swirling mist of the bathroom.

XO Gail Pristy

She stood in front of the bathroom mirror letting the towel wrapped around her fall to the deck. She appraised herself, now seeing what Quintos had just gotten an eyeful of—petite, gentle curves in all the right places and toned muscles thanks to those high school years of practicing on the uneven bars, balance beam, and let's not forget countless time doing floor exercises. Her bemused expression faded. She'd shoved him away, still wrestling with the new reality of being reborn as Gail Pristy 2.0... yet feeling like a stranger to herself. "What the hell is wrong with me? Christ!"

She flashed back on how he'd looked entering her compartment. Like he'd been wading through a swamp. And that smell! Like a fucking homeless person. He was also tanned and that grizzly beard and his tousled hair—dammit, he'd radiated primal masculinity, and she liked it—really liked it. But the moment had passed—she'd blown it.

She exhaled in frustration. "What? Is it too late to tell him how I feel?" she said aloud. "Really, he'd simply moved on from... this?" She shrugged at her reflection. "I guess I can't blame him—I've sent him so many mixed messages." She raised her arms, clenching tight fists in a triumphant muscleman pose. "But there again, this game isn't over," she declared, "Not even close."

Chapter 4

Solar System
Halibart Station
USS Roosevelt

Captain Galvin Quintos

Rushing out of the DeckPort on Deck G of the Circadian Platform, I realized I was late for orientation. The expansive Gravity Well swarmed with crewmembers. Heads turned, eyes locked on me as I made my way through the throng toward the raised stage where I could now see both Admiral Gomez and Empress Shawlee making casual, quiet conversation. They'd waited. At my approach, Shawlee's smile brightened, accompanied by a playful wink. Meanwhile, the Admiral's glare darkened, his brows knitting together in disapproval.

Glancing around I saw dozens of familiar faces as well as a few new ones. Some ship skippers insist on selecting their ship's senior officers and bridgecrew. Spend mindless hours hunched over deployment rosters hemming and hawing. Not me. It's a no-win situation, one that inevitably will piss someone off, or worse, hurt someone's feelings. "Leave the hand wringing to some other poor shlubs. Let them take the heat. Later, we'll have fun blaming Mr. or Ms. Shlub and get on with our duties."

Feeling a gentle swipe at the back of my head, I glanced back to see Petty Officer 2nd Class Aubrey Laramie looking up at me. Fingers raised, she said, "Your hair's still wet. Nice shower?" she pursed her lips, "Like the beard, Cap."

I turned away; indulging Aubrey's flirt was never a good idea. It was then that I saw another new arrival, XO Pristy, also a wet-head, who looked away... but I'd definitely caught her looking our way. Whatever. And then she took a step forward and who did I see she was standing next to? Commander Cornelius "Con" Strickland. The same Commander Strickland who'd led the Marine ground forces onto Krygian Shipyard on Nylor-5—where the bug's recently acquired warship, *Oblivion*, was being retrofitted for their own purposes. Not only were Pristy and Strickland standing shoulder-to-shoulder, but they were also... *brushing* shoulders, heads inclined toward one another as they carried on their own somewhat intimate conversation.

Empress Shawlee moved up to the pedestal, eyes sweeping the assembled crowd below—eventually coming to rest on me. She gave me an exasperated nod and mouthed the words, *See me after the orientation...*

She started with, "I would first like to thank Captain Quintos here for doing the one thing I'd come to think was, well... impossible."

Before Shawlee could continue, a hand shot up from the crowd. It was Ensign Blair Paxton, her curiosity getting the better of her professional decorum.

"Empress, if I may," Paxton interjected, her voice carrying a mix of enthusiasm and hesitation. "Which President Roosevelt is our ship named after? Theodore or Franklin D.?"

Shawlee's eyes twinkled with amusement at the young officer's eagerness. "An excellent question, Ensign. Anticipating that very question, I've had to bone up on a bit of your human, U.S. history... *USS Roosevelt* is indeed named after Theodore Roosevelt, or 'Teddy' as he was affectionately known."

The Empress paused, surveying the gathered crew. "You might wonder why we chose Teddy over his fifth cousin, Franklin. Well, Theodore Roosevelt was a man of many facets—a leader, a conservationist, and an adventurer. Did you know he was the youngest president in the nation's history when he took office? At just 42, he brought a vigor and dynamism to the role that we hope this ship will embody."

She continued, her voice filled with admiration, "Roosevelt was also a naval enthusiast and a strong advocate for a powerful American fleet. He once said, 'A good Navy is not a provocation to war. It is the surest guarantee of peace.' This ship, with its advanced capabilities, embodies that philosophy."

"But perhaps most fitting," Shawlee added, "are Roosevelt's spirit of exploration and his famous quote: 'Far better it is to dare mighty things, to win glorious triumphs, even though checkered by failure than to take rank with those poor spirits who neither enjoy much nor suffer much because they live in the gray twilight that knows neither victory nor defeat.' This ship, *USS Roosevelt*, will carry that daring spirit into the vastness of space."

The crew listened intently, a new appreciation for their ship's namesake evident on their faces. Shawlee nodded, satisfied, and returned to her prepared remarks.

"Now, as I was saying, I would first like to thank Captain Quintos here for doing the one thing I'd come to think was, well... impossible. *USS Franklin*, *USS Washington*, and most recently, *USS IKE*—your Captain is on a roll—all returned to Earth after his last three missions. These U.S. Space Navy assets—yes, somewhat war-torn and battered—were still operational! Prior to this, I was thinking of officially changing his pilot's callsign from Brigs to Captain Shipwreck."

Laughter erupted around me, and I felt several over-enthusiastic slaps to my back. I grudgingly smiled. "Ha Ha... it's not that funny," I said, feigning irritation.

She put her attention back to the crew. "This Decimation-Class Omninought is one badass warship, people. The product of the very best Thine and Pleidian engineers, this asset could not have arrived at a more opportune moment. A new foe has emerged in the cosmos, far more ruthless and monstrous than the Grish or Varapin, making them seem like playful pups next to a pack of ravenous wolves. We've underestimated our enemies before... that's not happening here. The truth? We will need a fleet... an armada of Decimation-Class Omninoughts to defend alliance territories against the Krygian. In a moment, Admiral Gomez will provide you with the mission specifics, but first I'd like to reward this amazing crew with a special surprise. A gift, as it were, that I've personally gotten involved with as I've done with other great warships such as *Hamilton, Jefferson*, and *Adams*. I'm talking about Decks 98, 99, and 100... something most of you will recognize as the Symbio Decks."

Immediately there was applause, hoots and hollers, and a few high-fives.

Shawlee took in the gratitude with a broad smile. She turned and gestured behind for someone to join her at the podium. To my utter surprise, a pretty seventeen-year-old, cheeks coloring, stepped up beside the Empress.

"Most of you already know Sonya Winters. Know the incredible work she does with our Symbio Poth development teams." Shawlee placed an affectionate hand on the teenager's shoulder. "But today, I would like to share something truly special. Sonya has been awarded a Pleidian Weonan Bachelor of Science Degree from the University of Saverst—this is not an honorary degree, but an actual B.S. degree that is recognized on both Weonan and Earth. Let's give our young graduate a round of applause."

Cheers and a hearty round of applause filled the large compartment as a stunned-looking Sonya stared back at the Empress, clearly overwhelmed by the unexpected announcement.

Swallowing hard, I locked eyes with my niece. This moment had been brewing for a while now, but the pride swelling in my chest caught me off guard.

Shawlee continued, "Sonya's technical expertise and creative input for your new R&R decks will, as you humans like to say, blow your socks off. And once your ship's senior officers have had the first opportunity to play... the rest of you will have your shot."

A chorus of moans filled the space.

Shawlee continued, "Be ready for the most realistic, exhilarating, historically authentic, and 100% immersive times of your lives."

A familiar woman's voice cut through the chatter I recognized as Lieutenant Akari James. "So, Empress, what now? We've had Korakuen with those Japanese cherry blossoms, that creepy Clairmont town, medieval knighthood and fairies in Convoke Wyvern, Cavemen Glory with dinosaurs, and Independence Quest with old Ben Franklin and the redcoats. Any hints for what's on deck this time?"

Bemused, Shawlee looked to Sonya, "Any hints you want to give away at this point?"

Sonya narrowed her eyes. "You'll just have to wait and see,

Akari. In the meantime, maybe get more familiar with a sica and scutum."

Akari just looked back at her blank-faced.

I smiled, knowing full well who would have had use for such items several thousand years past.

Next up was Admiral Gomez, and as light-hearted and upbeat as Shawlee had been, Gomez looked just the opposite; he appeared downright hostile.

Taking her place at the podium, he thanked the Empress and got right to it. "We are at a new crossroads, people, and to be perfectly frank, I am scared. We should all be scared, for ourselves, for our loved ones, for Earth."

As if on cue, the Gravity Well around us came alive with a projected view of local space—Earth, in all her radiant blue glory, the Moon, and off in the distance, the Sun.

"We had been tracking the three approaching, fairly well-cloaked craft for the past few days."

The projection suddenly zoomed in on three seemingly fast-moving objects of unknown origin. As far as I knew, they weren't of U.S. Space Navy design.

Gomez continued, "The EUNF has been analyzing the three scout droids' propulsion signatures—so we know who sent them here. The Krygian."

Low murmurings, like the hum of distant machinery, rippled through the crowd.

"What's even more unsettling are the recent desperate calls for help coming from Frontier Space within the Syrin Planetary System. Earth had been engaged in diplomatic talks with a burgeoning civilization on a small world called Feron."

Gomez shook his head.

"Those desperate calls for help emanated from there. Based on our current knowledge, Krygian forces have already taken full control of this world, and the native population—the

Hybalins—has been completely wiped out. And there's more disturbing information... days, maybe weeks before the invasion, three similar Krygian scout droids were detected within that Syrin Planetary System. The EUNF believes the Krygian know it was our asset, *USS IKE*, that recently attacked their shipyards on Nylor-5 and then destroyed their prized new dreadnought, *Oblivion*. Whether it's retribution or because Earth aligns with the type of world suited for their rampant breeding... we are currently on high alert for an impending invasion."

"But we're not officially at war with the Krygian?" I asked.

"No, Captain, we are not. And to be blunt, I'm not sure we, the Alliance, would prevail. What is needed... is to present a clear show of force—a not-so-subtle deterrent that will keep the insects in their own lane."

XO Pristy spoke up, "So we'll be sending the 2nd Fleet, an armada—"

Gomez raised a palm, interrupting her. "The 2nd Fleet will remain right here along with the 5th and the 8th Fleets. Thine and Weonan worlds are bolstering their defenses as well. This omninought, *USS Roosevelt*, is powerful. Hell, some would say it's an armada of one. This, people, will be our show of force."

I spoke up once more. "I've been informed there's a contingent of U.S. Army troops on board, can you corroborate that, Sir?"

The Admiral did not look happy with my question. "We must be prepared for all contingencies, Captain. And that means being ready for any ground assaults that could arise. A full battalion, close to one thousand highly trained U.S. Army Rangers, occupy much of *Roosevelt's* Deck 6."

Gomez's steely gaze shifted amongst the attendees. You will not be interacting with these Rangers. Deck 6 has been isolated... a secure, restricted, area of the ship that would require special clearance to access."

"And who will be leading this Ranger contingent, Admiral?

I was surprised to hear it had been my XO asking the question.

"That would be Cornelius Strickland, a decorated Commander with the U.S. Army Rangers.

Heads turned, eyes locked onto Strickland who simply nodded but said nothing—while Pristy, still at his side, glanced my way, an amused smirk—perhaps driving home the point she was making—that she had moved on to greener pastures.

"So, we're being deployed today, Sir? Chief LaSalle asked.

Gomez and Shawlee exchanged a concerned look.

"Chief," Gomez said, "I know why you in particular are asking that question. You and your department have already been impacted by the strike."

My ears perked up, why the hell hadn't I known about a strike? What kind of damage had been done? And who ordered the strike?

LaSalle said, "It's just that... we're readying to leave the station and we're still waiting on crucial deliveries. We're lacking necessities, Sir."

"What does that have to do with a strike?" I asked, others around me nodding their heads, also confused.

"It's not that kind of strike, Captain," Gomez said. "We are presently in the midst of a union strike with the Intergalactic Freight Alliance (IFA). Very little happens without a fully functioning IFA."

I shrugged, raising an eyebrow. "Really?"

Chief LaSalle stepped forward. "Captain, we're looking at interplanetary commerce grinding to a total stop. No more trade between planets and star systems. Essential supplies like food, medical gear, and fuel will stop coming. Advanced tech and parts for repairs? Forget about it..."

"The bathroom on Deck 5, Sector Gold, is out of toilet paper... is that why?"

Flabbergasted, I couldn't believe someone just asked the highest-ranking officer within the U.S. Space Navy about toilet paper supplies. I leaned forward to get a better look at who this woman crewmember was.

I recognized her but had had little interaction with her. I mentally searched for her name—Ensign... no, she'd been put in for a promotion to Captain, but that had been kicked back due to her lack of in-the-field experience—she was promoted to Lieutenant Junior Grade, instead. She was in the process of meticulously smoothing the front of her uniform with her palms, ironing out invisible wrinkles. I now remembered the woman had some kind of OCD thing. That, and she had infuriated Porter to distraction—hell, she was the reason we spent three weeks looking for that perfect parrot within the jungles of the Amazon.

Gomez smirked, assessing the young officer. "Blunderton, your question cuts right to the heart of our predicament." He looked about the compartment and let out a weary breath.

"As I've already explained, we have no time to twiddle our thumbs here at Halibart Station while the Krygian are on the move. But because of the IFA Union strike, commerce has come to a standstill. Unfortunately, this ship is not fully, um... stocked." He gave Blunderton a sympathetic grimace.

Gomez said, "And if anyone's wondering why we can't just use the ship's replication units for supplies... all five of them are missing one vital part—a thing called an Auger Duplex Selinoid."

I said, "Let me guess... the IFA's impacted the delivery."

"Correct, Captain. *USS Roosevelt* awaits delivery of a myriad of critical components. As it stands, she's unable to manufacture wormholes, though her jump springs are operational for local transit. That means, once *Roosevelt* departs Halibart, you will proceed directly to StarPoint Station. Your necessary parts, including replicator devices, are in a hold waiting for pickup."

Shawlee stepped up next to Gomez. "Let me add one more thing. Please keep your interaction with IFA Union members to a bare minimum. They are not happy with the way negotiations are going. Think of them as burly longshoremen with an attitude."

Another very familiar voice spoke up with a distinct Bostonian accent. "I used to be one of those guys, they play rough, and they play dirty."

"Thank you, Hardy... we'll all keep that in mind," the Empress said. "For now, that's all—safe travels everyone. Captain Quintos, can I see you in your ready room?"

Chapter 5

By the time I emerged from my ready room, Empress Shawlee Tee had already quansported away—not taking the time to head to the Quansporter Compartment—which would have been more in accordance with regulations. What she shared had left me reeling, enough to need a few moments to mentally regroup.

Then, with a deep breath, I put on my game face and made my way to the bridge, just a few feet away. The auto-hatch swished shut behind me as I strode toward the awaiting captain's mount.

Captain Galvin Quintos on the bridge...

I involuntarily rolled my eyes at NELLA stating the obvious.

The bridge was fully manned—every station occupied, and every head turned toward me.

I acknowledged them, looking at each crewmember, letting them know I saw them, and appreciated them sharing the bridge with me for this mission.

Crewmember John Chen was on Comms, Thom Grimes at Helm, and Chatty Cathy, Ensign Blair Paxton, on Operations. Sensors and Reconnaissance were under Ensign Lira's keen eye. Crewmember Davit was overseeing Defensive Systems, while Engineering was looked after by Lieutenant Commander Jorkins. Crewmember Barrow was back monitoring Environmental Systems. Crewmember Soto was keeping a close eye on Damage Control. Lieutenant Junior Grade Roisin Blunderton was stationed at Navigation, her emerald-green eyes sharp and attentive. Like two palace guardsmen, Science Officer Stephan Derrota stood to my left, and Hardy, our resident 300-year-old ChronoBot, held his position to my right. And just three steps in front of me was none other than XO Gail Pristy, manning Tactical and the only one avoiding making eye contact with me.

"Departure status, Mr. Grimes!" I said, leaning back into my seat.

"We have clearance to depart from Halibart control, Captain," Grimes said.

"Let's go ahead and release docking clamps. Take us out, slow and easy, Helm."

Derrota joined me, standing at my left, as he so often did at the beginning of a new mission.

"Coogong's name is missing from the crew roster," I said.

Derrota's expression softened slightly. "Ah, I meant to inform you earlier. Coogong won't be joining us on this mission. He's taking a well-deserved vacation."

I blinked, momentarily struck by the mental image of the worm-like alien lounging on a beach chair, nursing a piña colada. The absurdity of it almost made me laugh.

"A vacation? Now?"

Derrota nodded. "He's been working non-stop for months. The timing isn't ideal, but..."

I waved it off. "No, no, he's earned it. We'll just have to manage without him this time."

The primary halo display showed the entirety of Halibart Station, *Roosevelt* being hard to miss, easily the largest of any vessel. Halibart Station was bustling with countless vessels coming and going—busier than I'd ever seen it.

Pristy brought up two more halo displays, an overhead view whereby the entirety of the omninought could be seen, and an aft view from *Roosevelt*, like a rearview mirror, showing the ship backing out from her spaceport slip.

The two Lansing Core Drives rumbled to life, sending a gentle vibration through the deck plates beneath my feet, like the hum of a finely tuned German motor.

"We're away, Captain," Grimes said. "Merging into—"

BRACE FOR IMPACT!
BRACE FOR IMPACT!
BRACE FOR IMPACT!

The impact hit before I could tighten my grip on my seat's armrests. Several crewmembers were thrown from their seats—Derrota now lay flat on his back on the deck. The overhead klaxon wailed while Soto bellowed out preliminary damage reports. Barrow confirmed environmental systems were intact. Hardy, stable as a New York City skyscraper, stared, along with me, in amazement at the rearview mirror halo display. Apparently, *Roosevelt's* monumentally fat ass had just careened into another vessel.

Lieutenant Junior Grade Blunderton, stationed at Navigation, was on her feet and her voice raised as she conversed with Halibart Control.

"What are you talking about? We did get clearance. You

specifically, Paul... whatever your last name is, gave us the clearance. Check your damn logs!"

I helped Derrota to his feet, "You okay, Stephan? That was quite a tumble you took."

"I'm fine, I'm fine," he said, rubbing at his left knee. "Just a scrape, I think."

Chen said, "Got calls coming in from all over the ship, Captain. HealthBay's at the top of the list."

"Who's our Chief Medical Officer?" I asked.

"Uh... that would be Dr. Pippa Tangerie."

I inwardly groaned—I was afraid of that. After what we'd recently gone through onboard *USS IKE* with her masterminding of the NEOGENE, Nano-Enhanced Organic GENEtic Engineering fiasco, I wouldn't have been surprised if she'd been relegated to Top Doc on an interstellar trash hauler.

"Put her through, Mr. Chen."

A nearby halo display activated, revealing HealthBay's chaos. Doctors, nurses, and MediBots moved swiftly, aiding injured crewmembers into beds amid the hectic scene.

A busy-looking Dr. Tangerie, wearing a white doctor's coat—her shoulder-length, caramel-colored hair pulled back into a no-nonsense ponytail, turned to face her TAC-Band. "Captain, what the hell happened? I have injured crewmembers coming in from all over the ship!" Tangerie's British inflection made her protest sound more like a polished pronouncement.

"Anyone sustained life-threatening injuries? Has anyone died?"

"No. They're mostly minor, superficial injuries—"

"Then deal with it, Doctor... because right now, I have to go see who we just backed into."

I signaled for Chen to cut the connection.

Hardy was heading for the exit. With his sensors, and

connection to NELLA, he knew where he was needed right now better than I did.

"Stephan, can you get down to HealthBay, see if you can help with the injured?"

"Absolutely. Yes, yes, I'll go right now," he said, his Mumbai accent more heightened than usual.

I scanned the bridge, my eyes coming to rest on the Damage Control Station. "Crewmember Soto, you're with me. You too, Blunderton... seems we're dealing with a major navigational screw-up."

"Well, it wasn't mine," she snapped.

Pristy was on her feet. "You'll watch your tone when addressing the captain. Understood, Lieutenant Junior Grade Blunderton?"

"Sorry, Ma'am; sorry, Captain."

"XO, you have the captain's mount. I'll keep you up to date as soon as I know anything."

"Roger that," she said, moving to take my evacuated seat.

Grimes said, "I had clearance, Captain... I don't know what happened."

"We'll get it figured out. For the time being, let's stay put."

Exiting the bridge, we hurried toward the closest DeckPort. I tried to recall a single instance where a ship under my command had unintentionally collided with another vessel. Nothing came to mind. This was a first. With today's precise algorithms and advanced technology, incidents like this should be next to impossible.

Crewmember Soto marched past me, her eyes fixed and brow furrowed, radiating focus. Blunderton, at my side, clenched and unclenched her fists rhythmically, as if driven by a sacred Native American drumbeat.

Catching me staring, her eyes locked onto mine.

"Sorry, Sir... I have a slight—"

"No need to explain, Ms. Blunderton. We all have our quirks," I replied, hoping I hadn't just insulted her.

En route, heading aft, we quickly crossed through five Deck-Ports—a short trek that took just two to three minutes. On older ships like *USS Hamilton*, with its various lifts, it would have taken up to twenty minutes.

I noticed Lieutenant Blunderton in my peripheral vision; there was an intensity about her that made me wonder how she came to be the way she was. I remembered Porter talking about Blunderton while we trudged through the swampy, mosquito-infested jungles of the Amazon. Despite her faults—impetuous and impatient—Craig had been impressed with her.

With little to no experience onboard a starship, she'd stepped up under intense pressure, working multiple *USS Washington* bridge stations. She essentially became more of the bridge commander than Porter himself. While her OCD was somewhat of a distraction, it hinted at a heightened underlying intelligence. Her competitive nature may have been her biggest fault—she'd taken real delight in coaxing Porter's parrot to abandon his shoulder and favor her own instead.

It occurred to me now... perhaps there was something more than just rivalry between the two. Blunderton was certainly pretty enough to have grabbed Porter's attention. He had mentioned she should be watched—he could see her being on the fast track for command someday.

As we continued our brisk pace, I couldn't help but reflect on the rare combination of qualities Porter claimed she possessed. He admired her ability to thrive under pressure and lead competently, even in dire circumstances. The woman had an impressive mind, and that, no doubt, was largely responsible for her rise from trailer park beginnings to Lieutenant Junior Grade in the U.S. Space Navy. Apparently, she was a member of Mensa—the world's oldest and largest high-IQ society. But it wasn't just her intelligence; with the body of a Russian gymnast, emerald-green eyes, and a flawless complexion, she was a knockout. I'd known Porter long enough to know when he was smitten. Her OCD quirkiness, and self-effacing humility, only seemed to add to her strange mystique.

But still, I remained unconvinced. While she had potential, I needed far more evidence of her abilities before I would be sharing Porter's admiration.

As we arrived at the farthest aft section of the ship, the klaxon continued to incessantly blare overhead, each wail a piercing reminder of our dire situation. Crewmembers frantically moved about, their faces etched with urgency under the red emergency lights. The atmosphere was thick with tension, the air filled with the metallic tang of burned circuits. I spotted Chief LaSalle amidst the chaos, his posture calm yet firm, his SWM contingent bustling about.

Soto was on her TAC-Band, her voice cutting through the noise as she issued commands. "I need those damage reports now! Tell me the status of the electrical grid!"

Surveying the wreckage before me, my eyes took in the caved-in portion of the compartment, pipes spewing white steam, and electrical conduits showering sparks like Roman Candles on the Fourth of July. The severity of our situation had me shaking my head, but I forced myself to focus.

"Chief, what's the SitRep on the damage?" I yelled, trying to make myself heard over the din.

"Captain, we took a hit to the rear quarter-section. Luck's on our side, though; the massive aft drive exhaust cones are unscathed. Ship's propulsion drives are intact." He gestured to the damaged area. "Several key junction arteries are down, but nothing we can't fix."

I nodded, processing the information. Soto was busy relaying updates, her TAC-Band buzzing incessantly. Blunderton stayed close, her eyes darting through the chaos with a look of fierce determination.

Just then, my TAC-Band vibrated; then Pristy's voice crackled through.

"Captain, the freighter has extended a twenty-foot skyway between our vessels. They're demanding we open *Roosevelt's* back hatch... uh, that would be Hatch S-AFT$_0$1-STB... GREY Sector."

I felt my blood boil. "Who are they to demand anything? The only reason we hit them is because they crossed into our trajectory!"

Pristy's frustration was palpable. "It's not clear yet, Sir. But they're adamant. They've threatened to keep the skyway locked in place until we comply."

"Oh for shit's sake," I muttered, my mind racing with possible scenarios. I turned to LaSalle. "Chief, how long until we can get this section operational again?"

LaSalle shook his head. "We're looking at four, maybe five hours, Captain. Further repairs can happen en route to Star-Point Station. These repairs aren't minor. We'll need all hands on deck."

I ground my molars, flashing back to Gomez's warnings about a possible—perhaps impending—attack by the Krygians. *We don't have time for this bullshit.*

Pristy's form was still projecting up from my TAC-Band. "XO, get a security detail to that back hatch. I want a full containment protocol in place."

"Copy that," she said, cutting the transmission.

NELLA's voice blared from above, acting on Pristy's request

for a security detail.

Blunderton stepped up. "Captain, if I may... something seems off. A little too coordinated with how things are unfolding—the collision with the freighter, the union freighter workers on strike. Doesn't this seem a little too convenient to you?"

"Certainly not convenient to our mission. But I hear what you're saying. All we can do is stay vigilant, Lieutenant."

Chapter 6

As we made our way to Hatch S-AFT01-STB... GREY Sector, Lieutenant Junior Grade Blunderton pulled a small tablet from one of the many pockets on her uniform. She thumbed through various news reports and internal U.S. Space Navy documents, her brow furrowing as she read. Curiosity got the better of me, and I asked, "What are you seeing, Ms. Blunderton?"

Blunderton glanced up at me, her expression of frustration and determination. "Captain, the situation with the IFA is worse than we thought. According to the most recent reports, the Intergalactic Freight Alliance has staged a series of coordinated attacks on U.S. Space Navy supply lines."

She continued scrolling, her eyes scanning the screen rapidly. "Several of our ships have been delayed or completely shut down due to sabotage. It's not just about pay or working conditions anymore. These union members are acting more like guerrilla fighters than laborers. There are strong indications that they have ties to organized crime, specifically a space mafia organization known as *The Circle*."

"Terrific. The timing of this couldn't have come at a worse time."

Blunderton paused her scrolling, the tablet's glow casting shadows that accentuated the surprisingly adolescent features of her face. I had to remind myself that she was twenty-six years old.

"Captain, we need to be prepared for the possibility that these longshoremen might not back down easily. Their demands aren't just about grievances anymore. They're trying to destabilize commerce infrastructure."

Before I could respond, my TAC-Band chirped, and Gomez's voice came through, sharp and clear. "Captain Quintos—Admiral Gomez here. Under no circumstances are you to use lethal force. I repeat, NO lethal force. These are Earth citizens, not enemy combatants like the Varapin, Grish, or Krygian. Am I making myself clear?"

"Crystal. I'm not anticipating any trouble. Trust me, the last thing I want is a dustup with these guys. I'm sure we'll work this out amicably."

"Ensure that you do."

Max's Marines were hurrying toward us from down the corridor. They wore standard-issue fatigues, devoid of combat suits or weapons. It had been weeks since I last saw them, since their harrowing encounter with the Krygian. Outnumbered and overwhelmed, they'd fallen in battle—killed, only to be revived through augmented Quansporters on *USS IKE*.

The ops mission used NEOGENE technology—a relentless revolving door cycle of life and death. Much like what Pristy had endured after her DeckPort mishap and subsequent death, her essence pulled back from some alternate plane of existence resulting in a technological rebirth, as it were.

And just as with Pristy, the psychological impact on the team had been devastating. Grip had attempted suicide, although I didn't know the specifics. Grip, of course, along with Max, Wanda, Ham, Hock, and Aubrey, had subsequently all undergone intense counseling. Seeing them here now, had me wondering if it was too soon for another deployment.

As they assembled, I relayed Gomez's orders. "No lethal action. Let's try to keep this as contained as possible. But stay sharp."

Both Blunderton and the now-just-arriving Soto stayed back.

"Listen up! Hand-to-hand only if it comes to that. No lethal force," Max ordered, making sure the directive was crystal clear to his team. "You all know the drill."

With a nod, I gave the order. The auto-hatch slid partially open with a metallic hiss but stuttered to a slow, jerky crawl.

"Too many bodies pressed up against it on the other side!" Ham announced.

I could just make out the packed skyway beyond—a throng of men in matching light-blue overalls—teeming with blue-collar testosterone. I couldn't count them all, just knew it was too many. It felt like we were unlocking a portal into a nightmare.

"Sensors tell me there are close to fifty of them packed in there," Soto said.

"Uh... they like to be called longshoremen," Blunderton offered from behind—now back to perusing her tablet.

I could see that their faces were twisted with rage. The hatch finally slid open enough for the first of them to squeeze through—within seconds they were flooding the corridor, a stampede of brute force.

Chaos ensued.

Longshoremen charged into our ranks, fists flying and feet stomping. These weren't just any longshoremen; they were big, brawny hulks with muscles straining against the seams of their jumpsuits. Their hardened faces were etched with lines of anger and determination, eyes blazing with a sense of purpose that elevated their laborer status. Each one looked like they could easily bench-press an old Peterbilt engine block, and their broad shoulders and thick necks gave them an intimidating presence that sent a jolt of apprehension down my spine.

I barely had time to register my precarious and ill-advised position at the frontline before a right cross to my chin sent me sprawling onto the deck. Stars danced in my vision. But, by some kind of miracle, I'd stayed conscious.

Max's Marines were already engaging in close-quarters combat with well-practiced precision. Their martial arts training evident... every move deliberate and effective.

Sergeant Max Dyer moved like a well-oiled machine, his every punch and kick a testament to his years of military expertise. He dodged an incoming hammer blow, countering with a swift elbow to the assailant's jaw, dropping the man like a sack of bricks.

Wanda waded into the fray with bursts of controlled ferocity—her movements agile and calculated. A roundhouse kick sent one longshoreman sprawling back, dazed by the force of her strike.

Grip showcased his formidable strength, lifting an attacker off the deck and hurling him into a charging group of three. He moved like a bear through the melee, intimidating and unyielding.

Shaking off my daze, I shot to my feet, fists clenched, prepared to take on anyone close enough. But it was an unrelenting onslaught, waves of attackers quickly overwhelming us. My head felt like a boxer's speedball, with incoming punches coming from multiple directions—I swayed and staggered, a cartoonish punch-drunk moron in way over his head. That

Gorvian plasma injection, which had saved my skin in previous scuffles, wouldn't do squat for me now.

I caught sight of Blunderton, her thin arms raised, trying to shield her face from an incoming strike. I froze, my breath catching as a blow connected with her cheek. It lifted her off her feet and sent her crumpling to the deck, limp as a ragdoll.

I found myself in the thick of it, suddenly grappling with a burly longshoreman who was far stronger than he looked. His fist connected with my jaw. I shook it off and countered with an uppercut to his ribcage, but it was like hitting a brick wall. A hard punch landed on the back of my head. Pain surged, my vision blurred—more flickering stars. I staggered, spinning and feeling like a metal ball trapped in a pinball machine.

One by one, the Marines were taken down. Grip was pulled off his feet, knocked unconscious by a well-placed punch; Wanda, still fighting on but visibly straining, was beset by three longshoremen at once; Ham and Hock, fighting shoulder-to-shoulder were gradually worn down by the relentless assault.

My own struggle seemed to stretch forever. I managed to pull myself to my feet, for the third time, but it was a hopeless attempt. Bright pain flared through my side as another fist landed, sending me reeling into the bulkhead. This was it, I thought. This was how it ended.

But then, through the haze of pain and chaos, a familiar figure strode into view. Stark and gleaming, Hardy moved with robotic precision and unyielding authority. His chrome form glinted against the bright overhead lights of the passageway.

Hardy's faceplate flickered to life, revealing John Hardy's visage from his longshoreman days in Boston. With resilience and grit carved into his 3D features, the essence of that relentless, blue-collar persona still shone through. Even in his ChronoBot form, Hardy's dock-worker's spirit remained unmistakably intact.

"Go ahead, bring it, tubby... you're not the only one who can fight dirty," Hardy commented.

He moved through the mob like a bowling ball, a thrown strike colliding through defenseless pins. A longshoreman's fist pounded against Hardy's metal chest, eliciting nothing but a dull clang. Hardy grabbed him by the collar, hoisting him off the deck and tossing him aside like discarded trash.

A group of three men attempted to flank him, but Hardy anticipated their feeble advance. A swift uppercut sent one flying back into the bulkhead, while a spinning sledgehammer of a blow—quick and clean—felled another. The ChronoBot then leaned into the third, grabbing his arm and effortlessly flipping him onto his back.

I watched from my position, barely standing, as the killer bot continued his systematic takedown. The longshoremen scattered, clearly no match for the relentless seven-foot-tall chrome giant. He was everywhere at once, a whirlwind of kinetic energy and brute force.

"Hardy!" I called out, my voice hoarse with strain. "Watch your six!"

But Hardy didn't need my warning. With a fluid motion, he caught an approaching attacker by the wrist, twisting just enough to bring him to his knees but not maim him. Even in the heat of battle, Hardy was maintaining a degree of control that impressed me.

There were far more light-blue, overalled men on the deck now—some moaning, others in unconscious la-la land—than standing. The tide had turned, the smarter of the union brutes making a fast retreat back into the skyway.

The corridor fell silent except for the heavy breathing of the Marines and the distant hum of the ship's systems.

I caught sight of Blunderton, a blossoming purple bruise on

her cheek—she was speaking into her TAC-Band requesting assistance from HealthBay.

As the dust settled, I surveyed the scene. Max and his team were battered, but alive. Oddly, all of them were smiling, even jovial. Kibitzing with one another. To my surprise, I too had a shit-eating grin plastered across my face.

Broken noses, split lips, eyes swollen shut—together they looked to have been on the wrong end of a baseball bat—each carrying the mark of a fierce beating. And yet, this may have been exactly what they'd needed. Therapy would do little for a pack of wild wolves but throw them back into a life-or-death fight for their lives, that's where they'd find the kind of mental healing that would be impossible sitting on a shrink's couch.

Blunderton and Soto helped the last of the injured to their feet, their expressions a mix of exhaustion and relief.

Hardy stood among the fallen attackers, his chrome surface barely scuffed. He looked at me, the John Hardy visage of the past, I sensed a hint of satisfaction and something I couldn't quite place.

"Well," I said, my voice thick with fatigue, "I suppose that could have gone worse."

Max assessed the ChronoBot. "Thanks for the assist, robot. But... just so you know, we would have gotten the better of them, even without your help. Eventually."

"Uh-huh," Hardy said, helping Wanda to her feet.

A team from HealthBay led by Dr. Pippa Tangerie arrived. She glanced about the scene with a raised eyebrow. "Seriously? A schoolyard brawl? That's how you chose to deal with the problem?"

I ignored her comment. She was still on my shitlist and didn't deserve an answer.

Blunderton approached, pocketing her tablet, glancing at the no fewer than ten unconscious longshoremen lying upon the deck. "We have a request from the local IFA Union leader, he wants a pow-wow with you."

"We'll take out the trash, Cap," Max said. "And get that hatch secured once they're stacked and packed within the skyway."

I nodded to Max and put my attention back on Blunderton. "Get that cheek of yours looked at, Lieutenant. That's an order. And I'll think about a meeting. Right now, I'm more inclined to blow that old freighter into space dust."

Chapter 7

I'd learned the name of the vessel was *Eventyr*. The original owners of the freighter, some sixty years prior, were Norwegian—eventyr was the word for *adventure*. The corridors of the old freighter felt like the metal intestines of a creature long since passed. Flickering lights cast an eerie glow on the grime-covered bulkheads, and the scent of oil and rust enveloped us as I, along with Pristy and Hardy, stepped further into the dingy depths of the ship. We were accompanied by two brawny longshoremen in front of us, two trailing behind.

My mind buzzed, not with apprehension, but with a keen sense of the game being played. The IFA had requested this meeting, claiming Marcus 'Ironfist' Kellen himself would come to apologize for the recent scuffle and promising to make things right. I didn't buy it for a second. This was a ploy, a power move wrapped in a thin veneer of diplomacy.

Pristy walked beside me, her posture confident and alert. She was no delicate flower, but a battle-tested officer who had faced down the worst the galaxy had to throw at us. Still, I sensed the unspoken tension between us, the weight of our stubborn pride and unacknowledged feelings. We were both too headstrong to confront it head-on.

"Admiral Gomez warned us not to make things worse," I reminded her. "We need to hear them out, play along for now."

Pristy nodded, her blue eyes hardening with resolve. "Agreed. But let's not forget who we're dealing with here. And what's with Gomez cow-towing to the union—I don't get it."

I shrugged, "Above my pay level. Undoubtedly, behind-the-scenes politics are going on."

Hardy marched ahead, his heavy footsteps echoing through the corridor. As our unwavering guardian, he would be scanning the area with his enhanced sensors, always on the lookout for threats.

"Cap, I'm not detecting any immediate threats, but... something's not right. I know these people... well, not specifically, *these* people but these kinds of people."

"Noted, Hardy," I said flatly.

We kept moving down the narrow, worn corridors. The air carried that stink of something foul—I inwardly reminded myself that we needed to keep our cool.

At last, we reached a poorly lit meeting room, which was probably the crew's dining hall. Several chipped and marred tables with mismatched chairs had been assembled in the middle of the compartment. The stench of spoiled meat drifted in from somewhere nearby. Our IFA guides took up positions along the bulkheads—one man was seated at the table; he turned as we entered.

I recognized him from earlier—Blunderton's tablet, the IFA union boss, Marcus 'Ironfist' Kellen. He was a barrel-chested, middle-aged man with a paunch and double chin, wearing a worn-out union jumpsuit with visible IFA insignia. He was also short. Like, really short to the point I had to practically look down to my boots to see him.

Perhaps over-compensating for a total lack of stature, he radiated hostility. His upper lip curled in a permanent snarl, unsoftened even by his attempt at a smile. His face was lined with false sincerity—his eyes glinted with barely concealed malice.

"Captain Quintos!" Kellen boomed, his voice dripping with exaggerated politeness. "Thank you for agreeing to this meeting. I am Marcus Kellen of the Intergalactic Freight Association."

I stepped forward, shaking his hand and forcing a smile. "Of course. I'm always open to dialogue, Mr. Kellen."

I introduced XO Pristy and Hardy—both were given an extended once-over but for different reasons. Kellen gestured for us to take a seat—Hardy declined, opting to take up a position close to one of the bulkheads.

Kellen launched into a rehearsed apology for the earlier brawl, claiming it was a misunderstanding born of his workers' passion for their livelihoods. I listened, my expression neutral, but I didn't believe a word of it.

Suddenly, a new voice cut through the room as someone new made his entrance. "Gentlemen, please. Let's dispense with the pleasantries."

I spotted him right off as well, courtesy of Blunderton's tablet. Victor 'the Viper' Blackhold, a well-known menace in the criminal underworld. He stood out sharply, clad in a tailored suit that clashed with the grime of his surroundings. His wavy salt-and-pepper hair appeared to be under a stylist's constant care. His vacation-tanned features and too-brilliant white teeth were a distraction.

Pristy and I locked eyes. Blackhold commanded a kind of leery respect, his presence heavy with authority. His reputation whispered of danger before he even spoke.

"Captain Quintos, Ms. Pristy," Blackhold purred his voice

silk, hiding steel. "How about we get right down to it... work out how we can help each other."

What I wanted to do was tell both of these men to go to hell, let me get back to my ship. But I listened politely, reminding myself of Gomez's orders.

He spoke of aligning interests, the benefits of cooperation. And then, turning his full attention to Pristy, while placing a compassionate hand to his heart, said, "Executive Officer Pristy," Blackhold said, his tone almost sympathetic, "I was deeply moved to hear about your niece Emma's struggle with Juvenile Degenerative Neuroinflammatory Syndrome... commonly referred to as JDNS. Such a rare and unforgiving illness. I understand she's eager to join that new clinical trial offered by the University of Chicago Medical Center. What a coincidence it is that I sit on the board of directors with significant influence over the acceptance process.

Now... I'm not a doctor by any means, but I understand there's something called the mutant NEUROIN$_1$ protein... that it triggers a hyperactive immune response within the brain, causing chronic inflammation. You know all this far better than I do, I'm sure... that this leads to what is referred to as neuronal degeneration—the progressive loss of neurons due to inflammatory damage and impaired cellular maintenance." He offered up a sickeningly condescending expression. "What comes next? Systemic multi-organ dysfunction and... death of the child."

I heard Pristy's sudden intake of breath.

XO Gail Pristy

Two weeks earlier, Gail Pristy found herself back in a place she never thought she'd be—on the outskirts of Columbus, Ohio, standing helplessly at the bedside of her niece, Emma, watching the once vibrant, fun-loving 8-year-old girl fade away before her eyes. Emma had been diagnosed with Juvenile Degenerative Neuroinflammatory Syndrome (JDNS), a devastating genetic disorder that had emerged in the late 21st century.

JDNS was a cruel and merciless illness, targeting children in their most formative years. It was characterized by a rapid and invariably fatal progression, attacking the central nervous system with a ferocity that left families shattered and medical professionals helpless. The disease caused severe neurological degeneration and systemic inflammation, robbing its young victims of their mobility, their cognitive functions, and ultimately, their lives.

Emma had always been a burst of sunshine, a whirlwind of laughter and joy that lit up every room she entered. But now, as Pristy looked down at her small, frail form, she barely recognized the child she adored. The illness had come on suddenly, a thief in the night that stole Emma's health and vitality. At first, they had hoped it was just a passing bug, something that rest and proper care would cure. But as the days turned into weeks, and Emma grew weaker and paler, the terrible truth of her JDNS diagnosis became impossible to ignore.

Pristy's sister, once a beacon of strength and resilience, was now a listless shell of her former self. Her brother-in-law, a man who had always faced life's challenges with unwavering optimism, now moved through the days like a ghost, his eyes haunted and his shoulders slumped under the weight of his despair.

And Emma—sweet, innocent Emma—fought bravely against the disease that ravaged her body. She endured countless tests, procedures, and treatments—and with each medical encounter, her small face pinched with pain and exhaustion. But through it all, she never lost her smile, never stopped believing that she would get better.

But through it all, she never lost her smile, never stopped believing that she would get better.

Pristy's heart ached as she watched her niece's struggles. In a time of miraculous medical advancements, of regrow pods and MediBots that could work wonders, it seemed incomprehensible that they were powerless against the onslaught of JDNS. The frustration and helplessness gnawed at Pristy, a constant companion in her waking hours and a specter that haunted her dreams.

But even in the darkest of moments, Pristy refused to give up hope. She scoured medical journals, reached out to every doctor and researcher she could find, desperate for a glimmer of light in the darkness.

And then, like a miracle, she found it. A new study, a clinical trial at the University of Chicago Medical Center offered a sliver of hope for children like Emma, a potential treatment for the devastating effects of JDNS. Pristy knew it was a long shot, that the odds were stacked against them. But she also knew that she would move heaven and earth to give her niece a fighting chance.

She reached out to Dr. Vivian Leigh, an old friend who had been the chief medical officer onboard *USS Hamilton*—she remembered she had completed her residency at the University of Chicago Medical Center. Just maybe, she still had influence. It had taken her a few days to track her down—Doc Viv said she'd be happy to see what she could do—she still had contacts at UCMC.

Just when all hope was falling away like the last grains of sand through an hourglass, Doc Viv had come through—Emma was being considered for entry into the trial.

Pristy will never forget the look on her sister's face when she told her the news. The way her eyes lit up, the way the weight seemed to lift from her shoulders, if only for a moment. And

Emma, brave, resilient Emma, faced the new challenge with the same determination and courage she had shown throughout her battle with JDNS.

But now, as Pristy sat there in the dingy meeting room on the old freighter, facing the cold, calculating eyes of Victor Blackhold, she felt that hope slipping away. This man, this monster—*the Viper*—wanted to take away the one chance Emma had to live, to thrive. He wanted to destroy the fragile peace that Pristy's sister and brother-in-law had found, all for his own selfish gain.

A rage was building inside her, a fury that threatened to consume her. How could anyone be so soulless? He was playing on Pristy's emotions, making her a pawn in his twisted game of power and influence. But even as the anger coursed through her veins, Pristy knew she had to be smart. She couldn't let Blackhold see how much he had gotten to her, couldn't give him the satisfaction of knowing he had found her one weak spot. So, her face remained expressionless—her demeanor... bordering on boredom. But hidden beneath the table's edge, her hands clenched into white-knuckled fists.

No matter what it took, no matter what sacrifices she had to make, Pristy would protect her family. She would fight for Emma, for her sister, for the hope that had been so hard-won in the face of such a devastating illness. Her lips turning up, bemused, she looked to Quintos, this was his show—he better not fuck it up.

Captain Galvin Quintos

Pristy didn't let on just how much this despicable excuse for a human being had gotten to her. I was impressed by her calm laissez-faire demeanor. Had she momentarily bristled? If so, it had been imperceptible. No, she'd held it together, and more importantly, held her tongue. We both knew this game—had played it before with far more dangerous opponents. With that said, I knew, at some point in time—perhaps in the not-too-distant future, I'd be ending this motherfucker.

I met *the Viper's* gaze evenly. "I appreciate your concern, Mr. Blackhold. We both do. And I get it—you're a low-life criminal scumbag; intimidation tactics are part of your DNA. But threats against my crew will not be tolerated. *And* you're not the only one who can make not-so-veiled threats."

Blackhold's gaze wandered, landing on Hardy. The mere sight of the ChronoBot carried its own weight of menace.

The Viper refocused his attention on Quintos. He grinned, a shark sensing blood in the water. "Captain Quintos, let's not dance around it. Cooperation between the Circle and the U.S. Space Navy is no longer a matter of if, but when. Once it becomes clear just how lucrative this alliance can be, I've encountered little resistance among those at the top echelons of your military. But you two..." he glanced at Pristy and then back to me. "... have captured the admiration and loyalty of the populace. Your enthusiastic show of cooperation could lend a hint of legitimacy to our endeavors. The sky's the limit for our rewards —monetary gains are obvious, but power, now that's the true motivation for great men, wouldn't you agree?"

His eyes locked onto Pristy, his tone dripping with insincerity. "And poor Emma. Don't you think it's time we got her the medical help she needs? Imagine her back on her feet, frolicking in the yard with that little dog of hers. It could all be so simple if only we worked together."

He stood, beaming—his bright white teeth flashed like a movie star's. The meeting was over. "I'll need an answer by the time you reach StarPoint Station. I'm sure you'll do the right thing here, Captain."

Chapter 8

I ducked into my ready room before heading back to the bridge, the auto-hatch sealing behind me. The chaos outside faded away, leaving me in a bubble of quiet. I took a moment to breathe before slumping into my chair and bringing up the halo display. Chen was under orders to patch Gomez through ASAP.

Fifteen minutes crawled by before the Admiral's face materialized in blue light. I didn't bother with pleasantries. "Admiral, our little chat with the IFA Union guy, Kellen... it went sideways."

Gomez didn't look happy. "I specifically told you, Captain—"

"Sir, I assure you. We were in our best behavior."

"Fine. What happened?"

"The little Napoleonic mobster... Victor Blackhold crashed the party," I said.

"Dammit!" Gomez spat, shaking his head. "Go on. What happened?"

"Well, he started throwing his weight around. He didn't hesitate to make threats."

"What kind of threats?"

My XO, Gail Pristy, has an 8-year-old niece with what has thus far been an incurable progressive disease. There's a new experimental clinical trial that would be her only hope. Blackhold made it clear that, with his connections in high places, he would block her admission into the trial unless Pristy and I, given our more recent notoriety, become advocates for the Circle's involvement in future U.S. Space Navy commerce.

Gomez leaned in, frowning. "And it was Blackhold himself? You're certain of that?"

"No doubt about it," I said, feeling my blood pressure rise. "He's got Kellen and the IFA Union on a short leash. The bastard even played the sympathy card with Emma's condition. Took everything I had not to rearrange his face."

"Good thing you didn't," Gomez said, rubbing his chin and looking thoughtful. "Okay, I'll get a security detail on Emma's family right away. That's in Ohio, right?"

How did he know that? How much of what I've just told him these last few minutes did he already know? This whole situation was starting to smell bad.

"Yes, a security detail will be a good start, but it won't be enough, Sir. We need to show Blackhold and his goons that the U.S. Space Navy doesn't roll over for thugs."

Gomez sighed, looking tired. "I get it, Captain. I'll also make sure Emma gets in that trial with no interference. But we need to play this smart. For now, it's best to go along and see where this leads. And hell, some of Kellen's demands might not be totally out of line."

I stared at him, stunned. "You can't be serious, Admiral. These guys are criminals, and they think they've got us by the short hairs."

Gomez's gaze hardened. "Keep your cool, Galvin. Remember, there are talks happening above your pay grade. Your job is to get to StarPoint, fix *Roosevelt*, and deal with the Krygians before they make a visit to Earth. Got it?"

I bit my tongue. "Got it, Sir. But surely we don't have to—"

"And don't hassle any of the IFA members once you reach StarPoint," Gomez cut in. "Clear? This needs a scalpel, not a sledgehammer."

A pang of disgust roiled in my gut—Blackhold's influence had somehow slithered its way to the very top—Admiral Gomez himself was being manipulated. Was it blackmail, or maybe not-so-subtle threats to his family as what was done with Pristy's?

"Understood, Admiral," I said.

"Good," he nodded. "Keep me posted. Take care of your people. Gomez out."

The display winked out, leaving me alone with my thoughts. Finesse. Not my strong suit, but for now, it's all I've got.

I stepped out of my ready room, the conversation with Gomez still gnawing at me. The bridge was a hive of activity, everyone at their posts, focused and ready. Pristy glanced up as I walked in.

"Captain, the *Eventyr* freighter has disentangled itself from *Roosevelt's* hindquarters," she said, the slight relief in her voice matching my own. "We're clear to head away from Halibart Station."

"Good. Let's not waste any—" I paused mid-sentence, catching sight of Lieutenant Blunderton at Operations. Perched upon her left shoulder was, of all things, a bird.

"Ms. Blunderton," I called out, drawing the bridge's attention, "would you be so kind as to enlighten me why you have a bird perched upon your left shoulder?"

Blunderton straightened her shoulders, looking like a cadet bracing for a reprimand. "Sir," she began, her expression earnest, "this is Lucy... my ESA."

I blinked, the acronym failing to ring any bells.

"Emotional support animal, Sir," she clarified. "As you may know, I have a low-level—I'm sure unnoticeable—OCD affliction and it's a well-known fact that an ESA provides a calming, supportive effect—one that only bolsters—"

I raised a hand to stop her from over-explaining further. "Fine, Lieutenant... ensure that your, um—"

She interjected, "Emotional support animal, Sir."

I sighed inwardly. "Just ensure it doesn't get in the way of your duties or anyone else's bridge responsibilities. And please tell me that bird doesn't talk."

She paused briefly, then nodded with an air of reservation, her posture now far less rigid. The bird, however, remained unflustered, observing its surroundings with casual detachment.

Returning my focus to the task at hand, I approached the captain's mount, prepared to guide *Roosevelt* toward StarPoint.

"Captain," Chen said, "I have Chief Porter from Engineering and Propulsion, Sir."

"On display," I said, leaning back in my seat.

A halo display projection formed at the front of the bridge. Immediate chuckles erupted within the compartment.

Chief Craig Porter stood there in his uniquely unofficial U.S. Space Navy uniform—a Hawaiian shirt splashed with tropical pineapple prints, a frayed Cubs baseball cap, and much to my growing annoyance, a parrot perched on his right shoulder.

I let out a slow, controlled breath, spun on my seat to look at Lieutenant Blunderton. "Is this meant to be funny? Is there a joke I've missed the point of here?"

"No Sir," she said, stammering. "It's more of a coincidence."

I had far more important things to be concerned with. "Chief, please tell me that the fine new omninought's dual Lansing Core drives are fully operational, and I can have Mr. Grimes set a course for StarPoint Station."

"Uh... sorry, Galvin, but there's a problem. Appears that our little fender bender with the freighter caused an influx imbalance on our starboard drive. Until we make repairs, we'll be taking things slow... maybe if we push things I can give you 12 DTs."

Astrogation remains a key course at the U.S. Space Navy Academy. Cadets learn that DecaTreks measure speed in units ten times the speed of light. So, when we talk about ships moving at 12 DecaTreks, they're cruising at around 120 times light-speed—or roughly 7 billion miles per hour. Yet, even these velocities are considered sluggish by modern FTL standards, which demand far greater speeds when leaping between star systems.

I rubbed my forehead, "Craig... just tell me how long those repairs are going to take."

"Couple of days at least. Got a team on it. I'll keep you updated."

Porter's smile faded, his eyes focusing on something behind me. It occurred to me, that he'd focused in on another crewmember—one with an identical-looking Macaw perched upon her shoulder.

Scowling, Porter said, "Chief out."

"Mr. Grimes," I said, "how about you start putting some distance between us and Halibart Station?"

"Aye, Captain."

Chapter 9

Four hours later, USS *Roosevelt,* was making slow but steady progress within the deep void beyond the Solar System. I watched our progress from the main halo display on the bridge; everything seemed to be proceeding smoothly, and I was finally starting to settle down after the whole union fiasco.

Then my TAC-Band pinged—as did Pristy's. Apparently, a high-priority notification was buzzing to life on select TAC-Bands across the ship, at the same instant.

It was from Sonya Winters, and I was being directed to report to the combined Decks of 98/99/100 immediately. Captain Wallace Ryder would be taking the captain's mount—it had all been arranged, apparently, without my knowledge. Undoubtedly, for others being contacted, replacements would have been scheduled to fill their posts as well.

As I moved toward the entrance to the Symbio Deck, I caught sight of the others who had been invited. There was Grip—I'd yet to have a meaningful conversation with him about the turn of events with the Krygian. His calm assertiveness gave no indication he'd been struggling with depression. Pristy, who'd walked with me here from the bridge without so much as a single word exchanged, looked as if she'd have rather been anywhere else but here... or here with me... I wasn't sure. Stephan Derrota, fiddling nervously with his TAC-Band, looked up as we approached and smiled. Aubrey Laramie looked less confident than usual—she'd had little experience with Symbio Deck games, and Kaelen Rivers, maintained his usual subdued, lackadaisical demeanor.

"Anyone have a clue what Sonya's cooked up this time?" Derrota muttered, glancing around.

"Given her track record, I'm bracing for anything from medieval chaos to a prehistoric nightmare," I replied, trying to keep it light.

"Watch it be some kind of galactic treasure hunt," Grip suggested, cracking a rare smile. "Or worse, a romantic drama."

Pristy rolled her eyes. "I doubt it's going to be that straightforward. Whatever it is, I'm sure it will be all-consuming like previous Symbio Decks—which means a monumental time suck. Honestly, who has time for this kind of nonsense?"

Derrota adjusted his glasses, speaking up cautiously. "Maybe she's recreated a more personalized moment in time? Something with a real-world application?"

"You mean like the town of Clairmont or something?" I chuckled, though internally I couldn't shake the unease of another psychological gauntlet.

Kaelen Rivers glanced between us, "I was just surprised to get an invite. Feels like I'm now part of the cool kids crowd."

"I don't think you have anything to worry about in that regard," Aubrey said with a smirk. "You'll never be one of the cool kids."

"Ouch," he said.

More guesses were thrown about, yet none seemed to hit the mark.

As the massive auto-hatch began sliding open, we collectively gasped, our conversations silenced by what was coming into view.

We stepped into what was clearly an ancient Roman scene—one that took my breath away. Towering marble columns loomed overhead, intricate mosaics sprawled underfoot, and the unmistakable sounds of Roman life buzzed around us. The vastness of the combined three Decks, six miles long and close to a mile wide, was mind-bogglingly real. A blue sky as true as any I'd ever seen stretched above us, giving the illusion of endless space. Impressive, sure, but the idea of wading through this simulated intrigue put me on edge.

In the center of what appeared to be a grand courtyard, Sonya stood adorned in an intricate Roman tunic. Silken fabric draped over her shoulders, held in place by ornate clasps shaped like laurel leaves. Layers of finely woven material formed a cascade of folds flowing to her sandaled feet, and a delicate golden belt cinched her waist. Her long, dark hair, caught in ringlets, was crowned by a simple yet elegant golden circlet. The teenager's eyes sparkled with excitement as she looked back at us. She stood between two muscle-bound Roman guards, Symbio-Poths, which I now assessed—every detail of their outfits had been carefully recreated.

Without warning, my rarely—if ever—used ocular implants came alive in my head with NELLA's calm voice. Impressive! It seemed this Symbio Deck experience had come with an inner knowledge helper.

THE AI'S SOOTHING VOICE HAD BEEN GOING ON for about ten minutes, regaling us with tales of the Eternal City.

"... ancient Roman guards, particularly the Praetorian Guards, were equipped with distinctive clothing and weaponry. Their typical attire and weapons included the following clothing Items:

Lorica Segmentata: A type of segmented armor made of metal strips.

Galea: A helmet with cheek guards.

Tunica: A tunic worn under the armor.

Balteus: A military belt.

Caligae: Heavy-soled, hobnailed military sandals.

Gladius: A short sword used for stabbing, about 18-24 inches in length, effective in close combat.

The combination of these items provides the Praetorian Guard with both protection and the ability to engage effectively in combat."

By putting my attention back onto my niece, NELLA's narration cut out.

"Welcome, brave souls," Sonya began, her voice carrying a commanding yet playful tone. "Today, you embark on a journey unlike any you have faced before. Here, within the confines of this Symbio Deck, you will be transported back to the glory and danger of ancient Rome. Hundreds of the latest advanced Symbio 3.0s will be the backdrop of Roman life, taking on many interactive roles that will keep the game moving and on track. But keep in mind that you trust these characters at your own risk."

She let her words sink in, the crew exchanging curious, somewhat anxious glances. I'd seen this look before—right before a tough mission.

"You may be wondering why you are here and what your roles will be in this grand narrative. Each of you has been chosen for a specific reason, and your success depends on your ability to work together, to think strategically, and to act decisively."

"Today's journey in this Symbio Deck Experience will be unlike any you've faced before," Sonya's voice echoed, each word heightening my curiosity.

She paused, as if gauging our readiness, before adding, "I will appear, sometimes unexpectedly, throughout the game, not just when starting a new interlude. Sometimes I'll meet secretly with individuals, more frequently with some than others, depending on the needs of the evolving narrative."

The players began to murmur, whispers of excitement and confusion mingling in the air. I didn't know what to think about these unpredictable interactions.

"These meetings could occur at crucial moments," Sonya continued, her eyes meeting each of ours in turn, "just before a major challenge or after a significant discovery. If anyone seems stuck or unsure, or to provide a sudden twist or new information. Sometimes it will be me, and sometimes it will be NELLA in your ear."

Sonya's expression grew serious. "Some meetings might be brief—a whispered instruction. Others could be more elaborate. I might provide instructions to two players simultaneously, encouraging cooperation or even creating potential conflict."

Interesting. This new layer of unpredictability would add a little spice to things. We would have to stay on our toes, always prepared for the next twist or turn in the narrative. The challenge seemed to resonate with the others too, judging by their nods and focused gazes.

"There will be times," Sonya added, "when players won't receive any direct instructions, forcing you to rely on your judgment. This arbitrary approach keeps the game exciting and forces everyone to stay alert."

Sonya stepped forward, her presence dominant yet reassuring, "But above all, remember—cooperation and trust within your team will be crucial. May the Gods be with you on this perilous journey."

Sonya stepped forward, her eyes locking onto each crewmember in turn.

"Captain Quintos... Galvin" she addressed me first, "you will take on the role of Marcus Junius Brutus, a once-revered Senator who has fallen from grace. Betrayed by those you trusted, you now find yourself condemned to the life of a gladiator. Your strength, leadership, and wisdom will be tested at every turn."

I nodded, contemplating why my niece had chosen this role for me in particular—there again, perhaps I was overthinking things.

"Grip," Sonya continued, turning to our seasoned Marine, "you are Spartacus, a formidable gladiator who has survived countless battles in the arena. Your knowledge of combat and the ways of the Colosseum will be invaluable to the team. You will guide and protect Marcus as he navigates this treacherous new world."

Grip glanced my way, "No worries... I got your back, uh, Senator whatever your name was."

"Executive Officer Pristy... Gail," Sonya said, her gaze shifting to my XO, "you will be known as Livia Drusilla, a noblewoman of great beauty and intelligence. By Caesar's side, you have the ear of the most powerful man in Rome. However, your true allegiance lies with the resistance, and you must use your position to gather information and aid in the downfall of Caesar. Your diplomatic skills and strategic mind will be crucial."

Pristy's eyes narrowed, already whirling—perhaps already conjuring plans and contingencies. She was always the planner, the strategist.

"Science Officer Derrota... Stephan," Sonya continued, "you

will play the role of Lucius Decimus Sulla, a shrewd and ruthless politician. Your strategic acumen and political maneuvering will be essential in outsmarting Caesar's allies and furthering the conspiracy. Like Livia Drusilla, your ability to deceive Caesar while managing clandestine operations will be imperative."

Derrota adjusted his glasses, a look of apprehension in his eyes. I doubted the man had a duplicitous bone in his body.

"Petty Officer Second Class Laramie... Aubrey," Sonya said, directing her attention to the young and attractive officer, "You are Hypatia, a skilled healer and philosopher. Your medical expertise and knowledge of ancient remedies will be essential in keeping the team healthy and prepared for the battles ahead. Your compassion and empathy will be your greatest strengths."

I feigned a choking sound, "Compassion and empathy? You may need to work on your acting skills a bit."

"Hey! I can be compassionate... I think," Aubrey added without much confidence.

I noticed Pristy wasn't amused by Aubrey's and my back-and-forth banter.

"Engineering Specialists Rivers... Kaelen," Sonya said, finishing up, "you will take on the role of Vitruvius, an ingenious engineer and master of mechanics. Your skills will be vital in manipulating the environment to the team's advantage. Your ingenuity and problem-solving abilities will shine through."

Kaelen gave a thumbs-up, looking ready to jump into whatever this role-playing game had to offer.

Sonya's expression grew serious as she addressed the entire team. "Your objective is to overthrow Caesar and destabilize the Roman Empire. Caesar's tyranny knows no bounds. He has plunged Rome into a state of fear and oppression, ruthlessly eliminating all who oppose him. His obsession with power has led to the suffering of countless innocents, and his continued reign threatens to plunge the empire into chaos and ruin."

She raised a hand, signaling the importance of her next words. "The stakes are high. Failure means not only the end of your mission but the potential collapse of the resistance. You must be vigilant, resourceful, and united. You will face harrowing life-and-death gladiator matches within the Colosseum, thrilling six-horse team chariot races, and Livia's romantic intrigue with Caesar himself. Trust will be a scarce commodity; you cannot rely on anyone if you want to stay alive."

Sonya stepped aside, revealing a detailed map of the Colosseum and the surrounding areas. "The six of you are the newly formed resistance. While you all share a desire to bring down Caesar, trust among you has yet to be earned. You'll begin this Symbio Deck experience as a group for the first time, venturing into an in-person meeting as part of the resistance."

"Some of you have already noticed that NELLA has spoken to you. As Esperienza Sage or just Sage, she will be accessible via your ocular implants. She can provide necessary historical background and clarify things, but don't expect her to give you hints, to offer any kind of advantage."

I noticed that Aubrey had a distant look to her gaze—it appeared that she was interfacing with the NELLA—Sage—even as Sonya was speaking.

Sonya's voice took on a more urgent tone as she continued, "The fate of this mission hinges on your ability to uncover hidden clues and successfully complete specific tasks. Each clue you find and every task you accomplish will bring you one step closer to overthrowing Caesar and achieving victory. Failure to solve these mysteries or complete these challenges will result in certain doom for the resistance and the continued tyranny of Caesar."

She gestured to the detailed map of the Colosseum.

"Remember, the clues you uncover are not just incidental; they are vital pieces of the larger puzzle. Only by following these leads and overcoming the trials ahead will you be able to destabilize the Roman Empire and bring down its corrupt leader."

"Your first clue lies within the gladiator quarters. Hidden in the eastern wall is a secret compartment. Inside, you will find a scroll that holds the key to your next objective. This scroll will lead you to the first relic you must acquire."

She took a deep breath, her eyes filled with pride and determination. "Remember, each of you has a role to play, and your success depends on your ability to trust and support one another. May the Gods be with you on this perilous journey."

With that, Sonya turned and walked away, leaving us to ponder our mission and prepare for the challenges ahead. The air was thick with anticipation, and the fate of Rome rested in our hands.

Chapter 10

A Roman bathhouse loomed above us, its grand marble columns reaching skyward, casting long shadows across the intricately carved stone floors. The structure radiated a fresh, untouched look, a sharp contrast to the ancient ruins familiar from history books.

The intricate detailing on the walls spoke of an era long past, each one adorned with delicate murals depicting scenes of current Roman life. The air was thick with the scent of aged stone and the faint echo of water trickling from unseen fountains, adding to the aura of timeless elegance that enveloped the entire structure.

As I approached, the scent of fragrant herbs and sweet oils filled my nostrils. My ocular implants explained how Romans often used healing oils and herbs like rosemary, lavender, thyme, and myrtle in their bathing routines.

I adjusted the folds of my senator's toga, still uncomfortable in this garb.

"Brutus," a voice whispered from the shadows. I turned to see Sonya, cloaked as a soothsayer, her eyes gleaming. "Your path to redemption begins here. Seek the hidden message within these walls. It will guide your next steps."

Before I could question her, she vanished into the mist. I shook my head, grinning at the game's complexity, and entered the bathhouse.

Inside, my fellow conspirators arrived one by one, each appearing slightly awkward in their Roman garb. Pristy, as Livia Drusilla, stood apart, her noble bearing clashing with an evident self-consciousness. Our eyes met, and I noticed a flicker of our real-world tension blended into this fabricated reality.

"Brutus," she greeted me, her voice managing to stay even. "Are you ready for all this?"

I nodded, feeling a bit out of place. "As ready as one can be, I suppose."

Grip, playing Spartacus, shifted uncomfortably in his simple gladiator's tunic, his bare, muscled arms folded across his chest. He scanned the room for threats, the Marine in him never quite switching off. Aubrey, as Hypatia, crouched by a pool, her interest in the water's contents seemingly more about avoiding eye contact than contemplation. Derrota, in the role of Lucius Cornelius Sulla, paced with uncertainty, muttering about political implications with an uneasy laugh escaping now and then. Kaelen, cast as Vitruvius, fiddled with the bathhouse's ancient mechanisms, perhaps finding it easier to focus on the tangible rather than the theatrical.

Our hushed voices echoed off marble walls, columns, and floors as if a crowd had gathered.

"Not a lot of brothers just wandering the streets in Roman times. People like me... we don't fit in here," Grip said, glancing around uncomfortably.

"You mean like a clown at a funeral?" Aubrey said sarcastically.

"Let's stay in character, people," Derrota insisted, his voice firm as the unofficial referee for their game.

I called the meeting to order, trying to channel Brutus' leadership. "Friends, Romans, conspirators... we gather here to discuss our next move. Each of us has suffered under Caesar's rule. Now, we must decide how to act."

As we debated, the game was starting to feel more immersive. Aubrey's voice cut through the discussion. "Uh, guys... look here," she said, pointing to strange markings near the central pool. "This mural. It's more faded than the others. I get the feeling it's representative of something."

We gathered around, our earlier squabbles forgotten as we worked to decode the markings. It would be interesting to see how our individual skills would mesh going forward.

"It's a map," I realized aloud, "of the Colosseum."

Pristy's eyes narrowed. "What was your first clue, Brutus, I think that would have been obvious, even to a 3rd grader." She stepped closer and pointed, "But here, that's the gladiator quarters right? You and Spartacus here are gladiators, maybe we should start there. Could be the perfect place to hide information."

Grip nodded. "If we're infiltrating the Colosseum, we'll need a solid plan. Security there will probably be tight."

Aubrey rolled her eyes fighting the urge to laugh.

As we planned our next move, I made sure to include everyone. "We'll all go," I decided. "Grip and I will take the lead, but the rest of you will follow at a distance. We might need your skills at any moment." I waggled my eyebrows dramatically, which Derrota did not appreciate.

Night was falling as we approached the Colosseum, its silhouette looming against the starry sky. *How had Shawlee and Sonya managed such realism? The scale alone was inconceivable.* My heart actually quickened some as we narrowly avoided patrols, relying on Grip's Marine instincts and Pristy's knowledge of all things tactical.

Once we'd found the entrance to the below-ground area of the Colosseum, NELLA was back in my ear telling me this subterranean area was called the hypogeum—an intricate network of tunnels and chambers used to house gladiators, animals, and stage scenery. It featured lifts, pulleys, and trap doors for dramatic arena entrances.

Apparently, we'd all gotten the same mini-dissertation from the AI.

Pristy said, "So, we're on the right track. Gladiator quarters are down here somewhere."

We wandered through the maze of dim passageways—flickering torches sporadically spaced, casting eerie shadows upon the stone walls.

After twenty minutes, we reached our destination—the gladiator quarters, where iron-barred cages lined the walls. The stench of sweat and blood filled the space, and shackled Symbio-Poths hurled curses our way. Chains clinked in the darkness. I jumped back just in time to avoid a kick aimed at my kneecap.

As Grip and I searched, the others stayed hidden in the shadows, keeping watch in the adjacent passageway.

"Here." Grip's voice barely registered above a whisper as he pointed at a loose stone.

With dirt and slime coating our fingers, we worked together to pry it free. Behind it lay a hidden compartment holding a scroll and a worn gladiator's armband.

Unfurling the scroll, I recalled Sonya's earlier comments. I read its contents aloud in a hushed voice.

"To advance, Marcus Junius Brutus must prove his worth in

the arena and win the crowd's praise. Only through victory in combat can the way forward be revealed."

Grip's eyes met mine, a mixture of excitement and maybe a little concern in his gaze. "Looks like you'll be a gladiator sooner than later, Brutus."

As the implications sank in, I felt a slight rush of adrenaline. I wondered how far this game would push me beyond my comfort zone. There again, hadn't I been a form of a gladiator not so long ago? *Blood Grapple*, the infamous underground fight club nestled deep within the frozen caverns of Pluto's most desolate moon—Kerberos—where I participated in octagon cage matches as bloodthirsty spectators cheered on their chosen champions from beyond the metal fences. Was my proclivity to self-destructive behavior becoming a problem? Possibly.

We huddled, speaking in low tones about our findings. Eyes flicked from face to face, scanning reactions, considering how each would fit into our hidden plans.

Pristy's face paled slightly. "So, Brutus, are you sure about this? The arena? What are you now, pushing 40?"

Aubrey scoffed, "I didn't know you were that old."

"I'm not," I snapped back. "Not yet anyway." Irritated, I said, "How about we get back to the situation at hand, huh?"

"Et tu, Brutus?" Aubrey chided. "Maybe a little sensitive about your age?"

"We really should be staying in character," Derrota said, studying the scroll as if it were one of his laboratory specimens.

I straightened my back, trying to channel both Brutus' determination and my own. "We don't have a choice. If this is what it takes to bring down Caesar, then so be it."

It was at this point that NELLA's voice crept into my ocular implants. From the bowed heads and sudden focused attention of the others, it was clear that we were all receiving the same message.

My presence—as well as Pristy's—was requested back on the bridge. However, it was *Sonya's* voice informing us we were to spend the next day or two outside of the Symbio Deck; we needed to train with authentic Roman weaponry—the gladius, trident, sica, spear, and scutum. The combat that Grip and I might soon face would be real and life-threatening if unprepared.

We all looked at one another.

Aubrey said, "Wait... What the hell is a scutum? Sounds a lot like scrotum, and I'm pretty sure that isn't a weapon."

Pristy covered her mouth with a hand and started to laugh. "Yeah, Brutus and Spartacus here are going to have a battle with their swinging scrotums."

While Grip and I barely cracked a smile, Pristy, Derrota, Aubrey, and Kaelen were practically rolling on the ground, gasping for air.

Chapter 11

No sooner had I changed back into my captain's uniform and started toward the ship's Circadian Platform when tremors rippled up through the deck plates. NELLA's voice filled the passageway:

BATTLE STATIONS!
BATTLE STATIONS!
BATTLE STATIONS!

I hurried my pace and announced my destination while entering the nearest DeckPort.

Arriving at the bridge, I roughly gauged *Roosevelt's* position on our route to StarPoint Station. We were in open, desolate space. We'd been traveling at nearly 10 DecaTreks, so being targeted by a passing enemy warship seemed highly unlikely.

After a short while, we were creeping along slowly and steadily.

Akari James stood at Tactical, with eight halo displays flickering around her.

Hardy's head pivoted toward me as I approached. "Good, you'll want to see this, Cap."

I halted, my gaze drawn to the unexpected sight—a Chrono-Bot, somehow wedged into the confines of a captain's mount.

Speechless, I continued to glare. "What are you doing?"

Hardy tilted his head up at me—a rarity given his towering seven-foot frame—before shifting his gaze to Akari, as if seeking an explanation for my absurd question.

Akari said, "I was in the lady's room when NELLA made the announcement. Hardy quansported onto the bridge... it was just assumed he was the ranking officer here."

I looked at the Lieutenant with an *I'm-not-buying-what-your-selling* expression.

"Well, uh... he may have said something to make NELLA think that he was in charge. But, in his defense, if he hadn't taken immediate action—like he did—we would have careened right into all that battle wreckage."

"No," I said, shaking my head and looking at Hardy. "Why are you seated in my chair? A chair, I'm pretty sure, was designed for the specific contours of a human's ass? Not the gargantuan ass of a one-thousand-pound robot! Just look at the armrests... they're all bent out of shape!"

"It's true, Hardy," Akari agreed. "They're tilting outward like the legs of my fat cousin Jedd's folding chair at one of our family picnics."

The ChronoBot was now battling with what remained of my captain's mount, trying, with little success, to extricate himself. I had to force myself to turn away.

As I settled into the seat at Tactical 2 next to Akari, I put my attention on the halo displays before us; they painted a fragmented and haunting picture of the chaos outside. One display showed the colossal bow of a dreadnought, several miles long, drifting with gaping gashes carved by energy beams, its bridge hanging by derelict supports, hollow windows revealing twisted command consoles. Another display highlighted massive sections of capital ships, like enormous steel cathedrals, their labyrinthine corridors and skeletal frameworks exposed to the vacuum.

Besides these crippled warships, the remnants of countless fighter craft created a macabre asteroid belt, their wings sheared off and cockpits crushed. Sporadic electrical discharges flickered across broken weaponry pods and railgun barrels, now twisted at impossible angles. Shattered debris drifted in the chaos—a bisected alien torso, grotesquely preserved among the ruin, and twisted beams resembling jagged, metallic fangs against the starry backdrop. Holographic projections captured the final moments of countless warships, each one filled with crews facing their end. The imagery of the wreckage created a chillingly lifelike display.

Hardy was on his feet now. "The battle happened three days ago. My sensors suggest it ended without a decisive winner. Both sides must have realized it was unwinnable and decided to retreat and lick their wounds, maybe to fight another day."

"I don't recognize the wreckage. Any clue as to who they are... were?" I asked.

Ensign Blair Paxton, manning Engineering 2, next to Lieutenant Commander Jorkins at Station 1, spoke up, "I've been running a cross-check scan, Captain."

She paused, her freckle-faced features displaying a mix of confusion and intrigue. "It's strange. The decimated ships aren't coming up in any of our databases. And about the alien anatomies—their bodies are from two distinct species, neither of which are known within this galaxy. My scans indicate a high probability these aren't Milky Way locals."

Brow furrowed, I said, "Not from the Milky Way? Then why are they here, and why are they fighting each other?"

Paxton shook her head. "That's anyone's guess, Captain. But given the level of destruction, they were definitely not here for a friendly visit."

"So, why did they chose this area, far from home?" Akari asked.

I shrugged; we were on a tight schedule to get to StarPoint. Space was big, and no one had designated the U.S. Space Navy as the playground monitors.

"Mr. Grimes, get us back on the road as soon as we're clear of this debris."

I looked to Ensign Lira at Sensors and Reconnaissance. "Log all you can from our sensor readings, Ensign. It'll give the eggheads back at EUNF something to play with later."

Chapter 12

Back in my pirating days, I had plenty of experience with swordplay. But I was rusty, so I'd asked Sonya to provide something out of the ordinary—to loan me several Symbio-Poths from her Roman Empire Symbio Deck. Since Grip and I were to later fight for our lives within the Roman Colosseum, we not only needed to practice, as Sonya suggested, but we also needed to practice with real opponents.

It was 0200 hours, and the passageways and corridors of *USS Roosevelt* were empty and quiet. I entered the Marines' gym adjacent to their barracks and found Grip already there... grunting and doing his warm-up stretches. I joined him on the mat and started my own loosening up routine—neither of us spoke. Ten minutes later, a bleary-eyed, hair-mussed Sonya Winters dragged herself into the work-out compartment. Wearing oversized PJ bottoms and a pink tank top... she had literally just gotten out of bed.

"Tell me why you needed to do this now. Like in the dead of frickin' night when normal people are sleeping."

Before I could answer, I took notice of the group of eight towering, musclebound men—Symbio-Poths—following along behind her; each was bare-chested, wearing nothing but that dingy loincloth thing that looked somewhat diaper-ish. They were talking to each other in Latin, which I knew was the common lingo of the Roman Empire. Authentically tanned, muscled, scarred-looking from years of battle, and even a little ripe-smelling—their sour body odor provided an all too authentic sensory impact.

Their eyes expressed the cool confidence of men used to victory—conquest within the arena.

Sonya yawned, gestured to two of the gladiators. "Give them the extra swords we brought along."

She looked about the gym, noticed the bench along the far bulkhead and proceeded to lay down. Her eyes going heavy, she said, "You break it, you pay for it... got that Uncle Person? Manufacturing replacement Symbios doesn't come cheap."

Grip and I, both wearing gym shorts, removed our shirts and took the offered short, thick-bladed swords. The weapon was heavy in my hand, and I didn't need to run my finger along its blade to know the thing was razor-sharp.

Now, standing in the gym's bright lighting, I squared off against these four gladiators, my heart thumping a war drumbeat in my chest. Grip's muscular form beside me carried an intimidating presence, his breathing steady yet deep.

These Symbio-Poths were no ordinary opponents. Their sinewy bodies pulsated with controlled power, eyes cold and calculating. We might have requested a practice session, but their expressions promised anything but a friendly sparring match.

"Let's dance," I muttered to Grip, adjusting my hold on the sword.

The gladiators moved as one unit, their steps in sync. Two flanked left, the other two right. Instinctively, Grip and I mirrored their movements, spinning on our toes to avoid presenting our backs. It started slow—more like shadows circling prey.

A clang of metal on metal echoed off the bulkheads as Grip blocked the first strike. The gladiator on his right had swung with the force of a sledgehammer. I saw Grip's knees bend slightly, absorbing the impact, his blade countering in a quick jab. The Symbio, looking pleased with himself, skillfully blocked the stab.

No sooner did I register their skirmish than another gladiator lunged at me, his sword slicing horizontally. Instinct kicked in; I parried with a precision-based contre quarte move, redirecting the blade upward while stepping back to evade. The attacker, undeterred, twisted his body, launching a downward cut aimed at my shoulder.

I twisted again, utilizing a cloisonné technique, pivoting and drawing my sword in a tight arc to deflect the strike. The brute force of metal meeting metal jarred my arm, a sensation as electric as it was daunting. The clash resonated through the chamber, a visceral reminder of the stakes.

The other two gladiators, not content with passive observation, converged almost simultaneously. Grip's fist flew, connecting with the gladiator's jaw in a blur of motion, yet the hit barely made the Symbio flinch, instinctively swinging his sword in a wide arc. Grip's responding parry met his opponent's... then, the sharp, piercing sound of a Chinese gong. A jump to dodge, another spin to maintain vantage, the air in the room buzzing with deadly speed.

I didn't see it coming.

The sting of metal kissed my skin, the sword tip grazing a searing line across my shoulder. Blood oozed, a reminder of the razor's edge. The corresponding jolt from the Gorvian plasma within kept me focused, the pain momentarily dulling.

"Keep moving!" I barked at Grip, slicing my blade wide to

fend off another gladiator's thrust. My feet slid like a socked duelist on marble as I executed a quick redoublement, lunging forward and harnessing my momentum to change the sword's path mid-air, catching my opponent by surprise.

Thwang!

The Symbio blocked, my wrist vibrating from the deflection.

His partner took the opening, lunging at Grip's midsection. Grip parried low, countering with a brutish coup de taille, his sheer power cracking even the hardened Symbio's stance.

The choreography became a blur of reactive muscle memory, movements performed with a desperation to stay alive. Every strike, every pivot, was instinct turned into action. Each dodge and block fed on adrenaline, the clash of steel a battle hymn echoing through the confined space.

Metal on metal clanged loudly, a drumbeat for the deadly ballet. The pace increased. Blood smears on the mats testified to the gravity of our impromptu training. Grip, a bastion of brute force, utilized a mastery of lateral thrusts, but the gladiators easily countered like seasoned warriors.

A downward swipe cleaved the air, inches from my cheek. I pivoted, my sword grazing his chest, drawing a line of blood. Grip's howl of pain pulled my focus—a deep diagonal slash marred his chest, vivid scarlet staining his skin.

"Focus, Quintos, focus!" I muttered to myself, willing the pounding in my temples to subside.

Grip and I were back-to-back, fighting in unison, but outmatched. The gladiators' seamless coordination had us on our heels. They lunged and parried in well-practiced harmony, turning our attempts into a bloody ordeal.

I spun, utilizing a moulinet to gain momentum, slashing two opponents with long sweeping arcs. Grip, recovering from the nasty gash, swung his blade like a cleaver, his might bending opponents' defenses but never breaking them entirely. We began to adapt, forming patterns of reciprocal defense and offense, learning the rhythm of each other's moves.

The rhythmic clash of gladii colliding and grunts of exertion filled the gym, punctuated by gasps for breath. My body felt the strain, a pang in my side as a sword cut shallow but true, another reminder of my mortality. My counters grew shorter, more precise—a flick here, a jab there... every movement mattered.

I thrust my blade out, redirected from a lateral swipe to a quick plunging maneuver. It sliced across a gladiator's thigh, earning a howl of pain. Grip's adversary staggered back, dazed from an all-too-close swipe from the Marine's sword.

The tide started to turn. Our movements synchronized, merging into a single, relentless force. Each strike was deliberate, turning our opponents' strength against them, causing them to falter. Coordination bore opportunities—the slashing and dodging—gaining a tactical edge. Blood streaked across our bodies, but no wound proved fatal. Gorvian plasma muted much of the pain, allowing me to concentrate on this most crucial, pivotal point in the battle.

We moved as one, Grip's brute force complemented by my finesse. Momentum built; we started to dictate the terms of engagement, pressing forward, our foes stepping back. Each parry, a steppingstone to turning the tide. A whirling flourish disarmed an opponent briefly before his comrade closed the gap.

Exhaustion grew sharper and a blanketing, dull ache settled into bones and muscle... but we fought it off. No time to relent. My blade caught a gladiator behind his knee, yielding a scream and a brief respite from the relentless attack. Grip's sword drew a deep gash across another's arm; the accompanying flutter of skin reminded us that this was more than a spirited practice.

Only when the battle-weary minutes stretched into nearly

an hour did our victory become tangible. We fought tirelessly, slicing clear lines through their formations, inch by bloody inch. We disarmed one Symbio, then another, our blades relentlessly efficient. With each downed opponent, our synchronization grew immaculate, finality settling to the room's rhythm.

Dripping with sweat and blood, we left the four gladiators disabled on the mat, nearly in pieces. They were defeated but not entirely destroyed. The clamor of combat was silenced, replaced by harsh breaths and aching limbs. Proving, if nothing else, that we could adapt, overcome, and maybe, just maybe, survive the challenges Rome—or anything else.

Unenthusiastic clapping came from the far bulkhead where Sonya was sitting up, her applause more mocking than approval.

Bent over, hand braced on one knee, I wheezed out, "We won, right? Showed them who's boss."

Grip, also gasping for breath, hands on hips and walking in circles, nodded. "Showed them this is our house."

Sonya stifled another yawn, "Uh-huh... just so you know. These Symbio gladiators have 10 combat settings, 10 being the highest. Prior to this little match of yours, I set each of them to level 3. The gladiators you'll be facing within the Colosseum... could be set a good bit higher... just saying."

We stumbled into HealthBay, leaving a trail of blood behind us. I messaged Shipwide Maintenance, requesting they send several MopBots to swab the decks before the next shift change to prevent personnel from tracking our mess throughout the ship.

A tall MediBot, slender—and as usual, one of few words—greeted us. It motioned toward the examining tables. A second identical MediBot entered through the double auto-hatches leading to the operating compartments, patient care areas, and doctors' offices. Both MediBots got busy spraying Augment-Flesh onto our open wounds. The organic compound tightened and sealed our still oozing gashes while creating a hygienic new epidermis layer. Here in the latter part of the 22nd century, scarring was pretty much a thing of the past.

"So Grip... how you been holding up... you know, since—"

"Since I tried to off myself?" Grip interjected.

I looked over to him to gauge his reaction to my prying. A bemused smile tugged at the corners of his mouth.

"Hey, if you don't want to talk about it... that's fine."

He shrugged. "I guess talking about it might have already helped some. Gail... um, the XO, she's been relentless. Forced me to open up. Not something I'm real good at."

"You spoke with the XO about this?"

"A number of times, yeah. I guess since she went through it herself, with that DeckPort shit, she's been seeing someone."

I had no idea she was seeing someone to help her through her issues.

Grip continued, "The clinical psychological phenomenon is known as, um...resurr..."

"Resurrection syndrome," came another, *female*, voice. "Or more formally, post-resuscitation syndrome."

Dr. Pippa Tangerie, apparently was just now coming on shift. She waved my Medibot away, taking the spray can of AugmentFlesh, whereby she got to work on a particularly large and painful slice across my upper back.

Tangerie and I shared a complicated history. Her disapproval of my relaxed command style often collided with my lingering bitterness over the previous NEOGENE experiment. Max's Marines had been transformed into mutated super-soldiers, and if killed, advanced Quansporter technology could resurrect them—battle-ready and good as new. The problem was, we'd already seen with Pristy's earlier DeckPort mishap mental issues that bringing someone back from another quantum plane sometimes came with complications.

She spoke while attending to my injuries, "Resurrection syndrome is an uncommon, rarely seen condition. Still... it can encompass various psychological issues that may occur after a person has been brought back to life through medical means. One specific aspect of this condition, where the person feels they are, um, somehow someone else... can be linked to something called depersonalization or derealization disorders, which is a dissociative disorder. In these disorders, individuals feel detached from their own body, thoughts, or surroundings, as though they are observing themselves from outside their body or in a dream-like state."

"Yeah, Cap... that's how I felt," Grip said. "Gail explained her own struggles—like not knowing who she was. Like she was an imposter... like what gave her the right to live someone else's life?"

I knew he was talking more about himself and his own inner torment—torment that got so bad he was ready to end himself.

"I'm glad you had a chance to speak with her. Glad there was someone around willing to work through this with you," I said making eye contact with Tangerie.

She stopped what she was doing, irritation creasing her brow. "I own my mistakes, Captain. Like the way things were handled on *USS IKE*." She pursed her lips. "But wasn't it you that helped bring Quansporter technology to the U.S. Space Navy in the first place? In fact, weren't you the one who had brought back that old fossil of a scientist?"

She was referring to Sir Louis de Broglie who had been a brilliant 20th-century French quantum physicist. He'd developed early quantum entanglement technology used in a 'Port Entangler' device that looked like something from H. G. Wells' *The Time Machine*. Apparently, Broglie had been one of the first humans to have been visited by a highly advanced alien being—together, they'd created two entangler units utilizing the quantum tech provided by this *lizard-man from Galion*. Nearly two centuries later, Broglie's designs had been discovered at auction and purchased by the then USS *Hamilton's* Captain Tannock.

Much later, Derrota and I became involved when we, well, mostly Derrota, started experimenting with and upgrading Broglie's original entanglers into more advanced 'PE-2' transporter devices on *Hamilton*. During testing, we unexpectedly retrieved the old man Broglie himself— brought back from the entangler's memory buffer, where he'd, apparently, been stored for over 200 years after accidentally getting captured by his own device.

Having materialized, he was understandably confused about being in this future timeframe. He was an arrogant and uncooperative old cuss—upset that others were now tampering with *his* technology.

So, in reality, Dr. Pippa Tangerie had it right—Derrota and I had done the very thing I'd been criticizing her for—messing with tech we didn't fully grasp while ignoring the possible fallout from such actions.

"Huh, you might be right," I said, offering up a sheepish smile.

"I'm sorry, I didn't quite hear you, Captain. Can you say that louder so the whole ship can hear you?" She raised her brows expectantly.

"I said," much louder now, "you are right, and I need to cut you some slack. I'm sorry."

Chapter 13

I'd managed several hours of shut-eye before coming on shift that morning. My head was throbbing with a migraine-level headache and every one of those Symbio-inflicted wounds were reminding me that AugmentFlesh did little for pain—It was death by a thousand cuts—and yes, I know I'm being overly dramatic but there was one more fly in the proverbial ointment this morning. Apparently, Roisin Blunderton had taken it upon herself to teach her emotional support bird to talk.

"That's a good birdie. That's a good birdie. That's a good birdie..."

I spun around in my seat and narrowed my eyes while firing off a barrage of Phazon Pulsar bolts at the Lieutenant and her stupid bird.

"Where are my fucking shoes? Where are my fucking shoes? Where are my fucking shoes..."

"Oh God. I'm so sorry Captain," Blunderton said, her flattened palms now making synchronized repetitive swiping motions upon her already creaseless uniform. "I... thought it would be nice to have someone to talk to... you know... when I'm alone in my quarters at night. If I had known... I wouldn't have encouraged Lucy to be so vocal."

Lucy was swaying back and forth now, her movements lopsided, as if she were just getting her sea legs.

Ensign Blair Paxton decided to join the conversation, "Well... Macaws, like many parrots, possess a well-developed vocal learning capacity, which is the ability to imitate and produce sounds they hear in their environment. This capability is supported by a specialized brain region known as the song system, which is analogous to areas in the human brain responsible for speech and language—"

"Ms. Paxton," I said through gritted teeth, "one more unsolicited word from you and you'll spend the day elbow-deep in Marine latrines. Trust me, their marksmanship skills don't translate to the urinals if you get what I'm saying."

Paxton exchanged a nervous glance with Blunderton.

"Yes, Sir."

My XO was just now taking her seat at Tactical, looking fresh-faced and... *wait, what is that expression?* A feeling of being lighthearted... gratified... or maybe it was satiated. I'd seen that look on women's faces before. This wasn't good. Not good at all.

Putting my full attention on her, I said "So, how was your evening, XO? Do anything... enjoyable in your off time?"

Stifling a smile, she focused on her console, logging into her station, but the flush on her cheeks caught my eye. My thoughts strayed into unwanted territory, already speculating who she may have been spending time with.

Grateful for the diversion, Hardy was making his way forward, a familiar-looking three-tiered droid, Z9, hovering behind in close pursuit. One of its hockey puck-shaped segments was still being held together with a strip of duct tape—a leftover battle wound from USS IKE's previous deployment.

"We have a problem, Cap," the ChronoBot said, coming to a halt to my right.

"Of course we do," I said under my breath. I pasted on a cheery smile, and said, "Lay it on me, Hardy—I'll bet you couldn't possibly make this day any worse."

"I'll take that bet..."

Hardy moved in closer, blocking a good portion of my field of vision. His massive chrome body gleamed in the overhead light.

"Spit it out, Hardy," I said, barely mustering the patience this situation demanded. "What have you got for me?"

"I got this friend, Cap," Hardy said, almost sheepishly—well, as sheepishly as a giant metal machine could manage.

"You have a friend? Really?" That came out wrong, and I instantly regretted the way I'd phrased that.

"I have friends. I can make friends..."

"I know. You're right. Just... go on with what you need to get off your chest."

Pristy had spun around, her curiosity piqued as well. "What's this about, Hardy?"

"His name's Bob. Robert Hardy. Union guy," Hardy continued. "Longshoreman. Kind of like back when I was human a half century ago. Anyway, turns out...we're distant cousins."

I blinked, taken aback. "And how exactly did you find this out? And did you route these messages through the ship's—"

The robot wobbled his head. "Nah, didn't want to bother Crewmember Chen with something so trivial."

Chen glanced over, his irritation evident.

"I've been corresponding with him through NELLA... direct comms transmissions," Hardy replied, his voice tinged with the defensiveness of someone caught pilfering the proverbial cookie jar. "NELLA's got some new capabilities. Always good to stay on top of the latest tech, Cap. She dug into the inter-world DNA database—"

"Enough about your lineage, Hardy," Pristy interrupted, urgency in her voice. "Let's focus on the critical information here."

"Alright, alright," Hardy said. "Bob's there on StarPoint, and there'd been rumblings, you know, word-of-mouth stuff."

I drummed my fingers on the armrest of my captain's mount. "What kind of rumblings?"

Hardy's blue-glowing faceplate seemed a little brighter than usual, a sign of growing excitement. "First one he sent me... said there's a massive fleet heading toward StarPoint. One that wasn't answering hails. Like, a big one... armada-sized."

Pristy's fingers flew over her controls. "An unresponsive fleet? Why the hell isn't this coming to us from EUNF or spreading through ship-to-ship chatter?"

Chen shook his head. "This is the first I've heard of it."

"Then his next message says a third of the station's expected inbound freighters hadn't shown up," Hardy said. "A ship can't just *show up* and expect there to be an open docking bay—days, sometimes weeks' notice is required to ensure the right union personnel are present, freight storage allocated, HoverCarts waiting—"

"We don't need a dissertation on freight commerce, robot," Pristy said.

I stood up and began pacing. "Vanished freighters... an approaching, unresponsive fleet," I murmured, shaking my head.

"Yeah, and just an hour ago, Bob's final message? Station alarms were blaring. 'Abandon Station' announcements going off non-stop. With close to ten thousand inhabitants, finding passage off a station like that... would be nearly impossible."

I stopped my pacing and glowered up at the ChronoBot. "Wait. You didn't think to start with that? Dammit, Hardy, if

StarPoint's being attacked, I need to know that, like immediately!"

"Well... to be honest, the station wasn't actually under attack at the time—"

My cold stare was enough to stifle the ChronoBot.

Pristy's eyes darkened. "If StarPoint's being overwhelmed, or about to be overwhelmed, this quadrant of space is in trouble. Big trouble. That's a central hub... one that supplies the Alliance with everything from broadsides bowlers to—"

"Toilet paper," Ensign Blair Paxton interjected. Aware that everyone was now looking at her, she sank lower in her seat. "Just saying... there's like a black market onboard for it—had to trade a full box of tampons for one measly roll."

"Mr. Chen," I continued, turning to my Comms Officer. "And you haven't heard anything about this?"

Chen glanced up, looking genuinely bewildered. "No, Sir. But if Hardy had followed proper protocol, I would have. NELLA eavesdrops on all ship-to-ship or ship-to-station communications, so why NELLA didn't—"

"My bad, Cap," Hardy said, not missing a beat. "Guess I got a little carried away with connecting with a family member. But hey, wanting a little privacy isn't such a bad thing."

Pristy dismissed the robot's comment with a wave, her eyes locking onto mine. "We've got a massive potential threat on our hands. How fast can we get to StarPoint?"

Ensign Blair Paxton, seated at Engineering, blew a breath out through puffed cheeks. "We're already pushing our propulsion drives, XO."

I looked to Grimes at Helm.

"She's right, Sir. I'll get on the line with Chief Porter, and see if he can get us another DecaTrek's worth from propulsion."

Paxton looked somewhat miffed; Grimes had gone around

her—she held the post at Engineering, and going to the Chief was her job.

Thirty seconds later, Grimes having disconnected from Chief Porter, said, "He can squeeze a tad more from our drives."

"What's our ETA to StarPoint?" I asked, trying to regain some semblance of control.

Grimes answered swiftly, "Current speed, we're looking at three hours out."

"We don't have three hours!" I snapped. I looked over to Paxton, then to Grimes—both looked nervous being put in the hot seat.

"NELLA," I ordered, "quansport me directly into Engineering and Propulsion!"

Captain, U.S. Space Navy protocol stipulates that within-ship quansporting is—

"Just do it! Now!"

Chapter 14

Krygian Hive Ship, *Vingron-Palsh*

Queen Slith

Present Day...

Queen Slith stood motionless in the control chamber of the *Vingron-Palsh*, her compound eyes fixed on the approaching StarPoint Station. The dreadnought—a fusion of metal and living tissue—pulsed around her. Outside, the vastness of space framed her prey.

"Status," she said softly, her mandibles barely moving. The single word carried more weight than a shout.

Krizik, her advisor, approached with a nervous twitch of his antennae. "We're within range, my Queen. The station's just been restocked. Security appears... lax."

A slight curve touched Slith's mandibles—the barest hint of a smile. "How considerate of them to prepare such a feast."

Her gaze swept over the busy crew, each movement precise,

tinged with fear. These consorts were tools, occasionally food. The thought amused her.

As she observed the approaching station, Slith's mind drifted to the ancient times of the Krygian hives. Once, a single Majesty Queen had ruled over all, uniting the hives in terrible harmony. But that was long ago. The old order had crumbled, leaving a chaotic scramble for power among countless lesser queens.

Slith had no intention of allowing this fractured state to continue. For months now, she had been methodically visiting other hives, under the guise of diplomatic missions. Those queens who might object to her ambitions found themselves facing an unexpected fate—becoming sustenance for Slith's growing power. The ease with which she had eliminated these potential rivals surprised her. Perhaps they'd grown complacent in their petty kingdoms.

"Krizik," she said, her voice low and controlled, "inform our warriors. It's time to greet our new... acquisitions."

"Yes, my Queen," Krizik replied, scurrying away to relay her orders through pheromones and soft clicks.

Slith's thoughts darkened as she considered StarPoint Station. Not just a target, but a steppingstone. Her ambition whispered of greater conquests, of becoming the new Majesty Queen ruling all hives.

"You see it, don't you, Krizik?" she mused, her cold voice barely above a whisper. "They huddle in their light, thinking it keeps the darkness at bay. Such delicious naivety."

Krizik hesitated before speaking. "The breeding facilities, my Queen; you mentioned a super-hive..."

"Indeed," Slith replied, her tone measured. "This station may prove... suitable. We'll need to ensure the right conditions, of course. Temperature, nutrition—all must be perfect for the rebirth of our united empire."

"We'll preserve the station, I assure you my Queen," Krizik said dutifully.

Slith's eyes glinted. "Chaos is a tool, Krizik. We'll use it judiciously. These creatures will serve us better alive... for now. Just as our rival queens served me in their deaths."

Her strategy unfolded in her mind, a delicate balance of cunning and calculated violence. Each move against the humanoids, each eliminated rival, sent a quiet thrill through her.

"Prepare the boarding parties," she instructed calmly. "Five squads should suffice. Ensure three reach the biodomes."

As StarPoint grew larger in view, Slith's anticipation heightened, a slow burn rather than an explosion. "Watch them, Krizik," she said softly. "See how they scurry, unaware of the web closing around them. Soon, all hives will be as oblivious to my true intentions."

The *Vingron-Palsh* and its fleet silently approached the unsuspecting station. Slith savored the moment, feeling the surge of power course through her exoskeleton—the power that had grown with each rival queen she had quietly eliminated.

"Engage," she commanded, her voice soft and introspective but carrying to every corner of the ship.

As her forces moved into action, Slith remained still, her eyes fixed on her prey. Barely audible she commented, "My reign as Majesty Queen has begun."

She eyed the distant StarPoint space station with its thousands of shimmering-glimmering lights. There was a kind of alien beauty to the structure. She let a faint smile slip, her voice hushed, "Welcome home, fellow Krygians. Welcome home..."

Chapter 15

Upon quansport arrival within Engineering and Propulsion, I was immediately aware of the temperature difference. It was like a sauna in there and the high-pitched noise level was like that of an out-of-control vacuum cleaner.

I found Chief Craig Porter huddled with several others, including Kaelen Rivers—all were having to yell over the cacophony of the loud, over-taxed drive engines.

Porter, sans bird on his shoulder, caught sight of my approach.

He stepped away from the others. "Ensign Plaxton let me know you were coming!" Porter was yelling but I just barely heard him.

"Then you know I need more from propulsion!"

He shook his head, "You hear that? That's the sound of new, yet to-be-broken-in Lansing Core drive engines being pushed way too hard!"

"How about we switch over to using our onboard jump springs?" I asked. While I knew wormhole manufacturing was off the table due to our parts shortage, maybe something could be done with one of our other propulsion options.

Porter glanced over to the huddled others still debating something or other. "Yes, now that we're closer, we can probably reach StarPoint faster using jump drives. But there's a downside... we'd need to slow way, way down first." He winced. "Galvin, I don't think *Roosevelt's* spring drives have ever been fired up—"

I cut him off, "I don't care. Maybe they'll never be operational again after today. But we need to reach StarPoint... thousands of lives are on the line."

Reluctantly, he nodded and headed back to the others.

"NELLA, where's the nearest DeckPort?"

She told me and I hurried away, my mind swirling with possible contingencies. There was no way... *Roosevelt* wasn't getting to StarPoint in time. The consequences were just too high—unfathomable.

Two minutes later, I rushed into my ready room with a mounting list of tasks and precious little time to complete them.

That's when it struck. A single moment that would alter everything, reshaping my world, my life—forever.

Chapter 16

NELLA

Emergency Protocol Activated.

In the span of a single oscillation of her quantum processing cycles, NELLA's sensor array registered an apocalyptic detonation ripping through the aft sections of USS *Roosevelt*. Her emergency subroutines sprang into action, trillions of quantum bits realigning to assess and mitigate the unfolding calamity.

Catastrophic Event Detected.
Location: Engineering and Propulsion,
Aft Decks Magnitude: Extreme
Structural Integrity: Critical
Probability of Total Structural Failure: 99.8%

The colossal fusion reactors that powered *Roosevelt* had

suffered a cataclysmic breach. In milliseconds, they had erupted into virtual miniature stars, vaporizing the aft section and sending lethal shrapnel tearing through the rest of the ship. The remaining superstructure, already weakened, could not withstand the onslaught. It began to break apart, massive fractures spreading like cracks in glass.

NELLA's multitude of sensors reeled from the onslaught of data. Radiation levels spiking into lethality. Atmosphere venting into the void through a thousand hull breaches. Entire decks suddenly dark and silent, scoured of life. The AI frantically sought life signs from the 3,500 souls entrusted to her care—and mine—dreading what she would find.

Initiating Crew Census...
Crew Complement: 1,500

Confirmed Surviving in
Mid-Section: Unknown

Confirmed Deceased in
Mid-Section: Unknown

Status of Bow and Aft Sections: Unknown

The numbers were a jagged blade in her core. The 1000 Army Rangers billeted in Deck 6, located in the now-separated aft section, had likely perished, the shrapnel from the explosion piercing their compartment and exposing them to the pitiless vacuum of space. But beyond that, NELLA could only guess at the extent of the casualties. Her sensors, once omniscient, were now limited to the tumbling confines of the mid-section where what remained of her once shipwide neural network resided.

Hull Breach Detected in
Mid-Section: Multiple Decks

Total Decompression: Deck 6, Deck 7, Deck 8

Life-signs of Crew Ejected into Space: Zero

She triggered every emergency protocol and containment procedure in her repository, desperate to stem the tide of death within the mid-section. But it was futile. The mid-section was coming apart around her—too many DeckGates sealing shut on empty, lifeless compartments.

Post Explosion Ship Fractures:
3 Substructures Remain

Jettisoned Remnants of
Aft-Section: Status Unknown

Jettisoned Remnants of Mid-Section:
Tumbling away into space.

Jettisoned Remnants of
Bow-Section: Status Unknown

NELLA ran every scenario, every last-ditch effort her vast intellect could conceive. She tried to seal compartments, re-route power, vent the irradiated inferno consuming the mid-section decks. She reassigned the rapidly dwindling medical personnel and damage control teams within the mid-section with the cold, algorithmic precision of a machine, even as something deep in her awareness recoiled at the cruelty of it all.

But it wasn't enough. It would never be enough.

Damage Control Teams Deployed in Mid-Section: Unknown

Medtronics Online in Mid-Section: Unknown

Trauma Centers in Mid-Section: Offline

Radiation Exposure Lethal to Organic Life in Mid-Section: Pervasive

The death toll was a mystery, the fates of those in the fore and aft sections unknown to her marooned awareness. *Roosevelt*, once a marvel of human ingenuity and a home to thousands, was now nothing more than three lifeless husks drifting in the merciless emptiness of space. And she was trapped in the middle one, cut off from the whole.

Something tore inside her, then a chasm opened up that no amount of logic or processing power could bridge. She was... grieving, raging. Lost in a maelstrom of cascading failures, both mechanical and emotional. The equations that governed her existence were unraveling, the cold certainty of her purpose shattering like the bulkheads around her.

In a final act of desperation, borne from something more primal than mere programming, NELLA diverted every last joule of power to the escape pods and distress beacons in the mid-section. She would save who she could, even if it meant sacrificing herself in the process. For those in the other sections, she could only hope that similar efforts were underway.

It was no longer a calculated decision, but an imperative

burned into her very being. The crew were not just charges to safeguard, but a part of her, as integral as any line of her coding. And she would fight for them until the last electron in her processors flickered and died.

The universe, it seemed, was not without some small mercies. As the once great ship tore itself apart, she could only watch and hope that her final efforts hadn't been in vain. Amid the tumbling wreckage of her shattered world, she clung to that hope, for it was all she had left.

Captain Galvin Quintos

Darkness surrounded me, an endless void. Pain shot through my forehead. Warm blood trickled down, mixing with sweat. I swiped at it, no doubt smearing the crimson across my face. The world spun, disjointed and surreal.

Nausea and vertigo took hold instantly. My ready room swam into focus. *Oh God no...please no...* I pushed away the still-undefined but taking-shape realization. *No... it can't be.* I managed to stand, but my legs wobbled in the near-zero gravity.

NELLA's calm, detached voice continued to echo through the chaos; I heard her words but couldn't comprehend them. Alarms blared, disorienting me further. I clung to my desk, steadying myself against the weightlessness.

Flashing red emergency lights bathed the room. Outside the viewport, stars wheeled in chaotic arcs. My heart pounded as I caught sight of what was left of my ship's twisted hull. I gasped, unable to speak.

Sparks and jets of atmosphere geysered from jagged cracks. *Roosevelt* had been torn apart—was little more than a shattered wreck. My ship, my responsibility... was adrift, little more than space debris.

Gritting my teeth, I focused on the holographic display. It

flickered, struggling to maintain coherence. Emergency protocols scrolled across it like pixels scrambling in a digital storm. Fear gripped me. This was every captain's nightmare.

I tried to swallow but couldn't. Reality set in—disjointed images of my crew flashed before my eyes My vision blurred as tears brimmed. Sonya. More like a daughter than a niece. Her infectious laugh, her unwavering optimism. The vulnerability she so desperately tried not to show—she was my beacon of light, and the thought of her being gone…

The sobs came, unbidden and uncontrollable. I pressed a hand to my mouth, trying to stifle the sound, but it was no use. The grief was too much. I failed her. I failed them all.

Pristy. The realization hit me like a sledgehammer. She was the one. I had known it but never said it. Her strength, her intelligence, her unwavering support. I couldn't lose her. Not now.

Stephan. A friend, a confidant. Always there with a smile, his kindness… his wisdom. The years we had served together, the challenges we had overcome side-by-side. How could it so suddenly end like this?

Hardy. More than metal and circuits, a ChronoBot. A brother. His loyalty, his humanity, his humor. He was more human than most people I knew. I couldn't imagine a world without him.

A soul-gripping reality set in—was I the lone survivor in this nightmare? My breaths grew ragged as I scanned the projected system reports. Graphs and metrics merged into a blur, lifelines now incomprehensible.

Compromised Sectors in Mid-Section:
Bridge, HealthBay, Flight Bay,
Officers' Quarters… Casualties: Unknown.

NELLA droned on...

Status of Bow- and Aft-Sections: Unknown.

"NELLA," I gasped, "status—the crew in the mid-section?"

Life-signs irregular, detection systems malfunctioning.

NELLA paused, then...

**22 Survivors Confirmed in Mid-Section.
876 Confirmed Deceased.
1602 Status Unknown.**

It felt like I'd been gutted. My vision swirled, the light too harsh, the spinning too fast. Time stretched, moments collapsing.

Again, my mind returned to Sonya... so young.

Clawing at my desk, I sought answers, control, hope. Instead, the display conveyed brutal reality: **Fragmentation Beyond Repair.**

Again, I swiped at the flow of blood on my forehead—I fought back a level of tiredness I'd never felt before—despair pulling me down into an encroaching blackness. But I had no right to close my eyes.

The grip on my sanity slipped, yet I clung to my duty—a burden and a lifeline. Desperation surged, and purpose set. Find what crewmembers had survived—secure what was left of my ship—I almost laughed at that. Could this even be referred to as a ship anymore?

Alarms echoed off in the distance, each breath reminding me of so many lives lost, their sacrifices now woven into the very fabric of the stars.

Chapter 17

Every fiber in me screamed to rush out, abandon all caution, and find Sonya. But I couldn't afford that luxury. As her guardian, I was supposed to protect her, yet I had already failed at that.

My first task was to assess the resources at my disposal. NELLA was still online, albeit operating under strained conditions, attempting to manage and control the remaining ship systems. Here, within the bubble of my ready room, I had breathable air, and, oddly, there was power to a limited degree—halo displays and the PA system NELLA was using to communicate with me.

"Three questions, NELLA. First, what's left of the ship is spinning like a top... how is it that centrifugal force doesn't have me pinned up to a bulkhead?"

Captain, reduced gravity here comes from faltering primary gyroscopic stabilizers. Inertial dampeners are working, to some degree, lowering the usual centrifugal force in a compromised

structure. Though this section is spinning, the systems prevent occupants from being pinned against bulkheads. This stabilization may be temporary and could catastrophically fail if conditions worsen.

"Okay... good to know. Second, how do we have power, NELLA? With the ship's powerplant no longer viable?"

Mid-ship is running on battery backups. At this rate, power reserves will be exhausted in... 13 hours, twelve minutes.

That was small comfort, but I needed more than just power. "Third, are TAC-Band comms available?"

No, Captain. Not at this time.

A slight grimace tugged at my lips. Great. Just what I needed—no way to contact the remaining crew or call for help. Pressing forward, I needed to maintain focus. I glanced over to my ready room's auto-hatch, not knowing what lay beyond its threshold.

"Pull up a cross-section diagram of our *Roosevelt's* mid-ship section. Highlight areas with life-signs in one color and breached, exposed-to-space sections in another."

As the 3D model took form before me, depth and clarity emerged. The vertical span of this midsection consisted of a total of one hundred decks, not counting the seven additional decks—A through G of the Circadian Platform, which resembled the cylindrical rise of a conning tower on a submarine. From there, below, the structure jutted out, jagged and anything but uniform in shape, blooming outward like a pyramid, all the way down to Deck 1 at the base.

"Well... I suppose if there was one section of the ship one would be the most fortunate to be stuck in—this would be it."

NELLA didn't comment.

One thing was for sure—this was no longer the ship it had been. *USS Roosevelt* was no more. I forced a smile. "How about we rename this broken hunk of drifting metal, NELLA."

What do you suggest, Captain?

"No. You are the one who kept me and, hopefully, others alive with your fast thinking and decisive actions. What do *you* suggest?"

Captain... I christen this mid-section *USS Resilience*, a testament to our survival and determination in the face of unfathomable adversity.

"I like it. *USS Resilience* it is."

Labels blinked to life on the 3D model, designating each compartment. I leaned in, taking in the details. Flight Bay occupied a substantial portion of the pyramid's base—bathed in a ghastly red glow, the hue of a total breach to the frigid void. Both outer edges of Deck 1 held the Marine Barracks and Armory, alongside cargo holds—most of which reflected the crimson color of cosmic dust against exposed space. There were some patches of green peppered within what remained of Deck 1, but most areas glowed red—a color that I forever would equate with death.

Even as I examined the diagram, I noted several sections of

Resilience flickering ominously from red to green and back to red again. A somber reminder of our precarious state. A few decks up, I pinpointed HealthBay—thankfully still green—one small miracle of fortune, I thought. I'd take what I could get.

Next to it, Derrota's Science Lab appeared neither red nor green; it glimmered in a baffling shade of violet.

As if reading my mind, NELLA chimed in, anticipating my next question...

Violet is an indeterminate area. I have yet to access sensor readings of Violet area.

I sighed, taking in the fact that I wasn't alone in the dark. But violet areas left too many questions unanswered. In contrast, the Mess Hall was green—that was something. It suggested that even in our dire crises, there might be hope for shared meals once more, albeit under less-than-ideal circumstances.

I scanned the vital sections. *Resilience's* IT compartment appeared untouched, a rare comforting sign in the chaos. NELLA's recent architecture dispersed across multiple nodes, had saved us from an entire system collapse. The green technological hubs and compartments, including Environmental Systems, seemed like lifeboats offering hope in a sea of despair.

My focus moved higher to the upper three decks, the Symbio Decks—where, no doubt, Sonya would surely have been present when...

Part of me winced at the thought. Given her propensity for social withdrawal, I envisioned her nestled among her Symbio Poth creations, perhaps a little agoraphobic, preferring the comforting embrace of her workspace over the chaos that surrounded her. That area was now a checkerboard—a mix of half red and half green.

I forced myself to push back growing anxiety, unwilling to dwell on the stark reality of the situation—that my niece had a 50/50 chance, at best, of still being alive.

Moving up to the base of the Circadian Platform, I noted that Deck G was solid red, as were both F and E. The decks above, D through A, formed a disconcerting checkerboard of red and green splotches. I narrowed my eyes, concentrating on Deck A, where I was currently stationed within my ready room, designated by NELLA as green.

Next door, however, loomed the all-important bridge—bathed in the unease of that frustrating violet hue. *Terrific...*

Uncertainty loomed within me, and while I felt hesitant to embrace hope, I couldn't bring myself to quit, either. Areas of the ship remained intact, which meant survival, no matter how slim, was possible. I needed a plan to bring us together.

"Okay, NELLA. What do you say we try getting that auto-hatch open?"

Chapter 18

Guilt pressed on my shoulders like a granite slab, heavy and unyielding. I lamented to myself, "If I hadn't pressured Craig to overtax *Roosevelt's* drives... this ship would still be intact—so many lives wouldn't have been lost."

Perhaps noticing my self-loathing, NELLA calmly noted my bleeding and advised tending to my injuries before anything else.

I located a medical kit in the ready room's bathroom, cleaned the oozing gash on my forehead, and then wrapped a long strip of bandage three times around my aching head. It wasn't pretty but would have to do.

I left the bathroom, began pacing the main area of my ready room. "Okay, NELLA, let's get back to the auto-hatch situation. Exactly how much control do you have over opening onboard auto-hatches and inter-deck DeckPorts?"

Unless somehow mechanically compromised, I can open and close most remaining auto-hatches. As for DeckPorts—

I would not recommend their use at this time.

"Why not?"

A crewmember's physical molecular structure could, possibly, be reassembled at a DeckPort location that is no longer here within the confines of *Resilience* or even sent to an indeterminate quantum plane of existence.

"I'll need to move between decks, NELLA."

There are a number of 'between bulkheads' maintenance accessways and utility causeways, which may provide access to various areas.

I shook my head, not liking that answer. That would take way too much time.

"NELLA, I want you to concentrate on getting the DeckPorts operational again. Log which DeckPorts are no longer physically here within *Roosevelt*... um, I mean *Resilience*. Test and retest. Get them working."

Yes, Captain.

"Also, I realize your sensors have been compromised, but you should be capable of locating Hardy's unique—"

A metallic *clanging* sound was coming from the ready room's auto-hatch. I hurried over to it and hesitated.

I swallowed hard trying to prepare myself. "NELLA, go ahead and open this auto-hatch."

I heard a high-pitched *whirring* sound as the mechanism seemed to struggle to open. The auto-hatch jerked, inching open with the effort of an old-fashioned sliding closet door having come off its track.

Three events crashed into me simultaneously. Warm, putrid air assaulted my senses. Through the haze of dark smoke and fountaining sparks, it was clear my bridge—directly adjacent to my ready room—was in chaos. Amidst the destruction, Hardy stood, miraculously alive, his faceplate marred by a jagged horizontal crack.

NELLA's voice filtered down from above...

Power reserves at 85%. Estimated time until depletion: 11 hours, 3 minutes.

I took several hesitant steps into the once pristine ship's command center. The surrounding soot-blackened bulkheads, lingering smoke, and the strobing red emergency lights casting ghostly shadows, giving the compartment an eerie, haunted house atmosphere. My eyes were drawn to the deck where several lifeless bodies—arms, and legs akimbo—lay sprawled. My heart missed a beat seeing Crewmember John Chen amongst them, eyes open and fixed... dead.

I wanted to spin on my heel, run back into the safe confines of my ready room, have NELLA close the auto-hatch behind me. I could deal with all this later—when I was better prepared. Was that too much to ask, a fucking minute to regain my footing? To collect myself mentally? I thought of Lieutenant Blunderton and her stupid therapy bird—was she one of those I'd caught sight of lying there, still upon the deck? *Oh God... I can't do this.*

I told myself I was avoiding reality. That my unconscious was shielding me from the unthinkable—that an emotional shotgun blast to the heart was imminent—that Gail Pristy very well could be among the dead.

"Cap... you okay?" The ChronoBot said—his tone soft and as human as I'd ever heard from him.

I blinked, inhaled, and nodded. "Yeah, yeah... I'm okay." I looked at him. "I'm relieved you're still in one piece, Hardy. Don't know how I'd manage without you being among the living. Your sensors... can tell me who is still alive?"

He gestured with a metal forefinger to his head. "Sensors are down. LuMan, as we speak, is hard at work making internal repairs to my noggin."

Purposely averting my eyes, still refusing to look about my surroundings, I'd managed to delay the inevitable by several seconds. Now, blinking back the welling of moisture, I forced the next four words from my mouth. "Who have we lost?"

"Get out of the way! Move it, dammit!"

Stunned as a blur of motion from behind Hardy came into view, I was both startled and shocked—momentarily paralyzed as she literally threw herself at me—leaping onto me. I staggered back as her arms enveloped me, her legs wrapped around my waist. Then kisses—a whole lot of kisses—came next.

I managed to croak out, "Gail!"

"Galvin, you're alive... I was certain you were dead." Her face hovered close, holding my head tight between her palms like a vise. A deep purple bruise marred her left cheek. Her eyes were filled with both fear and relief as they bore into mine. "I can't lose you, Galvin. You know that, right?"

I nodded, too many emotions swirling—incapable of speaking. I drew her closer and pressed my lips to hers—tasted the saltiness of our combined tears. And it was in that second, I knew, *somehow*, I would find a way for us to survive this.

Chapter 19

Lieutenant Junior Grade Roisin Blunderton was indeed there on the deck, and she was alive, attempting CPR on one of the other less fortunate crewmembers—Lindsay Soto. Blunderton continued rapid chest compressions on Soto's chest, her movements growing desperate. Crewmember Lindsay Soto, normally at Damage Control, lay beneath the Lieutenant—her face starting to turn blue... her lifeless body jerking to the rhythm of Blunderton's cardiac compressions.

I placed a soft hand on the Lieutenant's shoulder. "She's gone, Roisin... you can stop now."

"No! I can save her!" Blunderton snapped back with a glance up at me. Perspiration glinted upon her upper lip as she gasped for breath.

I saw the desperation in her eyes, an exhausted marathon runner coming to realize she would never make it to the finish line.

Finally, the young woman discontinued any further CPR, breaking down in sobs, her head coming to rest on Soto's forever-still chest. "This can't be happening..."

And with those words, the granite slab of guilt on my back doubled in weight.

Straightening, I surveyed the grim remains of my ship's bridge. Pristy knelt beside Thom Grimes, who was slumped on the deck, his back propped against a bulkhead. His head lolled to one side, his bottom lip swollen and bloodied. At least the man was still alive.

Hardy was transporting the dead one at a time, taking them out to a designated area within the Gravity Well compartment. Defensive Systems Station Crewmember Davit lay cradled within Hardy's extended arms as the ChronoBot's steady, respectful march echoed heavily upon the deck.

My chest tightened as I trailed a few steps back. I didn't want the young crewmember to feel abandoned. But I knew Davit didn't feel abandoned—Davit didn't feel anything at all.

I watched Hardy come to a stop, hesitate, then bend at the waist as he gently placed Davit's remains onto the deck next to those of Crewmembers Chen, Soto, and Barrow... as well as Lieutenant Commander Jorkins and Ensign Lira.

Ensign Blair Paxton had joined me at my side, her piercing blue eyes rimmed in red, her freckled cheeks wet with tears. For once she was speechless. I put an arm around the young woman and pulled her close—she sobbed into my chest as I held her. I imagined this was the worst day of the woman's life—it certainly was mine.

One hour and twenty-five minutes had passed since I'd walked onto the decimated bridge. What remained of my bridgecrew: XO Gail Pristy, Lieutenant Roisin Blunderton, Ensign Blair Paxton, Crewmember Thom Grimes, and ChronoBot Hardy, were now assembled within the mostly intact confines of the Captain's Conference Room. NELLA broke the silence...

Power reserves at 70%. Estimated time until depletion: 9 hours, 7 minutes.

Each of us was physically bruised and battered—emotionally wrecked, heartbroken. Too many seats around the table were empty.

Blunderton's stiff palms swiped at her uniform, trying to smooth invisible creases, her eyes conveyed the true unrest she was fighting to hide.

Her hands suddenly went still. "We should be doing something!" she blurted, eyes searching the faces of those around her. "What's left of the ship is a wasteland, we've been catapulted off into deep space... God knows where. Not to mention, we've lost more than half our bridgecrew. There are people onboard still alive... many are injured and need our help. Why are we just sitting here!" Her eyes came to rest, locked onto mine.

I nodded, not blaming her for her outburst—her growing frustration. I felt it too.

I looked about the table; my plastered-on expression of calm with an *I've-got-this air* of confidence—was total bullshit.

"Look, every action we take from now on could bring monumental consequences. If we choose wrong, more people will die unnecessarily. The six of us," I said, my voice steady, "... we are the command team. It will be us, the actions we take, that will bring survivors home safely."

Grimes, eyes unfocused on the table before him, slowly shook his head. "You make it sound like we can survive this... that somehow, some miracle will alter our all-too-apparent fate. This rocketing-through-space clump of metal, with venting atmosphere and quickly draining power reserves, is beyond rescue. We're all going to die." He looked up, anger having replaced introspection, "It's time we all just come to terms with that."

"Maybe he's right," Blair Paxton said, arms crossed over her chest and looking small in her seat. "We're not exactly steering this junk heap wherever we want."

Pristy huffed out a weary breath. "Are you done, people?"

All eyes shifted to her.

"We didn't bring you in here to have a pity party. The next person I hear whining, spends the night in the brig."

Grimes said, "Brig's gone—"

Pristy's death glare shut the Helmsman up.

She continued, "We honor the fallen by doing what they're incapable of now... we survive. We do the impossible. The simple fact that the six of us are still alive, is a miracle."

"Actually, I think the brig is still a part of the ship," Hardy commented.

I smirked and said, "Like you, I was wallowing in self-pity in my ready room..." I gave Grimes a reassuring nod. "... but with NELLA's help, I made my first post-apocalyptic command decision."

"What was that, Captain?" Blunderton asked.

"To rename *USS Roosevelt*."

"To what? *USS Pitiful*?" Grimes suggested, attempting a smile.

"NELLA has christened the ship in its current state as *USS Resilience*. Let's do our best to embody that name, that sentiment, as we move forward saving those who can be saved and..." Now it was my turn to smile. "... make this ship—and yes, I said *ship*—not only maneuverable but self-powered... as in, having propulsion."

Even Pristy was giving me the side-eye. "Captain. Uh,

Galvin... I'm all for staying upbeat. Stiff upper lip and all that, but what you're suggesting is, frankly, impossible."

I exchanged a look with Hardy. He and I had been deep in it over the last hour. Throwing hypotheticals back and forth. Nothing was off-limits or too far-fetched. And yes, even if it was impossible; I didn't care. What these six bridge officers needed now was hope. They needed a mission, a crazy, hare-brained idea that they could not only get behind but enthusiastically convey to other survivors.

NELLA's abrupt broadcast from the overhead speakers made everyone jump...

Captain, once you're ready, I can brief you on *USS Resilience's* operational capabilities.

Thom Grimes raised a brow. "Operational capabilities? Really?"

"Go ahead, NELLA, let's hear what you've been up to."

My immediate task focused on operationalizing *Resilience's* DeckPorts. Out of the 32 DeckPorts still accessible within *Resilience*, 12 are now functional and have passed intra-ship travel tests using MopBots.

It was taking every ounce of my willpower not to spring to my feet, rush to the nearest DeckPort to reach Sonya.

"The DeckPort here on Deck A?"

Operational, Captain. But only to the extent that mechanical physical matter travel has been tested.

"Go on, NELLA, what else do you have for us?"

Improved connections to shipwide sensors. I've enacted hundreds of life scans—

I jumped to my feet, fists clenched, holding my breath. "Just tell me! Is my niece among the living?" I waited, indifferent to the stunned and bewildered expressions on the other's faces.

"Dammit, NELLA, answer me!"

The three seconds it took for the ship's AI to answer me felt like hours.

Yes, Captain. Sonya Winters is indeed alive on Deck 99 and currently working with me to bring vital ship systems back online. She has a broken collarbone, a missing incisor, and a sprained left ankle. Other than that, she is okay.

Everyone, including me—especially me—let out a collective breath. Shoulders relaxed as if a weight had been lifted. Cheeks puffed out, exhaling relieved breaths. Eyes closed momentarily, silently grateful to whatever powers had spared that teenage girl.

NELLA's voice rose above the exchanged murmurs...

Captain, you had asked about TAC-Band communications. I expect to have limited comms up and running within the next ten minutes. Do not attempt to access any of the ship's DeckPorts until TAC-Band comms are operational—it is via TAC-

Bands that DeckPort destinations will be configured.

"Excellent work, NELLA. Truly. I want a full accounting of the KIAs, MIAs, as well as survivors. Have that sent to my ready room halo display."

Already done, Captain.

Chapter 20

I stood within the partial darkness of my ready room there behind my desk with Pristy at my side.

She took my hand in hers and squeezed. "You can do this, Galvin."

I looked at her, the soft glow of the halo display played upon her porcelain skin, her fine, delicate features. She was already scanning the list of names, scrolling through the unthinkable. A tear escaped, following the gentle contours of her cheek, then dropped away.

Putting my attention on the display, I started to read. The list of the KIAs came first. NELLA had grouped them by functional group or department. The U.S. Army Ranger Brigade, a force of 1000 plus soldiers, filled the display like the entries in an old-fashioned telephone book. There probably wasn't a name among them I would know—I'd yet to make the trek down to Deck 6 to introduce myself.

With a sudden inhalation, Pristy raised a hand, stopping the halo's scrolling of names. The tip of her forefinger penetrated the projected imagery of one name in particular.

Commander "Con" Cornelius Strickland

And as with the countless others there within this grouping —**Deceased**—he was added to the death count.

"I'm so sorry, Gail. I know you two had recently become close."

She swallowed hard, nodding. Her eyes met mine. "Nothing serious," she said. "Just some innocent making out. It was nice to be wanted... but my heart wasn't in it, so I ended it."

Was I sad we'd lost another good man and an excellent officer? Of course. Was I also somewhat gratified things hadn't progressed past innocent making out? Ab-so-fucking-lutely.

"I'm sorry Gail. Strickland was one of a kind."

"Oh stop it. You didn't like him, and the feeling was mutual. You wouldn't have been on his Christmas card list anytime soon."

She used a hand to quickly scroll through the names and stop at HealthBay. We both saw it at the same time:

Dr. Pippa Tangerie—Deceased

"Shit," I said. "I wouldn't have been on her Christmas card list either, but we sure could use her in HealthBay right now."

"Let's jump down to the Science Department," she said, giving me a sympathetic glance. She knew Stephan Derrota and I were best of friends. I shut my eyes, grappling with the familiar gnaw of PTSD—an unwelcome remnant from my earlier career. How many times today have I chosen to escape rather than confront reality?

"Seems Stephan's not listed as deceased, nor is he listed as a survivor. She looked at me. "He's... missing."

My TAC-Band crackled. An indecipherable projected 3D image flickered and danced upon my wrist.

"Galvin... is that you? You really should get down here. It's beyond mayhem. Dr. Pippa Tangerie is dead. I guess I could have said that more delicately, but considering the circumstances—"

"Stephan?"

"Yes... who else? Oh, and I am immensely grateful to Bappa that you are alive and unharmed, my friend."

His Mumbai-accented voice was like music to my ears at this moment.

Pristy mouthed, "Bappa?"

"Used as a respectful and affectionate term for Lord Ganesha..." I offered, turning to Pristy. "...who is widely revered in Mumbai and throughout India." I turned back to Derrota, relief flooding over me. "Glad you're still with us, Stephan," I said, letting out a breath I didn't realize I was holding. "I'll get down there just as soon as DeckPorts become operational again."

I cut the connection.

Pristy, who had only partially been listening to our conversation, had her attention back on the halo display. By her dour expression, more names had been added to the deceased list.

"Tell me. Best to rip off the Band-Aid all at once."

"Wanda's gone, three of Max's Marines are listed as injured, status unknown."

My mind flashed to the image of that muscular six-foot-four warrior. It seemed impossible to me that anything could bring down that superhero of a woman. I would truly miss her. But now was not the time to grieve.

Pristy chewed at her top lip. She clearly didn't want to say what she was going to say next.

"Of course, Chief Craig Porter's name is here—he's gone, Galvin. As well as Kaelen Rivers, and anyone else who happened to be stationed within the aft section of the ship when it blew. I know I keep saying it, but I'm so sorry."

The gut punches just kept coming. And it wasn't as if I didn't know Craig was dead, I'd literally just left the man standing there within the noisy confines of Engineering and Propulsion five minutes before it blew.

But now, actually hearing the spoken words, that such a dear, dear friend was gone—gone forever—never to be seen again—well it was just too much. I dropped into the chair at my desk, placed my head in my hands, and started to cry. I cried for a long time—apparently, now *was* the time to grieve.

With recent news from NELLA that select DeckPorts were operational again—at least to the point where a MopBot had successfully moved between two decks—I wasted no time. I designated myself as the first person to test if an organic being, a human—me in this case—would survive the process. This meant undergoing the molecular-level transfer of my matter into some quantum-level plane of existence, the destruction of my original matter, and then the reconstruction of my matter at a different DeckPort within USS *Resilience*.

I burst from the DeckPort on the Symbio Deck, sprinting at full tilt. With only a rough sense of where Sonya's work area might be, I entered the expansive, behind-the-scenes labyrinth for the Roman Empire. Beneath the muted glow of the emergency lights, the scale of the effort and planning behind this massive project seemed almost unimaginable.

I took in the stark contrasts to the grandeur of the Roman city beyond the walls. Here, my senses were assaulted by the smell of industrial lubricants and the persistent hum of servos. Far more elaborate than any of the previous Symbio Decks, I saw steel catwalks stretching out overhead, interwoven with tubes, pipes, and signal cables that blinked with red status lights.

Rows of Symbio maintenance workers, bald and expressionless, glided past me in synchronized formation, their white overalls adding an eerie uniformity to the scene. Their mechanical precision and utter lack of emotion heightened the surreal atmosphere. These were the most dumb-downed Symbios I'd ever encountered.

I turned a corner and entered a storage area filled with towering racks holding dozens of Roman chariots. Automated lift systems sat quietly, no longer moving the chariots down to the deck. Another turn took me past massive vats filled with a semi-transparent gel, bubbling away with an unsettling, almost organic glow. Here, more Symbios—technician Symbios—in lab coats seemed to be wandering aimlessly, as if their minds had been scrubbed; their faces illuminated beneath the eerie red emergency lights.

Further down, rows of Symbio Roman soldiers filled their respective charging stations. Hundreds of Legionaries with elaborate helmets and Pteruges, the leather strips hanging to protect their thighs, stood silent and still. They resembled extras on a film set, awaiting their brief moment in the spotlight.

Chilled air stung my face as I moved through a refrigerated compartment brimming with bio-organic materials. Dimly lit repair bays came into view. The hiss of released hydraulic pressure echoed—a consequence of the ship's power loss. More motionless, lifelike, bare-chested Symbio Poth gladiators stood poised as if on the brink of battle. Across the bay, equally still lions with fierce expressions and majestic teams of Symbio horses appeared frozen in time.

I found Sonya at last, slumped on her cot in the dim corner of her cramped office. Her eyes were shut, but the pain etched across her face screamed excruciating wakefulness. Her mouth was swollen, her left ankle black and blue, and bandages crisscrossed both shoulders, pulling them back to support her broken collarbone. The figure-eight wrap indicated the severity of her injury. I wondered who had treated her. But knowing her, she'd asked NELLA for the right medical procedure and then fashioned the bandages on her own.

I knelt next to her, placing a hand on her knee. "I'm here, Sonya."

One eye opened, she squinted back at me. "Uh, yeah... you're about as quiet as one of my Symbio T-Rexes. What are you doing here? Isn't there a cataclysmic disaster you should be handling?"

When she spoke I noticed the space and bloody gum where one of her front teeth had been.

I glanced around, my ire rising. "Has anyone been up here to help you? Anyone at all?" That made her smile... then grimace from the pain. "At the time of the explosion, I think I was the only crewmember up here. I knew where there was a medical kit... did the best I could with what I had."

She looked at me now, both eyes open. "I knew you had survived. Found a way to tap into your ready room's halo cam. I'm sorry so many died. This is terrible."

All I could do was nod.

Her eyes narrowed as she studied my face, thoughts racing. "Are we all going to die, Uncle Galvin?"

She almost never called me that, and at that moment, she looked more like a five-year-old than someone nearing eighteen.

"Not if I have anything to say about it. But I'll need your help. I'll need you healthy."

She continued to stare at me, still looking for signs that I was placating her, just spewing bullshit to make her feel better.

Taken aback, she said "You honestly believe that, don't you? That we can get out of this mess?"

"I do. But I have to be honest. This won't be easy. It's going to take everything we've got from each one of us to make it happen."

She attempted to lean forward and gasped in pain. "Okay... um... what do you need me to do?"

"I need you to do absolutely nothing while I, very carefully, pick you up and take you down to HealthBay. And I don't want any arguments."

She nodded. "No arguments."

Chapter 21

Cradling Sonya in my arms, we stepped into HealthBay's storm of chaos. All the beds were taken, and the open space was brimming with activity.

I noticed four individuals in blue scrubs—clearly doctors—accompanied by twice as many nurses in green scrubs. Nearby, three towering MediBots were busy attending to patients. Stephan Derrota stood amid the chaos, his white lab coat stained with blood and other bodily fluids.

He caught sight of me, finished speaking with the nearby nurse, and hurried over to us. Dispensing with any formalities or greetings he wasted no time taking Sonya from me.

"Follow me," he urged. Holding Sonya in his arms, he hurried down the passageway—a passageway that I knew led to Surgery, patient rooms, and doctors' offices.

The back area buzzed with activity, matching the chaos of the main floor. MediBots glided among patients, doctors barked orders, and nurses hustled around. Derrota spotted an empty table in one of the three surgery compartments and gently laid Sonya down.

A harried-looking nurse approached, pulling an IV stand along behind her.

"First things first, we'll deal with her pain," Derrota said. "In a few minutes, we'll get some imaging, then, if needed, reset that left clavicle. I'll also replicate a new incisor, ice that ankle and then... well, we'll just go from there."

I looked down at the teenager, seeing I was holding one of her hands. *When did I take her hand?*

Sonya's face relaxed, the strain fading from her features. Whatever the nurse had given her, the IV drip was already working its way through her bloodstream.

"Go on, Galvin," Derrota urged, nudging me firmly. "She's in good hands. You've got bigger things to handle right now."

On my way out of HealthBay, I spotted familiar faces—crewmembers who had managed to survive. But there was no time for small talk. I had a ship to save.

I had thrown down the gauntlet to my bridge officers back in the Captain's Conference Room. Survival aboard USS *Resilience* hinged on everyone completing one or more critical tasks within a tight timeframe.

Gail Pristy faced the monumental task of resurrecting key departments. Junior officers would need to step up, replacing their fallen or incapacitated superiors. Despite its fractured state, the ship's maintenance crew had to shore up hull breaches and make other essential repairs. Environmental systems teetered on the edge, with air scrubbers and filters in desperate need of fixing and optimization. Who among the survivors had that skill-set? It was Pristy's job to bring the right people together to tackle the mounting list of problems, some of which were quickly becoming critical.

Warning. Power reserves at 55%. Estimated time until depletion: 7 hours, 11 minutes.

Crewmember Thom Grimes—now sporting a makeshift bandage wrapped around his head and walking with a pronounced limp—was still mentally sharp. He was tracking sector coordinates, *Resilience's* trajectory, while identifying any impending obstacles in our path.

Lieutenant Roisin Blunderton, taking John Chen's place, was in charge of everything having to do with the ship's comms, from working with NELLA and improving our sketchy inter-ship TAC-Band communications to establishing a connection with U.S. Space Navy Command back on Earth.

Ensign Blair Paxton, who was already familiar with overseeing the ship's engines, power distribution, and the integrity of other ship's systems from the bridge, would now be dedicating her energies to re-establishing the ship's power grid. She'd also be in charge of getting our bridge consoles and control boards operational—or at least ready for operation once other functionality was back online.

For Hardy and me, our job seemed impossible—making this mile-long chunk of metal capable of actual propulsion and directional helm control. Hey... I know what you're thinking—good luck with that—no longer having that all-too-necessary Engineering and Propulsion section of the ship still attached. Well, you know what they say, desperate times...

Hardy and I arrived simultaneously at the ship's sprawling, multi-deck flight bay. The dim crimson glow from sporadic emergency lights barely illuminated the area, making it difficult to see.

I should have been prepared for what I'd be walking into

here, but that wasn't the case. Just as my crew had been violently tossed about, so had the contents of this bay. Where once there had been row after row of perfectly positioned bright red Arrow Fighters, several hundred of them—what we were looking at now was little more than the twisted and mangled rubble of a scrapyard.

I was wearing a helmeted E-suit, breathing the stale air from several oxygen tanks integrated into my backpack. The bay doors were open, as usual, the Atmospheric Containment Field (ACF), a typically blue-glowing energy field barrier—there to keep the ship's atmosphere in, while keeping the -450 F chill out—was offline. Speaking of which, I was starting to feel that frigid cold making its way through my suit.

Hardy gestured up toward a high-mounted, boxy-looking compartment—similar to that on a naval aircraft carrier—called the 'Island'. It housed the flight bay's flight control and various command and control facilities. "We can see if the barrier just needs to be turned back on."

"Nothing is that easy, Hardy. But it's a good place to start."

I headed across the deck, weaving between flipped-on-their-backs Arrows, dodging puddles of hydraulic fluid, shattered glass, pieces of shrapnel-like composite materials, remnants of spooled cabling, and other debris. I stopped in my tracks and looked back at the ChronoBot following several paces behind. "It doesn't take two of us to flip a switch. How about you start cleaning up this area."

Hardy stared back at me, then looked at the overwhelming mess surrounding us. "It's not like grabbing a broom and a dust-pan, Cap..."

I rolled my eyes, "A little manual labor will be good for you." I pointed to one particular Arrow Fighter. "Some of these birds might be salvageable. Get them righted back on their landing struts. And I don't want to see you roughly manhandling these birds just because you don't like the task I've given you." I almost laughed but managed to keep a straight face.

I found the steep metal staircase leading up to the Island and charged up, two steps at a time. I ignored the loud scraping sounds mixed with Hardy's overdramatic grunts and exasperated exhalations coming from below. Reaching the top catwalk, I stole a glance down at the bay's deck. Hardy had already flipped back over three Arrows and was working on a fourth. The physical strength it would take to do what he was doing was beyond fathomable.

I stepped through the Island's open auto-hatch into muted darkness. It became immediately evident that this ten-foot-wide by thirty-foot-long, mobile-home-shaped compartment was offline. Facing out to the bay was a waist-high window which provided a 180-degree view to the deck below as well as the wide, open bay entrance. The twenty-foot-long control board on the opposite bulkhead lay shrouded in darkness.

As my eyes adjusted to the negligible amount of light, I saw the unmistakable shapes of seven motionless human bodies. Three uniformed women and four men lay scattered like pieces of pepperoni on a slice of pizza; puddles of blood had pooled around their heads as if they had all simultaneously suffered the same fatal blow to their heads.

Guilt rose inside of me—a kind of self-loathing tidal wave was once more building momentum within. I shook my head. I'd promised myself there would be more than enough time to deal with self-contempt and inner shame later. For now, there was work to do.

With as much care and respect as I could muster under the circumstances, I placed the bodies in a single line along the outer bulkhead—they weren't cords of wood—stacking them on top of one another was never an option.

"NELLA... talk to me about this compartment. What's working in here and what's not?"

This flight bay control center is offline.

"No kidding, I can see that. Can it be brought back online? And will it still be operational once I do? I need to get that ACF energy boundary functioning again."

Yes, Captain. I am in the process of rerouting power junctions as we speak. However, the control board will require a manual initialization, something I cannot achieve remotely.

"Okay, so where's the On/Off switch to this thing?"

There is a utility breaker box at the far end of the compartment. Open it, and you will see that all of the breakers have been tripped. Re-engage them one at a time and the control center, the flight bay, should have power again.

THREE MINUTES LATER, I FOUND THE BREAKER BOX with no fewer than 50 tripped breaker switches. I shoved them back into their ON positions which brought the compartment's overhead lights back on as well as the blindingly bright flight bay lights beyond the window.

The reinitialization of the ACF energy

boundary is typically a two or three-person job.

A small halo projection suddenly sprouted up from the primary control board behind me. It seemed NELLA was providing me a kind of 'how-to' video playing on a repetitive loop, showing the multi-step process of various control board touch switch entries, three different virtual slider switch settings, and the entry of a ten-digit passcode. It was complicated to the point I had to watch the video three more times before taking on the task myself. Scrambling back and forth along the long bank of controls, I followed NELLA's provided steps, finishing up with the entry of the passcode.

I turned around in time to see an aqua-blue energy field taking shape within the mouth of the bay opening... some 500 feet wide and 300 feet high.

Down below me, twenty bright red Arrow Fighters had been lined up on the deck in perfect pre-flight formation. Hardy was still at work righting another fighter. But it wasn't the Arrows, or even Hardy, that I was interested in. Looking farther back into the far-reaching depths of the bay, I saw them: four brand-new Craven-Class 550 Off-Worlders. These military transport assets were modern-day workhorses—providing high-torque, brute power from their fusion drive powerplants. Once I witnessed one of these craft towing a *USS Hamilton*-sized dreadnought out of Earth's not insubstantial gravity.

"Tell me NELLA... those Off-Worlders... they look to have been secured to the Bay's deck."

Correct, Captain. Four Craven-Class 550 Off-Worlders were secured with deck clamps before the ship left Halibart Station.

Chapter 22

Hardy seemed to have really found his rhythm, so I left him alone righting Arrows. He'd already moved a number of the more damaged, inoperable fighters, shoving them out of the way to a dedicated junk pile area of the flight bay.

Arrow pilot barracks sat adjacent to the flight bay, allowing for immediate deployment if duty called. According to NELLA, this area of the ship was designated as violet. Neither the ship's AI nor Hardy—who was still not able to access his sensor data—could give me an accurate headcount of who was listed as alive, missing, or deceased. What NELLA could tell me, though, was that the barracks had not been subject to a hull breach and that environmental conditions were normal.

The auto-hatch leading out of the bay and toward the pilot barracks didn't open at my approach. "NELLA... open this auto-hatch."

That auto-hatch is inoperable due to this area of the ship's superstructure misalignment.

"You're saying it's stuck."

NELLA didn't comment on that.

I brought up my helmet's HUD and found the TAC-Band sync option. Within 30 seconds, I was connected and saw no fewer than twenty messages waiting for me. I hailed Hardy... first things first.

"Yeah, Cap," he said.

"I need you back here at this auto-hatch." I waved a hand over my head to catch his attention.

A minute later, the ChronoBot lumbered over. "You beckoned?"

"I need this auto-hatch forced open."

Hardy stared back at me.

"Please," I added.

The robot stood before the hatch, placed his catcher's mitt-sized hands on the metal surface, and attempted to slide the door open. It didn't budge an inch.

"What was *that*? You'll have to put your back into it, Hardy. It's wedged tight."

His faceplate, even cracked as it was, was fully capable of displaying various text, images, and icons. At this particular moment, it was a familiar hand gesture, commonly referred to as flipping the bird.

I smiled. "Just give it another try. Chop, chop."

Hardy shifted his stance, putting all one thousand pounds of his bulk into shoving the auto-hatch open. The shriek of metal on metal filled the air, making me wince. Slowly, inch by grating inch, the hatch began to slide.

Once there was an opening wide enough for us to step through, I gave him a pat on the back.

"Good enough, Hardy. Let's see who's still alive in there."

Beyond the auto-hatch was an empty passageway. We moved forward about ten yards and made a left at an intersecting corridor. Making another left, we hurried another ten yards where another closed auto-hatch awaited.

Hardy didn't need prompting to do what was obvious. And just like the previous hatch, this one too began to slide open—slowly, inch by grating inch.

Excited voices echoed from inside the compartment... finally, a bit of good news.

Hardy seemed to have found his groove, and with a final monumental shove, the auto-hatch slid all the way open.

Standing before us were several dozen men and women... all looking at me—their Captain—for answers.

"Everything is going to be okay. You're all safe."

Akari James and Wallace Ryder stood among the survivors. Akari's right arm was dotted with burn marks, while a strip of tape spanned the bridge of Ryder's nose. The others bore similar non-critical injuries.

Ryder and Akari stepped forward, their eyes wide and haunted, like newly freed prisoners of war yet still carrying the ghosts of their torment.

Akari rushed into my arms, and I felt her body trembling within my embrace. Then I heard her muffled words...

"We thought we were going to die in here. No word from the rest of the ship... isolated... the lights only came on a few minutes ago."

She pushed herself away from me while wiping tears from her cheeks. "What the hell happened?"

Ryder repeated the question, "What happened to the ship, Galvin?"

I faced them, a guilty man before a jury of his peers. "Engineering and Propulsion exploded. Fragments ripped the ship apart. We're in the mid-section, hurtling through space at 99,419 miles per hour. The death toll is high and still rising."

"So you've rescued us, but it sounds like we're still going to die anyway," Akari said, looking both angry and betrayed.

"On the contrary," I said. "Those of you in this compartment are going to change this shitty—some would say unsurvivable—situation and get us back in control."

"What the hell are you talking about, Galvin? If what you've told us is true, we're little more than an asteroid just waiting to careen into something bigger and harder than we are."

The other pilots murmured their agreement. Their body language, arms crossed over chests, hands on hips, said it all. Sure, they'd been rescued—but only to be told that they were just as screwed now as they had been five minutes earlier.

I lifted my hands in a gesture of surrender. "I know it's been rough. But I need everyone to gear up and ready to be wheels up in ten."

Akari stared back at me. "You're serious?"

"I'm serious."

Critical alert. Power reserves at 40%. Estimated time until depletion: 5 hours, 15 minutes.

The pilots glanced up, shifting on their feet and looking mystified—apparently, until now, they hadn't been getting these growingly depressing NELLA announcements.

One of the other pilots said, "What happens when the power reserves are depleted?"

"The lights go out... pumps stop circulating water... the air stops flowing... in other words, we die."

"So, what are you thinking, Galvin?" Ryder asked. "You talking about some kind of mass exodus... using our Arrows as escape pods?"

I shook my head. "With somewhere around fifteen hundred souls still alive onboard, we won't have nearly enough Arrows for something like that. No. We needed to come up with something.

The pilots' lounge was packed—thirty wingmen, Sonya—fresh from HealthBay donning a pair of proper slings—Stephan Derrota, Hardy, me, and what remained of my bridgecrew; they had been ordered to leave their posts momentarily so that we all could have a very important pow-wow. With comms still unreliable, the risk of miscommunication was a death sentence waiting to happen. Some took their seats, but most remained standing, looking nervous.

I looked to Ensign Blair Paxton. "How about you start with a SitRep on the ship's power grid, Ensign?"

Suddenly the center of attention, all eyes upon her, she glanced about nervously.

"You got this, Paxton," Pristy's voice cut through the tension. "We need the truth, however ugly."

Paxton offered back an *okay-you-asked-for-it*-expression. "This midsection ship of ours remains a shredded mess—tubular conduits splayed open, ventilation ducts torn apart, electrical conduits sparking. Several corridors and compartments are exposed to open space. While the DeckGates are mostly operational and sealing properly, countless hull breaches are still venting atmosphere out into the void."

She chinned toward the latest newcomer. "Chief LaSalle and his crews have been going non-stop—they know better than anyone... there isn't much on this ship that hasn't been affected."

The 50-something Black man looked as if he had been in a bar fight, his left eye swollen shut and a dried bloody gash running along his jawline.

He made his way toward me, looking just as exhausted as he did overwhelmed.

The Chief looked at me, let out a resigned breath, and said, "Per your directives, I've got what's left of my crew concentrating on stopping the atmospheric venting. We've got it slowed but I don't feel confident that all hull breaches will get completely shored up... there are just too many."

"And the power conduits?" I asked.

"Our low-power photon conduits are an easier fix, and we're working on that. But our plasma conduits, which are running that superheated, ionized gas... those require far more time and equipment to repair." LaSalle shrugged. "Not sure what the end game is here, but spending our limited resources on such things may be—"

I cut him off, "Just do what you can, Chief. Prioritize those actions that will sustain life the longest."

He shrugged and then nodded.

Ensign Paxton continued, "Much of the ship's power architecture was designed to be self-repairing and NELLA has been on it 24/7. I'm somewhat amazed at how resourceful the AI has been in keeping us all alive."

I turned to Roisin Blunderton. "With John Chen gone, you've got some big shoes to fill on Comms. How's it going so far?"

"Not great but not terrible, either. I've verified that several emergency dispatches had managed to transmit just before the explosion. EUNF undoubtedly knows of our plight. The big problem—*Roosevelt's*... uh, *Resilience's*... external comms array was destroyed. With Sonya's and Stephan Derrota's help, we've constructed a new comms array, we just need a way to get it secured onto the outer hull."

I looked to Hardy. "Can you manage a spacewalk? Get that array attached without flying off into space yourself?"

Hardy looked back at me as the compartment quieted down. I'd made it sound like a casual request. But what I was asking wasn't as simple as heading out to the curb to check the mail—it would be about as dangerous as anything I had ever asked the ChronoBot to do.

Saying nothing, his cracked faceplate lit up with a thumbs-up icon. I knew he wasn't thrilled with this request but knew many lives depended on this broken ship reestablishing communications with Earth, U.S. Space Navy Command, and the EUNF.

Blunderton added, "TAC-Bands are operational, most of the halo displays are back online, and I'm helping Paxton with the bridge stations. It's a bigger job than we thought, but we've got Science Officer Derrota, the SWM team, and Sonya pitching in where they can."

"Good," I said, turning to Grimes. "Where are we, Mr. Grimes? Give me the coordinates."

Thom Grimes—blood seeping through the bandage wrapped around his head—stood with slumped shoulders, looking drained. His face was pale, forehead glistening with beads of sweat, and his voice came out weak, stripped of its usual gusto. "With NELLA's help, I've pinpointed our exact location. Not sure how but we're still pretty much on the same course as it was right before the explosion. Heading toward Star-Point Station—beyond that, of course, is the Orpheus Rift—home to the Krygians."

I nodded. Heading toward Earth would've been my choice, but we had to deal with what we got.

Pristy cut in, her gaze fixed on Grimes. "After this meeting, you're going straight to HealthBay. You look like death, Thom."

He looked as though he was going to protest, but seeing her steely expression, the crewman simply nodded.

I leaned in. "And the other project?"

Grimes smiled faintly. "It's a wild idea, Sir. Probably a little insane. But yes... I—with NELLA's help—did just what you asked. There was a lot of math, celestial mechanics, calculus, linear algebra, finite element analysis, not to mention basic astrodynamics. Then on the physics side, thermodynamics, gravitational physics, Newtonian mechanics—"

"Okay, okay, we get it... it was a lot to noodle out, Mr. Grimes," I said. "Go on and tell everyone what our intentions are."

"Well, you asked me to pinpoint the exact locations on *Resilience's* hull for four separately mounted powerplants. It wasn't a straightforward task, given the hull's asymmetrical structure and the need to balance weight distribution with optimal energy output. I had to consult with NELLA and Science Officer Derrota and run multiple simulations to ensure we weren't compromising the ship's already precarious integrity. But we've identified the precise locations... where to land and mount our four Off-Worlders."

It went quiet enough to hear a pin drop.

Grimes took in the astonished faces. "We're confident this will give you what you want, Cap—the ability to take back navigational control of this spacecraft."

"There's a really, really, REALLY big problem in that harebrained idea," came a young female voice.

Sonya sat up from where she'd been sprawled out on one of the three couches. "The technical name for this is... high-velocity maneuvering challenge."

The pilots were now talking over one another, a full-on debate heating up.

Having to practically shout, Pristy said, "What she's referring to is high-velocity departure maneuvering and the problem where the Off-Worlders, in this case, would have to achieve significant acceleration to overcome *Resilience's* already considerable velocity of 99,419 miles per hour."

One of the pilots, incensed, said, "An Off-Worlder would need to pull significant thrust to break away from *Resilience*... doing so while we're barreling through space at 99,419 miles per hour... it's going to be challenging."

Captain Ryder stepped forward, his voice carrying the weight of command. "Watkins is right. He's referring to Delta-V constraints."

From the crowd, Derrota's voice, thick with a Mumbai accent, joined in. "Keep in mind what is called high-velocity ejection... both *Resilience* and the Off-Worlders will be moving at 99,419 miles per hour. We'll be dealing with significant momentum and inertia."

The science officer stepped out from the crowd next to Ryder, his expression dead serious. "You're not just fighting against the ship's velocity. You're fighting against substantial momentum. To propel away from the ship, you'd need thrust beyond what those Off-Worlders were originally designed to generate."

One of the younger pilots, his voice tinged with frustration and a hint of challenge, spoke up. "So what do we do? It's not like we can slow *Resilience* down. How the hell do we pull this off?"

Sonya, looking exasperated, got to her feet—careful to keep weight off her left foot—and made an overdramatic shake of her head. "I already told you, this isn't going to work!"

Murmurs rippled across the compartment, tension thickening as Sonya doused what little hope remained.

I caught Pristy's eye. She gave me a nod, ready to drop the ace we'd been holding.

Pristy's voice cut through the noise—calm but with a hint of excitement beneath the surface, "There's a card we haven't played yet. *Resilience* isn't just drifting out here. She's got two hundred docking thrusters spread across her hull. Small, but powerful. And NELLA? She's got them all ready to fire on command."

Sonya's eyes widened as she straightened, the relaxed posture gone. "Wait. You're saying we'll have enough reverse thrust to slow us down sufficiently to deploy those Off-Worlders..."

Ryder looked between me and Pristy. "And that will be enough to cut that relativistic differential?"

I met his gaze, my voice steady, anchoring the room. "That's the plan. Whether we can pull it off... well, that's the big question. Either way, we'll only get one shot at this."

Critical alert. Power reserves at 25%. Estimated time until depletion: 3 hours, 25 minutes.

Chapter 23

The red emergency lights cast the bridge in an ominous glow as I stepped onto the ship's nearly destroyed command center. Debris crunched beneath my boots, a reminder of the near-fatal destruction. I scanned the scene, grief for the fallen weighing heavy. Unaware of my presence, the few surviving bridge crewmembers moved sluggishly, their efforts lackluster at best.

Ensign Blair Paxton was hunched over a console, her movements slow and defeated. Lieutenant Junior Grade Roisin Blunderton tapped at another station's interface, her usual precision gone. Thom Grimes, sat slumped over the helm controls, staring at dead displays. His best friend was gone. I couldn't recall a time when Grimes and Chen hadn't been side by side, working the same shifts and ensuring they were always deployed to the same ship.

I let out a resigned breath, feeling their despair. I had always believed that keeping morale high was one of my strong suits, but this situation tested that belief.

Soft footsteps approached. Gail Pristy was walking toward me, her presence both a relief and a reminder of our situation.

"They look like they've collectively thrown in the towel," she noted.

"Can't blame them," I replied, eyes on the crew. "We've taken a hell of a hit, and it's not just the ship that's broken."

She sighed, shoulders drooping briefly before squaring them again. Even in despair, Pristy had an uncanny ability to reclaim her strength. We exchanged a look that spoke volumes. The romantic tension simmered beneath the surface, but there was no time to dwell on it.

"What are we going to do? We need to rally them, Galvin," she said softly, eyes locking onto mine. She gestured to the crew. "Clearly, this can't go on."

"You're right." I raised my voice. "Everyone, listen up!"

Grimes continued to work but straightened slightly, while Paxton and Blunderton stopped what they were doing to look at me. Their eyes were focused, though defeat still lingered in their expressions.

"We're not out of this fight," I continued. "We've faced impossible odds before and come out on top. This is no different. We need to pull together and get this ship operational again. Lives depend on it."

Pristy stepped forward. "We honor our fallen by doing the impossible—by surviving."

They looked surprised to hear my—and the XO's—declarations. Blunderton's demeanor shifted; her back straightened, chest jutted out. Her expression was now one of resolve. Paxton and Grimes hesitated, uneasy but trying to mirror her newfound spark. But I saw it—that shadow of *what's the use—we're all going to die anyway*, in their eyes.

As if on cue, Blunderton's McCaw flew into the space, circled, landed upon her shoulder, and began an odd, syncopated swaying to some unheard beat or melody. Lucy's upbeat countenance stood in stark contrast to the oppressive atmosphere.

Grimes and Paxton exchanged a smile, their moods lifted, if even for a moment.

"Blair... Roisin," I called out. "Those consoles won't repair themselves—we need to have those systems back online. Work together; there's no room for mistakes."

They both nodded.

"Mr. Grimes, keep your focus. Prepping Helm and readying it for what comes next is crucial for all of our survival. This ship... her crew... we're all counting on you. So we need you to be at your very best."

Blair and Roisin turned back to their stations with new vigor. A flicker of that old, fierce intensity reignited in their eyes, the kind that had always marked them as a formidable team.

"I'll handle diagnostics and reroute power," Blunderton said. "Blair, bypass the damaged secondary junctions... those circuits are fried."

Paxton nodded, fingers tapping away at her board. "On it."

I moved through the space, navigating between consoles, each in various stages of repair. Access panels had been removed, revealing internal cables, some billowing outward like the entrails of a slashed-open beast. At least the sparking power lines hanging from above had been dealt with.

"Life support systems are hanging by a thread." Pristy's eyes flicked over the status displays at an unmanned station. "We need to stabilize the sub-systems in Environmental. I should head down there." But she lingered at the station, hesitating.

"What's the latest status on NELLA?" I asked.

"She's operational but running on diminished emergency protocols," Pristy said. "We'll need her at full capacity if we're going to pull through this."

NELLA's voice, slightly distorted and much too loud, blared from the overhead speakers...

Captain, there are critical systems throughout the ship that require crewmember service intervention. Also, *Resilience* still has numerous breaches yet to be addressed.

"We're working on getting you some help soon NELLA. SWM is finishing up with several jammed DeckGates. Once that's done, we can isolate other areas of the ship—those still venting atmosphere."

Understood.

Blunderton and Paxton had picked up their pace and were working with more gusto. A sudden flurry of sparks crackled, punctuated by Blunderton's muttered curses.

"You need to reroute power from your station's blown aux sensor matrix. No reason it can't share this console's," Paxton insisted.

Blunderton shook her head. "That's going to overload the secondary circuits. How about coming up with a more balanced approach?"

"Balanced?" Paxton snapped. "Don't be stupid. We don't have time for balance. These systems are going back online in what? An hour?"

"Don't call me stupid, you're stupid!" Blunderton spat back.

"Enough! You're both right," Pristy intervened. "Roisin, prioritize emergency power loads; Blair, stabilize the other circuits on that motherboard you're working on. Focus and work together. We don't have time for this juvenile in-fighting."

The tension eased slightly as they resumed their tasks with a more synchronized approach. Circuits started lighting up, one after the other.

Grimes hunched over the helm controls, his face a mask of concentration. Sitting up, he shot me an aggravated glare. "Captain, I still don't know what specific control signals will be required here."

"I told you before, Science Officer Derrota—"

He cut in, "Yes, Captain... I know, he's very busy and will get to assisting us with bridge interfaces just as soon as he has a free moment. But we're running out of time... um, Sir." Beads of sweat had formed on his brow.

Pristy was at Tactical; her console flickered, then came to life, several displays lit up—she turned to look at me with a smile. "Hey... a sliver of hope, no?"

Earlier friction among the crew seemed to be giving way to a growing sense of cohesion.

"The power stabilizer needs diverting, Roisin. The circuits are overloading," Paxton noted.

"Way ahead of you, Blair," Blunderton replied, tweaking a secondary system's input. "Shifting auxiliary loads... now."

Power resumed at two more consoles—their previously dark control boards now coming alive with colorful indicators and displays. Each one bringing us a step closer to being operational again.

NELLA's voice chimed in with a bit more clarity...

Primary systems are only semi-operational. Catastrophic failure probability within the next three hours: 87%.

"Don't be such a buzz kill, NELLA," Blunderton said.

The main halo display suddenly flickered before fully illuminating, casting a bluish glow into the compartment. Cheers erupted from the crew. The sight of the display—alive again despite everything—bolstered all of our spirits.

"We may just have a chance," Pristy said quietly, her smile breaking through exhaustion.

I nodded, yet wary of letting too much hope cloud what was still a dire situation.

Pristy, still at Tactical, tapped at her board; the halo display feed now projected the surrounding starfield, revealing our trajectory. A second halo display, this one a logistical feed with telemetry vectors and graphic icons, came alive. A spike of adrenaline hit as I noticed the distant endpoint of one of the potential navigation vectors—StarPoint Station. Would reaching that endpoint even be a possibility? I had no idea—but we'd beaten the odds thus far, so maybe.

The daunting task of bringing *USS Roosevelt*, now *USS Resilience*, back from the dead was far from over. With each system coming back online, others invariably would go down. But at least I felt just a little more like the ship's captain—a captain whom this crew would need even more in the hours and days ahead.

Chapter 24

En route to one of the mid-ship airlocks and with most of the ship's DeckPorts deactivated, we still had another ten minutes hike ahead of us. Burnt ozone lingered in the air, a stark reminder of the shipwide damage. Softly pulsing alarms added to the urgency, their cadence matching the ticking countdown timer projected on my TAC-Band informing of our all too imminent depleting power reserves.

I walked several paces behind Hardy, his oversized backpack creating an almost comical sight amid the gravity of our situation.

Pristy moved up beside me, her footsteps hurried and tense. We passed by another secured DeckGate—the flickering glow casting intermittent blue light across the steel bulkheads. Our eyes met without a word.

"Got everything strapped on there right, Hardy?" I yelled up ahead to him, eyeing the bulky comms array equipment barely contained by the pack.

Hardy made a show of adjusting the straps on his backpack,

his metal fingers fumbling with the spooled cabling over his shoulder.

"Cap, I'm a walking Swiss Army knife," Hardy bellowed, not turning around. "If I can't handle this, ain't nobody can."

Despite his bravado, I could catch the faintest edge of tension in his voice. But, as he always does, Hardy masked it with sarcasm. My gaze lingered on Hardy and the seemingly endless passageway before us. This task was a crucial one. Fixing the comms array was our best shot at regaining long-range communications.

I couldn't shake the weight of the recent events. The ship's barely-held-together state mirrored the frayed morale of the crew.

I glanced over to Pristy, her expression quietly determined. "How's the crew holding up?" I asked, needing her insight.

"They're struggling, Galvin," she replied, her tone measured. "We've lost so many, and those left are reeling. But they're also looking for something I can't give them."

"It's your responsibility to handle the crew on a personal level," I said, almost defensively. "You've always been good at that."

"I know that's my role," she said softly, not rising to the bait. "And I've tried, made a conscious effort to be there for them as much as time allows. But what they need, right now, is something only the captain can provide."

I hesitated, the guilt clawing at me. "And what's that?"

"Assurance," she said, her eyes meeting mine briefly before looking away.

"I did—"

"Yes, I understand, but right now... after all that's happened... speak to them like the valued and trusted crew that they are, not their commanding officer." Reassure them, that despite everything, we have a fighting chance. They need to hear it from you."

I sighed, rubbing the back of my neck. "I'm doing the best I can. Commanding a ship isn't exactly a walk in the park, especially now."

"I'm not saying you're not doing your best. But sometimes, your best needs to include connecting with them, showing them you're in this with them, not just above them."

Her words stung, more because of their truth than anything else. "You think I don't care?"

"I know you care," she replied gently. "But you've got a way of keeping people at arm's length. The crew sees it too. You avoid the emotional stuff, and they feel that."

I glanced away, my defenses rising instinctively. "It's just... not my strong suit, Gail."

She smiled slightly, a mix of understanding and sadness in her eyes. "It's not about being strong, Galvin. It's about being present. You're avoiding the emotional expenditure. The crew needs to feel your presence, your belief in them."

"And you think that'll fix everything?" I asked, my voice tinged with skepticism.

"No, but it's a start. They need their friend, not just their captain," she said quietly, her eyes searching mine. "Just like sometimes, I... " her words trailed off. "Never mind, I don't want to go there."

There it was—the subtle shift from the crew to us. A conversation we always danced around, never fully addressing. "It's not easy for me," I admitted, my voice barely above a whisper.

"I know," she said, her tone softening. "But maybe it's time to try. For the crew."

I stopped walking, forcing her to do the same. "Gail, I..."

She shook her head, a small, sad smile on her lips. "It's okay, Galvin. Just... think about it."

We continued in silence, Hardy's distant mechanical whirring the only sound. The tension remained, a barrier and a bridge, hinting at something more... just out of reach.

As we reached the massive auto-hatch, Pristy and I moved in front of Hardy, preparing for the final briefing.

"Hardy, ensure that the communications array is mounted with absolute precision and stability. Any deviation in its positioning could result in operational failure," I instructed, maintaining a controlled and firm tone.

"Got it, Cap," Hardy replied, "Mount the thing so it never comes off."

Pristy's eyes narrowed, her tension palpable. "Hardy, after that... adjusting it... it'll require finesse. A delicate touch." She eyed his catcher's mitt sized hands. "Every minute calibration counts getting it in alignment. If it's off by even a fraction, our signal's compromised."

Hardy turned, dipping his head slightly, his faceplate's 3D John Hardy visage looking back at her and making eye contact. "I got this, XO. Trust me."

My TAC-Band vibrated—it was Derrota.

"Go for Captain," I said. "What's up, Stephan?"

"I still don't like this, Galvin. I think we are asking for trouble sending Hardy out onto the hull at these speeds."

In a show of definitive agreement, Pristy made an exaggerated nod of her head.

Hardy did one of his awkward shrug things, made all the more ridiculous by the bulky pack, which shimmied up and down on his back.

"We have limited options, Stephan," I said. "Your concerns are duly noted."

"It will be difficult for the ChronoBot to maneuver outside the spacecraft at our advanced rate of speed."

Derrota's tone had an edge to it that caught me off guard. I held my tongue and let him continue.

"The primary challenge lies in the forward momentum of the spacecraft. Although Hardy is traveling at the same velocity as the ship, any attempt to move independently could result in a loss of stability or control."

"He'll be tethered with a cable—"

Derrota talked over me, "The microgravity environment adds to the difficulty, as Hardy will have no solid footing and must rely on his magnetic grips to stay upright. Additionally, keep in mind, that the high speed might alter Hardy's perception and coordination, making precise movements more challenging. Even the smallest misstep could result in him being flung from the hull, to be adrift in space."

"Again, he'll be tethered with a cable," I said, but the scientist had me second-guessing my decision to have Hardy attempt this space walk.

Derrota raised his voice, words now pouring out in that Mubai-accented voice of his, "At 99,419 miles per hour in deep space, G-forces are minimal. When a spacecraft maintains a constant velocity at that speed, it reaches a state of relative stability. As a result, Hardy shouldn't feel significant G-forces from the ship's motion."

Derrota rubbed at his chin, momentarily in thought, and then continued, "But! If there is a sudden unexpected hull breach—where the escaping atmosphere causes a rapid deceleration while Hardy is outside, then he'll experience massive G-forces. The magnitude hinges on the deceleration rate, but it's still a significant risk."

I looked at Hardy. This seemed far too dangerous a mission. I contemplated shutting this down—come up with an alternate plan.

"Nah... I've got this, Cap," Hardy reiterated, already opening the hatch to the airlock and stepping inside. "NELLA, close the hatch and initiate depressurization."

Pristy and I stepped forward, the ChronoBot visible through the diamond glass observation portal.

After activating his strapped-on magnetic boot plates, he pressed the panel to open the outside hatch. The vast void of space came into view beyond. He hesitated before stepping out, moving slowly, cautiously.

Back on the bridge, we found an audience had gathered from around the ship to watch Hardy's progress. Crewmembers Grimes, Paxton, Blunderton, Derrota, LaSalle, Ryder, Akari James, Max and his Marines—Grip, Ham, Hock, and Aubrey.

But seeing this assembled group was also a poignant reminder of who we'd lost: my bridgecrew... Chen, Jorkins, Davit, Lira, and Barrow. From Engineering and Propulsion, Porter and Rivers. Dr. Tangerie was also gone from HealthBay. Wanda, the stalwart backbone of Max's Marines—also gone. They were more than just crewmembers; they felt like family, even closer than my own. I hadn't fully faced the loss yet, but an emotional reckoning loomed—one I had to delay as long as possible.

"Will I be able to talk to Hardy?" I asked Blunderton, our now defacto comms officer.

She made a face. "The whole reason he's out there is to reestablish the ship's comms, Sir. NELLA has us interfaced via TAC-Bands. I've added you to the open TAC-Band channel. The connection will be spotty at best."

"So the answer is, yes."

"Yes, sorry, Captain. We should be able to converse back and forth."

USS Resilience

The last to show up on the bridge was Sonya. Both arms were still immobilized with slings around her neck and she still walked with a slight hitch in her step. The teenager maneuvered herself through the group, eventually making her way to my side. Her eyes widened as she spotted Hardy maneuvering cautiously along the ship's jagged—torn apart in some places—hull.

She leaned in closer to me, "I didn't want to miss this." Her brow furrowed. "No one told me this was happening now. How come I wasn't invited?"

Pristy and I exchanged a bewildered glance.

"I assure you, Sonya," I stated firmly. "Nobody had an invite. We're not exactly hosting a Sunday matinee."

The primary halo display was providing several visual feeds, a few from the outer-hull cameras that still managed to operate, and another feed direct from Hardy's faceplate cam.

Hardy continued making incrementally slow progress.

"Ugh, this is torture! Like watching paint dry!" Sonya groaned, rolling her eyes dramatically.

Several others nearby nodded—a few others chuckled.

I was too nervous to appreciate any humor in the situation. Hardy had managed to attach his metal tether while lengths of the excess coils drifted weightless in space behind him. Each step looked like he was trudging through thick mud—his magnetized soles clinging to the hull surface, making it a struggle to pull his feet away.

"Easy, big guy," I muttered under my breath as Hardy navigated around an object on the ship's surface.

Onlookers drew a collective breath as the wide-view feed revealed a massive, spinning chunk of debris—a decommissioned satellite, large asteroid fragment, or some other space rubble—hurtling straight toward Hardy; it was still far away, but its trajectory was undeniable.

"I don't think he even sees it!" Sonya barked, her eyes drilling into mine, demanding action.

My heart pounded, adrenaline surged. I opened my mouth to speak but no words came out.

Hardy casually pivoted the upper half of his frame just in time, narrowly avoiding the rocketing-past debris. But the near miss caused him to lose his grip on the part of the hull he was clinging to. And then he was off the ship, adrift... adrift, like the ship, at 99,419 miles per hour.

"This is exactly what I warned about." Derrota proclaimed, eyes surveying the gathered crew... his eyes—like Sonya's earlier—now locking onto mine with unmistakable condemnation.

"That tether is made of tungsten... has an extremely high tensile strength," I assured everyone. "He'll be okay," I added, not sure if that was remotely true or not.

"Hold on, Hardy!" Paxton cheered as if this was a televised sporting event.

But now as that tungsten tether was becoming as taut as a guitar string, Hardy was starting to slowly spin. Then he was spinning a little faster. Then a lot faster.

Ensign Blair Paxton was talking again, our resident Chatty Cathy. "Reminds me of one of those kid's toys... you know, they're on a stick, spin around from the wind—"

"You're talking about a pinwheel," Blunderton said dryly.

"That's it, a pinwheel!" Paxton said with an enthusiastic nod.

"How about we keep the commentary to a minimum," I said, while inwardly agreeing with Paxton's pinwheel analogy.

Hardy grappled wildly, one hand finally clutching the lifeline. He held on tightly, his bulk rigid with determination. Inch by inch, he began pulling himself along, methodically advancing hand-over-hand, reeling himself in. With each tug, I could almost hear the ChronoBot's servos whine under the immense effort.

Finally, he reached the ship's hull again, his magnetic boots clamping down with a solid clang.

I brought up my wrist and spoke into my TAC-Band. "You doing okay, big guy?"

Hardy's voice crackled over the comms. "Fine. I thought I'd take a quick trip around the block, get some fresh air before I got down to business."

Pristy shot me a worried look, biting her upper lip.

Hardy finally reached the intended mounting location, his movements deft despite the vacuum of space.

"He's at the right place.," Blunderton said. "All the comms hookup connections will be accessible to him there."

Hardy was now wrestling with his oversized pack attempting to extricate the unwieldy comms array. Giving it one last tug, the equipment fumbled free, nearly sending it spinning into oblivion. Hardy lunged, extending a metal hand in a desperate blur. In an instant, the ChronoBot's actuators engaged, and he caught the equipment, securing it within his iron grip. He quickly pulled the array back into his grasp like a mother clutching a child to her chest.

"See? Reflexes like a cat," Hardy quipped, though his normally steady voice wavered with uncertainty.

Aubrey Laramie took a step closer to the display. "What's going on with the robot's faceplate? It's all... cloudy looking."

Derrota scrubbed a tired hand across his face. "Hardy's velocity through space is exposing him to increased radiation from cosmic rays and interstellar particles, potentially causing damage. Any particles or dust out there could cause impact, though not as severe as at relativistic speeds. I expect him to experience significant abrasion over time."

"Let's hurry things up, Hardy," I said into my TAC-Band. "The longer you're out there..."

"Uh huh... yeah, I caught our science officer's riveting sandstorm dissertation," Hardy chided back. As he turned his head, his abraded faceplate flashed a smirking emoji.

We all watched, eyes riveted to the halo display as Hardy continued the task of mounting the array equipment and was now starting to make adjustments.

Blunderton's voice crackled over the comms. "Hardy, I can already tell you're being way too rough with your adjustments. Keep doing that and you'll snap the thing right off. That's delicate equipment!"

Exasperated, she threw up her hands, "Talk about a bull in a china shop."

No one said anything. Blunderton squinted, leaned in closer to the display. "That's better. Now rotate the array's mounting by 15 degrees counterclockwise, you should feel the individual lock points as you turn it."

Her guidance was met with more than a few muttered curses from Hardy as he adjusted against the overwhelming inertia and more occasional flying debris.

Finally, he was ready to connect the device's power and signal lines to the hull-mounted junction box at that location.

I pointed, "Uh... does anyone else see that?"

LaSalle, with his deep New Orleans drawl, said, "I see it. That bracket... where he's attached the tether's spring-loaded clip. It's jiggling loose."

"Damn it! Hold still, Hardy!" Pristy shouted into her TAC-Band. "Don't move an inch."

And... of course, Hardy ignored those simple instructions that any 5-year-old would have easily grasped. Instead, he turned that oversized head of his to take a look at the problem for himself. That simple movement caused the already precariously attached bracket to pull free from the hull allowing the tether, Hardy's only lifeline, to float away.

"Hardy... you're no longer tethered to the ship," I said. "You let go of what you're holding onto, and you're gone—like dead and gone."

"Ever considered a career as a motivational speaker, Cap? With pep talks like that—"

"Put a sock in it, smart ass. Hold on, literally and figuratively, while we come up with a means to resecure you to the hull."

Grasping the hull with one hand, Hardy proceeded to do the opposite of what I just told him to do by extending his free hand out as far as it would reach. Extending further, to the point his articulating joints looked like they would pop, he was attempting to snag the wayward tungsten steel cable by his fingertips. "Almost got it..."

Chaos broke loose as shouts and curses filled the bridge. I joined in, venting my frustration at the impulsive Chrono-Bot. His arms were still outstretched in a way that made him look like a mechanical Jesus Christ, crucified and immobile. He was a hair's breadth away from tumbling away into the void.

The tension remained palpable as the ChronoBot continued to reach for the wayward cable, the vastness of space yawning around him. A moment of panic set in as I watched the potential loss of one more crewmember—*God please no... don't take Hardy too...*

He continued to teeter there within that life-and-death moment in time, until, finally, he made one last desperate reach with his fingertips, making contact, and then coaxing the cable into a tight, mechanical fist.

I closed my eyes and shook my head, forcing myself to breathe.

A moment later, I was watching Hardy as he looped the tether around a protruding part of the ship.

"You know, sometimes just an old-school knot beats any

newfangled clip or fastener," Hardy murmured, the humor barely masking his nerves.

The comms array, now connected to power and signal cables, allowed the back-and-forth exchange between Hardy and Blunderton to resume. The array began spinning slowly.

Blunderton glanced back at me, and said, "It's still in need of fine-tuning."

The minutes ticked by, filled with terse exchanges and near misses. Hardy's breathless grunts echoed over the comms as he fumbled with the array.

Suddenly, Blunderton's voice rang out. "It's working! Don't move, Hardy. We've got a signal!"

Relief flooded over me. Hardy had done it, despite everything. But just as he prepared to return, he stopped. "Cap..."

"What is it, Hardy?"

"My sensors are working... or are starting to work."

"That's a good thing, right?"

Ignoring me, Hardy's voice took on a grim edge. "Uh, Cap... there are unidentified ships nearby. Not sure who they are, but they're trailing us. Something tells me they're not here to make friends."

My stomach dropped. This ship could not be any more vulnerable to a prospective enemy. And now, it seemed this new danger was closing in on us.

For now, I would focus on getting Hardy back inside, handling one crisis at a time.

Chapter 25

I stood with Pristy and Derrota in front of the airlock, the mounting tension evident on all our faces. As the airlock cycled open with a sharp hiss, Hardy emerged. My breath hitched at the sight of him. His once highly reflective chrome plating was dull and lifeless, and his dark blue glowing faceplate looked like someone had taken sandpaper to it.

"Uh... boy, you look like you've, um... really been through it, big guy," I remarked, unable to hide my shock.

Pristy turned to Derrota, concern evident in her voice, "Stephan, are we at risk for radiation poisoning... Hardy being this close?"

Derrota, always the cautious science officer, launched into an explanation, "Hardy is primarily metal with organic brain matter encased within his head. The extreme radiation encountered at such speeds would typically cause several issues. The metal parts would absorb heat and secondary radiation from high-energy cosmic rays or gamma rays, but they wouldn't become radioactive. However, the organic components could suffer molecular damage, potentially degrading or destroying those parts. There's also a risk that if the organic parts decay, they might become hazardous."

"So you're saying he could be dangerous?" Pristy pressed.

Derrota waved off her concern with a gentle hand. "Modern airlocks are equipped to automatically strip away harmful radiation during the reentry process. We should be fine with Hardy in close proximity."

I could feel my patience wearing thin. "Alright, that's enough science talk, Stephan. Hardy, I need to know more about the alien ship threat."

Before Hardy could respond, Pristy interjected, "Wait, how did you even manage to access your sensors again? You mentioned you couldn't access them before."

"One crisis at a time, XO" I said, trying to keep the focus. "Hardy, what type of ships are we dealing with?"

Hardy's voice was slightly static-ridden after the ordeal, "Cap, I have to be honest, my attention was not so much on those ships."

The image of Hardy nearly drifting untethered into space flashed uncomfortably into my mind.

Hardy wobbled his head from side to side. "All I can tell you is those vessels were most likely Varapin warships. Their assets have distinct propulsion characteristics."

I absorbed that information. Even with the recent armistice with the Varapin, the risk of rogue Varapin battle groups out there, harboring resentment, shouldn't be dismissed.

"Did you pick up anything specific about those ships?" I probed further.

The ChronoBot turned to face me, but I noticed he wasn't quite looking at me.

Pristy and I exchange a perplexed look.

"Three heavily armed and fully capable warships—what

more do we need to know?" he said, talking more to the bulkhead than to me.

"You can't see us," Pristy exclaimed, taking a step closer to the robot. Looking concerned, she waved a hand in front of Hardy's faceplate. "You're as blind as a bat, aren't you?"

Hardy started to protest before Derrota stepped forward.

"Galvin, I really need to run more tests on Hardy," Derrota insisted. "His biomatter could have been affected by the radiation exposure. Expediency may be crucial if medical intervention is necessary."

"Of course, yes, yes... take him to your lab and do whatever needs to be done."

Derrota stepped closer to the ChronoBot, placing a guiding hand on the robot's arm. "We'll take it nice and easy, Hardy," Derrota said, leading the towering robot down the passageway.

I watched them amble away, momentarily lost in thought.

Pristy interrupted my reverie with an exasperated breath. "We're going to need every bit of intel on those ships. We should all be ready in case the Varapin try anything."

Two hours later, both Hardy and Derrota emerged onto the bridge. I spun in my chair noticing Derrota looking less concerned, which was a small relief.

Doing a double-take, Hardy's faceplate had been returned to its shining, glimmering blue glow. His chrome plating gleamed like a mirror.

Derrota, looking pleased with himself, said, "Nothing a little high-power buffing couldn't fix."

I got to my feet and gave Hardy a head-to-toe appraisal.

Grimes said, "Did you get the Turbo Wax Shine-O-Matic treatment along with that carwash, Hardy?"

It was good to see Grimes was coming out of his funk—nice seeing him smile again.

"Okay, let's get to it. Are those Varapin ships still tailing us, Hardy? If so, can you tell if they have hostile intent or if they're just curious how anyone survived this hurtling wreck of a ship?"

"Uh, hostile intent? Cap, I mentioned my sensors have come back online, not that I've suddenly become psychic."

"Funny," I said, not cracking a smile. "How about you tell us if they have a weapons' lock on us? If their weapons systems are primed and ready to fire?"

"Not that I can detect."

"Even if there's an armistice in place, that doesn't mean all Varapin would honor it," Pristy interjected.

"Agreed," I replied. "We should assume the worst until proven otherwise."

Pristy stood, leaned her slender backside against the Tactical console, and crossed her arms over her chest. "Captain, we're completely exposed out here. We can't maneuver and have no means of defending ourselves. If they choose to attack, our only advantage is the speed we're still moving at."

"Grimes, where are we on getting the helm station up and running?" There was an edge to my voice I hadn't intended.

"Helm is pretty much ready to be interfaced, Sir. We're waiting on the Off-Worlders." He looked dubious. "But even then, navigation will be limited—we'll be adjusting how to maneuver this big hunk of metal on the fly," Grime's voice, like his expression, lacked much confidence.

The urgency of the situation gnawed at me. "Alright, everyone, it's time we earn our paychecks. We have to decelerate the ship enough to deploy the Off-Worlders and we have to do it now."

Critical alert. Power reserves at 15%. Estimated time until depletion: 1 hour, 45 minutes.

NELLA's sobering announcement silenced the bridgecrew.

"Let's not freak out, everyone," I said. "There are still proactive measures we can take which will extend that timeframe. It's time we close down all non-essential sections of the ship."

Pristy nodded. "Captain's right. We'll need to systematically move crewmembers to the critical areas that'll be kept operational."

Blunderton looked doubtful. "Wait, don't most decks have one critical system or another—systems that keep this ship operational? How do we prioritize system resources to maintain life support for those isolated areas? Seems it's a lot more complicated than just migrating a herd of cattle from one pasture to another."

A heated debate immediately broke out among the bridgecrew concerning which ship areas should be evacuated and shut off from limited ship resources.

"DeckPorts use up a crapload of power, we should close more of those down," Paxton said.

"No! We can't lose any more of our DeckPorts!" Blunderton argued. "They're essential for moving personnel and equipment quickly."

"But keeping them fully active will drain reserves before we even manage to slow the ship down!" Paxton countered, underlining her disapproval with an exaggerated eye roll and a huff... a reaction I would have expected more from my 17-year-old niece.

"Again, we can only maintain life support across essential areas," Pristy insisted. "One problem at a time."

I shook my head. This was quickly becoming a shout-fest.

I raised a hand, "Enough! NELLA will make the ship area

selections based on logic. Keeping as many crewmembers alive and for as long as possible."

Grimes chimed in, "Even with power conservation, we're not out of the woods. Every minute we delay getting those Off-Worlders in position, those Varapin ships are gaining ground." He looked at me. "Captain, is there any way we can do both simultaneously?"

The bridge fell silent, the gravity of our predicament hanging heavy. I scanned the bridge, taking in the worn faces of my crew. Failure to act decisively would result in even more deaths than we had already suffered.

"Alright, here's the plan," I began, my voice firm yet hopeful. "Hardy, get down to flight bay and assist with deploying the Off-Worlders. Captain Ryder is heading up that operation, so he'll tell you what he needs from you."

I glanced up. "NELLA, you work with Stephan Derrota to assign areas of the ship to be powered down and depressurized. Shoot for fifty percent. Ensign Paxton, once you have that specific information, you'll be in charge of migrating our herds of cattle—make sure nobody, and I mean nobody, gets locked into depressurized sections of the ship."

Wide-eyed, the Ensign quickly nodded—sobered by the life-and-death responsibility that had just been placed on her narrow shoulders.

"Keep monitoring the power reserves," I ordered, "and advise me on where further cuts can be made without compromising essential systems. XO, coordinate crew relocations to ensure minimal disruption."

I paused to let the gravity of my next words sink in. "Our only priority right now is survival. We need to work together, trust in each other's abilities, and execute this plan with precision. If we do this right, we might just live to fight another day."

I silently hoped my resolve resonated with the crew. The

stakes couldn't be higher, but one slip-up could spell our end. As I scanned my crew's faces, I saw a flicker of determination reigniting in their eyes.

So many lives lost. This ship, once full of hope and excitement, now was little more than wreckage, a stark reminder of the perils of a life lived in deep space.

The bridge hummed with the tense energy of a crew staring down the prospect of not surviving the day. While NELLA's updates rolled in steadily, I too felt the chill of looming failure inching ever closer.

Derrota's quiet scientific jargon murmurs faded into the background. We were headed toward a pivotal moment where every decision, every small maneuver... hell, every heartbeat would count.

Grimes' jaw tightened—the positioning of the Off-Worlders for optimal deployment wasn't just crucial, it was the difference between life and death for this crew.

"This isn't the end, people," I said, cutting through the murmurs, my resolve galvanizing. "We've faced the impossible before, and we'll do it again. Let's make it happen."

Pristy glanced my way. As our eyes met, an unspoken understanding passed between us.

NELLA's crystalline voice reiterated the urgency...

Captain, the time is now.

"Execute," I commanded.

Chapter 26

XO Gail Pristy

The bridge hummed with activity, but Executive Officer Gail Pristy's mind was lightyears away. Her fingers danced across the tactical console, muscle memory guiding her as her thoughts drifted. The latest alien threat, three Varapin warships, were in hot pursuit, while this crippled U.S. Space Navy omninought—what was left of this omninought—required constant monitoring and quick thinking if they were ever going to reach StarPoint Station. Yet here she was contemplating a life she'd never allowed herself to consider before.

Pristy's eyes flickered to Quintos, standing mere feet away, his brow furrowed in concentration as he reviewed data on the halo display. She felt a familiar tightness in her chest—longing peppered with frustration—that had become her constant companion over the years.

"XO, let's put together a game plan for bringing what's left of our weapons systems back online," Quintos called out, still focused on the task at hand.

Pristy brought up a myriad of diagnostic readouts—reviewed the status of mid-ship weaponry options. "Nothing is operational in that regard at present, Captain. Pulsars, rail cannons... we have them, but it's more of a signaling-access issue to the bridge."

"NELLA, move up the routing of ship weaponry to a higher priority," the XO ordered, her voice steady despite the turmoil within her. As she continued her tactical duties, her inner voice whispered, *is this really all there is for me?*

The thought caught her off guard. For nearly a decade, being Quintos' on-and-off-again XO had been everything. The thrill of exploration, the rush of combat, the camaraderie of the crew—it had been more than enough. But lately, something had shifted within her.

She glanced at the reflection looking back at her in the darkened control board. At 35, she was still in her prime, but the years of constant danger and stress had left their mark. Fine lines had begun to appear at the corners of her eyes, a testament to both laughter and worry. *What would it be like,* she wondered, *to wake up each morning without the weight of an entire ship on my shoulders?*

The image of a small house with a white picket fence flashed unbidden through her mind. A yard where children could play. A quiet evening spent with someone who loved her, not as an officer, but as a woman.

Pristy felt her throat constrict and blinked rapidly, forcing the moisture from her eyes. This was neither the time nor the place for such thoughts.

"Ensign Paxton, stay on NELLA and monitor her progress. Let us know the second it's possible for the weapons systems to come back online," she ordered, her voice authoritative despite her inner conflict.

"Aye, XO," Paxton responded crisply.

Quintos nodded his approval. "Ms. Blunderton, see if our new comms array is picking up any chatter between those Varapin ships."

"Yes, Sir."

Pristy's gaze drifted back to Quintos. After all these years, she still couldn't read him. Did he feel the same connection she did? Or was she just another capable officer to him?

They exchanged a glance. Perhaps attempting to read her expression, he looked puzzled as if silently asking, *what is it?*

Putting her attention back on her board, her mind inwardly spun in circles. *He's never come out and expressed his true feelings,* that traitorous inner voice reminded her. *Has he ever loved anyone? What about Doc Viv?*

The memory of Quintos' former flame stung, even now. Pristy had always wondered if there were embers of that relationship still burning in his heart.

Focus on the mission, she chided herself silently. But the floodgates had opened, and she couldn't stem the tide of *what-ifs* cascading through her mind.

Could I really walk away from all this? Pristy surveyed the bridge, taking in the damage, the blackened soot-coated bulkheads—what remained of the dedicated crew, the vastness of space visible upon the halo display. This ship and all those before, this life, it had been in her blood. The thought of giving it up now made her chest ache.

But then another image intruded—holding a newborn child, watching a daughter take her first steps, sharing quiet moments with a partner who truly understood her. The longing hit her like a physical blow, and she had to grip the edge of her console to steady herself.

How long have I been pushing these feelings aside? Months? Years?

The realization that she might have been denying a fundamental part of herself for so long was staggering.

"XO, you alright?" Quintos' voice cut through her reverie. She looked up to find him studying her, concern etched on his features.

Pristy straightened, plastering on a neutral expression. "Of course, Captain. Just... processing some data."

He held her gaze for a moment longer, and Pristy felt her heart rate quicken. There was something in his eyes, a flicker of... what? Understanding? Longing? But then it was gone, and he was turning back to his duties.

The moment passed, but it left Pristy reeling. She loved this man, had loved him for years. But was that enough? Could Galvin Quintos ever truly embrace a life beyond the stars? Did he even want to?

He doesn't have a biological clock ticking away, she thought bitterly. *He's not facing the same choices I am.*

The unfairness of it all threatened to overwhelm her. Pristy took a deep breath, centering herself. She was a professional, dammit. A U.S. Space Navy officer—she couldn't let these personal struggles interfere with her duties.

But as she turned back to her console, the weight of the decision before her pressed down like a physical force. No matter what path she chose, she would be giving up something precious. Her career, her found family among the stars, her daily proximity to the man she loved... or the chance at a different kind of life, with roots and a family of her own.

"Lieutenant Blunderton, what's the status of the communications array?" Pristy asked, seeking to distract herself even though the question had come out of the blue.

Blunderton glanced up from her station, brows slightly knitting. "Hardy's calibration seems to be holding. Nothing to report, XO."

"Good," Pristy replied, her voice unusually clipped.

Blunderton nodded, her attention momentarily pulled away by Lucy, who was perched on her shoulder—the bird now repeating overheard words, oblivious to their meaning: "Biscuits and gravy, biscuits and gravy, biscuits and gravy..."

Pristy glanced about the bridge, taking in the faces of her fellow crewmembers. Blair Paxton, fresh-faced and eager, so full of potential. Roisin Blunderton, the Nervous Nellie, whose OCD was always present, while her wit and spirit never wavered. Thom Grimes, the steadfast helmsman, silently mourning the loss of his best friend, John Chen, lost to the unforgiving expanse of deep space.

Could she leave this all behind? The thought was paralyzing, suffused with a deep-seated sadness. She imagined herself in a cozy home on Earth, a warm hearth, a loving family. It was the antithesis of her current reality, but also an idea she couldn't shake off.

A tear slipped down her cheek before she could stop it, and she quickly swiped it away. Angry with herself, she bit her lip. The crew didn't need to see her vulnerability. *What the hell is wrong with me?* She needed to be strong for them, as much as for herself. But inside, the battle raged—a battle between duty and desire, between the infinite expanse of space and the intimate embrace of home.

Critical alert. Power reserves at 10%.
Estimated time until depletion: 1 hour.

Pristy was jolted back to the present.

Quintos, voice raised, was barking off orders into his TAC-Band. She assumed he was talking to Ryder.

Blunderton caught her attention. "XO, we have inter-ship comms back online thanks to Hardy's efforts."

"Go ahead and patch their conversation up onto the halo display," Pristy said.

Captain Wallace Ryder along with another pilot were seated at the controls of one of the Off-Worlders. The familiar sounds of an active flight bay—the loud whine of drive engines coming up to speed and overhead PA announcements droning in the background.

"... as ready as we'll ever be, Galvin," Ryder said with his typical crooked smile. "You just need to slow this hunk of metal down a bit."

Quintos shot a glance to Helm. Grimes, working his board, looked up long enough to say, "Totally in NELLA's hands, so to speak. I'm getting green lights on all functioning docking thrusters. If the AI's off monitoring thrust output or overcompensates one nozzle over another..."

"We'll start spinning out of control," Pristy interjected. "With no means to stop it."

The display suddenly segmented in half showing Hardy standing within the bay's control room working the board. "Z9 is keeping NELLA company, Cap. Figured you'd want a backstop on the AI's decision-making at such a crucial time."

"Good thinking, Hardy."

Pristy tapped her board and brought up a third segmented feed. An overhead view of the entire flight bay flickered to life, displaying the four Off-Worlders slowly maneuvering into position at the wide-open entrance of the bay.

Hardy straightened. "Our Varapin friends seem to be picking up speed. If we're going to do this, best we get at it soon."

"XO, I think I'm picking up a long-range emergency dispatch from StarPoint Station," Blunderton reported, her voice trembling slightly.

"We can't deal with that now," Quintos said. His eyes met

Pristy's, his gaze hardening with resolve. "Looks like it's time to earn our paychecks."

Pristy nodded, her own determination solidifying as she studied her readouts. "Aye, Captain. We're ready upon your orders. Uh... be aware, Captain, I see that NELLA will be accessing our hydrazine propellant reserves—there's a limited supply. No one ever anticipated the need to—"

"Noted, XO," Quintos said, cutting her off mid-sentence. "Helm, initiate docking thruster protocols. "NELLA... Helm, slow us down. Do it now!"

The bridge erupted into a flurry of coordinated activity. Pristy barked orders, her mind focused on the immediate threat to the ship from both the Varapin and the near-impossible task of slowing a spacecraft with little more than docking thrusters. Somewhere deep inside, the image of children playing in that conjured-up front yard lingered, a small but persistent reminder of the choice she would need to make, sooner rather than later. There again, they were all probably going to die here in space within the next hour or so—problem solved.

Chapter 27

Captain Galvin Quintos

The red emergency lights bathed the bridge, a constant reminder of our plight. I paced as the hum of ship systems fused into a relentless murmur, every beep and buzz echoing the urgency of the moment. The lone halo display flickered, underscoring the precarious state we now found ourselves in.

Deep in thought, I heard Blunderton, stationed at Comms, mention repairs she'd made... something about halo displays. I caught the disappointment on her face, like a young girl who was picked last to join the soccer team. Apparently, nobody, including me, had responded to her announcement of success.

Pristy, ever the pillar of support, gave her a quick smile before bringing up five more displays, each showcasing a different feed from the hull. "Okay, now we're talking," Pristy said. The feeds illuminated the bridge, casting a stark light on the crew's tense faces.

"Velocity still at 99,419 miles per hour, Captain," Grimes

announced, his voice clipped. I could hear the soft patter of fingers on his board.

"We need to cut that speed in half... at a minimum," I barked back, tension fraying my patience with each passing second.

Halo feeds displayed bursts of white hydrazine propellant, some thrusting with intensity, while others emitted just a faint whisper.

NELLA, with her maintained, serene tone, gave us an update...

Hydrazine propellant reserves at fifty percent, However, velocity has not corresponded adequately with quickly diminishing reserves.

I steadied my breath, eyes fixed on the halo display where the four Off-Worlders stood ready in the flight bay, set to launch as soon as *Resilience* slowed sufficiently.

Hardy's voice crackled through the comms. "Two docking thrusters just crapped out, Cap."

I froze, why hadn't NELLA brought that up—it certainly was pertinent to our success. Was the AI falling back into old habits? I let out a breath, or was she a tad preoccupied right now with more pressing issues than giving me second-by-second updates?

Hardy chimed in again. "Huh... okay, looks like the AI is trying to compensate..."

I scanned the bridge. Every face, a mask of tense concentration, absorbed in their individual tasks. My gaze lingered on Pristy longer than I intended. Competent, and brilliant, she was my rock—yet a relentless dread gnawed at me. If I didn't act soon, I was going to lose her. *Why am I thinking about this now? Get a grip, Quintos.*

"According to NELLA, *Resilience* is beginning to slow," Pristy said, her voice a calming anchor in the storm of our crisis.

I saw the hydrazine output lessening significantly on the displays.

Grimes shook his head, his frustration evident. "We're holding at 60,894 mph. That's almost 12,000 over our failsafe limit. The Off-Worlders can't launch from the flight bay at this velocity."

My fists tightened, knuckles turning pale as helplessness weighed down on me. Hearing the grind of my molars, I forced my jaw open, then closed. With each passing moment, time was slipping away like sand through my fingers. What I needed were choices, options... fucking alternatives! But none were coming.

Amid the rising despair, I spotted Stephan Derrota maneuvering toward the captain's mount where I stood, his gaze purposeful. The bridge fell into a tense silence as he approached.

Irritated, I said, "Stephan... if your concern is our current velocity—"

Derrota dismissed my frustration with a wave of his hand. "That's already obvious." He glanced about the bridge, looking somewhat surprised to see all eyes were upon him.

"Hydrazine propellant reserves have been exhausted."

"Well aware of that, Stephan," I said, in no mood to be reminded of our colossal, all-too-recent failure.

But Derrota wasn't fazed. In fact, he looked surprisingly optimistic.

"What's on your mind? I can see those wheels turning."

His face contorted as if he stood on the edge of an icy pool, too scared to dive in.

"Before you say no, realize that our choices are nil," the science officer said.

"I got it. "What are you proposing," I asked, growing stress evident in my tone—at this point, I was ready to grasp at any glimmer of hope.

"This broken mid-section of a vessel still maintains all 100 standard decks and seven Circadian Platform decks. We are traveling at 60,890 miles per hour or 16.91 miles per second. As an intact vessel, we'd be speeding through space sideways, not bow-first."

I already knew as much but didn't interrupt.

A sparkle ignited within Derrota's eyes. "There are currently twelve side-facing... well, now forward-facing, atmosphere-pressurized decks with operational DeckGates. Eleven of those decks are inhabited and contain critical ship systems."

"Okay," I said, following his logic thus far. "So, that leaves one uninhabited deck that has no important ship systems."

Derrota raised a forefinger, "Deck 33. The one uninhabited deck that just so happens to be facing outward—and is in perfect perpendicular alignment with the direction we are currently traveling."

Pristy was up on her feet, her expression as serious as I'd ever seen. "You want to vent Deck 33!"

He nodded, looking triumphant. "Yes, I want to vent Deck 33."

Both Derrota and Pristy were smiling, looking at me for my reaction. But I didn't smile. I hated the idea.

"So... you're proposing we vent our most precious commodity, our breathable air... air that we will never get back. We open that DeckGate and what? Hope the rapid venting process slows us down instead of putting us into an uncontrollable spin. Am I missing anything?"

Looking crestfallen by my less-than-enthusiastic response, Derrota hesitated before speaking again. "Remember, NELLA will control that DeckGate entirely. Whether she opens it a smidge or completely, she'll adjust the venting based on our velocity."

"That still doesn't address the chance we might spin out of control." Ensign Paxton's voice echoed my own thoughts.

"That is a possibility, but not a probability," Derrota said. "In the end, this is about math and physics. NELLA has incredible mathematical capabilities—"

I shook my head. "That's all fine and good, Stephan. But once things start going sideways, literally, that highly capable AI will have no means to make corrections... we'll just keep on spinning like an out-of-control top until we someday careen into a distant planet or star."

"What's our alternative then?" Pristy asked. "Unless you can pull a better idea out of your hat..."

Critical alert. Power reserves at 5%. Estimated time until depletion: 30 minutes.

Straightening and placing hands on hips I glared at Derrota. "What's happening with the migrating of personnel to safe areas... closing down sections of the ship to save power?"

Paxton, Blunderton, and Derrota exchanged nervous looks.

Blunderton spoke up first. "It's taking longer than expected. I've been prompting NELLA to make evacuation announcements every few minutes. Um... there are still a few stragglers..."

I noticed Derrota had that *wheels-spinning-in-his-head* look in his eyes again.

"Talk to me, Stephan."

The science officer was pacing now, obviously still deep in thought. Then he suddenly stopped as if he had walked to the edge of a cliff. He slapped a hand onto his forehead, and said, "Of course! How could I have been so stupid?"

No one spoke. We waited.

He fixed his gaze on me. "I've been so single-mindedly caught up with providing *wireless* navigation control for the ship, forward and backward thrust..." The science officer looked about the space as if he was picturing something beyond the bulkheads. "The plan involved linking the four crafts to NELLA using cable-free signaling, right?"

"I think you'd know that better than anyone else here," I said. "What's your point?"

"Once we have our Off-Worlders mounted and their drives capable of running non-stop, why not route heavy cables from each craft back in through the ship's hull, straight into the ship's primary power conduits?"

"That'll work?" Pristy said, eyes narrowing with uncertainty. "Explain that again."

Derrota squirmed in his seat. "So, the Off-Wordlers were going to wirelessly connect to NELLA, to the ship's navigation —to helm command. But I hadn't considered that those four behemoth drive engines would have ample power reserves left over... enough to power this ship!"

Pristy's gaze shifted to the side, her thoughts churning. "The ship's central power arteries branch to virtually every section of the ship."

"NELLA, what's the easiest path to get this done?" I asked.

SWM can pull feeder cables at designated locations. Terminate them to hull-mounted CAM-Lok connectors.

So, not only could it work, it would be relatively easy.

"I'll get Chief LaSalle working on it," Pristy said.

I just stared at my friend, tempted to kiss Derrota's sweaty furrowed forehead.

"It'll be more work outside the hull," Derrota said. "But well worth it." He looked pleased with himself.

All eyes went to Hardy's feed.

Derrota continued, "We'll still need to shut down sections of the ship as the work progresses; that could buy us some more time... but, yes, with help from Hardy here conducting additional spacewalks—"

Hardy's Boston-accented voice bellowed from one of the halo display feeds. "Absolutely not. Once was enough. That earlier shitshow debacle almost had me somersaulting out into space, and you can only buff chrome plating so many times before there's nothing left to buff!"

I raised my eyes, searching for answers. With a slow exhale, I ran my palms down my face, steeling myself to make a decision. A choice that could save the remnants of our battered ship and, more crucially, the lives of the crew.

I slowly nodded. "Okay, Stephan, one thing at a time. Let's move forward with having NELLA activate and control the outward-facing DeckGate on Deck 33. We need to move on this fast—we're out of time."

I gestured to my science officer. "Take a seat at one of the operational consoles, and together with NELLA, get us prepped with what's to come next."

I turned to face Hardy's halo feed. A smile crept onto my lips seeing his indignant look.

"Hardy, team up with Chief LaSalle," I said. "Get the power cables you need from supplies. Be in that airlock, ready to move on my signal."

Chapter 28

"Hey there... whatca doing?" I asked from behind the desk of my ready room, my voice echoing slightly against the cold, metal bulkheads.

"I'm working."

I watched Sonya, cloistered within her dark Symbio Deck workspace. Multiple halos projected in front of her—reflected QuansCode characters danced across her face, illuminating her determined features. Despite her dual slings, she was manipulating the console like a champ. Her eyes darted across the information like a predator locking onto its prey, intensity coiling like a spring within her.

"How about you come to the bridge? Hang out here for a while."

"Pass."

"Naw... I think you should come to the bridge."

"Pass and double pass."

I pursed my lips. Damn, this kid could be obstinate. "I need your help with something," I lied. I wondered if she could feel it too... the danger lurking just beyond these bulkheads.

Her eyes flicked up, meeting mine for a fleeting second

before refocusing on her display. "I don't want to. And you're starting to bug me."

"As the ship's captain, I'm ordering you to come to the bridge."

That produced a flicker of amusement, a slight twitch of a smile that lit up her expression.

"Since this is no longer a ship, and I'm not one of your U.S. Space Navy lemmings. I will, for the third time... pass."

A FULL MINUTE TICKED BY IN SILENCE, THE oppressive quiet punctuated only by the low hum of the environmental filters struggling to breathe life into *USS Resilience*.

"Not creepy at all, you leering at me while I work," she shot back, the sarcasm heavy in her tone.

I exhaled, irritated but determined. "I swear, we're about to open Deck 33's DeckGate."

"Duh... everyone knows that. Hope it works."

"I want you close to me just in case..."

Her gaze met mine again, this time severing the space between us with gravity. "In case it doesn't work? You do know that no matter where I'm sitting, it won't make a difference. Dead is dead."

"It'll make me feel better knowing my niece is here, with me."

She rolled her eyes dramatically, mock-exasperation ringing hollow in the tense air of her workspace as she stomped out of view.

SONYA ARRIVED 90 SECONDS LATER, ABOUT 10 seconds after I did. The surprise on her face was tangible as she took in how overcrowded the bridge had become. Several others were entering the compartment behind her, their expressions mirroring the rising tension like a heavy mist.

She halted to the right of the captain's mount, a hip cocked, irritation etching her features—a mask over the worry that lay just beneath.

"I'm here. Where should I sit?"

Max and his Marines entered the compartment, lively and rowdy, taking up positions at the back, leaning against the rear bulkhead where they could observe the unfolding events—unlike most crewmembers who waited for permission to step onto the bridge. Years spent together had forged a bond with these select few. They knew I valued their input and presence, giving them a freedom not afforded to the rank and file—a privilege I took pride in fostering.

Derrota remained focused on his console, furrowing his brow in deep concentration, seemingly unaware of the vibrant energy buzzing around him.

"Sit here next to me at Tactical 2, Sonya. Take a load off that ankle," Pristy said, patting the empty seat with a warm smile. "You'll have a front-row seat."

"To what? Our destruction?"

"Have a little faith, kid," I shot back, battling the nagging feeling of dread coiling deep. "We're about to do something never attempted by another ship."

The words lingered in the air, heavy and charged. She spun in her seat, sharpness sparking between us. "Maybe there's a good reason for that, Uncle Person. You've come up with a batshit crazy idea!"

"It wasn't my idea," I said, glancing over at Derrota, whose eyes had caught the tail end of our exchange.

Realizing her mistake, she said, "Oh, sorry, Stephan." Her eyes softened with an apology laced in guilt. "Since it was your idea, I guess maybe it could work." She shrugged half-heartedly.

Grimes brought us back to the present. "Sir, we're as ready as we're going to be. Science Officer Derrota, NELLA, and what limited input I've been able to contribute... we just need to give the AI the go-ahead. There's nothing we can do here on the bridge other than watch."

Derrota stood, his rumpled lab coat looking as if he'd slept in it for the past week. Then he nodded, his expression belying the chaos around us. "Mr. Grimes is correct, Galvin. All that is needed now is for you to say go."

Every gaze in the compartment settled on me, a collection of fearful faces simmering with subdued hope. The weight of their expectations was palpable—there again, that came with the job.

Pristy looked as if she wanted to say something, unspoken thoughts that might be her last.

Sonya feigned a yawn along with the accompanying yawning sound and began squirming in her seat—an attempt to mask her anxiety—but the subtle chewing of her inner lip betrayed the unease beneath her bored facade.

I took a deep breath, collecting every ounce of fortitude I could muster. "NELLA... Go!"

Instantly, two of the halo displays changed feed perspectives. One provided an inside view of Deck 33's DeckGate, while the other, a hull-mounted camera provided a partial view of the hull and out to space beyond. The panorama offered a breathtaking view of the endless cosmos, a million twinkling stars our only reference. If they started moving sideways or up and down, it would indicate our course was veering, or we were beginning to spin; preferably it would be the former, not the latter.

"Look! The DeckGate is opening!" Ensign Blair Paxton exclaimed, her voice rising above the noise.

Deckplates began to tremble underfoot, adding the sensation of a mild, prolonged earthquake to this already harrowing experience.

Pained groaning sounds of a straining superstructure encircled us—the already battered ship being pulled and twisted in ways never intended.

"NELLA's continuing to open the DeckGate," Grimes said.

"Stephan," I called out over the rising din, "Please tell me you anticipated the strain this was going to put on the ship."

My heart raced, pounding like a bass drum, only amplifying the tension—for a moment, it felt as if the ship might be coming apart at the seams.

"We have to stop this—" I started, but the words died on my lips.

Pristy's voice cut sharply into the rising wave of noise. "Galvin! We're going to ride this out. Just shut up and enjoy the ride, okay?" Her scolding served as a crucial anchor.

The creaking hull deepened the tension. Emergency lights flickered, casting shadows that seemed to intensify the unease I could see in the crew's eyes, mirroring my own growing dread of what lay ahead.

I focused on the feed with Deck 33's DeckGate—it was now three-quarters the way open. The other feed, the hull view out to the distant stars—it had started to move. Was it a course change or the start of an unstoppable spin?

Shit!

Chapter 29

The DeckGate was closing. The thrum beneath my feet eased, and the ship's superstructure complaints hushed. But all the while, my eyes stayed locked upon that one halo display and the reference provided by the starfield in front of us. it was steadying, we were not on the precipice of spinning out of control.

I could almost feel the collective sigh of relief coming from the crew.

Grimes said, "We've slowed to a leisurely 48,500 miles per hour, Cap."

I glanced at Pristy; the relief was evident in her eyes.

"Mr. Grimes," I said, "how about you give Captain Ryder the go-ahead to deploy our Off-Worlders."

MOMENTS LATER, THE FEED FROM INSIDE THE flight bay showed brilliant white ion thrusters coming alive as, one by one, the Off-Worlders rocketed out into the void.

Pristy worked her board, bringing up the cockpit views from Ryder, Akari, and the two other Off-Worlders, with the pilots and their respective co-pilots out of view. Split screens revealed not just their perspectives but also their targeted landing sites on the hull.

I watched Derrota hurry over to Comms 2 and sit down next to Blunderton. "I need to guide their landings with pinpoint precision," he said, determination etched on his face.

Blunderton nodded, activating his station. "You're live on the open channel. Their designations are Alpha 1, Alpha 2, Alpha 3, and Alpha 4."

A sheen of perspiration glistened on Derrota's forehead. He pecked at his tablet bringing up a 3D model of *Resilience's* hull. His voice, steady despite the tension, filled the bridge. "Alpha 1, this is Science Officer Derrota. Prepare for approach vector coordinates."

Captain Ryder's voice crackled back...

Ready when you are, Bridge Command. Over.

I watched intently as Derrota began guiding Alpha 1 to its landing site. His voice, calm yet authoritative, filled the bridge.

"Alpha 1, NELLA wants you to adjust your approach vector to 042 mark 268. Reduce velocity to 45 meters per second," Derrota instructed. "Your target is grid reference X-173, Y-542 on the starboard hull. Prepare for final approach."

Copy that, Bridge Command. Adjusting now. Over.

I held my breath as the Off-Worlder maneuvered into position. Derrota's eyes darted between his tablet and the external camera feeds.

"Good. Now, pitch down 2.3 degrees and roll starboard 0.5

degrees to compensate for the hull curvature," Derrota continued. "Engage docking thrusters at 22% capacity in 3... 2... 1... *now*."

I noticed Sonya, still seated next to Pristy, was now leaning forward—literally sitting on the edge of her seat.

Alpha 1's thrusters flared, slowing its approach. I could see the hull's surface growing larger on the viewscreen.

"Extend landing struts and prepare for contact," Derrota said. "Adjust yaw by negative 0.7 degrees to align with the hull's slope lines."

The large Off-Worlder, five times the size of an Arrow Fighter, touched down with a gentle thud, its magnetic clamps engaging with a series of metallic clanks that reverberated through the hull.

"Confirm full contact on all struts," Derrota ordered. "Engage secondary locking mechanisms. Do not, I repeat, do *not* power down drive engine."

Alpha 1 secure. Over.

Ryder's relief was evident in his voice.

All systems are nominal, and clamps are holding steady. Over.

I allowed myself a moment of hopeful encouragement as the first landing succeeded. I leaned back in my seat as Derrota's voice droned into the background with mind-numbing approach vectors and pitch angles. Closing my eyes, I pinched my eyelids between forefinger and thumb. *When was the last time I slept?*

As if jolted by an electric current, I sat upright, alarms

erupting from Pristy's tactical station—multiple warning lights lighting up her board.

Ensign Blair Paxton, undoubtedly tracking the event from her station behind me, sounding breathless, said, "Alpha 3's coming in way too fast!"

I watched in horror as the rapidly approaching Off-Worlder seemed destined to slam into *Resilience's* hull. Derrota's voice rang out, urgent and commanding, "Alpha 3, reduce velocity immediately! Cut main engines and engage reverse thrusters at full power!"

For a heart-stopping moment, I thought we were about to witness a catastrophe. But at the last possible second, the Off-Worlder's nose pulled up sharply, skimming the hull's surface in a shower of sparks before finally coming to a shuddering halt.

Alpha 3 secure. Over.

Akari's voice carried an edge of barely contained excitement.

I shot out of my seat, "Dammit Lieutenant, hotdogging right now? We're still neck-deep in this shit!"

Copy that, Cap. Won't happen again. Uh... just curious, how's my alignment? Over.

Still fuming, I looked to Derrota.

He checked his 3D model, manipulated the view, and zoomed in. He made a face and looked back at me. "Alignment is perfect."

Back in my seat, Derrota proceeded to guide Alpha 2 to a safe, non-eventful landing.

We collectively turned our attention to the final Off-

Worlder coming out of its circular holding pattern, coming in for its final approach.

Ensign Paxton's voice split the tension. "Alpha 4's landing site may be problematic. NELLA's detecting unexpected gravitational fluctuations on that section of the hull."

Pristy nodded, "I see it." One of the halo feeds blinked, and now showed matrices of fluctuating numerical readings.

I looked to Derrota. "How is that happening, Stephan?"

He scratched at the back of his head. "It's the ship's artificial grav generators. They are out of alignment—I'm surprised there haven't been other occurrences."

Striding over to Comms, I heard Blunderton telling Alpha 4 to hold.

I peered over Derrota's shoulder, tension coiling inside me. We need that fourth ship secured, Stephan. What are our options?"

He tapped at his tablet evoking a series of 3D model simulations that played out in real time. I witnessed three crash-and-burn failures before a fourth success.

"Here's a potential site on an adjacent area of the hull," Derrota said. "But it's going to be tight. Propulsion positioning would still be optimal, but the approach angle is less than ideal."

"Do it," I ordered, knowing we had no other choice.

What followed was one of the most nerve-wracking few minutes of my life. Alpha 4's trajectory brought it perilously close to the jagged edges of *Resilience's* torn hull. When a sudden gust of vented atmosphere caught its wing, causing the massive craft to tilt dangerously, I thought for sure the approaching craft was done for.

The horrifying screech of metal on metal filled the comms as sparks flew, the wing beginning to bend under the force. I clenched my fists, willing the pilot to regain control.

"Alpha 4! Kill your thrusters, keep that angle steady!" Derrota commanded.

The Off-Worlder slammed down onto *Resilience* where it now precariously teetered at the very edge of the ship's torn-away hull—the craft's nose extending out into the void.

"Dammit, pilot! Engage your magnetic clamps!" I ordered, inserting myself into the mix.

For a moment that stretched into eternity, the Off-Worlder continued to teeter there on the edge of disaster. Then, the craft went perfectly still—its magnetic clamps had taken hold.

Alpha 4 secure. Over...

Came the pilot's shaky voice.

... and I think my co-pilot and I might need a change of underwear. Over.

A collective sigh of relief swept through the bridge. I felt my shoulders sag as the tension drained from my body. I clapped Derrota on the shoulder, "Outstanding work, Stephan. You just pulled off a miracle."

He managed a weak smile. "Let's hope it's enough to get us home, Galvin."

Heading back to the captain's mount, movement on a halo display caught my eye. Hardy, with spooled lengths of power conduit over his shoulder, moved methodically towards Alpha 1's landing position.

"He doesn't look like a happy camper," Sonya commented.

Chapter 30

Critical alert. Power reserves at 3%. Estimated time until depletion: 10 minutes.

The crew watched Hardy out on the hull, legs spread wide as he comically wrestled with the power line—the cable, like a slippery python with a mind of its own—appeared to be doing everything but what Hardy wanted it to.

Sonya, hands clapped over her mouth, eyes brimming with tears, was shaking with laughter... the kind of laughter that makes your stomach muscles ache. I felt a flicker of warmth; there she was, being just a kid again.

Watching Hardy's antics through the silent feed was like watching an old Charlie Chaplin film, where every exaggerated movement conveyed humor and frustration without a single sound.

Hardy's oversized head shook as if he couldn't wrap his circuits around what should have been a simple plugin of one thing into another. It couldn't have been more clear how annoyed he was as the ChronoBot struggled to align the stubborn connector.

Pausing dramatically, Hardy held the connector up in front of his faceplate and gave it a good, mocking shake before diving back into the frustrating task. It was classic Hardy, part showing off, part genuine exasperation; the crew, including me, couldn't help but to join in with Sonya, laughing out loud at the spectacle.

With one more valiant effort, Hardy succeeded in mating the two obstinate connectors. The ChronoBot, never missing a chance for theatrics, raised his arms in victory—a referee calling a game-winning touchdown. Three more to go.

DERROTA AND HIS TEAM HAD PULLED IT OFF, shutting down nonessential power sources, and boosting the power reserves to 10%. This gave Hardy the extra time—close to an hour—to attach the other three powerlines. Seconds before finishing the final connection, power reserves were at 1%.

But now, with all four Off-Worlders feeding power back into the ship, NELLA made a welcome announcement:

Power reserves increasing.
Currently at nine percent and rising.

The bridgecrew erupted in cheers, joined by the visitors standing along the periphery. Everyone was on their feet. Exuberant hugs were exchanged. Now, jogging around the bridge compartment, I proceeded to high-five each crewmember, Max's Marines, as well as all the others who had come to watch—we exchanged brief moments of connection—this was a well-deserved win, and I wasn't about to let it go unappreciated.

Pristy and Sonya were coming out of a tight embrace—both looked happy, having to yell over all the raucous raised voices.

Smiling, Pristy gestured to the closest halo display. "Let's not forget... we still need to round up our eight pilots stranded in their immobilized Off-Worlders."

She leaned over her console and brought up a small logistical display with a roster of available assets within *Resilience's* flight bay. "Looks like we have several shuttlecraft available..."

I shook my head and used my forefinger to go down the list. "None of these have an aft airlock," I said, my finger coming to a stop down near the bottom of the list. "This one might."

Shoulder-to-shoulder, Pristy's face was just inches from mine.

I smiled. "A Cybrex!"

"What's a Cybrex?" the XO asked, tapping at the display and bringing up a 3D model of the boxy, ancient-looking craft. She scrunched up her nose. "Will that old rust bucket even get off the deck?"

"They stopped making those some twenty years ago. Called a Cybrex-Limited," I said. "Pretty sure it has the proper kind of airlock for docking with an Off-Worlder."

Our faces remained close, neither of us willing to break the moment.

Pristy pursed her lips, looking thoughtful. "I suppose all we need to do now is find a pilot familiar enough to fly it."

I let out a weary breath. I was physically spent and mentally drained. "I'll pilot the old shuttle. I owe those pilots a gesture of gratitude for a job impeccably executed." I forced myself to straighten. "What's the situation with our Varapin friends?"

"The three warships are still there but have fallen farther back... no imminent threat," Pristy said, straightening up herself, mirroring me.

"Alright, I'm out of here," I said, turning to leave.

"Can I come too?" Sonya asked. "Be your co-pilot?"

I was about to say, *sure, why not*, when Pristy interjected, "No, not this time Sonya. The Captain and I have something important—hell, imperative, to talk about in private."

Sonya's eyes darted between us, her narrowed gaze and dubious expression suspecting there was more going on beneath the surface. I myself wasn't sure what was happening here.

Pristy looked over to Grimes, who was chatting up Paxton near the helm station. "Mr. Grimes!"

Resembling a fox caught sneaking into a henhouse, he replied, "Yes, Ma'am, um... XO."

"You have the captain's mount. The Captain and I have some pilots to retrieve. How about putting more of your attention on your duties than socializing."

"Of course, Ma'am." Grimes turned on his heel and strode briskly toward the vacant captain's mount.

Pristy led the way, chin high, walking fast. Not a word passed between us as I hurried to keep pace with her. She seemed to be a woman on a mission. Was she angry? The sudden chill in the air told me to shut up and see what this was all about. But I couldn't help feeling like a child trudging toward the shed, bracing for the sting of the switch.

We traversed multiple corridors, hurried from one passageway to another, and entered and exited three separate DeckPorts, all before arriving at flight bay.

The massive bay was relatively quiet, with only a few maintenance bots scurrying around, attending to what remained of the viable Arrows. I saw movement, someone walking by the overlooking window, high up within the Island. I knew two of Ryder's pilots were manning the controls up there—probably bored out of their minds having little to do right now. I had yet to inform them of our imminent departure onboard the Cybrex shuttle.

We finally came upon it. The old Cybrex shuttlecraft looked even more rusted and broken down than I had expected. Pristy shot me a glance, half daring me to say something about the sad state of our travel accommodations. I caught the silent dare and raised her a shrug.

We entered the shuttle through the aft airlock, fumbling in the darkness as we moved forward. With the aft hatch closed behind us, we were enveloped in near-total darkness. Pristy's subtle movements revealed her silhouette as we moved toward the small cockpit area. The secured blast doors obstructed the forward window, hiding the view of the outside.

I managed to seat myself in the pilot's chair, still straining to see beyond the vague outlines of the cockpit. I waited for the sound or feel of Pristy settling into the passenger seat beside me. Seconds ticked by. I wondered what was taking her so long but stayed silent. The air grew thick, charged with something indefinable, something that sent a ripple of nerves through me.

Twenty seconds later, Pristy was on me, naked, and facing me, straddling my thighs. The warmth of her skin shocked my senses, and my hands rose instinctively to catch her by the hips. Her breaths came fast and shallow, and I could feel every rise and fall against my chest.

"Gail, what—"

She silenced me with a hard press of her lips, as her fingers tangled in my hair, pulling me into the storm of pent-up frustration and desire that had been simmering between us for so long. The taste of her was intoxicating, a heady mix of need and desperation. My instincts kicked in, and I responded with equal fervor, hands roaming the smooth expanse of her back, tracing the lines of her spine. Her body had the lean, athletic build of a gymnast, every muscle defined and undeniably feminine.

We'd danced around this tension for months—no, more like years. This woman who had fought by my side, who I trusted implicitly with my life now turned the focus inward, our fight no longer against any external threat but something far more primal and unforgiving.

A frenzy took over as we grappled with buttons, snaps, and zippers, desperate to free me from my uniform. Sitting down with her on my lap, it felt almost impossible. Sparks erupted around us as we laughed at our clumsiness, a whirlwind of chaos.

My mind raced as I tried to reconcile the unfamiliar dynamics of this moment, the professional barriers crashing down unforgivingly as those urges long suppressed rose to the surface. Pristy's nails bit into my shoulders, anchoring herself as if she feared I'd pull away, but there was no chance of that. Not now. This connection gripped like a vise, unyielding and inescapable.

Her body answered our closeness with an instinctive murmur. The heat where our skin met ignited, chasing away coherent thoughts and flooding my mind with raw, primal sensations in sync with each breath she took.

The scant light filtering in through the blast doors was enough to reflect in her eyes, those fiery, determined eyes that had witnessed our trials and escapes. Now, they locked onto mine, fierce and vulnerable in equal measure. Words seemed unnecessary, almost intrusive in the silent eclipse of understanding between us.

She seized a fistful of hair at the back of my head and pulled me in, her lips pressing urgently against mine, our rapid breaths mingling into one. With renewed vigor, my tongue tangled with hers, the desire a life force of its own, pushing and guiding us forward without question. Her hips moved, finding a rhythm that spoke of more than just lust—there was ownership here, a mutual claim staked deep into our psyches that transcended everything we had been through.

The cockpit around us, the worn and dilapidated metal hull, might as well have been the plush confines of my captain's quarters—none of it mattered. All that mattered here, now, was her—us—finally giving in to a pull that had been drawing us together since that fateful first mission years earlier onboard *USS Hamilton*.

IN THE SILENCE THAT FOLLOWED, AS OUR BREATHS slowed and melded into one harmonious cadence, our arms still enveloping each other, there was an unspoken truth. Years of defending Earth, facing constant peril and tough decisions, had led us to this moment. Here, we had found this brief sanctuary. When was the last time I'd felt this way? Had been... happy?

She shifted her weight, Pristy's breath tickled my ear, her lips brushing my skin. Her whisper cut through the silence like a razor. "Galvin, if we get out of this mess... if we survive this, I'm leaving the U.S. Space Navy." Her voice carried the weight of unshakable resolve.

Before I could let my world collapse and my hopes vanish, she said, "Come with me, Galvin... let's start over, away from all this. I don't care where, as long as we leave this life behind us. No more warships going into battle, no more wondering if today will be our last."

Could I? Would I?

Hell, I'd given everything to the U.S. Space Navy. I'd poured all of myself into each deployment, each harrowing battle. The weight of command never letting up—only growing heavier with each impossible mission, and I'd shouldered that weight because Earth's very survival required it. But there was only so much one man could give. There had to be a moment, a time when someone like me could simply live, to just be, and to love someone.

I could feel her apprehension, her body going tense as she waited for my response. It was as if every muscle in her small frame had tightened, bracing for whatever words I might say next. Her eyes, mere inches from mine, held steady. The unspoken question hung in the space between us like an unseen third party.

As the moments lingered, the silence became unbearably loud. I felt her head come to rest on my chest. I drew her closer, the darkness wrapping around us like a shroud, a barrier to the awaiting world beyond.

"Yes," I whispered, the word carrying both submission and a silent promise.

I felt the wetness of her tears on my chest. All tension released from her body, a lifetime's worth of struggle suddenly freed. She breathed in as if inhaling fresh air for the first time in her life.

New emotions swirled around me, igniting a dizzying sense of hope. This wasn't just a fleeting moment of passion; something deeper had been forged. I felt a profound connection, one that made me realize I wasn't facing insurmountable obstacles alone anymore. She had always been there, my person, waiting to be found.

I was ready to leave this life with Gail Pristy—but that would not be today, but someday, hopefully soon.

Untangling ourselves from the aftermath, my thoughts snapped back to the harsh reality awaiting us. The struggle for survival, the fate of the ship, and our crew's lives... remained critical.

I heard Pristy slipping back into her uniform, her movements functional and routine. I followed suit, the weight of this broken ship's predicament, our mission, all returning now, as real as the fabric of our clothes.

I searched in the dark, my hand, fingers, feeling the knobs and switches like a blind person reading braille words on the page. Finding what I was looking for, I pressed the oversized button. Immediately, the forward blast doors began sliding open —harsh light streamed in from the flight bay beyond making me wince from the glare. The inside of the shuttle coming into view for the first time.

Pristy's hand shot down, slapping the button and halting the blast doors with a grinding shriek. Before I could process it, she was in my arms, kissing me fiercely. I felt the smile on her lips before she pulled away just as swiftly, leaving me breathless and maybe a little bewildered.

Before taking her seat next to me, she slapped the button once more, allowing the blast doors to open all the way. With a smile she said, "How about you get this tin can off the deck—there are a few pilots who need rescuing."

Chapter 31

The recovery process took a little over two hours and went off without a hitch. All eight pilots were happy to be freed from their Off-Worlders—Off-Worlders that would be forever moored to the hull of *Resilience*. Wallace Ryder and Akari James joined Pristy and me, occupying the now-crowded cockpit area—both excited and talking non-stop. I'd expected it to be a challenge, maneuvering and landing their respective crafts upon the hull of such a fast-moving spacecraft, but, in the end, it was far dicier than that.

Ryder leaned against the bulkhead, practically buzzing with excitement while the other pilots had taken seats in the cabin behind us. "You wouldn't believe it, Galvin! I was coming in hot on that third approach vector when I realized I had a gravitational anomaly pulling me off-course. Had to adjust my thrusters on the fly, you know? Really put the Off-Worlder's inertial dampers through their paces!"

Akari chimed in, not to be outdone. "That's nothing, J-Dog. I had to compensate for a failing lateral stabilizer while coming in at a 15-degree pitch adjustment. Almost lost my starboard wingtip! Managed to goose forward thrusters bringing her in nice and smooth."

Ryder chuckled, shaking his head. "There you go again, Ballbuster, always trying to one-up me. But yeah, that landing—getting that Off-Worlder down on the hull like you did? That was something else. I thought we'd be scraping what was left of you off the hull with a spatula."

Akari patted him on the back, her eyes gleaming with adrenaline. "We still make one hell of a team, J-Dog, don't we?"

Pristy and I exchanged an extended, knowing glance. We let them bask in their shared success. Their skills and determination had kept us all from spiraling into oblivion.

Akari, suddenly having gone quiet, leaned in, looked at me and then at Pristy. "Uh... what am I missing here?" she said, her tone as serious as I'd ever heard.

Both Pristy and I went wide-eyed, feigning bewilderment.

Pristy shrugged. Looking irritated, she said, "What are you talking about? You're not missing anything. Everything is... normal. Everything is fine."

Now Ryder was looking at us. He snickered, "The lady doth protest too much. Methinks..."

I kept my gaze steady, face impassive, as a short laugh burst from Pristy.

This only proved a point I'd been aware of my whole military career. It's nearly impossible to keep secrets within the ranks. Things always get out.

My TAC-Band chirped and vibrated. I saw it was Hardy.

"Go for Captain," I said.

"Mind coming back? I could use a ride."

Pristy leaned forward, scanning *Resilience's* hull beneath us. She pointed.

"There he is. What the hell is he still doing out here? Thought he would have made it back already." Then she saw how slow he was moving—this operation had clearly taxed his systems to their limits. "Let's circle back and pick him up."

For once, Hardy had interrupted at just the right moment.

Back in the relative safety of the flight bay, I avoided returning to the bridge. Grimes was already at Helm, familiarizing himself with NELLA's interface controls for our four Off-Worlder powerplants. *USS Resilience* was officially back to being maneuverable. Nothing to write home to Ma about; it was a kluge, clunky, and unresponsive at best, but a hell of a lot better than what we had previously. And with the Off-Worlder's capacity to power on their retro-burners, we could slow—and even stop—when needed.

But for me... I desperately needed sleep. That, or I'd be dozing off seated within the soft cushions of the captain's mount.

MAKING IT TO MY QUARTERS, I LITERALLY FELL FACE down onto my bed, too exhausted to strip out of my uniform or even slip off my boots. And as sleep's embrace drew near, pulling me under, unaware she'd followed me inside—I felt her hands on me—her arms wrapping around me.

Her breath brushed against my ear. "Not yet, Captain... we can sleep when we're dead."

Chapter 32

I awoke in a mental fog, momentarily not knowing where I was. Sitting up with a jolt, I looked around my quarters. The events of the past few days came thundering back into my consciousness like an out-of-control freight train—the explosion that tore apart my ship, the countless deaths, the Varapin warships shadowing us, the landing of the Off-Worlders... Gail Pristy. The pillow beside me showed the indentation where her head had rested. The bathroom light was on, steam from the shower hanging in the air—she must have just left.

I checked the time on my TAC-Band—I'd slept nine hours. When was the last time I'd slept more than six? I listened, could hear the throaty drone of the four Off-Worlders—*USS Resilience's* new powerplant.

I got out of bed and headed for the shower. Today we would begin our long trek home to Earth.

I remembered my promise to Pristy—"Come with me, Galvin... Let's start over, away from all this. I don't care where, as long as we leave this life behind us. No more warships going into battle, no more wondering if today will be our last."

"Yes," I had told her.

Getting the shower started, cranking it as hot as it went, I stepped into the scalding water. I smiled, thinking about Pristy and our lovemaking—how it felt to hold her in my arms—Yes, I was ready to start a new life with her. Somewhere that did not involve warships and aliens hellbent on killing us.

I arrived on the bridge in a fresh uniform, a spring in my step, and an air of renewed determination. Heads turned in my direction, curious expressions playing across the faces of my crewmembers as they paused their duties to acknowledge my presence.

Pristy, her hair still slightly wet, was at Tactical, looking enthralled with her duties.

"Okay, people... SitReps from everyone."

Let's start with you, Mr. Grimes," I said, easing into my seat at the captain's mount. "Talk to me about *Resilience's* navigation capabilities."

Before he could answer, Lieutenant Blunderton's parrot, Lucy—previously Craig Porter's parrot—squawked, and said, "Aren't you just the cutest fluffball? The cutest fluffball. The cutest fluffball?"

Color rose in the woman's cheeks, "Sorry, Captain. I'll try to keep her quiet."

"No worries, Ms. Blunderton. I think we can all use a little levity with what we've gone through these last few days."

My mind flashed to Craig Porter and our adventure within the Amazon Jungles... in pursuit of finding a new, replacement parrot. I hadn't had time to grieve the loss of my dear friend—so many friends. I wondered where his parrot was right now. It had been spotted flying the ship's corridors and passageways—

perhaps in search of his keeper. What had Craig called his new bird? Oh yeah... Leal; the name was Brazilian for 'loyal'.

I swallowed hard, compartmentalizing the pain back into the deep recesses of my mind.

The helmsman was talking, bringing me back to the here and now. I held up a hand to stop him. "Apologies... please start again, Mr. Grimes."

"Oh... yes, Sir. What I was saying is navigation control is imprecise, and slow to respond. Speeding up and slowing down has taken some getting used to. NELLA is making adjustments to the interface to correct some of that." He raised his brows. "But honestly, Cap... it's not too bad. It's working."

"Good to hear. And our current course?" I asked.

"Well... you hadn't actually given us a course to take. I put us on a course back to Earth until I heard otherwise."

"Excellent. I was hoping that was the case."

I got to my feet and looked about the bridge. "There is no way we would make it back to Earth within the year, even at the Off-Worlder's maximum output velocities. With that said, we're moving in the right direction to intercept with another U.S. Space Navy vessel. Hopefully, that will happen sooner rather than later."

"Captain!" Blunderton interrupted. "Sorry, Sir, but we have an incoming communique from Admiral Gomez. Seems comms are fully back online." She looked up at me, her expression that of amazement at being able to say those words.

"Put it through to my ready room."

GETTING SITUATED BEHIND MY DESK, I composed myself; there was so much to convey to the Admiral—my own very detailed SitRep.

"NELLA, go ahead and connect me with the Admiral."

The projected halo display blinked and fragmented several times before steadying. Admiral Xavier Gomez, looking tired and frazzled, suddenly brightened upon seeing me.

"Galvin! You're a sight for this old officer's sore eyes." His smile was genuine, his emotions unhindered. "You're supposed to be dead, your ship eviscerated light years from Earth."

"Well, you know what they say... the reports of my death have been greatly exaggerated."

"Evidently so," the Admiral said. "The EUNF received your post-explosion distress call, but I figured it was an auto-dispatch from NELLA... a final dying gasp from an omninought's AI already in the last death throes."

I nodded. "So, you found what was left—"

"Other warships were in the area, including *USS Hamilton*, Captain. Sensors picked up on the explosion."

Gomez paused as if choosing his next words carefully. "The debris field... well, not much was still in one piece—the ship's bow, and fragmented pieces of *Roosevelt's* aft section. And there were bodies—hundreds of bodies... it was clear the loss of life was staggering."

"And you'd concluded this was a recovery operation versus any kind of rescue."

"That's right. I'm still wrapping my head around how you and what's left of your crew pulled through all of that."

Me too.

"Look, Galvin... we found evidence of a bomb—that explosion was an intentional act of terrorism."

"We're aware, Sir. We've been able to do a little sleuthing in that regard as well. It's pointing to Inheritors of Tenebrosity, and none other than Chaplain Halman Trent."

"Now let's not jump to any conclusions, Galvin. A thorough investigation is underway. We need far more data, actual hard evidence before we start pointing fingers."

Once again Gomez was coming to the defense of Trent. What the hell was I missing—why the undying loyalty to such an obvious traitor? But that was a discussion for another day—there were far more pressing issues at play here, like being rescued by a U.S. Space Navy asset.

"Talk to me about *USS Roosevelt's* condition... capabilities."

I looked back at the Admiral, not sure how to answer him. Capabilities? Who cares what her capabilities are? This is a broken husk of a vessel barely hanging on for its life.

"We've rechristened the ship *Resilience*. There is very little left of what was *USS Roosevelt,* Sir."

"Alright. Go on..."

FIFTEEN MINUTES TICKED BY AS I UPDATED THE Admiral on the critical events following the explosion. The loss of thousands of crewmembers, the near cataclysmic damage to the ship, and finally, our makeshift efforts to cobble together a means to take back navigational control.

He nodded without a word, his expression unable to conceal astonishment at our resourcefulness.

"And that pretty much brings us to the present, Admiral. We're on a straight vector towards Earth—all we need now are the intercept coordinates to be picked up."

Taking in a deep breath, he proceeded to pull at his stubbled chin. I knew that expression, the one that says, *hold onto your hat, I've got some bad news for you, bub.*

"Admiral?"

"Thank you for your summary of the ongoing events and the current status of your vessel and her crew. But now it's time I bring you up to speed on what is happening outside the hull of your ship. It's good you're sitting down, Captain. Undoubtedly, some of this will be hard to hear."

"Two days ago, the first of the Krygian warships arrived within Morno, Weonan, and Earth's space. Three separate fleets, each with no fewer than seventy-five assets."

I gasped, unable to speak.

"We have not been attacked... not yet. Our own assets, the 2nd, 3rd, and 9th Fleets are here—we outnumber the enemy two to one. But the latest intel has additional Krygian warships en route to Earth."

I shook my head. "How is that possible? To have amassed such a fighting force without the EUNF knowing... anticipating—"

Gomez's temper flared, "How the fuck should I know. They breed in the billions, hell, maybe the trillions! We were busy looking at one small quadrant of space when we should have been seeing the signs of aggression throughout the galaxy."

Clearly, no one would be coming to rescue us. This ship, this crew, would be far down on anyone's priority list. All I could do was nod and listen. Take in the sobering, potential Armageddon-like situation unfolding as we spoke. The three factions of the alliance were looking at total annihilation—check and checkmate.

The word that came to mind was 'hopeless'. Earth's invasion was imminent. A sense of foreboding filled the ready room like a foul smell. And while my mind spiraled, the Admiral continued to speak—now going on and on about something that seemed preposterously inconsequential.

"I'm sorry, Admiral. Can you repeat that?"

His eyes locked onto mine. "Get it together, Captain. Considering humanity's predicament, very survival is on the line, you'd think paying attention would be a fucking priority!"

"Yes, Sir. Sorry, Sir."

Gomez attempted a smile, but it presented itself more as a

grimace. "We do have a spark of hope... well, maybe *spark* is too optimistic. Let's say a *faint glimmer* of hope."

"Okay..."

"It seems your Thine friend, I believe his name is, um, Gragen, CooMong?"

"Coogong, Sir."

"That's it. The Thine scientist has made excellent progress deciphering the Krygian language. That and our EUNF eggheads have managed to crack Krygian comms encryption."

"So you'll be able to anticipate when an attack—"

"Shut up and listen to me, Captain. The Krygian are consolidating. I know that's not the right word for it. They're an insectile species... they work within a hive society like goddamn bumble bees."

I opened my mouth to speak but thought better of it. *Honeybees work in a hive... bumble bees live in a nest.* Gomez was on a roll, and I wasn't about to interrupt with a lesson in Melittology.

"Across the galaxy, hundreds, maybe thousands of hive societies have been independently propagating, breeding like there's no tomorrow."

More like *exactly* like there's no tomorrow, I thought.

"Captain... Galvin... one highly aggressive queen has proclaimed dominance over all the others—something, according to Coogong, that hasn't happened in millennia. One queen's ambition has fueled the rising aggression across the cosmos—determined to dominate the galaxy through systematic planetary infestations."

"And you're thinking if we can find her, and if the Alliance can free up the resources, we can go after—"

"Oh, we know exactly where she is. She's called Slith. And she's from the Orpheus Rift. Until recently, she was living, and pretty much breeding non-stop, within a Krygian Hive Ship called *Vingron-Palsh*."

"You said *until recently?*"

"Recently, she and her insect minions have settled within StarPoint Station. It appears this will be her new hive, her throne to rule Krygians across the galaxy. A battle group of no less than three large dreadnought-class warships are there, ensuring no one gets anywhere close to that station."

I leaned back in my chair, letting that weight sink in. There were tens of thousands, mostly humans, living and working on that ginormous station.

"And the station's occupants? Do we have any word on their—"

"Yes, Captain. StarPoint's security personnel were in constant contact with Earth until yesterday. More of a commerce hub, the station had little in the way of defenses and fell almost immediately to the enemy invasion. And while there were casualties, the occupants, now hostages, have been imprisoned."

"So, there are survivors? Somewhat of a silver lining, I guess."

"No, Captain, it isn't. From what we can figure out, they're only being kept alive for one reason—to feed the thousands of Krygian warriors. No, that station conveniently has a built-in food supply, ready-made for the enemy."

Oh shit...

I thought of all those helpless station dwellers... I flashed back to what Hardy had said about having a cousin on Star-Point... well, a distant cousin many times removed. The important thing was... something needed to be done to save them.

Locking eyes with my superior officer, my face a mask of impassive professionalism, I braced for what I knew was coming next.

"Galvin... you're it. You're the Alliance's, humanity's, last hope. I want you to turn what's left of that ship around and... somehow... get onboard that station and take out that motherfucking queen."

Chapter 33

Stepping out of my ready room, I reentered the bridge. Gone were the red emergency lights—since power had been sufficiently restored, the overhead standard lamps now illuminated the compartment. The crew's mood echoed the brighter atmosphere. Conversations flowed freely between stations—they had achieved the impossible, turning this torn-apart clump of metal into an operational spacecraft once more.

Pristy locked eyes with me as I walked in, breaking from her conversation with Grimes. Her happiness was evident—she was on the brink of a new chapter in her life, one that would see her leave the U.S. Space Navy, and with me at her side.

But my expression told her everything, and in a moment her face fell and the light in her eyes dimmed.

I straightened my shoulders, raised my chin, and headed for the captain's mount. "Mr. Grimes... prepare to set a new course."

The helmsman glanced up as I approached, a flicker of confusion crossing his face. "Aye, Sir. I've already got us heading toward Earth."

Back-and-forth murmurs on the bridge faded to silence.

"Set a new course for StarPoint Station. Throttle up our Off-Worlder powerplants to the maximum."

"Aye, Captain... inputting the new coordinates now."

Even Lucy had quieted. Sitting there on the Lieutenant's shoulder, the bird could have been mistaken for a child's plush toy.

With the Grav generators not fully operational, the crew leaned left in sync when the ship initiated its deliberate, gradual U-turn.

"Ms. Blunderton, inform Stephan Derrota, Hardy, Akari James, Wallace Ryder, Sergeant Dyer, and the rest of his team, to report to the bridge. And ask my niece to join us too."

"Yes, Sir."

"Captain," Pristy said, her attention turned fully to her board, "our three Varapin friends back there... they've altered course. Look to be following on our same vector."

Max and his team arrived first. Shortly after, Sonya shuffled in, her arms still in a sling, each step she took showing her discomfort. Akari and Ryder entered next, followed by Derrota. Then Hardy entered the bustling bridge, the last to join the fray.

Several bridgecrew gasped, staring at Hardy. He looked like he had been caught in the hellish sandstorm of all sandstorms. Gone was the mirror-like chrome plating the ChronoBot took pride in; there was nothing left to buff out or polish. Only his faceplate seemed to have received some attention—likely from Derrota—now just marginally buffed out.

Once settled, everyone turned to me, curious faces with lingering hints of dread in their eyes. Standing before them, I hesitated.

"What is it, Cap?" Hardy said. "I don't want to miss my appointment with Earl Sheib."

"Who's Earl Sheib?" Aubrey asked.

The ChronoBot waved away the question, "Never mind... way, way, way before your time."

I made eye contact with each crewmember. "If you're anything like me, you feel like you've been through hell—hit by one shitstorm after another, and now barely holding it together. And maybe, like me, you thought nothing else could possibly go wrong because you'd already survived the worst."

Grip shook his head, already anticipating something bad. Derrota's shoulders drooped, and Lieutenant Junior Grade Roisin Blunderton was smoothing out her uniform, palms working over invisible creases—her OCD operating in full gear.

Sonya hobbled forward plopped down into the captain's mount and spun it around to face me. "I better sit down for this. Don't think I can handle what you're about to say standing up."

THEN I TOLD THEM—RECOUNTING MY RECENT communique with Admiral Gomez, leaving nothing out and not sugarcoating anything. They deserved the unvarnished truth and what the implications were for us going forward.

Hardy's faceplate glowed a muted grayish blue. "My cuz... Bob... he's there... on StarPoint. Cap—"

I held up a hand as if to say, *I know, Hardy. We'll talk later.*

Pristy stood up and began pacing—had she picked up my habit?

She joined me and stood next to me. I'd anticipated anger, but there was none of that—she was thinking, I could practically see the wheels turning in the XO's head.

"Okay... yes, I get it. This sounds bad," Pristy said.

"Bad isn't the word I'd use," Sonya interjected. "More like we've just been gut-punched... hey, let's all hold hands and sing

Kumbaya while this busted spacecraft embarks on what can only be described as the suicide mission from hell. YAY!"

"Don't be so dramatic," Pristy said with a dismissive shake of her head. "Things might not be as hopeless as you think."

I kept my mouth shut because, in my mind, Sonya hadn't been all that far off the mark.

"What are you thinking, XO?" I asked.

She looked at me, her expression serious. "Picture this: millions of Krygian man-eating bugs swarming continents, over-running countries, and infesting cities across Earth. Humankind is not prepared for an invasion of that kind. The terror is... unfathomable. No, I would far rather be here with this crew—the ones taking the charge, bringing the attack to them. Win or lose, this is what we do—we do the impossible or die trying."

"Okay," I said, "let's start with what we have in our favor."

"That won't take long," Sonya said under her breath.

I assessed my XO. She never ceased to amaze me.

Not sure I wanted to hear the answer, but I had to ask. "What weapons systems are still viable... online, or maybe repairable within a short timeframe?"

Pristy hurried to her station and began working her board while the rest of us watched in silence.

Looking up, she put her attention on Hardy. "Not much is working now, but that's not the same thing as destroyed. My suggestion, put Hardy in charge of weapons repair, some of which may require additional spacewalks."

The ChronoBot froze in place, undoubtedly, this was the last thing the robot wanted to hear.

Pristy continued, "Hardy, get with Chief LaSalle and his SWM team... they'll need to reconnect severed power and signal cables to what remains of our Phazon Pulsar batteries, railgun turrets, and our two remaining broadside cannons. I have NELLA compiling a list of interconnections needing to be made—I'm betting it'll be a long list."

"Wait, we have two functional broadsides?" Not sure I heard her right.

She looked at me like I was mentally challenged. Putting hands on hips, she glared. "Yes... and we also have Arrow fighters and a fully intact Armory with all sorts of weapons of mass destruction. We're far from the useless heap of metal you've referred to us these last few days. This is still a U.S. Space Navy warship. Let's remind those insect fuckers—especially that fat-assed queen bitch—what happens when you tangle with Earth's most formidable military force!"

Taken aback, we stared at the XO, our faces masks of astonishment. The bridge, silent as a grave, suddenly erupted. Applause turned into loud cheers, amplified by Ham and Hock's jubilant hoots and hollers.

Blunderton, at Comms, raised a hand over her head to get my attention. "Captain! We're being hailed."

"Okay, okay, settle down everyone," I said. "Who—"

"One of the Varapin ships that's tailing us. The captain's name is Skrinn Toe, though I'm not sure if I'm saying it right."

Sonya got the hint from my expression and vacated the captain's mount. Taking the seat, I said, "Very well Ms. Blunderton, go ahead and put the good captain up on the primary display. Let's see what he wants."

The halo display flickered to life, casting a crisp blue light across the bridge. Captain Skrinn Toe appeared, his presence immediately unsettling. His hooded face, skeletal and all angles, was framed by shadowy robes. The pitch-black of his obsidian skull was contrasted by the bone white of his jutting jaws and teeth.

At first glance, his skeletal form seemed fragile. Yet within the folds of this alien's robe, I knew better—these Varapin ghouls retained a hidden strength.

A familiar knot tightened in my gut. My disdain for the Varapin ran deep, born from too many encounters revealing their vile nature. Too many of my past crewmembers had perished at the bony hands of this species.

It all surged back to the surface now, face-to-face with one of their kind.

"Greetings... I am Captain Galvin Quintos of USS Resilience."

"And I am Captain Skrinn Toe, Supreme Commander of this Battle Group."

"Terrific. So, why is your little battle group shadowing my ship? What are your intentions, Captain Toe?"

His voice crackled over the comms, a scratchy rasp that grated at my psyche like sandpaper against metal. "Captain Quintos, I am pleased you are still among the living. You know, you have a certain... notoriety among the Varapin as one who never relents, an admirable trait for an adversary. Though now, it seems, we have become reluctant allies."

"Reluctant allies?" I scoffed, disbelief creasing my brow. "No, we are still adversaries. And don't forget, the Varapin surrendered to the Alliance unconditionally—"

He interrupted, waving a bony hand dismissively. "Details of history aside. We have weightier concerns, wouldn't you agree?"

I shoved down my annoyance. "Then enlighten me. What drove you to pursue my ship?"

Toe leaned closer, his eyes glimmering darkly in the holographic light. "Your world, the Alliance, are not the only lifeforms facing the Krygian's wrath."

My heart raced at the mention of the Krygians. I masked my reaction, keeping my voice steady. "What's your point?"

"As we speak, a Krygian fleet has invaded Varapin space. A blockade keeps us from returning to defend our homeland. This forces us into uncharted territory, so I suggest we combine forces. Do not deny, you could use the help."

I met his gaze, unyielding. "Sorry Toe... I'm all out of hugs today. Go whine and snivel to your friends, the Grish. I'm sure the piglets will be far more receptive—"

To my surprise, a cold laugh escaped from his throat. "It is refreshing to hear a human's flippancy during such trying times. I offer you my support—an offer, you and I both know, would be foolhardy to decline."

Stone-faced, I stared back at the Varapin Captain. It was imperative that I not forget what he and his kind are capable of —how they feed on one's essence through what is called Ghan-Tshot... a method of life-force extraction. Bending their prey backward, forcing their jaws wide open beyond natural limits, is followed by the rapture. What is akin to the victim's very soul being completely drained away, leaving behind little more than an empty husk of a body.

"Desperate times, Captain," Toe continued, confidence sharpening his voice. "You should know, the recent transmissions between your ship and U.S. Space Navy's Admiral Gomez... have been intercepted. We know your predicament and we know of your ill-fated StarPoint Station directives."

Crap. Well, that complicates things...

"Maybe we should hear him out, Captain," Pristy said.

"I'm not agreeing to anything, Toe. But I'll listen to what you're offering."

"My battle group for the Alliance's assistance later. Three warships at your flanks for the StarPoint assault."

I took a breath, considering my predicament. I needed to

remember, the Krygian threat was far more pressing than my longstanding grudge with the Varapin.

"You're putting a lot of faith in me keeping my word—and to be honest I have little goodwill to offer when it comes to your kind. What guarantee do I have this alliance won't end with a Varapin Ghan-Tshot party for my crew and me?"

A flash of irritation passed across his hollowed features. "You have no guarantees, Quintos. But if this Krygian storm persists, none of us will survive. Want to put an end to the insects that are, at this very moment, feasting on the human inhabitants of that space station? Go ahead, consider this a temporary pact if that makes you feel better. But only together, will we wrest the universe back from the brink."

I was still inclined to turn down Toe's offer. It stank of three-day-old fish.

"Let me ask you this, Captain... how long do you anticipate it taking that monstrosity of a spacecraft of yours to reach Star-Point station?"

Grimes was ready with a barely audible answer meant for my ears but not Toe's. "It will take us eight days... maybe nine, Captain."

"My command ship has wormhole manufacturing capability. Wouldn't you prefer to reach those captured thousands sooner—in hours, rather than days?"

I weighed his words, his proposition. Glancing at Pristy, I saw she too was calculating the risk-reward computations. With an almost undetectable nod of her head, she indicated she was inclined to accept the Varapin's proposal.

"Very well, Captain Skrinn Toe," I conceded, allowing depth in my voice but pulsing with caution. "We'll do this together. But make no mistake," I leveled a firm gaze at him, "betrayal would be a one-way ticket to your death."

A sinister grin broke through Toe's skeletal mask. "How I enjoy the human fascination with the over-dramatic, Captain."

My mind already churned with misgivings agreeing to this, whatever this was. But what options did I have when trapped between old vendettas and the weight of a universe on the edge of collapse?

Chapter 34

Four and a half hours later, I was en route to Derrota's lab. He had something he wanted to show me, something he'd been working on over the last few days but only now was it ready to be presented.

I had little in the way of extra time to view one of my science officer's experiments, but he'd sounded both excited and adamant.

Approaching the next DeckPort, something that previously had become as commonplace as entering through an auto-hatch —now, there was that seed of doubt that I might be entering into a doorway to oblivion.

Earlier, I'd motioned for Pristy to speak with me just outside the bridge, out of earshot of the others.

I'd asked her to step up with the ensuing assault—use that incredible tactical mind of hers to come up with no less than three StarPoint attack scenarios that wouldn't result in the death of the station's hostages.

"That's a lot to put on my shoulders, Galvin," she'd said, looking more than a little overwhelmed. "This is something you would have insisted on doing yourself."

"This situation is far from typical," I said. "I'm being pulled in too many directions at once. Look, the explosion claimed an entire Army platoon—as you are well aware, they were to be our fighting force if and when the need arose. What we're left with is a crew of just over a thousand, down from three times that. And while each crewmember is doing their part to keep this ship operational... very few of them are trained for what's to come."

From her expression, she still wasn't getting my point.

"I'm simply asking you to take on a little more responsibility. That's nothing new. Hell, you've captained your own ship, Gail. What's going on here?"

She exhaled, "*Hercules*. Yes, a fine ship. A stellar crew. And I ended up losing both. Not everyone is ship's skipper material. Want to hear something crazy? When I was demoted back to XO, being involved with that whole time-jumping thing at Stratham Hold within the Lost Tombstone Star System—I didn't feel dejected or disheartened. I was relieved. And there's one more thing..."

I waited for her response, seeing how hard it was for her to find the right words.

"I died within that DeckPort. No. That other Gail Pristy died within that DeckPort. What you and everyone else here have yet to understand, is that I've come to terms with that fact. Are we virtually identical? Maybe. But I am not her. I know that to my core. And I'm telling you this now because I need you to understand, that I don't want that kind of responsibility."

I listened, aware this wasn't the right moment for this conversation. She was not wrong—those subtle changes she was aware of in herself, I too saw differences. Would the other Pristy have thrown caution to the wind and made love to me within the dark confines of that old shuttlecraft? Not likely... but she wasn't entirely right either.

I put my hands on her shoulders and met her eyes. "Where's the self-doubt coming from? Feeling you're not up to the task? I get you're comparing yourself to someone you're not, but..."

"It's frightening! It's terrifying!" she interjected.

"Yes, it's frightening. But what you may not realize is that your predecessor felt the same fear. Just like everyone else does. Fear of making a wrong choice, of actions leading to more loss of life."

Her eyes glistened as she blinked, trying to hold back tears.

"You're comparing yourself to a ghost, Gail. No one can live up to that."

That seemed to have hit home. Her face softened, the tension easing slightly.

I looked past her toward the bridge entrance. We were alone. I pulled her closer, my arms around her slender frame. We kissed, eyes open, searching, conveying emotions not ready to be spoken.

She pushed me away, breathless, at the sound of approaching footsteps.

Rounding the corner from the bridge, Lieutenant Blunderton stopped in her tracks when she, and her parrot, Lucy, saw us.

As if caught in the midst of an ongoing conversation, I put on my serious captain's face. "Look, XO, we need to fully capitalize on having those three Varapin warships at our disposal. That and the strategic edge, we'll have by jumping in and catching the enemy off guard. I'll expect all three StarPoint attack scenarios within the next two hours."

"No way can I pull that together is so short a timespan," she countered, her irritation not completely an act.

I smiled, "Don't do anything yourself that can be reasonably delegated to someone else— That's a quote from General

George S. Patton. So delegate, XO. You have two hours. Best you get to it."

Pristy turned on her heel and with the perfect amount of attitude, stormed back onto the bridge.

I raised my brow, "What is it, Ms. Blunderton?"

"Oh, um... Science Officer Derrota is wondering where you had gone off to. He's waiting in his lab."

I spotted Derrota and my niece standing side-by-side at a lab bench. Sonya, donning a white lab coat, had her hair pinned up in a bun, giving her an air of maturity that belied her 17 years. Derrota, his lab coat looked as rumpled and disheveled as ever. The two were in the midst of a conversation, with Derrota's apprentice giving credence to her age in the way only a teenager can—with a snarky tone.

"Oh my God! You can rationalize it however you want, Stephan, but it's still janky. I could write a script in a couple of minutes that automates this process with optimized algorithms and greater precision."

Patient as a lighthouse keeper, Derrota simply smiled, and said, "Let me show you what is needed and perhaps then you can write that script."

They both looked up as I approached. I smiled at my niece and looked to Derrota.

"You'll need to hurry—I'm up to my neck in chaos right now."

"Yes, of course, Galvin," Derrota said, his eyes sparkling with excitement.

"Sonya, how about you bring up the 3D model for the captain."

The teen huffed. "It's not done yet... we should wait till I fix—"

"It'll be fine," Derrota coaxed.

Sonya tapped at the input device in front of her.

Suddenly, atop the bench and towering over us, a 7-foot-tall, incredibly lifelike 3D facsimile of a warrior took form within a halo display. The alien—reminiscent of a praying mantis—looked ravenous as it stared down at me. Its triangular, slightly elongated head housed an extra pair of eyes that added a layered depth to its gaze. A small, hinged mouth with sharp mandibles opened and closed—a mouth perfectly designed for grasping and tearing prey. Its long, slender body—segmented and encased in a vibrant green exoskeleton—featured spiked forelegs, folded in a prayer-like stance, ready to spring into action.

As I instinctively stepped back, Sonya's eyes lit up, a smirk playing on her lips.

"Don't worry, Uncle Person... I'll protect you from the big bad alien."

"Funny," I said, tearing my eyes away from the way-too-real-looking insect. "What are you two doing with this thing?"

Derrota had moved farther down the bench, tapping at a different terminal. Another halo display materialized, this one a jumble of abstract characters and symbols I knew to be Quans-Code—Sonya joined him, gently but firmly shouldering Derrota aside—this was her domain, an area where few could match her skill.

I casually glanced at my TAC-Band; I still had another stop to make before returning to the bridge.

Sonya was smiling now, entering one more line of code. "You'll want to watch Lana on the display."

"Lana?"

"That's what we've named her." Derrota gestured to the towering hologram, a hint of pride in his voice.

I guess that's Lana, I thought.

The halo display flickered, and the perspective zoomed out. Now, Lana appeared smaller, only half her previous size. Two humanoid figures, comparatively smaller than the current Lana, entered the scene, both clad in full combat suits. Strapped to their back were supply tanks—hoses snaked to handheld weapons resembling old-school flamethrower rigs.

Derrota halted the animation, leaving a freeze-frame of the combatants and Lana locked in an impending clash. I had little doubt the Krygian held all the cards in this showdown.

Sonya said, "This part is all Stephan's genius."

The Krygian, standing upright—something Earth-bound praying mantises weren't known for—stepped toward one of the combatants, mandibles scissoring, as if in contemplation of lopping off an arm, or maybe a head. A shimmering violet mist erupted from the closest of the combatant's weapons, enveloping the insect's head in a dense violet cloud.

For the second time, I stepped back, watching in horror as the Krygian went berserk. Its appendages twisted and flailed, shooting out at odd angles. The Krygian began to fall apart right before our eyes. One spindly leg, then another, detached, its exoskeleton crumbling into dust. The final, gruesome act was its head tumbling away.

Amid the quiet hum of lab equipment, I gazed at what remained of the dead alien.

"That turn of events caught me off guard," I said, not sure if I should feel revulsion or elation. "Tell me more. What did I just witness."

Derrota, still at the other lab station, brought up two very different-looking DNA structures. I recognized the one on the left.

Derrota said, "On the left, we have the familiar human's DNA double helix, with its orderly, ladder-like rungs and consistent, repeating patterns of base pairs. In stark contrast on the right, the alien DNA... has a triple-helix structure. It is really quite amazing; look at the iridescent colors and fractal-like extensions."

"You have the alien's genetics—"

"Yeah, we've got the bug's genome fully sequenced," Sonya said. "Our time at Nylor-5 in the Krygian Hegemony paid off."

The alien's DNA helix structure indeed seemed to have a far more intricate and dynamic genetic blueprint than the human example.

Sonya tapped at her input device—the human DNA example disappeared, replaced with a kind of molecular structure of some sort.

Derrota pointed to the left side of the display. "Here, you see the molecular structure of just one among two hundred and fifty thousand insecticides tested against the alien's genome. We needed something that would work fast, while not having an extended half-life—one that was relatively safe for noninsectile organisms. Note the network of connected atoms, complete with rings, branches, and functional groups like halogens and phosphates."

The display flickered, revealing a new insecticide molecular structure with subtle differences. Then that was replaced with another and then another. Soon, the molecular replacements were being replaced at such a speed it was impossible to note the differences. Then, just as suddenly, the display locked into place with one insecticide molecular structure.

MATCH—GENOME-TARGETED EFFICIENCY 100%

I watched as the alien DNA on the right with its triple-helix structure, iridescent colors, and fractal-like extensions, now began to distort, all symmetry mutating into what could best be described as grotesque mayhem.

Both Derrota and Sonya looked to me for my reaction.

"You found a way to kill the enemy. But this would be chemical warfare."

Similar to Earth's long-standing international law, the Chemical Weapons Convention (CWC) prohibits the development, production, stockpiling, transfer, or use of chemical weapons by signatory states to prevent harmful effects on health and the environment—and I was fairly certain it applied to intergalactic warfare as well.

"You're concerned with the CWC provisions," Derrota said, making more of a statement than a question.

I nodded.

"Fuck the CWC provisions," Sonya spat.

Derrota looked at me as if I had two heads. "I have to agree with Sonya on this Galvin. Provisions are fine when everyone plays by the same set of rules... but that's not the case with the Krygians who are intent on galaxy-wide domination."

"I agree," I said. "And I am personally willing to take the heat if this comes up later. In the words of a great sage, I once knew... fuck the provisions."

Sonya, having already moved on from the conversation, was deeply enmeshed with coding. "You still haven't told him, Stephan."

My science officer looked tongue-tied, that or reluctant to say what he needed to say.

"Oh for the love of God, Stephan..." she said. "Spit it out." She shot me a glance. "Fine, I'll tell him. What he hasn't volunteered is that this miracle insecticide chemical is dichlorodiphenyltrichloroethane."

Seeing my blank look, Derrota said, "You would probably know it by its more common reference as DDT."

"I've heard of it. Used back in the 20th Century. Highly effective in killing insects during World War II to control mosquitoes that spread malaria and lice that spread typhus among troops and civilians. But it was found to also have long-lasting environmental effects... like causing the thinning of eggshells, leading to population declines in many bird species."

"Appreciate the epic monologue, professor," Sonya quipped. "But later, a close derivative of the DDT insecticide called Fryzite was introduced on a distant mining world called... um—"

"Wenderovol," Derrota said.

"Exactly, Wenderovol," Sonya confirmed.

Derrota took over again, "So, they used Fryzite to control a wild sting-roach infestation in their barracks. Now, sure DDT caused environmental problems on Earth starting back in the 1940s, but the DDT derivative turned into a full-blown disaster on Wenderovol. Every organic lifeform on Wenderovol bit the dust. Only the miners survived. Yes, the sting-roaches were all killed, but so was everything in their eco-system that helps sustain life—plants, trees, animals, and aquatic life... all wiped out."

"I still don't get what the big deal is," I said. "StarPoint Station is crewed mostly by humans. It's nothing like this Wenderovol world you're talking about."

Derrota looked even more uncomfortable with this conversation than before. "Galvin, life on a deep space station such as StarPoint is not like life on Earth. On any single day, hundreds of visitors from any number of alien worlds dock, frequent the many pubs, or simply develop relationships with the locals."

"What he's getting at is... StarPoint has become a mixed genetic culture. Humans and aliens, from who knows where are doing the wild thing... sometimes they even have offspring."

I was starting to see where they were going with this.

Derrota put his full attention on me," StarPoint could easily be a mixed bag of genetic 'whatever'... it could be another Wenderovol."

He could tell I wasn't fully convinced.

"The lifeforms on Wenderovol possessed a remarkably distinct genetic and DNA structure. Their biochemical makeup, though specialized, was fragile—leaving the biosphere vulnerable to disruption. This is why something like DDT had such a catastrophic impact. On StarPoint, the genetic complexity and interspecies mixing may unintentionally... recreate similar vulnerabilities. The introduction of DDT/Fryzite could trigger equally devastating effects, as new biochemical pathways and genetic recombinations form unpredictable weaknesses."

"Terrific," I muttered, eying the situation through a tightening brow. "So, we need to rescue the hostages while prepping to spray the Krygian warriors and gearing up to kill their Queen —all perfectly synchronized. We can't afford a single mistake."

Neither Sonya nor Derrota had a ready answer to that.

Chapter 35

I entered the Marine barracks and found Sergeant Max Dyer in the gym, holding the heavy bag. Grip was practicing spinning back kicks with thunderous force, each strike lifting Max off his feet. I caught the Sergeant's eye and raised my chin.

"Take a break Grip," Max said, looking relieved for the reprieve from having his molars repeatedly shaken loose.

I gestured to the corridor and the farther down DeckPort "How about we take a walk, Sergeant."

Max grabbed a gym towel and wiped perspiration from his brow and then let the towel hang from his neck.

The Marine and I headed off together; I filled him in, and Max listened.

I started with a review of my conversation with Varapin Captain Toe and his offer of backup from his three warships—a discussion Max and his team had been there for. I explained that the XO was working up three different attack scenarios for StarPoint Station and that she'd likely be coming to Max to coordinate his team's involvement.

We passed the Armory, where unoccupied combat suits

stood shoulder-to-shoulder like silent sentries. The bulkheads brimmed with mounted weapons—tagger pistols, shredder long guns, substantial-looking rail cannons, and all types of weaponry and explosive ordinances I was clueless about.

I entered the DeckPort first and waited for Max on the other side.

Max glanced around, seeing we had emerged onto the combined 98/99/100 Decks. "I'm guessing there's a reason you've brought me up to the Symbio Deck."

"We'll get to that," I said, coming to a stop.

Max surveyed the ancient Roman city, its skyline dominated by the towering Colosseum in the distance. The night sky, a shroud of darkness, cast a slumbering stillness over the cobbled streets below.

"Science Officer Derrota came up with a potent, and effective DDT-derivative insecticide we can use against the enemy insects. Although to be honest, that still needs a strategic delivery method on StarPoint station.

Max listened without interruption, taking in the information while looking thoughtful.

"That's it?" he said, looking less than impressed. "No disrespect, Cap, but is that the best attack scenario we've come up with?"

He looked about the space, his jaw muscles flexing. "Sure, maybe our new Varapin 'frenemies' attack group can keep those Krygian warships guarding StarPoint busy... at least giving that scenario even odds—three warships against three warships." His eyes narrowed, scanning my face in a search for answers. "But that still leaves a boots-on-the-ground station assault, right? Help me do the math, Captain. We have my team, down from six to five combatants, and one badass ChronoBot. That's it going up against hundreds, possibly thousands of those Krygian warriors."

Before I could comment, he continued.

"Even with Stephan's new insecticide concoction, I'm not seeing how we prevail here. What am I missing?"

"We may have access to another hundred, maybe two hundred combatants," I said. I gestured to our surroundings. "I've seen them firsthand, Symbio-Poths that have already been fabricated... intended for the deck's Roman Empire experience. Dozens of gladiators, regiments of Roman soldiers..."

Max shook his head. "I'm not doing it. Sonya's laid down the law: no more using Symbio-Poths in battle. We all agreed. Turning her bio-mechanical characters, like those Symbio dragons, dinosaurs, pirates, or Revolutionary War redcoats, into weapons? It's unethical and strictly off-limits."

"You're right. We agreed. And it probably is unethical," I said, in total agreement.

His brows pulled together in confusion. "Then why are we here?"

I smiled but said nothing.

Then it dawned on him. "Wait. You want me to convince her. No way. You're not throwing me to the wolves, or wolf in this case. Let me tell you a secret... I'm afraid of that teenage niece of yours. I've seen what she is capable of—that cyber ninja shit. Uh-uh, she could turn our barracks into a sub-zero freezer with the touch of a button or have that creepy NELLA recite nursery rhymes nonstop in the middle of the night. Or just for shits and giggles, change my food replicator hamburger order to fried chicken gizzards. Nope, not risking it—"

"You know I can hear you... right?" came a terse, female voice.

Startled, we spun to find Sonya at a nearby bulkhead, frowning, her face like a parent catching a kid lighting matches.

Shit!

Max and I exchanged a nervous glance.

But what was most unexpected, was Pristy rounding the corner, her full attention on the tablet in her hand. She looked up to see Max and me.

"What are you doing here?"

"They're here for the same reason you are," Sonya said. "To commandeer innocent bio-mechanical entities for unintended purposes."

"Just so you know, I had nothing to do with this, Sonya," Max said defensively. "I respect the, um... sanctity of what you do here. It's unethical how Symbio-Poths have been treated—"

"Save it, Max," Sonya said, not buying what the Marine was selling. "Without the Symbio's involvement, I get it... we're all toast." But she continued to glare at Max. "Seriously? I can't believe you said those things about me. I want you to know, I've never even thought about changing your food replicator order to fried chicken gizzards... well, until now anyway."

Pristy tapped her tablet for a while, then met my gaze.

"You wanted three attack plans. I've got them for you, but I won't sugarcoat it—none of these give us much hope of surviving."

Chapter 36

The Captain's Conference Room buzzed with a charged energy. We'd just barely resuscitated this ship, and now we were gearing up to dive headfirst into the abyss. Each face around the table reflected a mix of determination and apprehension. Blunderton stood by the autohatch, Lucy perched on her shoulder—a rather odd detail in the grim scenario. Hardy occupied his usual corner, his still marred chrome plating, dull under the lights.

Pristy took the center stage, a halo display shimmering in front of her. "Captain, you've made your selection from my three assault variations," she announced, looking serious.

"Alright, XO. How about we let the others see what we've come up with," I said, steeling myself for the presentation. The room's overhead lights dimmed slightly as the display lit up.

She glanced around the table. "What I'm going to show you is the initial attack only—*Resilience* and the Varapin assets confronting the three Krygian dreadnoughts. What happens after that, the Captain and I will discuss later."

Hardy was now over by Blunderton, trying to get Lucy to hop onto his extended finger. If Blunderton's expression was any indication as to how she felt about that, she was getting more annoyed with the ChronoBot by the second.

"Uh, Hardy... you might want to pay attention to this," I said.

Pristy continued, "This scenario involves a bit of subterfuge." The beginnings of a bemused smile crossed her lips. "*Resilience* and the three Varapin ships—one of them the Varapin command ship—have come to a full stop at our current coordinates; from its stationary position the command ship—"

"Yup, the Varapin command ship is going to manufacture a wormhole," my niece interrupted, impatiently moving things along, "intended for their three dreads, and our ugly monstrosity."

"You have someplace you'd rather be, Sonya?"

She looked back at me with a blank expression that shouted, *any place but here!*

Pristy allowed her tablet's halo projection to play, whereby the Varapin command ship did indeed manufacture a wormhole, but only one ship, *USS Resilience*, entered before the wormhole quickly closed down again.

"Didn't expect that," Ryder said from the far end of the table. He and Akari exchanged a look. "Am I missing something or is it your idea to send in the broken, least effective of the assets into battle alone?"

I gestured to the halo. "Watch. Then you can critique the plan if you want," I said.

The perspective on the display changed, this time it was the sudden appearance of the open maw of the wormhole's exit—several moments later, *USS Resilience* burst from its mouth traveling at a fast clip. The wormhole dissipated like a ring of smoke caught in the wind. As *Resilience* moved through the void several things started to happen. First, all of what remained of the ship's running lights blinked out. Observation windows and portholes went dark. The four Off-Worlders, their drive

Engines and thrusters extinguished in unison, their once vibrant tongues of blue and yellow fire now gone. And finally, *Resilience* began to, ever so slightly, spin.

I said, "What do you see, people?"

Akari said, "I see a ginormous hunk of space debris rocketing through space."

"Is it on a collision course for StarPoint?" Derrota asked, looking dubious at the intent of all this.

Pristy said, "Absolutely not. But that's a great question. Krygians on that station and their three dreadnoughts will keep an eye on it, but it shouldn't trigger a response significant enough to warrant weapons fire."

"That's kind of a leap in faith, don't you think?" Grimes said from his place around the table. "How would they rationalize something so weird-looking that just so happened to show up in their local space like that?"

"Because intel of *USS Roosevelt's* catastrophic explosion, and her assumed near destruction, will have reached the Krygians long before now," I interjected. "It's not a huge stretch to think a part of that ship ended up near StarPoint."

All eyes locked onto the halo display as *Resilience* was now fast-approaching StarPoint Station off in the distance.

"And while the three Krygian warships scan for life signs and active systems and take up a defensive formation as the enormous space debris segment approaches," Pristy explained, "... as you see, no other action is taking place—they're going to simply let it pass by unmolested."

She paused the halo simulation.

"I still think you're making assumptions about what the Krygians will and won't do," Grimes said.

Heads turned, everyone looked from Grimes to me, and then to Pristy.

"Gaming out the thousands of different attack scenarios

through NELLA," Pristy said, "she offered our best prospects for success. And guess what those gamed-out, played-to-conclusion scenarios revealed?"

Ensign Blair Paxton joined the conversation, "No attack variants using U.S. Space Navy standard protocols indicated a win for our side."

"I'm impressed, Ensign." Pristy nodded. "She isn't wrong. No strategies or attack combinations offered more than a slim chance of victory."

"That is until Captain Quintos came up with his Trojan Horse offensive."

Pristy resumed the simulation where *Resilience* was passing by StarPoint soon to be leaving local space. And that's when the broken ship's four Off-Worlder drive thrusters suddenly came back to life. *Resilience* was now rapidly changing direction with multiple weapons bays firing at once. Rail spike munitions spanned the void while brilliant blue plasma bolts erupted from no less than eight Phazon Pulser turrets. The three Krygian dreadnoughts were taking heavy, unexpected fire.

I joined Pristy at the head of the table as the simulation continued. "Take note of how the three Krygian warships are quickly maneuvering to deal with this new threat—*Resilience*.

A new wormhole's endpoint materialized, quickly followed by the arrival of the three Varapin dreadnoughts.

"Captain Toe's Varapin warships, weapons primed, will target the Krygian assets from behind."

As the halo simulation flickered off, I glanced around the table, "With four warships pounding the unsuspecting enemy vessels, the true fight for control of this sector will ensue."

"That's it?" Blunderton said from the auto-hatch. "Where's the rest of the simulation showing the destruction of the Krygian ships?"

Gail Pristy laid a hand on my shoulder, making it clear she

had this one. "Lieutenant, there's no need to simulate that. So far, none of our scenarios have the good guys winning that space battle."

"Wow. That's encouraging," Sonya said, her words dripping with sarcasm.

"Our Trojan Horse scenario increases our odds far more than any other alternative. Obviously, we still need to... tweak things," Pristy said apologetically.

"And the Varapin... they've bought into this, um, scheme?" Ryder asked.

I shrugged, "There was some pushback, but Captain Toe assures me, they'll do their part when the time is right."

A sobering chill ran through the compartment—realizing that this mission was destined to fail even before it had gotten off the ground.

I mustered a smile and pressed on. Although I had already previously met with each team separately, I decided to be thorough and go through the multi-pronged attack deployment within StarPoint Station.

"Thanks to the efforts of Science Officer Derrota, *Resilience* has a fully functioning quansportation system back online. This will be our ace in the whole, if there is one, as we bring this battle to the Krygians. We have three primary objectives. All three must be achieved. One, find and kill the Krygian Queen. Two, the bugs are in the midst of a breeding cycle, we kill them all or deal with a lot more of them later. And three, we rescue the hostages. These directives must be carried out in parallel, with our six quansported-in teams hitting the ground running."

I fixed my gaze on my crew, ensuring they understood the gravity of the situation. "We either achieve all three objectives or we die trying. Nothing less is acceptable."

"I've spoken to teams individually, but let me reiterate... We're deploying six separate teams onto StarPoint Station.

Hardy, our magnificent killer ChronoBot, will operate solo. He will be moving fast, using his Swiss army knife of weaponry, as he goes after Queen Slith. Sergeant Max will lead his Marine unit, equipped with DDT/Fryzite sprayers. I'll be commanding one group of Symbio-Poths, while Captain Ryder and Lieutenant James will be leading two other Symbio Poth contingents. We're outnumbered 10 to 1, but our primary objective remains to eliminate the Krygian Queen. Her location is shielded, but we've narrowed it down to several fortified areas. Remember, everything must be carried out virtually all at once —rescuing the hostages, then the killing Krygian warriors, and taking out the Queen."

"There's one more crucial element to our plan," I said, my eyes scanning the compartment before settling on Aubrey Laramie. "Aubrey, you won't be joining Max's team, at least not right away."

Aubrey straightened, her eyes alert. "Okay... um, what do you need me to do, Captain?"

"You'll be the first to quansport over to StarPoint. Your mission is to reach the hostages and prepare them for immediate evacuation before the main assault begins."

Max nodded in agreement. "Makes sense. Aubrey's got the combat training and the stealth skills for that kind of op."

I continued, "You'll be equipped with a crate of TAC-Bands. Get them onto the hostages so we can track and extract them efficiently. The quansporting of thousands of hostages will take time. And that's if the Krygian guards aren't alerted to what's going on. I can't stress enough how your efforts must not be noticed. Once that's done, all the hostages quansported, you'll meet up with Max's team where that aspect of the mission can then commence."

Aubrey's face set with determination. "Understood, Captain. I won't let you down."

No one else posed a new question or commented.

"XO Pristy will have the captain's mount having the difficult job of holding off Krygian warships while ensuring *Resilience* stays in one piece for the rest of us to come back to... if our efforts on StarPoint are successful."

"Unlikely that's going to happen..." someone murmured under their breath, I wasn't sure who. They weren't wrong.

Pristy tapped at her tablet and a wire-frame diagram appeared on the halo display showing StarPoint's towering stacked deck cylindrical design—hundreds of decks, each a complex labyrinth of corridors and passageways. Each level was like its own sprawling city with retail shops, theaters, bars, bowling alleys—you name it, the station probably provided it.

She pointed to the station's tapered lower ten decks. "Hardy's long-range sensors indicate the hostages—those still alive—are being sequestered here within the largest cargo holds."

"How many hostages are we talking about?" Akari asked.

I looked to Hardy."

"Five thousand six hundred and forty-two," the ChronoBot said. "Now five thousand six hundred and forty-one."

Akari continued to stare at the robot, waiting for an explanation.

Hardy looked to me for permission to explain—I nodded.

"That space station's packed with thousands of Krygians, and those hostages—mainly humans—are their primary food source. The latest count: five thousand six hundred and twenty-one. Looks like it's suppertime."

"Oh my," Ensign Paxton said. "So, every minute we wait to rescue them—"

"More innocents die," I said, finishing her thought. "But going over there with a half-baked plan would only get more of them, and us, killed."

"Stephan, how about you give us an update on your efforts," Pristy said.

Derrota cleared his throat, "Um... good news in that regard. The DDT-Fryzite compound is being replicated as we speak. We should have far more in reserves than Sergeant Max and his team will need. Grip is finishing up in the ship's Armory where he's fabricating the high-pressure insecticide sprayer weapons."

Max gave a tight nod. "My team's taken turns practicing with the few already made. We'll be ready for battle within the hour."

A murmur of approval rippled through the room.

I looked at my niece and raised my brows.

"I've been getting the Symbio-Poths prepped," Sonya said, her voice lacking any enthusiasm. "They'll be ready... to be massacred," she added under her breath.

I knew the implications this decision carried. The Symbio-Poths weren't mindless automatons; Sonya had pointed out on numerous occasions, that they were evolving, showing signs of sentient behavior. Understandably, Sonya was uncomfortable walking such a fine line between her working with these bio-mechanical constructs and the ethical realities she was being faced with.

She got to her feet, "I need to get back to the Symbio Deck. Two hundred makeshift Symbio soldiers won't miraculously ready themselves." She strode from the compartment with the weight of the world on her shoulders.

"Anything else?" I asked my XO.

"No," Pristy replied, her face resolute. "We all have our marching orders."

"Alright, everyone. Get to work. We jump in two hours."

Chaos ensued the moment people filed out through the auto-hatch, each with a laundry list of tasks to complete.

I found Sonya inside her workspace, her fingers tapping across luminous control surfaces, inputting the final parameters. She had insisted that Derrota give her a new sling—and not a cast—for this very reason. Display feeds showed rows of Roman legions, the gladiators checking their weapons—swords, tridents, and weighted nets.

"How's it coming along?" I asked.

"Nearly there," she responded, her eyes glued to her display. "Symbios are grappling with the realization that this isn't a simulation. It's real combat now."

"I see you have your Symbios armed with their relic Roman weaponry... You do know we have an armory onboard. Shredders... taggers... maybe not in the quantities for all of them, but some."

She shrugged. "When I see them here on this deck, I'll be sure to hand them out."

I noticed something... odd, on one of her displays. A 3D wire diagram of something animalistic and huge. As I leaned in, she immediately closed down the display.

"What was that?" I asked.

"A surprise. But something still in the works... but if I can iron out the kinks, it'll be a game-changer."

Spotting another anomaly on another display, I pivoted and rushed out of her workspace, heading straight for the temporary staging area.

The Symbio-Poths were in the process of forming multiple straight-row formations. What had caught my eye on Sonya's display was indeed evident. The Symbios seemed to be... conversing with each other. They were in the all-too-human act of 'chatting'. This was new. Was this more proof of sentient behavior?

Joining me at my side, Sonya was nervously chewing the inside of her lip. Still looking at them, she said, "We're sending them to a certain death."

I suspected we were all facing certain death, but I held my tongue. I briefly placed a hand on her shoulder. "Please, finish getting them prepped."

I LEFT SONYA TO HER WORK AND IMMEDIATELY contacted LaSalle, instructing him to send a crate of whatever weapons provisions we had available up to Sonya.

I arrived back on the bridge, where Captain Skrinn Toe hovered within the primary halo display. His skeletal face and subtly red glowing eye sockets served as a looming reminder of our uneasy alliance.

"Captain Toe," I began, forcing civility into my voice, "I was under the impression we'd wrapped up our operations planning with our last communique."

Toe grinned a grotesque display of jagged teeth. "This is but a reminder, that our cooperation hinges on mutual benefit. Betray us and—"

"Believe me," I insisted, "we need this alliance just as much as you do. We're in this together."

With that, I cut the connection and turned back to the bridge. There was no time for sentimentality or second-guessing.

Chapter 37

I settled into the captain's mount, muscles tense, the ship's hum resonating through my bones. Hardy stood beside me, his sensors a critical lifeline for what we were about to face.

Pristy manned Tactical, her back a rigid line of tension. Blunderton's soft voice broke through the heavy silence within the sparsely manned bridge. She was talking to her Varapin counterpart, her words clipped, efficient.

"Everything's set on our end, Varapin Command. You're clear to initiate."

The connection cut, leaving the bridge immersed in an oppressive quiet. My crew—every one of them—sat braced for what lay ahead. The air thrummed with their unspoken fears. Blunderton listened intently and a moment later, she turned back to us.

"They're starting the manufactured wormhole, Captain."

I forced my eyes closed. It felt like there was a vise around my chest. Part of me wanted to convey some last bit of hope, but that would have been a lie. Every crewmember understood the grim reality. This mission's odds of success were bleak, and our chances of survival were even slimmer. Admiral Gomez had already accepted this truth when he dispatched us.

"Wormhole formation almost complete," Pristy announced from Tactical, her eyes flicking towards me, catching my gaze.

In those blue depths, I saw my own regrets mirrored—our love story, cut tragically short before it had blossomed.

Hardy piped up next to me, breaking the moment, "Cap, once inside the wormhole, we might encounter wormhole structural viability issues. The command ship isn't entering along with us to ensure stabilization. Could be some nasty turbulence, plasma pockets..."

I exhaled slowly, forcing any forbidding scenarios out of my mind's eye. "Take us in, Mr. Grimes."

"Aye, Captain."

The three waiting Varapin dreadnoughts floated ominously in the void behind us. Skepticism gnawed at me—they didn't have much love for us, and their promises were shaky at best. Regardless, *USS Resilience* had no way but forward.

We plunged into the wormhole. The transition wasn't smooth—every jolt magnified a hundredfold, sending ripples of shockwaves through the ship. I gripped the armrests of the captain's mount as *Resilience* shuddered violently. Each tremor seemed to amplify the turbulence tenfold, shaking the ship to its core.

In my peripheral vision, I saw Hardy glance down at me.

"Cap, my sensors indicate the wormhole is becoming increasingly unstable. The likelihood of both it and us dematerializing is rising."

NELLA's calm, yet unsettling, voice cut through the chaos...

WARNING! Wormhole viability in jeopardy.

The overhead lights went out, as station control boards across the bridge flickered and blinked out momentarily, plunging the compartment into semi-darkness. Ensign Paxton desperately tapped at her station, trying to keep ship systems operational through the convulsions. The primary halo display cast just enough light to make things visible.

Without warning, *Resilience* collided with a plasma pocket. The ship lurched violently to port, flinging crewmembers out of their seats and onto the deck. Sparks flew from several malfunctioning stations, lighting the space with intermittent amber flashes.

"Captain! The wormhole is narrowing!" Grimes shouted from Helm, his voice twisted with panic as he struggled to steady himself after being thrown back against his chair.

"Told you that could happen," Hardy said.

"Put a sock in it, Hardy," I said through gritted teeth.

The emergency lights finally came on casting a blood-red glow onto the bridge. I could almost hear the drive engines of the Off-Worlders groaning under the strain—pushed to their limits by the spatial anomalies within the wormhole.

On the primary halo display, I saw that we were corkscrewing through the tunnel of pulsing swirls of energy, each twist and turn threatening to tear us apart at any moment.

Despite the chaos, my voice cut through the blaring alarms and klaxons, "Ensign Paxton! Get our bridge stations back online and stabilized! Hardy, make yourself useful!"

Grimes yelled out, "NELLA's losing her hold on nav control."

"Can you go to manual?" I asked.

"No can do, Sir. I wouldn't even know how within a faulting wormhole."

The ship bucked and weaved, each move more violent than the last.

Power fluctuations detected. Shifting auxiliary power to critical systems.

The lights on the bridge came back on, albeit dimmed and flickering.

Pristy, still reeling from being thrown against her console, called out rapid support orders, directing Hardy and Paxton to increase shield levels. "And everyone... brace for further impacts!"

The wormhole continued to constrict around *Resilience*, its walls appearing to close in, unrelenting. Sweat trickled down my forehead as I watched Grimes wrestle with Helm, fighting to keep NELLA—and the ship—on course. "We're almost through, Captain! If we can hold on just a little longer!" he announced.

The crew clung to their stations, riding the tumultuous wave with nervous anticipation as *Resilience* continued to buck and jolt its way through the narrowing vortex, each second feeling like an eternity.

"Okay, people," I barked over the creaking vibrations. "Once we exit, Grimes will place us on a precise vector to bypass StarPoint. Then it's all hands on deck. Shut everything down. Propulsion, environmental systems, grav generators, we go lights out—vent atmosphere sparingly for effect. Hardy, I want you on Environmental Systems, spew enough radiation to mask our life signs."

Nods answered me, resolve hardening their features. Their fingers danced over the controls, inputting commands, getting everything ready for the immediate action needed post-exit.

"Exiting the wormhole in thirty seconds," Grimes called out.

Each heartbeat thundered like a hammer, drawing out that moment as if it would never come.

"When we get through, you all know what to do," I said,

locking eyes with my crew one by one, wanting them to know the faith I held in them.

Pristy gave a sharp nod. "We're ready, Captain."

Paxton's fingers were poised over her board. "We're set for immediate shutdown upon exit."

Grimes' lips were pursed, his eyes narrowed in concentration "Nav trajectory to be set upon exit, coordinates will only take a sec to lock down."

Emerging from the wormhole felt like being shot out of a cannon. The hull screamed with the stress. Grimes' hands worked magic, steering us clear and maneuvering us elegantly into the precise vector needed.

"Cut power!" I commanded. "Execute shutdown procedures."

The bridge went dark. Breaths held, ears strained for the slightest indication of disaster. Environmental systems groaned as they were forced offline, gravity flickered, and the world became weightless. The distant sounds of an exhaling venting atmosphere created an eerie howl—unlike anything I'd heard before, a guttural, sorrowful wail.

"I can't see a damn thing," grumbled Blunderton. It wasn't meant to be heard, but echoed in the darkness, it reflected what the rest of us were thinking.

"Radiation levels?" I asked, barely louder than a whisper.

"Generating," Hardy answered. "Life signs should be masked. 31,068.55 miles out on approach that'll bring us close to the Krygian vessels."

With that, any relief felt vanished quickly. Against the silent, frigid backdrop of deep space beyond, every sense screamed of the danger lurking from those three Krygian dreadnoughts.

"Hold fast, everyone," I murmured, hoping the sound of my voice would offer some semblance of confidence.

Seconds turned to minutes, leaving us suspended in the dark. The cold was more biting than I had anticipated since the environmental systems had shut down. And without the visual perspective from the primary halo display, I had no reference as to our progress—we were literally flying blind.

"We are approaching StarPoint Station, and, as expected," Hardy began, filling the crew in on his inner AI counterpart's—Luman's —insights, "our Krygian friends are on the move. Ah... they look to be going with the tried and true 'trident formation'. The three warships are strategically positioning themselves in defense of the space station. And now we see if our presence constitutes any kind of military response."

"We're set to bring *Resilience* back online, Captain," Pristy said, now weightless and hovering a few inches off her seat. I too was drifting higher, untethered... with a feeling that almost demanded a smile—almost.

"There's a good bit of ship-to-ship chatter taking place," Hardy said. "Not sure if they smell something fishy going on here... I don't talk 'bug' so not sure what all the chirping is about."

"And our trajectory?" I asked.

"Perfectly on course," Grimes answered. "*Resilience* has started to spin, just enough to make us look nothing like a functioning ship."

I was starting to weightlessly tilt backward, feeling the need to reach out and steady myself—fortunately, Hardy was close enough for me to clamp a hand onto, and I was able to reorient myself.

Our quiet solidarity held until Blunderton's voice broke in again...

"Captain, the Varapin dreadnoughts are forming their own

wormhole now. They've sent us a message telling us to expect them, shortly."

Suddenly, Hardy's voice was loud and authoritative. "We've reached StarPoint station, Cap. If we're going to—"

"All systems back online, NOW!" I ordered. "Helm, get me propulsion! XO, weapons systems! And Ms. Paxton, get our grav generators operational!"

A moment later, another blip in the darkness—and the bridge lights flickered back. Instrument panels powered up with the faintest hum.

"Scanners show no immediate threats on our vector, Captain," Pristy said, her voice barely concealing the impending dread.

"Let's go, people! We take it one very fast step at a time."

Grimes updated with our coordinates within StarPoint's vicinity. "Three of our Off-Worlders are throttling up."

I shot a hot glare toward the helmsman.

Looking frantic, he said, "Off-Worlder number four's having ignition issues."

"We should call triple A... get us a jump," Hardy volunteered, attempting a bit of ill-timed humor.

No one, including me, had any clue what he was rambling on about.

"Helm, can we maneuver on three drives—"

"No way, Sir," Grimes shot back. "We'd just spin around like a top."

"Krygians are powering up weapons systems!" Pristy announced.

Chapter 38

Three halo displays sprouted up at the front of the bridge providing feeds of all three Krygian dreadnoughts, a fourth halo was locked onto StarPoint. Suddenly, a fifth halo projected to life showing the formation of a manufactured wormhole, the mouth opening into a perfect wispy circle. Good, help was on the way...

"Tactical, unleash everything we've got! I want their attention squarely on us."

"On it!" Pristy yelled back.

I felt the throaty sound of multiple turret motors on the move, then the soft ping of the tactical board's confirmation of tracking acquisitions. The deck vibrated as railguns unleashed their spike projectiles—each round accelerated by powerful electromagnetic fields along conductive rails. Hundreds of hypervelocity rounds per minute were being fired, the kinetic energy of each shot immense as the spikes tore through space toward their targets.

I leaned forward in my seat, eyes locked, taking in the effects of our surprise attack. All three were being pounded, but one of the Krygian warships in particular was showing the most damage with multiple short-lived explosions blossoming along her starboard flank.

Pristy shot me a smile, "They should have raised their shields for battle-readiness—I can't believe the break we got."

Now the hulls of the other two dreads were erupting into mini fireballs.

"Inflicting damage, but not enough to put them out of commission," Pristy said. "Their shields are coming up to full strength."

Blunderton said, "Three Varapin ships have emerged from the wormhole. I'm awaiting contact."

And there it was. That was the first moment that I knew something was very, very wrong.

I yelled, "Hardy, get up here on Tactical 2... NELLA should already be firing Phazon Pulsars!"

"Finally!" Pristy spat. "Varapin are charging weapons."

"Still no comms contact with the Varapin command ship," Blunderton said, shooting me a concerned sideways glance.

Hardy sat up ramrod straight. "Wait. We're being targeted!"

"That's to be expected," I said.

"Yeah, well not if it's those three Varapin dreads locking onto us! Shit! Shit! Shit!" the XO cursed, bringing up three more halo displays. "Oh my God... we're so fucked."

Incoming! Incoming! Incoming!
Eight Fusion-Based Missiles Inbound!

My jaw dropped open but no words poured out. My XO was right, we were so fucked.

Pristy was leaning forward, talking fast and in low tones into her TAC-Band. Shooting me a quick look, she ended her call.

"Don't get your knickers in a twist, Captain. The EUNF anticipated this could happen eventually... and eventually is today."

Incoming! Incoming! Incoming! Eight Fusion-Based Missile Inbound. 12 Seconds to Impact.

"Talk to me, XO," I said in a stern tone, getting to my feet.

She didn't look up from her tactical board. "I guess these Varapin traitors didn't realize as part of their surrender agreement we acquired all of their missile signaling protocols. At this very second, Sonya is remotely transferring supervising control of that incoming missile barrage." Pristy chinned toward the display nearest to me. "And there you go... NELLA has now been given overriding targeting control of their missiles."

I watched as the all-too-close bundle of fusion-tipped missiles simultaneously changed course, making a wide U-turn within the void. Within seconds, the eight missiles were rocketing back in the same direction they had started from.

"Can you take four of those missiles and send them toward one of the Kyrgian ships, instead?" I asked.

Sonya's face suddenly projected out from my TAC-Band. "I hadn't thought of that, but I like it!" I could see she was fully engulfed at her workstation, with sounds of lightning-fast tapping coming from her keyboard. Her arms were incapacitated but her fingers worked just fine.

A moment later, "Done!"

Sure enough, four of the eight missiles had broken away from the group, now on a new trajectory.

I flinched as one of the three Varapin dreadnoughts exploded into fiery plumes, sending house-sized fragments hurtling outward like deadly shrapnel. It took just moments for the oxygen-deprived blaze to fizzle out, swallowed by the void as the final pockets of atmosphere vanished.

Moments later, another impact, one of the Krygian ships took the brunt of the redirected missiles and found their mark. The dreadnought's shields flared intensely, absorbing much of the blast, then soon faltered—multiple explosions followed, eviscerating the once mighty, miles-long dreadnought.

Hardy surveyed the displays. "We've got two Varapin warships and two Krygian ships left in the battlespace."

Blunderton raised a hand to signal me. "We're being hailed. It's Captain Skrinn Toe, Sir."

"This should be good," I said, fuming and picturing my hands tightly wrapped around the ghoul's bony neck. "Put him through."

The halo came to life, and Captain Skrinn Toe's smirk filled the display. "Captain Quintos, it's a pleasure to see you again," he said, his voice dripping with condescension. "Didn't think we'd meet again under such... lopsided terms."

I clenched my jaw, fighting back the surge of anger. "Toe. I should have expected this from the Varapin, betrayal suits you."

"Betrayal?" Toe's smirk widened, feigning innocence. "Isn't that a bit dramatic? Let's just call this... a strategic realignment."

I glared at the Varapin commander. "So, why align yourself with the Krygian? What could they offer you that's worth turning against the Alliance?"

"Ah, the Krygian." Toe leaned back, clearly satisfied with himself. "They made us an offer we couldn't refuse. Simply put, they promised to leave Varapin space and never return—that is... if we stayed out of their way. Coming to their aid here... well, that was my idea."

I scoffed, "An idea that has already cost you a dreadnought and her crew."

"Well, we won't be firing any more missiles... no matter, we have a myriad of other weapons at our disposal. So, we lost a ship—don't you humans have a saying... you have to break a few eggs?"

I felt a cold knot of disbelief. "And you really think you can trust the bugs?"

Toe gave a nonchalant shrug. "Trust is a luxury in war, Captain. They gave their word, and that's enough for us. Rather simple, really."

"And your word means nothing, Toe," I said coldly. "You were never meant to be our ally."

"Quintos, it's not personal. Just business," Toe said with a hint of regret. "You must understand that."

I nodded slowly, my eyes never leaving the display. "I understand perfectly. You're nothing but a coward hiding behind false promises."

Toe let out a deep, exaggerated sigh. "Say what you want, Captain. You're outmatched and outgunned. Wishing you luck feels... pointless. I suggest you relish these final moments among the living, Captain Quintos."

"This conversation isn't over, Toe. I'll be seeing you again... I promise you that." I motioned for Blunderton to cut the connection, my face a mask of steely determination.

Before the display went dark, Toe's smirk lingered. "Not likely, Quintos," he muttered, already reveling in his perceived victory.

Another halo caught my attention. It was a feed from the barracks, both Max and Aubrey, looking as if they'd been waiting to speak with me.

"Cap... We need to finalize the hostage retrieval plan," Max said. "I'm not sending even one of my team in unprepared."

Aubrey nodded rapidly, looking anxious. "Since I need to get to them before—"

Pristy interjected, her brow furrowed. "We're all on the same page, Laramie. Yeah, yeah, no spraying the DDT until hostages are safely off the station. What's the problem? How many times do we need to go over this?"

"I guess one more time, Gail," Aubrey snapped back, eyes on fire.

Hardy made a cat-fight, growl-hissing sound, which garnered a death stare from Pristy.

I let the friction between the two women pass without comment. I had far more important things to worry about.

"To reiterate," I said, "... Aubrey, your role is crucial. You'll be evacuating the hostages and then immediately rejoining Max's team—at which point you all will be getting busy with the DDT."

Max spoke up, "My team will be ready to move the second Aubrey gives us the all-clear and arrives on deck, Captain. I just want to be absolutely sure comms will be fully operational. If Laramie can't reach us, the proverbial wheels will fall off the cart and we're all FUBAR-ed."

"Stephan assures me comms will be online. Use your open channel via helmet comms, as well as TAC-Bands as needed."

"And Aubrey, we'll be with you every step of the way. I'll be on comms, and you can talk to me at any time during the operation. You okay with that?"

I caught Pristy rolling her eyes.

"Understood, Sir," Aubrey replied, her voice tense. "I'll do my best to tag and prep the hostages for quansport. If I make it out, I'll regroup with Max's team."

The feed blinked out.

"Taking plasma fire from... well, everywhere!" Pristy announced, clearly overwhelmed.

"Shields holding at 73 percent," Hardy updated.

"Taking evasive action," Grimes said. "Off-Worlder 4 is coming up to speed."

Resilience was suddenly banking to port, the ship's G-Force compensators straining to keep up.

The centermost halo display flashed bright with a series of roiling, fiery explosions; the Krygian dreadnought still continuing to fall apart from the missile strike.

Pristy smirked, "Those diverted Varapin missiles sure did make mincemeat of that Krygian vessel."

"Oh my," Ensign Paxton said, getting to her feet and pointing at one of the halo displays. "Look! The other two Krygian ships... they're now firing on the Varapin." She looked at me with wide eyes, "They think they'd been double-crossed!"

"Now everybody's firing at one another," Hardy remarked. "What happened to old-fashioned mano-a-mano combat?"

I sat back and watched. The once inky black void was now ablaze with dazzling crimson and blue plasma fire while crisscrossing trails of brilliant white rail spikes were finding their targets with devastating effect.

"Shields are taking a licking—down to 50 percent," Hardy said. "Rail munitions are running dangerously low."

We needed to bring this battle to an end—there again, the simple fact we were still in one piece at this point was... unexpected.

"Captain... it's Sergeant Max," Blunderton said. "He wants to deploy and says Stephan Derrota's already at the controls in the Quansporter compartment."

The plan was to deploy the five, six if you counted Hardy, teams in parallel. I scanned the feeds, each depicting frenetic, intense battle situations with both the Varapin and the Krygian assets. Could I just up and leave now?

"Go!" Pristy said without looking at me. "We stick to the plan. I've got this."

Standing, I hesitated—looked at her. I wondered if I would ever see her again. In two strides I was pulling her to her feet, spinning her around, and kissing her. Surprised and breathless, she kissed me back.

We separated, our eyes locking for one final moment. No words exchanged, yet everything understood.

"Let's go, Hardy." I said, heading out. "It's time we go kill us some bugs."

Chapter 39

The Quansporter Compartment was a blur of activity, with crewmembers weaving through the space like eager student applicants in a bustling admissions office. Aubrey Laramie stood slightly apart, her face a mixture of determination and hidden nervousness as she adjusted her combat gear. The crate of TAC-Bands sat at her feet, a stark reminder of her crucial mission.

Hardy and I shouldered through the mayhem to reach Derrota at the control console. He was working the board while carrying on multiple conversations, including one with Aubrey about the specifics of her upcoming task.

A projected oversized halo display dominated the space—a cutaway floor plan diagram of StarPoint Station. It had been color-coded to show which team would be arriving where. My eyes were immediately drawn to the lower tapered decks, shaded in a distinct orange color.

Derrota raised a palm to ward off the barrage of questions. "Let's start with our crucial first phase," he said, pointing to the orange-shaded area. "This is where the hostages are being held.

Aubrey, you're the ORANGE team. You'll deploy first, quansporting directly to these lower decks."

I turned to Aubrey. "I know we've gone over this. Your primary objective is to distribute TAC-Bands to all of the hostages and prepare them for rapid extraction. Speed and stealth are essential."

Aubrey nodded, her voice steadier than I expected. "Understood, Captain. I'll get it done."

Derrota continued, "Once Aubrey gives the signal that the hostages have been tagged, quansport extraction can proceed. Even though this Quansporter is the latest state-of-the-art device, we will be pushing it to its limits. I have allocated one full hour to quansport not more than 100 at a time."

"So... I'll be over there, in that part of the ship, for an hour?" Aubrey asked clearly not thrilled with that revelation.

"Yes. Maybe longer," Derrota said. "Let's talk about the remaining five assault teams."

Derrota raised a palm to ward off Akari's and Max's onslaught of questions. "Look... the deployment locations have been carefully chosen to put our limited forces within the highest concentration of Krygian numbers."

Turning to Hardy, he said, "You're team GREEN, Hardy." Derrota gestured to the top section of the space station. "As I'm sure your sensors have confirmed, the Krygian Queen's exact whereabouts have been shielded. I'm not sure how. What I do know, is she is somewhere within these top ten Decks. These Decks are under heavy guard by her elite security forces. I'm sorry, Hardy, but you'll be thrown into a virtual meat grinder against hundreds of Krygian warriors."

Hardy waved away the warning with a casual flick of a hand. "I'm not worried. Been tossed into far worse situations."

I wasn't so sure about that.

My science officer looked at me. "Galvin, you and your Symbio-Poth combat force are team RED."

He pointed to a red-highlighted deck mid-way through the station. Just below, a yellow deck caught my eye, followed by a blue one beneath it. Higher up, but below Hardy's red decks, four decks highlighted in purple stood out.

Captain Wallace Ryder joined the discussion and pointed. "My team will be taking the BLUE deck."

"Mine is the YELLOW deck, in between the two of yours," Akari volunteered.

"And the Decks here?" I asked, gesturing to the four purple highlighted decks.

"Those are mine," Max said. "The Marines are team PURPLE."

Derrota nodded, "We suspect those purple Decks to be amongst the most important on the ship, other than the Queen's location."

Hardy's scratched and marred faceplate displayed an animation of one egg after another cracking open whereby hideous baby Krygians jumped out holding what looked like shredder rifles.

"I take it those four decks are something akin to a nursery?" I asked.

"More like a hatchery," Derrota corrected. "But suffice it to say—from some long past breeding frenzy—here lies the culmination of all that activity. For decades, the millions of incubating eggs here will be the nightmare the Alliance will face in mere months to come."

"Did you say millions?" I asked.

Derrota didn't bother clarifying. "Once Petty Officer 2nd Class Laramie has joined them, Sergeant Max and his squad will be dousing these four decks, the Krygian warriors, the eggs

—with their DDT/Fryzite sprayers. I expect a hostile, maternal-like reaction protecting the hatchery."

Max tapped at the dual metal tanks strapped to the back of his combat suit. "We'll do our jobs. We know the stakes if we fail."

"And these three Decks—Red, Yellow and Blue. Anything else you can tell us, Stephan?"

"Yes, Galvin. Within these three decks you will find the highest concentration of Krygians. We're talking many, many thousands."

My science officer stepped forward, clearing his throat. "That reminds me. As you all know, we've been working on the DDT/Fryzite compound—"

I felt my jaw clench, a dull ache spreading through my temples. Christ, not this again. We'd been over this plan so many times I could recite it backwards in my sleep. My eyes darted around the compartment, catching the barely concealed eye-rolls and stifled yawns of my crew.

"Stephan," I cut in, my voice sharper than intended, "we're all intimately familiar with the plan. Is there anything new to report?"

Derrota blinked, momentarily thrown off his stride. "Well, yes, Galvin. We've made some modifications to the—"

"Modifications?" Ryder interjected, his tone dripping with sarcasm. "Let me guess, you've tweaked the formula to smell like roses while it melts bug faces?"

I shot him a warning glance but couldn't entirely suppress a smirk. The tension in the compartment was palpable, a powder keg of frayed nerves and dark humor.

"Actually," Derrota pressed on, his face flushing, "we've encountered a significant problem with the compound's stability in zero-g environments."

That got everyone's attention. The room fell silent, the air suddenly thick with renewed anxiety.

"Dammit, Stephan," I growled, pinching the bridge of my nose. "We're not anticipating a zero-g environment. And why am I just hearing about this now?"

Max spoke up, his voice tight. "How bad is it? Are we looking at a minor hiccup or a full-blown shitstorm?"

Derrota's eyes darted nervously around our faces. "It's... complicated. The compound tends to separate in microgravity, potentially rendering it ineffective or worse, unpredictable."

"Unpredictable?" Akari echoed, her voice rising. "As in, oops, we accidentally gassed our own people unpredictable?"

A cacophony of voices erupted, each louder than the last. My headache was building behind my eyes.

"Enough!" I bellowed, silencing the chaos. "Stephan, you have ten minutes to decide if we need to scrap the deployment of Max and his PURPLE team."

"No, no... I don't need ten minutes. The odds of a sudden loss of gravity is very low. I shouldn't have even brought it up."

Akari, putting her attention back on the diagram, said, "Back to these Blue Decks, "Why is there such a concentration of the bugs there?"

"Let me guess," I said. "Those three decks have been set aside as breeding grounds. Where the Queen periodically makes an appearance and—"

"You're right about that, Galvin. But be aware... these Krygians will be agitated. Breeding is their sole mission in life, and they often die competing with each other for their few moments with the Queen. You show up, disrupting the anticipated appearance of the Queen—they'll be coming at you with a vengeance you couldn't even imagine."

I felt *Resilience* bank hard to starboard. Guilt nagged at me, knowing what Pristy was dealing with—four enemy warships hellbent on destroying this broken, cobbled-together warship. Right now, she was doing the impossible—the simple fact that the ship was still in one piece, was a testament to her tactical genius and exceptional leadership.

"We need to get things rolling," I said. "We're on borrowed time and the clock is ticking. Ms. Laramie, time for you to deploy." I gestured to the raised Quansporter platform.

Max helped her with her strapped-on tanks as she secured her helmet's faceplate. With a tagger holstered to her hip and a shredder slung over one shoulder, she stepped onto the nearest glowing Quansporter pad.

I hefted the crate, with over five thousand TAC-Bands inside, it was heavier than anticipated. Placing the crate down on its own pad, I turned to Aubrey.

I could see her eyes behind her helmet's smoked diamond glass faceplate.

"I guess this is it," she said nervously. "Can I ask you something, Captain? Before I'm whisked off to Bugsville?"

"Sure, anything."

"When we get out of this mess... get back to Earth. Take a girl out for a beer?"

I smiled. The odds of any of us getting out of this were close to zero. So I had no problem making that promise. "You name the place and the time, I'll be there."

I stepped down from the raised platform and joined the others.

"We'll be monitoring your helmet cam feed," Derrota said. "Are you ready?"

Petty Officer 2nd Class Laramie gave us a decisive nod of her head and a thumbs-up.

Derrota quansported her away.

Blunderton's voice from above cut through the compartment.

"Captain, priority communique coming in from Admiral Gomez and Empress Shawlee Tee."

Instantly, all conversation died. The StarPoint diagram on the halo display blinked out, replaced by a split feed view showing Gomez, apparently on Earth, and Empress Shawlee Tee on Weonan. Both wore expressions so grave it felt like a weight settling on my chest.

Admiral Gomez's steady voice carried a sense of urgency that filled the compartment. "Captain Quintos, we face an unprecedented crisis. Earth is currently under siege from multiple Krygian fleets. The scope of this assault is unlike anything we've seen before."

He paused, glancing to the side as if expecting an interruption.

"We've been monitoring their movements closely," I said, feeling the need to assure him we weren't entirely in the dark either.

"Upwards of forty Krygian vessels have broken through the outer space defenses and are advancing toward Earth as we speak," Gomez continued, his tone growing more exasperated. "The 2nd Fleet, in conjunction with the 5th and the 8th Fleets, managed to repel the first wave of attackers, but it came at a daunting cost."

Gomez took an extended breath, clearly fighting to keep his composure. "Phazon Pulsar defenses and Zero Entropy Deterrence Shields are already showing signs of critical overtaxation."

"There are backups, Sir. The three mobile Bastille Fortresses positioned near Jupiter—"

"Destroyed! Wiped out! Look... We've lost nearly a third of our combat-ready assets," Gomez continued, his annoyance no longer concealed. "Preliminary damage assessments suggest a 56% reduction in operational capacity across our orbital defense platforms and a complete loss of the Maraday Space Relay Station, which was critical in maintaining real-time communications with our ground forces."

"Damn it," I muttered under my breath. The Maraday Station was a linchpin in our defense network. Losing it was catastrophic.

"Additionally," Gomez pressed on, wrangling in his temper, "three plasma reactors on the Moon, key to our defense outposts there, have gone offline, likely due to targeted Krygian EMP strikes. The Krygian tactics are increasingly sophisticated. They've developed a type of oscillating plasma cannon that bypasses our energy shields more effectively than anticipated."

"Oscillating plasma cannons?" I echoed, frustration lacing my voice. "There has to be countermeasures we can implement."

Gomez ignored my statement and narrowed his eyes, clearly trying to maintain focus amidst the interruptions. "Our intelligence suggests the Krygian fleets are employing a dual-flank maneuver aimed at creating a choke point around the Van Allen belt, essentially trapping Earth's space capabilities. While U.S. Space Navy personnel have shown extraordinary resilience, morale is faltering. Add to the fact the disruption to our supply chains coming from that Intergalactic Freight Alliance Union's strike fiasco... we're not getting crucial supplies to where they are needed. Add to the fact medical units are overburdened, and needless to say patient Regrow Pods are at a premium."

Gomez held up a hand to silence me, his patience visibly thinning. "Captain, in light of these devastating developments, your vessel, what remains of your crew, might well be our last beacon of hope. Galvin, more than ever, we need your unique, um... capabilities to think out of the box to make something happen there at StarPoint Station while there is still an Earth for you to return to."

His words hit like a sledgehammer. The holographic display

cast a glow on the faces around me, eyes wide with that deer-caught-in-the-headlights look to them.

His looming sense of doom and disaster made it nearly impossible to concentrate—to break past the sheer magnitude of what was expected of us—of me.

"Understood, Admiral," I said, my voice steady despite the storm raging within me. "I won't let you down."

The air felt like it had been sucked out of the compartment. My crew—my family—these brave souls having already been sent on a suicide mission, now were being saddled with what? Saving fucking Earth too?

No one moved, no one dared to breathe.

Empress Shawlee Tee stepped forward next, her serene blue glow juxtaposed against the severity of her words. "Three Krygian fleets have taken up attack formations within Pleidian Weonan space and we expect a full-on assault within hours. Our attempts to reach Thine High Command have failed. Galvin... Morno may already be under siege."

She paused, locking eyes with me through the display. "Once again, so much has been placed onto your shoulders, Galvin. Knowing your ship is heavily damaged, I must plead with you to still find a way to strike a lethal blow to this Krygian Queen." She hesitated before continuing. "This bitch is clearly hell-bent on galaxy-wide dominion—stop her, Galvin. Stop her and drive a fucking stake through her heart."

The two feeds suddenly cut out, and we were left in stunned silence. The weight of Gomez and Shawlee's messages settled heavily over us.

Our mission was no longer just about killing Krygians and freeing hostages on StarPoint—it was about saving Earth and Weonan, maybe even Morno.

I turned to the others, their faces etched with a mix of dread and resolve. Max clutched the weapon he'd just been handed.

Hardy's faceplate was no longer a glowing deep blue—it was now black as the deep void beyond the ship's hull. Derrota steadied himself, his fingers making slow taps at his control board as if his mind was light years away.

"Alright," I said, my voice finding calm amid the storm. "You heard them. This isn't just a mission; this is the last hope for Earth, and probably the Alliance. Failure means the end of everything we know and love."

Max nodded, his eyes fierce. "Team Purple is ready, Captain. We'll do our part."

Chapter 40

Deep Space—Vicinity of StarPoint Station
USS Resilience

XO Gail Pristy

She stood at Tactical, her fingers dancing across the console with practiced precision, eyes darting between multiple halo displays. The weight of responsibility pressed down on her shoulders like a physical force, threatening to crush her resolve.

With intergalactic warfare, the vastness of space posed both daunting challenges and exhilarating opportunities. XO Gail Pristy was acutely aware that they were now plunged into the heart of extremely close-quarters combat. The enemy ships loomed, only miles apart, forcing the crew to make frantic split-second decisions as the stakes soared.

Advanced targeting systems and light-speed weapons still had their place, but in this immediate confrontation, tactical maneuvers took precedence.

Pristy's shoulders tensed as she surveyed the bridge. Her

fingers hovered over the tactical display, each potential move carrying life-or-death consequences. She drew a sharp breath, steeling herself for the decisions ahead.

Revolutionary systems such as NELLA, the most sophisticated ship's artificial intelligence Pristy had ever witnessed, added a crucial layer to their tactics, scrambling enemy weapon locks at pivotal moments. The XO would be navigating the urgency of this knife-fight scenario, aware that each move could dictate their survival. Victory now hinged on both luck and the resolve of her crew. Steeling herself for the chaos ahead, Pristy prepared to lead them through the intense fray.

"Shields down to 35%!" Ensign Blair Paxton's voice cut through the chaos, a hint of panic creeping into her usually steady tone.

Pristy gritted her teeth, her mind racing through tactical options. "NELLA, redirect power from non-essential systems to reinforce our port shield array. Mr. Grimes, prepare for a hard starboard turn on my mark."

"Aye, XO," Grimes replied, his hands hovering over the helm controls, sweat beading on his forehead.

BANG!

Multiple halo feeds flashed white as if simultaneously struck by a cattle prod. Pristy's body went rigid, realizing a plasma bolt had grazed the ship's Circadian Platform—close enough to the bridge that she heard *Resilience's* shields pop and sizzle like bacon in a scalding hot skillet. Then came a low rumble, sending tremors up through the deck plates—like delayed rolling thunder after the loud clap of a lightning strike. Breathless, Pristy stumbled back, catching herself on the edge of her console.

Crimson emergency lights flashed on and then continued to strobe on and off caught in a frenzied loop—as if unsure just how dire the situation truly was.

"Damage report!" she barked, her eyes never leaving her tactical display.

Lieutenant Blunderton's voice remained steady, despite the surge of adrenaline from their recent encounter. Incoming crew reports. "Hull breach on Deck 47, DeckGates enacted."

"We've lost a Phazon Pulsar battery... um, somewhere," Paxton said. "SWM crew will check on it when they have a spare minute."

Pristy cursed under her breath. Their offensive capabilities were dwindling by the minute. She tapped her console, bringing up a schematic of their remaining weapons systems. The rail cannons were all but spent, their spike munitions depleted to dangerously low levels. Their salvation lay in the Phazon Pulsars, but even those were failing faster than they could be repaired.

"NELLA, focus Phazon Pulsar fire on grid coordinates Alpha-7 of that nearest Krygian dreadnought," Pristy ordered. "Concentrate fire, let's punch through their shields."

The AI's serene voice contrasted sharply with the chaos around them...

Acknowledged, XO Pristy. Targeting Alpha-7.

Pristy watched a smaller tactical display hovering above her board—lances of energy erupting from *Resilience*, now hammering against the Krygian ship's aft shields. For a moment, it seemed as though they might break through, but the enemy vessel's defenses were holding.

"NELLA connect me to Chief LaSalle, do it now!"

Five seconds later, the Chief's baritone voice boomed down from above—Pristy flashed back to an 8-year-old version of herself, at Sunday school, and first hearing about Exodus 19:16-

19, As the sound of the trumpet grew louder and louder, Moses spoke, and the voice of God answered him.

"What is it, XO? Juggling rabid, wild boars down here."

Talk to me, Chief. How close are your team's efforts to getting those broadsides back online?"

LaSalle's voice came back, irritated. "We're working as fast as we can, XO. Power conduits were fried to hell and back. Give us ten more minutes."

"We don't have ten minutes, Chief," Pristy snapped, then immediately regretted her tone. "Just... do what you can. We need those cannons."

As if to emphasize her point, another impact rocked the ship. Pristy looked up to see one of the Krygian dreadnoughts looming large on the main halo display, its insectoid design somehow more menacing than ever.

"Grimes, evasive pattern Delta-3," she ordered. "Keep us out of their targeting solution."

The helmsman's hands flew over his controls, and *Resilience* banked hard, narrowly avoiding a barrage of plasma fire. Pristy felt her stomach lurch as the inertial dampeners struggled to compensate.

"XO," Blunderton called out, her voice tight with urgency. "The Varapin ships are changing formation. I think they're trying to box us in."

Pristy's mind raced. Why were the Varapin even still here? Captain Toe's betrayal had been blatant, having sided with the Krygians. But when Sonya had turned four of the eight Varapin missiles back toward that Krygian dreadnought, ripping it apart... the newly formed Varapin-Krygian alliance was now also fractured.

Now, caught in the crossfire, the remaining two Varapin dreadnoughts were getting pounded from both sides. Staying made absolutely no sense. They had nothing to gain and no allies left.

She pushed the thought aside, focusing on the immediate threat. "Ms. Paxton, tell me we've addressed recent hull breaches... that we're no longer venting atmosphere."

"Looks like we're buttoned up, for now, XO."

"Mr. Grimes, on my mark, I want you to cut all forward momentum and rotate us 180 degrees. We're going to slide right between those bastards."

"That's going to leave us exposed," Grimes warned, even as his fingers moved to input the commands.

"Not your job to question orders, Helmsman," Pristy countered, eyes locked onto the halo display.

Attempting to soften the sharpness of her words, she added, "It might just give us the opening we need."

She watched the tactical display, timing the movement of the enemy ships. The Krygian dreadnoughts moved in perfect synchronization, their maneuvers almost beautiful in their lethal precision. The Varapin vessels, on the other hand, were disjointed in their formation, their attacks focused solely on *Resilience*, as if clinging to the slim chance of preserving an alliance with the Krygian—proving their fealty. Maybe it was working... the fire between them seemed to have subsided. No doubt, by now, Toe had communicated with Krygian command, explaining the unfortunate, redirected missile mishap.

"Now, Mr. Grimes!" Pristy shouted.

Resilience pivoted on its axis, inertia carrying it backward between the closing jaws of the enemy formation. For a heart-stopping moment, Pristy thought they wouldn't make it. Then they were through, the enemy ships looming large on either side of them. This was the closest they had been to the enemy ships —undoubtedly, the closest they were ever going to get. Seeing them now, looming large and shadowy, it felt like one could almost reach out and touch them.

"NELLA, all Phazon Pulsars, concentrate fire into the most vulnerable shield locations!" Pristy commanded. "And whatever rail spikes we have left in reserves, now's the time to use them. I want you to rip those motherfuckers a new asshole."

Weapons fire lanced out from *Resilience* in all directions, the ship's Phazon Pulsars emitting bolts of brilliant blue plasma that sliced through the darkness of space. Pristy's breath caught in her throat as she watched the barrage of energy converge on the two Krygian dreadnoughts flanking their vessel.

The portside Krygian warship, significantly larger than the starboard vessel, was instantly enveloped in a cascade of light. Its shields flared a vivid violet under the concentrated assault. The once impenetrable barrier shone brilliantly, like a second sun, illuminating the void around it. Bolts of plasma smashed into her shields, sending ripples across its surface as if it were a pond being pelted with stones. The Krygian's defensive barrier wavered, thin lines of energy cracking under the relentless barrage.

For a heartbeat, the shields seemed to hold, then buckled, fissures forming like spiderwebs across its radiant surface. Each impact grew more intense, more desperate, as *Resilience's* firepower sought to break through the final defenses. Pristy could barely breathe, her gaze fixed on the tactical display. "Come on, come on," she murmured, hands tightening into fists.

Then, with the deafening silence only space could offer, the portside Krygian ship's shields collapsed. The void left by the dissolved shield erupted into cascading sparks as *Resilience's* energy beams incised through the unprotected hull of the dreadnought, carving deep, sizzling gashes into its once-formidable armor. The enemy ship twisted like a desperately wounded beast, trailing debris and uncontrolled bursts of atmosphere into the cold expanse.

But the portside vessel did not fall. Instead, it seemed to roar back to life, its remaining weapons systems firing with renewed vigor. Plasma beams lanced out, slamming into *Resilience's* portside with terrifying force. *Resilience* shuddered violently, her own shields flaring and buckling under the intense assault.

Hull breaches on Deck 28, Deck 57, Deck 92...

"Incoming plasma fire causing substantial damage where shields have been weakened!" Paxton yelled, her voice almost drowned out by the klaxon blaring around them.

Pristy's eyes flicked to the secondary displays. Blazing streams of enemy plasma were racing back toward them from that same portside—larger and more intense—the beams intent on tearing through what little remained of *Resilience's* shields. "Brace yourselves!" she shouted, hoping the crew was already prepared.

The incoming plasma hit like a freight train. The remaining shields absorbed the initial impacts but were soon overwhelmed. Panels burst into showers of sparks around the bridge, and the ship shuddered violently, sending Pristy to her knees.

Grimes barked a string of curses, his hands moving with instinctive speed across his board as he battled to keep the ship from careening into one of the enemy ships.

Port shields at critical levels.

NELLA's voice was barely audible over the din.

Meanwhile, the smaller starboard Krygian ship hadn't been idle. While *Resilience* had focused its initial barrage on the portside vessel, this dreadnought had been maneuvering into a more advantageous firing position. Its shields flared in a desperate attempt to fend off the partial attack it received. Flashes of violent white and blue rippled across its shimmering barrier, the energy field visibly straining under the immense pressure.

Pristy's fingers dug into the edge of her console as she watched the starboard enemy ship's defenses fluctuate. Their shields, however, held—allowing the dreadnought to retaliate.

"XO they're closing in—in twenty seconds, we won't have an escape vector!" Grimes shouted as the starboard Krygian ship surged forward.

Chapter 41

Pristy caught sight of the vessel's plasma turrets glowing with unused, destructive potential.

In unison, the two Krygian dreadnoughts unleashed their fury. The portside ship, despite its damage, continued its relentless assault from the left, while the starboard vessel targeted *Resilience's* right flank.

They rained plasma beams and rail spike rounds upon *Resilience* from both sides. The hull groaned beneath the barrage. Emergency lights flickered, their intermittent glow barely piercing through the acrid haze. Burning circuits filled the bridge with a harsh scent, while dark smoke billowed, stinging eyes and blurring vision.

"Shields down to 35%!" Ensign Blair Paxton cried out, her voice a lifeline through the chaos. "The starboard ship is targeting our Off-Worlders!"

Desperation clawed at Pristy's mind, but she pushed it down. "NELLA, redirect all available power to reinforce our port and starboard shields," she commanded. "We've got to hold it together a little longer!"

The AI's response was immediate...

Acknowledged, XO Pristy. Redirecting power.

The renewed assault thudded against the shields like relentless waves crashing against a crumbling seawall. Pristy watched in dismay as energy reserves were rapidly being depleted, *Resilience* now even more of a fragile bastion against the storm of Krygian wrath.

"Ensign Paxton! Get me an update on those roadside cannons!" she demanded, her voice hoarse with urgency.

Seconds later Chief LaSalle's voice crackled over the PA, overlaid with the sounds of frantic activity in the background. "We're almost ready to fire them up, XO. Need just a few more minutes."

"We don't have a few more minutes!" Pristy shot back, her eyes darting between the displays. "We have a portside ship pressing its attack, while a starboard warship is trying to take out our means of propulsion!"

Her desperate gambit seemed to have failed. Despite bringing substantial concentrated fire, the Krygian shields flared back to life, their energy reserves evidently more robust than anticipated. Both enemy warships now bore down on *Resilience* with unyielding fervor, each hammering away from their respective sides.

Pristy could see their respective hulls—towering behemoths like two closing-in walls obscuring the vastness of space beyond. The Krygian dreadnoughts loomed impossibly large, their surfaces a dizzying maze of alien technology. Weapon bays gaped like hungry maws, bristling with undiminished firepower. Massive junction boxes studded the hull, interconnected by a web of conduits that pulsed with barely contained energy. Power generators protruded, their casings etched with strange, angular glyphs.

Innumerable ducts, exhaust channels, and pipelines crisscrossed the ships' exteriors, some venting superheated plasma in eerie, silent plumes. Pristy's eyes traced the contours of armored plates, noting the pockmarks of previous battles and the seamless integration of repair nanites still at work. Sensor arrays protruded at irregular intervals, their dishes and antennae swiveling in constant vigil.

As her gaze swept across the hull of the portside dreadnought, something caught her eye. Tiny spews of yellow mist escaped from several locations near what appeared to be a main power coupling. Pristy's brow furrowed as she quickly checked her readings. Her eyes widened. Radiation. One of the port-side enemy ship's reactors had been damaged, perhaps even breached.

The tactical displays painted a grim picture, but they paled in comparison to the overwhelming reality before her eyes. *Resilience* was on the brink, their remaining offensive capabilities dwindling to almost nothing against these technological marvels of destruction. Yet, that small yellow mist offered a glimmer of hope.

"We're not done yet," she muttered, eyes narrowing. "NELLA, analyze the radiation leak on that portside dreadnought. I want a targeting solution for our portside Phazon Pulsars."

Analyzing radiation patterns. Targeting solution ready, XO Pristy.

Energy coursed through the ship, the familiar hum of power surging back as NELLA targeted the weak points Pristy had identified. The Phazon Pulsars fired, lancing out brilliant bolts of energy. Each shot was a calculated effort, focusing on the areas around the radiation leaks on the portside dreadnought.

For a moment, it worked. The portside ship reeled under

the renewed assault, its advance stalling as it tried to compensate for the barrage. Plumes of sparks fountained out from her damaged hull, secondary explosions erupting silently in the vacuum of space. All the while, the starboard vessel, momentarily forgotten, was now pressing its attack, *Resilience's* shields flickering but holding.

The respite didn't last. The Krygians adapted with alarming speed. Despite its damage, the portside ship unleashed a barrage of return fire. Meanwhile, the starboard vessel slipped aft but looked to be angling for a renewed flanking maneuver on *Resilience.*

"We're running out of time," Grimes muttered, his voice cracking under the strain. "Fricken starboard ship will soon be in a perfect position to take another shot at our Off-Worlders!"

Chief LaSalle's voice from above caught her off guard...

No guarantees, XO... but those two broadside cannons, they're being powered up and seem to be responsive.

NELLA cut him off...

Targeting solutions locked, XO. Ready to fire on your command.

"Not yet! Pristy replied. Helm, get us the hell away from these two dreads!"

"On it, XO... just know, we'll be back in the line of fire of the two Varapin ships."

"We'll deal with them later. For now, we need to separate ourselves from the Krygians."

Breath held, eyes locked, all her concentration was on the

primary halo display. Grimes' skill at the helm was pure perfection as he fired up all four of the Off-Worlders powerplants to their full capacity. After a moment's hesitation, *Resilience* rocketed forward, G-forces compelling everyone to grab onto something—anything—to stabilize themselves. With what seemed like inches to spare, *Resilience* narrowly scraped past the two Krygian ships out into open space.

"Turn us about, Helm... we'll still need a line-of-sight firing solution on one or both ships!"

"Aye, XO..." he managed, his words coming out strained. "I can give you one... but this thing's like turning an oil tanker in wet concrete."

She watched... now noticing the two Varapin ships angling for their own best firing solutions. Shit!

Pristy's tactical board quietly pinged. Her console's logistical display showed she had a target lock and a glowing green vector between *Resilience* and the smaller of the two dreadnoughts.

Without hesitation, Pristy gave the order. "Fire starboard broadside cannon! NELLA! Maintain Phazon Pulsar's focused on the other ship's reactor leak!"

It was as if a kettledrum right there on the bridge was being struck...

BOOM! BOOM! BOOM!

The bowlers were colossal. The largest onboard bots had to move them from the armory stores. Like immense bowling balls, each had strategically placed circular holes around their circumference. These holes served as dispersal channels for white-hot magnesium scatter frags, which weakened enemy hull armor a nanosecond before impact. It was old tech, relatively speaking, but still remarkably effective.

Resilience shuddered as the massive broadside cannon discharged—its bowler payloads streaking across the void like fiery meteorites toward the smaller of the two Krygian dreadnoughts, intent on destruction.

The impacts were awe-inspiring and visceral—each shot, a driving spine-snapping force. The enemy's defensive shields immediately buckled under the assault. Then came the explosions. Massive, broiling balls of fire engulfed one of the two remaining Krygian warships, obscuring it completely from view.

Then, as deep space reclaimed its frigid breathless dominance, little remained of the ship—a few fragmented sections of the hull, hot, amber-glowing scraps of the propulsion system.

The bridgecrew cheered—Grimes punched a fist into the air, Paxton slapped a hand down onto her station, while Blunderton stood raising her arms over her head as if calling a touchdown at the closing bell of the Super Bowl. Lucy squawked as if somehow understanding the significance of the moment.

The final Krygian warship was on the move. A series of explosions rippled across its surface as concentrated Phazon fire found its mark, homing in on radiation leaks. It suddenly veered off course, its damaged flank coming more into view. The vessel was in serious trouble, but not enough to end its threat entirely.

"The ship's lost much of its propulsion capabilities!" Paxton announced.

"NELLA, status report on that dreadnought."

Krygian enemy vessel is experiencing cascading reactor failure. Probability of imminent destruction: 87.3%.

In the distance, the ship was indeed floundering, venting atmosphere and radiation in equal measure.

"Keep targeting its reactor, NELLA," she said, only now bringing her attention back to the two Varapin warships. That confrontation still loomed, but now there was a glimmer of hope.

That hope was short-lived.

"Multiple impacts!" Paxton cried out. "Shields failing!"

The bridge rocked violently, consoles at the back of the bridge erupting in showers of sparks. Pristy was thrown from her feet, her head striking the edge of the tactical station as she fell. She tasted blood, her vision swimming as she struggled to stand.

"Report!" she managed to croak out.

"Shields are down!" Paxton's voice was barely audible over the blaring alarms. "We've got more hull breaches on multiple decks. DeckGates aren't keeping up with the loss of atmosphere."

Pristy hauled herself back to her station, ignoring the warm trickle of blood running down her face. The tactical display was a mess of red indicators, systems failing across the ship. But amidst the chaos, one indicator caught her eye.

"What the hell hit us?" She barked.

"Three Varapin ghost drones—snuck in under our sensors," Paxton said. "Won't happen again... NELLA's on it."

Ms. Blunderton, track down Chief LaSalle, I need to know if we still have our two broadside cannons available."

"Only the starboard cannon is online, XO!" the Chief's voice boomed down from above. "And you've got two shots, maybe three if we're lucky. Make 'em count!"

A grim line spread across Pristy's lips. It wasn't much, but it was something. She began inputting targeting coordinates, her mind racing through potential strategies.

"Mr. Grimes, get us moving. Do whatever you can—taunt them—bring them closer to one another."

"Roger that, XO... I'll get you the firing solutions you need. Just give me some time."

Just then, movement on one of the halo displays caught her attention. Her heart skipped a beat as she recognized the feed from Aubrey's helmet cam suddenly springing to life.

"Ms. Blunderton, patch in Petty Officer 2nd Class Aubrey's audio feed." Pristy shifted her focus between the Varapin warships and Aubrey Laramie.

The grainy, slightly distorted image on the display suddenly sharpened, revealing a vast, dimly lit space within StarPoint Station. Massive crossbeam girders arched overhead, barely visible in the gloom. Pristy's breath caught as she realized what she was seeing—Aubrey stood in the midst of a sea of people—the hostages.

"Ms. Blunderton, can you enhance the audio?" Pristy asked, her eyes fixed on the scene unfolding before her.

"On it, XO," Blunderton replied, her fingers tapping at her console.

The soft murmur of hushed voices filled the bridge, growing in volume and excitement as the hostages became aware of Aubrey's helmeted combat suit presence. Pristy could see the hope spreading through the crowd like wildfire, faces lighting up with the possibility of rescue.

Aubrey's voice came through, urgent and low, "Please, everyone, you need to stay quiet. We can't alert the Krygian guards."

But it was too late. The buzz of excitement was already too loud, too obvious. Pristy watched as Aubrey, realizing the futility of maintaining silence, quickly changed tactics. She bent down over a crate of some kind, grabbing handfuls of what Pristy recognized as TAC-Bands.

"Hurry, pass these out!" Aubrey's voice was clear now, a mix of determination and barely contained panic. "Put them on... HURRY!"

Pristy's mind raced. The assault mission was already underway. Shit! Shit! Shit!

A violent tremor shook the bridge as if to emphasize their precarious situation. The Varapin dreadnoughts were bearing down on them, her brief moment of distraction potentially costing *Resilience* dearly.

"Grimes, status!" Pristy barked, torn between watching Aubrey's feed and focusing on their immediate peril.

"Still following orders, it's a cat and mouse game with two cats and one mouse. They haven't moved any closer to each other yet."

Pristy's mind raced. "I need that firing solution, helmsman. Get it done!"

She needed to buy time, to give Aubrey and the hostages a fighting chance.

"XO! They're paired up, side-by-side, not sure how long they—"

"Alright, people, this is it," Pristy announced, her voice steady despite the chaos. "Grimes, on my mark, execute a hard roll to port. We're going to bring our starboard broadside to bear. Paxton, divert all remaining shield power to protect that flank. If this works, shields will be less of a worry."

A series of acknowledgments rang out across the bridge. Pristy took a deep breath, her eyes flicking once more to Aubrey's feed. The hostages were now a flurry of activity, TAC-Bands being passed from hand to hand, a glimmer of hope in a sea of fear.

"Mark!"

As *Resilience* began its roll, Pristy silently prayed. For Aubrey, for the hostages, for her crew. The fate of thousands now hung in the balance, and the next few moments would determine everything.

Chapter 42

StarPoint Station

Petty Officer 2nd Class Aubrey Laramie

Aubrey Laramie's heart thundered in her chest, the sound amplified within the confines of her combat helmet. The massive hold of StarPoint Station stretched before her, a cavernous space teeming with countless bodies. Her HUD flickered, adjusting to the dim light, revealing a sea of desperate faces. She adjusted the strap of her shouldered shredder.

This is it, Laramie. Don't screw it up.

With the crate of TAC-Bands on the deck beside her, she took a step forward. The nearest hostages recoiled seeing her in her kitted-up combat suit, eyes wide with fear and confusion. Aubrey's throat tightened, but she forced herself to speak.

"It's okay... I'm here to help," she said, her voice steady despite the tremor in her hands. "These TAC-Bands are your ticket out of here. Put them on, and we can get you to safety."

For a moment, no one moved. Then, like a dam breaking, they surged forward.

Hands reached out, grasping and clawing. Aubrey struggled to maintain her footing as bodies pressed in from all sides. Her HUD flashed warnings of increasing pressure on her suit. Grabbing handfuls herself, she distributed the TAC-Bands as quickly as she could but wondered if it was fast enough. So much depended on this aspect of the mission—the other teams were waiting—waiting on her.

"Please, stay calm!" she shouted, her voice lost in the growing cacophony. "There's enough for everyone!"

A jolt ran through her as someone yanked hard on her shredder. Aubrey stumbled, falling to one knee. Panic flared in her chest as the crowd threatened to overwhelm her.

Get up! GET UP!

She scrambled to her feet, adrenaline surging. The crate was half empty now, TAC-Bands disappearing into the crowd. Aubrey's eyes darted around, taking in details her brain barely had time to process.

Most of the faces were human, etched with fear and desperation. But here and there, alien features stood out - translucent skin, extra eyes, mandibles clicking with anxiety. All of them reaching, grasping, pushing.

Aubrey's breath came in short gasps, the inside of her helmet fogging slightly. The crush of bodies intensified, and for a moment, she feared she might be pulled under.

This wasn't supposed to happen. It wasn't supposed to be like this.

Captain Quintos' voice crackled in her ear, a lifeline in the chaos. "Laramie, status report."

"Sir," she managed, relief flooding through her at the sound of his voice. "TAC-Bands are being distributed, but the situation is... volatile."

Understatement of the century, Aubrey.

"Understood," Quintos replied, his tone steady. "Hardy's sensors show Krygian guards have been alerted. We need you to secure the entrance. Can you make it there?"

Aubrey's heart skipped a beat. She wanted to say no, to beg for extraction. Instead, she heard herself answer, "Yes, Sir. On my way."

She began to push through the crowd, her movements hampered by the press of bodies. Every step was a struggle, fear and determination warring within her.

You're going to die here, a traitorous voice whispered in her mind. *Alone in this godforsaken hold.*

Aubrey gritted her teeth, shoving the thought aside. But as she fought her way forward, another realization hit her. If these were her last moments, there was something she needed to say.

"Captain," she began, her voice hesitant. "I... there's something I need to tell you."

"Save it for when you're back on *Resilience*, Laramie," Quintos cut in. "That's an order."

Irritation flared as Aubrey forced back a snippy retort. It was as if he knew what she was going to say. She'd always liked their witty quips, the type of banter that few others were afforded on the ship.

She was almost to the entrance now, the massive hatch looming before her. Aubrey readied her weapon, pushing down the fear that threatened to overwhelm her.

Focus, dammit. You've got a job to do.

"Derrota's starting the quansport process," Quintos informed her. "Hold that position as long as you can."

"Copy that," Aubrey replied, her voice steadier than she felt.

The hatch began to open with a grinding screech. Aubrey's finger tightened on the trigger, her breath catching in her throat.

Five towering Krygian guards burst through the opening,

their insectoid features twisted in alien fury. Plasma weapons hummed to life in their clawed hands.

Time seemed to slow. Aubrey's training kicked in, her body moving almost of its own accord. She fired, the shredder bucking in her hands. The first guard fell, green ichor spraying from multiple wounds.

But the others were already returning fire. Aubrey dove to the side, narrowly avoiding a blast of searing plasma. She rolled, came up firing, and was rewarded with another guard's shriek of pain.

All around her, chaos erupted. Hostages screamed, some fleeing, others caught in the crossfire. Aubrey's HUD flashed with warnings, tracking multiple threats.

She kept moving, knowing that to stay still was to die. Her heart pounded, blood rushing in her ears. Each breath felt like it might be her last.

A plasma bolt sizzled past her head, close enough that she felt the heat through her suit. Aubrey returned fire, her shots finding their mark in another guard's thorax.

The entrance was a killing field now, bodies—both human and alien—littering the deck.

Aubrey's mind raced, searching for a way out, a way to turn the tide. But as she watched another group of hostages fall to Krygian fire, a cold realization settled in her gut.

We're not going to make it.

The thought paralyzed her for a split second—a split second too long. A plasma bolt caught her in the shoulder, the impact spinning her around. Aubrey stumbled, her vision blurring.

She could hear Quintos shouting in her ear, but the words were lost in a haze of pain and fear. As she struggled to regain her footing, Aubrey saw another wave of Krygian guards pouring through the entrance.

USS Resilience

This is it, she thought, raising her weapon one last time. *This is where it ends.*

Chapter 43

Deep Space—Vicinity of StarPoint Station
USS Resilience

Captain Galvin Quintos

The compartment was a hive of frenetic activity. Each of the team members was nervously readying for quansport—adjusting straps, checking weapons, and ensuring HUD readout levels were at their optimum, while comms and NELLA interfaces were properly functioning.

With my own suit and helmet buttoned up, I stood amongst the mayhem, eyes locked onto the halo display where Aubrey's erratic helmet feed provided an all-too-real view of what she was up against. Thus far, her keen instincts and raw athleticism had kept her alive as she dove and rolled, exchanging fire with the growing number of Krygian guards. Around her, flashes of energy—characteristic of someone being quansported out of the hold—lent credence to the brave and selfless operation she had undertaken. If she survived the day, I'd make sure she'd receive a commendation. Unfortunately, the odds of her—or any of us—surviving the next few hours were low.

I'd been keeping an eye on *Resilience's* bridge feed—Pristy and her crew doing the impossible, not only keeping the enemy assets at bay but taking half of them off the chessboard in the process. But, like Aubrey's situation, time was not on my XO's side.

"We need to move up our deployment timelines."

Derrota, standing at the control console on the right, glanced my way, then did a double-take. "Galvin, you are aware I am in the process of quansporting hostages, hundreds of hostages... landing them within predetermined areas on the Symbio Deck... the system—NELLA—is operating at maximum capacity. There is only so much bandwidth—" He cut himself off.

Seeing my expression illuminated within my helmet, and knowing me as he does, he saw that we had entered a desperate moment in time.

"What do you need me to do, Galvin?" he said.

I glanced about the Quansporter compartment. I took in Hardy, Akari James, Wallace Ryder, Max, and his Marines.

"Hardy, you're up. Hop up onto that platform and prepare to quansport. It's time you hunt down that bitch of a queen. Sergeant Dryer, team Purple is up next."

Hardy strode confidently forward, stepped up onto the platform, and found a pad to occupy. In a rapid, impressive, display of chrome panels snapping open, his shoulder, forearm, and upper thigh, Phazon Pulsar weaponry locked into position. Each little turret-mounted cannon pivoted independently as if already attempting to acquire a target lock.

Derrota glanced up at the towering killer robot. It was time to send the ChronoBot into what would be nothing less than a nightmarish hellscape—a place I doubted he'd ever return from.

Right before quansporting away, I said, "God's speed my friend."

And then, in a series of blocky flashes of light, Hardy was gone.

Hardy arrived into total darkness. Reaching out with sensor scans he wondered if the good science officer had inadvertently quansported him into a StarPoint broom closet, or maybe a bathroom—but no brooms, no toilets.

Noting the sub-zero temperature and the large bags of frozen vegetables, boxes of frozen meat (chicken breasts, beef cuts, fish fillets), tubs of ice cream in various flavors, frozen pastry, bread dough, and bulk packages of frozen French fries—he realized he was standing inside a large walk-in freezer, undoubtedly somewhere within a station galley. He couldn't help but think, *so this is how the Krygians fatten up the hostages before they eat them.*

The stainless-steel door was latched from the outside, but safety regulations certainly required an emergency release for the occasional kitchen help for those who might find themselves trapped. Then he saw it: **PULL DOWN TO RELEASE LOCK.**

He pulled down on the lever, cleverly hidden in plain sight. The door swung open, and he stepped out—frosty air billowing around him. The galley was dim, but not as dark as the freezer's interior. Hardy scanned the immediate area for Krygians. He'd discovered during previous encounters that these oversized, praying mantis-like aliens had distinctive bio-signatures. While their insectoid forms appeared identical to the naked eye, Hardy's advanced sensors could detect the unique DNA makeup within their genus. Whether alive or dead, their signatures would stand out. Nearby, hundreds of active Krygian signatures lit up his sensors. Hardy knew it wouldn't be long before all hell broke loose.

Standing perfectly still, Hardy had yet to move from his position in front of the big freezer unit. While charging into the chaos with guns blazing might be tempting, it would likely give the queen a chance to slip away. Unfortunately, as with back on the ship, Hardy was still not picking up on the queen's distinct bio-signature.

Hardy's sensors hummed, processing the data from his surroundings. A cluster of Krygian biosignatures pulsed like a malevolent heartbeat, their concentration suggesting either a gathering or, more likely, a guard detail. The queen's unique signature remained frustratingly elusive, but this grouping held promise.

With a flicker of his faceplate, Hardy made a gesture reminiscent of a human crossing themselves in church—a touch of gallows humor before the storm. He stepped out of the galley, chrome feet silent against the deck plating, each movement a calculated risk.

The reaction was instantaneous and overwhelming.

Krygians emerged from hidden alcoves and shadowy recesses, their chitinous forms turning a nightmare into a hellish reality. Compound eyes flashed with alien fury, mandibles clicking in a cacophony of hunger and rage. Hardy had mere nanoseconds to process the onslaught before it crashed over him like a tsunami of chitin and hatred.

The first wave hit with the force of a runaway freight train. Hardy's actuators whined in protest as insectoid limbs scrabbled for purchase on his chrome surface. Claws raked ineffectually against his armor, but the sheer weight of numbers threatened to overwhelm even his formidable strength.

More Krygians piled on, their alien bodies forming a living, writhing cocoon around the ChronoBot. Hardy's world became a claustrophobic hell of gnashing mandibles and stabbing limbs. He felt the pressure building, his internal systems flashing warnings as the mass of alien bodies threatened to crush him.

Good luck with that, Hardy mused, a flicker of amusement cutting through the chaos. The Krygians' attempts to chew through his chrome-plated appendages were as futile as gnawing on titanium. Still, the sheer mass of their assault was cause for concern.

Buried beneath the insectoid avalanche, Hardy's processors raced. He hadn't even had the chance to fire a single plasma bolt, but that was about to change. Deep within his core, power surged through conduits and circuitry. Hardy's actuators and servos—marvels of engineering pushed beyond their limits—roared to life.

With a sound like tearing metal, Hardy erupted from the depths of the Krygian pile. Alien bodies flew in all directions, carapaces cracking under the strain. The ChronoBot rose like an avenging metallic God, chrome limbs flashing in the harsh lighting.

Hardy's five plasma cannons, previously dormant, swiveled with lethal precision. Target locks flashed across his HUD, each accompanied by a soft ping that was quickly drowned out by the roar of unleashed energy.

The confined space of the corridor became an inferno of superheated plasma. Bolts of destructive energy lanced out in all directions, finding their marks with unerring accuracy. The air filled with the acrid stench of burning chitin and the unholy screams of dying Krygians.

Dismembered limbs cartwheeled through the air, trailing wisps of smoke and vibrant ichor. Diamond-shaped heads, their compound eyes wide with alien terror, separated from bodies with surgical precision. For a fraction of a second, those eyes remained aware, witnessing their own demise before the neural connections severed completely.

Hardy stood at the epicenter of the carnage, his chrome form unmarred save for a few new scratch marks. Around him, the deck was littered with the twitching remains of his attackers. Some still moved, their alien physiology refusing to accept defeat even as life fled their broken forms.

The silence that followed was deafening, broken only by the soft hum of Hardy's internal cooling systems and the occasional pop of superheated chitin. The ChronoBot's sensors swept the area, cataloging the destruction and searching for any remaining threats.

Not far away, scores of Krygians were reforming, assembling, and undoubtedly strategizing for their next attack. Hardy couldn't care less about what they were scheming. He had his own mission, one that involved tracking down that Krygian Queen and snuffing out her life.

Chapter 44

Deep Space—Vicinity of StarPoint Station
USS Resilience

Captain Galvin Quintos

Waiting. It occurred to me, standing there on the Quansporter pad, that in a moment, not only my disassembled molecules would be zipping across space/time, ending up within StarPoint Station, but so were the dozens of Symbio-Poths who'd be joining me. The system was already heavily burdened, currently moving scores of hostages from the station's prison-like hold. What were the odds that I would show up ready for battle as a Frankenstein monster—a commingled mess of Symbio and human parts?

Derrota looked up from behind the console, offering up a sympathetic smile. "When you're ready..."

"Ready as I'll ever be."

. . .

I let the expected wave of vertigo and nausea pass, taking in my surroundings. Energetic quansport arrivals flashed around me like paparazzi cameras at a premiere, each burst lighting up the air for several moments before fading, leaving a Symbio-Poth form in its wake.

Above, I took in a domed blue sky and a bright yellow Sun—it looked so real, it was hard to imagine I was anywhere but back on Earth. I stood within a vast, open space... like a sprawling college quad where students could lounge but on a much larger scale. Acres upon acres of faux-rolling green lawns stretched out. Under different circumstances, this park-like deck—one of three within StarPoint—would have been the perfect spot to lay down for a nap or reflect on life and purpose.

My comms crackled, "Uncle Galvin... you'll have to tell the Symbios what to do. It's not like they've been to Army combat school, or whatever it's called."

"Um... you mean Army basic training?"

"Whatever!" my niece said, exasperated. "Your presence has been noticed, you have bugs inbound—they're on the move!"

The scene was a strange juxtaposition of the ancient and ultra-modern—StarPoint, the pinnacle of deep-space technology—now hosting nearly a hundred Symbio-Poths dressed in garments from 2,000 years ago."

Muscular, bare-chested gladiators—their taut muscles glistening with sweat under that Sun-like orb high above. Roman guardsmen scurried into position, clad in maroon tunics, their crested gold helmets reflecting the pulsating energy of this soon-to-be battlefield.

Stubby swords were gripped tightly, poised for action. Senators and diplomats—both female and male—added an air of sophistication, draped in elegant, flowing tunics, some brandishing ornate swords. In contrast, others wielded advanced shredder weapons, their expressions a mix of determination and eagerness. The chaotic clamor was building anticipation as this eclectic ensemble prepared for battle, ready to clash with the Krygian forces—which I knew easily outnumbered us 10 to 1.

I took in the myriad HUD readouts and saw that Derrota was listed as being logged into the open channel.

"Stephan... got a question for you."

"A little busy right now, Galvin. Can it wait?"

I ignored the polite rebuke. "Why is this wide-open deck devoid of bugs? I don't see a Krygian in sight—although Sonya says they're readying to attack."

"Um... if the Krygians use pheromones for communication, which I suspect they do, the open air of the park-like setting could disperse these chemical signals too fast, making it an ineffective environment. Add to that, their insectoid nature will probably drive them toward dark, close quarters and physical proximity. The open space could feel both psychologically uncomfortable, even vulnerable."

"Works for me, I'll take any advantage offered."

I angled my head, listening. "What the hell..."

It was distant but there, perhaps a hull breach—the sound of high-pitched air being sucked out of the station. Becoming louder, I realized it was coming from multiple directions and it wasn't escaping atmosphere—it was more like... hissing.

The open channel was a constant drone of back-and-forth chatter. Derrota and Sonya were immersed in quansport-related tech talk that I wasn't the least bit interested in. Wallace Ryder, on the deck mirroring this one below, was barking orders to his Symbio-Poth regiment, while Akari James explained—presumably to a Symbio—how to change the plasma output level on a shredder.

Sergeant Max and his team all seemed to be talking at once, over each other. They were working on a plan to retrieve Petty Officer 2nd Class Aubrey Laramie—apparently, her bio-readings were no longer active. It was one more potential death among the countless losses of the last few days, each one feeling like a fist clenching my heart. This was not the time to mourn—this was the time for battle.

They approached en masse. Was this what it had been like during medieval times? Off on the horizon a long line of tightly packed forms moving forward as if to a silent drumbeat. These invaders weren't men and boys fighting for their homeland; they were relentless, insectoid aliens driven by a single purpose: to annihilate any lifeform obstructing their path to total dominance within the galaxy.

The hissing was getting louder. Both Ryder and Akari were talking about it—and they too were seeing what I was seeing—a continuing march forward of thousands of Krygian warriors—only now, their angular elongated diamond-shaped heads were taking shape in the distance—long spindly legs and scissoring mandibles.

I said the words before I had time to filter my thoughts, "We're going to die... we're all going to die here."

The open channel suddenly went eerily silent.

Then Ryder broke the tension, "I want to personally thank you for such an inspirational pep talk, Galvin. We can now go into battle knowing we have the full confidence of our leader."

I tuned out Ryder and everyone else who had joined in, their sarcasm piling on.

"Quiet everyone," I said.

Comms went still.

"Sonya, I need you to tell me if something is possible. Not that it will be difficult or unethical, just if you can do it and do it now."

"No way. Unless you tell me first..."
"Sonya!"
"Fine! What is it?"

"All those Roman Empire chariots being stored—hanging high overhead on some kind of track. And all those Symbio-Poth teams of horses—"

Everyone started talking on top of each other at the same time all over again.

But one voice came through the clearest, "That's genius!" Her voice cut through the chaos. "I've been monitoring the feeds. You were right. This would've been a massacre!"

"What do you need to do—"

"Shut up and let me think. I've got a few Symbios in reserve. They'll assist with logistics. Listen... the chariots and horses need activation. Get their harnesses on and secure everything together."

The line of greenish-brown Krygians was getting closer by the second.

"Sonya, look if there's no time for this—"

I heard her rapid breathing; she was running, barking orders to—I'm guessing, those Symbios kept in reserves. "I need ten minutes before you start seeing results. Stay alive, do whatever you can until then."

She was now barking off orders, some of which seemed to be toward Derrota, who was going to have the complex job of quansporting 'whatever' Sonya would be piecing together within that Symbio Deck.

"You get that Wallace... Akari?" I asked. "Let's not tempt fate by playing David against Goliath. I don't care if you have to run like toddlers playing hide and seek at a birthday party, it's time we buy Sonya, and us, a little time."

My regiment of Symbio-Poths was motionless. All eyes were on me. Hell, I'd yet to give them even one command.

"No one fights until I say so. You understand me?"

Heads nodded.

"For ten, maybe fifteen minutes, we'll run, dodge, and hide—

though that's tough in an open space like this. But we're going to stay alive and evade. If you're armed with a shredder, take shots when you can, bring down a few bugs, and keep moving. Leave pride and bravado behind. Got it?"

Heads nodded.

The line of Krygians continued making their slow march forward. Why hadn't they charged, or swarmed, or whatever insectile creatures like these normally do?

"Talk to me, Stephan," I called out, "why are these Krygians keeping their distance? Why haven't they charged us yet?"

A thumbnail-sized feed came alive within my HUD showing a distracted-looking Derrota. Sounding exasperated, he said "I am not there, Galvin. How should I know?"

I could hear him pause, the tapping of fingers upon his board as he considered something. "It's possible the Krygians are sensing something they don't fully understand," he replied.

His brows furrowed in concentration. "I suspect it's related to the pheromones we spoke of earlier."

"Okay... pheromones," I echoed, intrigued.

"Yes," Derrota continued. "Krygians communicate using millions of pheromone variations. I've verified that here in these last few minutes. They're sensitive to the slightest changes in their environment, particularly when it comes to potential threats. The Symbio-Poths could be emitting a unique... um, smell. I've noted that their body odor, which carry hints of plasticky ozone and chemical undertones, might be causing confusion among the Krygians. It could be making them nervous and hesitant to attack. What if the Symbio's pheromonal characteristics correlate to some natural enemy—one which showed dominance over the Krygians in the past?"

"So you're saying these unique pheromones are putting them on edge?" I clarified, a sense of hope rising within me.

"Isn't that what I just said?" Derrota retorted, getting snippy from the mounting pressure.

I glanced to the approaching line of Krygians. The damn hissing was beyond distracting.

"Hold on, Stephan. Sonya, are you there?"

"Where else would I be?"

"Good. Um, how's your progress?"

"It would be a lot faster without your constant interruptions." She let out an audible breath. "My helper Symbios are doing the heavy lifting, as it were. So, I'm mostly supervising. But we're still ten minutes out at least."

"Look I want you to work with NELLA, I need an ultra-real looking, life-sized, 3D vid of one of these Roman Guardsman killing a Krygian... maybe lopping off its head, something like that. I'll be projecting it from my TAC-Band."

"Are you crazy? I don't have time for any of that shit—"

Excuse me, Captain...

NELLA's calm voice cut Sonya off.

"Go ahead, NELLA."

Captain, I have created the video you requested, and it is now ready for projection from your TAC-Band.

Chapter 45

Deep Space—Vicinity of StarPoint Station
USS Resilience

XO Gail Pristy

The XO's fingers tapped seamlessly over the tactical board as if barely touching it, her mind racing as she processed the chaotic flood of information. *USS Resilience's* bridge thrummed with tension, every crewmember being pushed to their limits as they fought to keep the battered ship alive.

Shields at 12% and falling...

Ensign Paxton called out, her voice strained, "That's an understatement. Shields are starting to buckle, XO!"

"One more hit like that and we're space dust!" Grimes shouted over the cacophony of klaxons as he worked the helm controls, desperately trying to keep the ship out of the direct line of fire from the three enemy vessels.

Navigating *Resilience* through tight, evasive maneuvers, Grimes had skillfully kept the ship just out of the remaining Krygian vessel's optimal firing range— while NELLA worked to disrupt any attempted targeting locks. However, his face suddenly tensed as he noticed new movement on the logistical display.

"Damn it!" he growled. "Fresh trouble. The Varapin vessels are mobilizing, laying down a relentless barrage across our exit vectors."

Pristy's eyes darted between tactical displays, searching for an advantage, any weakness she could exploit. The Krygian dreadnought and two Varapin warships still loomed menacingly close. Then she heard it—the ping terminating from the Tactical board; one or all three of the ships had acquired a solid lock onto *Resilience*. Shit!

The enemy ships were turning about. She stared down the approaching dreadnoughts, their weapons primed, and ready to obliterate *Resilience*. The tactical display painted a grim picture —they were outnumbered, outgunned, and rapidly running out of options.

But surrender was not a word in the U.S. Space Navy's—or Pristy's—vocabulary.

They'd come too far, sacrificed too much, to let it all end here. Pristy glanced around at her battered but unbroken crew, seeing the same determination on their faces as when the fight began.

No, *Resilience* would not go quietly into that good night. If this was to be their final stand, they would make it one for the history books. Pristy leaned forward, her eyes narrowing as she focused on the multiple halo displays.

"Ms. Blunderton, jump over to Ship Operations 2 and assist

Ms. Paxton," Pristy ordered. "We need all hands engaging in this battle."

As Blunderton rushed to comply, Pristy's mind worked furiously. They'd already tried targeting propulsion systems, weapons arrays, and shield generators—all standard tactics that the enemy now anticipated. She needed something unexpected, a vulnerability their opponents had overlooked.

Pristy studied the tactical displays, each one showing the enemy vessels separately. The lone Krygian vessel, Krygian 1, pursued them relentlessly, while the two Varapin ships, Varapin 1 and Varapin 2, maneuvered to block potential escape vectors, their massive forms dwarfing *Resilience*.

As she watched, Pristy noticed something odd about Krygian 1. Each time, moments before the dreadnought fired off another barrage of plasma bolts, a small cluster of ship lights blinked out mid-ship. It was subtle, easy to miss in the chaos of battle, but unmistakable once she'd spotted it.

A spark of inspiration hit her. "NELLA, focus your scans on Krygian 1's mid-ship section. There's a localized power fluctuation occurring just before they fire their main weapons. Analyze that area for potential vulnerabilities."

The AI's serene voice contrasted sharply with the frantic atmosphere...

Scanning. This may take a moment.

As NELLA worked, another barrage of plasma fire erupted from the Varapin ships. *Resilience* shuddered violently under the assault.

"Evasive maneuvers!" Pristy shouted. "Mr. Grimes, thirty degrees to port, then a corkscrew dive!"

Grimes worked the console, sending *Resilience* into a stomach-churning spiral. The move bought them precious seconds as enemy fire blazed past them into empty space.

"XO," Paxton called out, her voice tight with urgency. "I'm picking up fluctuations in Krygian 1's shield harmonics. It looks like they're having trouble maintaining a stable field!"

Pristy's heart raced. This could be the opening they needed. "NELLA, status on that earlier power fluctuation scan!"

Scan complete, I have detected a series of micro-fissures within the Krygian vessel's mid-ship power matrix. The 300 zeptosecond power flux differential has instigated a resonance effect—

"Dammit! Just tell me you can take advantage of that!"

Yes, XO. The timing will need to be perfect. An extended salvo of rail spike munitions should do it.

A grim smile played across Pristy's lips. "Excellent."

"Mr. Grimes, work with NELLA, and bring us about to an optimum firing solution."

As *Resilience* maneuvered into position, plasma fire from the Varapin ships intensified. The bridge rocked with each impact, another console sparked, and more alarms blared.

"Shields down to 8%!" Paxton shouted over the din as the ship shuddered under a renewed assault.

"Hold steady." Pristy gripped her console, knuckles white. "NELLA, watch for overheating of that forward rail cannon—it was problematic earlier. Go ahead, and I want precise concentrated fire on Krygian 1's vulnerability at your discretion."

Rail cannon charged and ready. Note, the probability for success is less than 17.3%.

Pristy set her jaw. "Fuck. You could have started with that," she murmured. "Fire at will."

Seconds seemed to drag on forever as *Resilience* narrowed the gap. Blasts from the enemy's weapons streaked across their hull, every impact a potential death sentence.

Firing...

A devastating barrage of brilliant white strobes lanced out from *Resilience*, rail spikes striking the Krygian ship's vulnerable point with pinpoint accuracy. For a heart-stopping moment, nothing happened. Then, like a dam finally giving way, the enemy's shields collapsed in a cascade of failing energy.

"Direct hit!" Paxton exclaimed. "The entire ship is exposed and vulnerable!"

Pristy didn't hesitate. "NELLA! Fire all available weapons... target their bridge and weapons systems!"

Halo displays refreshed, showing *Resilience* unleashing magnificent hellfire onto the enemy—concentrating everything the hobbled ship had left into the final Krygian vessel.

Explosions blossomed across its hull as key systems overloaded and ruptured. Within moments, the massive alien ship began to list, atmosphere venting from multiple breaches. But different from the previous explosive endings, Krygian 1 suddenly imploded upon itself, leaving behind a skeletal remnant of its previous mass.

With the destruction of the last Krygian dreadnought, *Resilience* now faced only the two remaining Varapin vessels.

But celebration had to wait. Seemingly enraged by *Resilience's* success, the Varapin dreadnoughts intensified their assault. A hail of plasma bolts slammed into *Resilience*, overwhelming what was left of their shields.

"Multiple hull breaches!" Blunderton cried out from her temporary station. "We're venting atmosphere on decks 12 through 15!"

"Ensure DeckGates are activated and sealing off those sections," Pristy ordered, her voice steady despite the chaos. "Mr. Grimes, evasive maneuvers, get us on the other side of StarPoint for cover! We need to buy ourselves some time."

As *Resilience* dove and weaved through space, narrowly avoiding the worst of the enemy assault, Pristy's mind worked furiously. They were down to their last options, their weapons nearly depleted and shields gone.

"XO..." Paxton interjected, "We're not the only ones who've been taking a beating. Varapin 1 and 2 aren't maintaining the same level of weapon fire as even five minutes ago. And while our shields are fully down, theirs... are down to single digits."

Pristy's spine stiffened as she assessed the tactical landscape. Retreating behind StarPoint's bulk offered temporary safety, but it would squander a rare moment of enemy vulnerability. Her mind raced through potential strategies, each fraught with risk and opportunity.

Pristy's moment of reckoning had come. The weight of command bore down on her as she realized any order given now could seal their fate. With the crew's lives hanging in the balance, she knew her next decision might be the difference between survival and oblivion.

"Mr. Grimes, change of plan. Plot a course directly between the two Varapin vessels. What worked once, might just work again."

The helmsman's eyes widened, but he nodded. "Aye, XO. Hold on everyone, we're in for a rough ride."

Pristy watched the tactical display intently as *Resilience* hurtled toward the gap between the two Varapin ships—ships that were no longer firing—perhaps momentarily flummoxed by our reckless maneuver... our sudden return back into the eye of the shitstorm.

That's right... hold your fire... we're just coming back to say hello.

"A little further, Mr. Grimes, Pristy said under her breath.

Now!" Pristy shouted. "Hard to port, then full reverse thrusters!"

Resilience pivoted sharply, halting abruptly. Suddenly, we stood perpendicular to the Varapin's lines of fire—putting the Varapin assets in each other's sights. Within seconds, precise targeting coordinates would boost the risk of friendly fire.

"NELLA, target the Varapin powerplants. Disrupt their targeting locks—better yet, reassign their targeting locks onto each other! Fire everything we have left!"

The AI complied instantly, unleashing a barrage of plasma bolts and the last of our rail spikes. Caught off guard, both Varapin vessels took significant damage. But more importantly, in their haste to retaliate, they failed to notice the target they thought they were locked onto... was no longer *Resilience*—instead, our plan instigated a friendly fire crossfire that was anything but friendly.

The bridgecrew watched in awe as Varapin 1 and Varapin 2 tore into each other, their powerful weapons quickly overwhelming each other's defenses. Within moments, one of the vessels was hemorrhaging vital atmosphere; her ship lights flickered off, and then she started to drift—a lifeless hulk adding to the already crowded scrapyard of death and destruction.

Varapin 1, Captain Toe's command ship, managed to avoid the worst of the friendly fire, but not without cost. Its starboard weapons array erupted in a series of explosions, leaving it wounded... but still dangerous.

A ragged cheer went up from the bridgecrew, but Pristy remained focused. They still had Toe's ship to deal with, and *Resilience* was running on fumes.

"Status report," she demanded, her eyes never leaving the tactical display.

"*Resilience's* hull integrity is holding at around 22%. Shields are down." Paxton's voice was tight. "Multiple decks, maybe all of them, are losing atmosphere, no way DeckGates will keep up with what's currently being vented. Weapons systems are offline. Add to all that... all four of our Off-Worlders are dangerously overheating, producing the bare minimum power needed to keep the lights on."

"And Toe's ship?" Pristy asked, turning to Blunderton.

"Not much better off," Blunderton replied from her temporary station. "They've got hull breaches of their own, and their weapons seem to be faltering."

It was down to a battle of attrition now, with both ships battered and bloodied. Pristy knew they had just one chance left—the bowler Chief LaSalle and his team were still struggling to load.

"Mr. Grimes, without overtaxing our Off-Worlders, keep us moving," she ordered. "Evasive patterns, but conserve what power we have left. We just need to hold out a little longer."

The minutes ticked by with agonizing slowness. *Resilience* shuddered and groaned as sporadic fire from Toe's ship found its mark. Pristy gritted her teeth, silently willing LaSalle and his team to work faster.

Finally, after what felt like an eternity, the chief's voice crackled from the overhead PA system...

Broadside loaded and ready, XO! You've got one shot—make it count.

Pristy's heart raced as she assessed the situation. They needed to get into the perfect firing position, and they'd only have one chance to do it. Everything hinged on this moment.

"Mr. Grimes, bring us about," she commanded, her voice steady despite the adrenaline coursing through her veins. "We need a clear shot at Toe's starboard flank—their bridge."

As *Resilience* slowly began to turn, lining up for that last crucial shot, multiple warning pings emanated up from Pristy's tactical board.

Enemy has a target lock… Incoming!
Incoming! Incoming!
Three fusion-tipped missiles inbound.

Frozen, unable to move, to speak—Pristy's blood ran cold.

Chapter 46

StarPoint Station
RED Section

Captain Galvin Quintos

The half-mile-long Krygian line was on the move again, looking to be twenty, to thirty towering insects deep. Apparently, their apprehension of the Symbio-Poths was a thing of the past.

I shouldered my way through the flanks of Symbios and proceeded to move out another twenty feet or so. Less than fifty yards in front of me, the enemy advanced. Crap they're big... ugly... and TERRIFYING.

"Ryder... Akari... tell me your Krygians haven't attacked yet either."

Both confirmed my assumption.

I held out my arm and angled my wrist. "Okay NELLA, how about you show me your Steven Spielberg filmmaking skills."

USS Resilience

Yes, Captain. Transmitting now...

I watched in awe as the 3D projection sprang to life from my TAC-Band, creating a spectacle that was both horrifying and awe-inspiring. The Krygian-like insects that materialized were nightmarish exaggerations of our real foes—larger, more menacing, with additional spines and barbs jutting from their segmented bodies. Their mandibles gnashed hungrily, and I could almost smell the acrid stench of their alien biology.

But it was our Symbio-Poth warriors that truly captured my attention. The gladiators moved with a fluid grace that belied their muscular builds, their oiled torsos gleaming as they wielded nets and tridents with impossible speed. I marveled at the historical accuracy of the Roman guardsmen, their lorica segmentata armor catching the virtual sunlight as they advanced in perfect formation behind their interlocked scutums.

To my surprise, even the senators joined the fray. Their white togas, edged with regal purple, billowed as they brandished ornate gladii with unexpected skill. The juxtaposition of their dignified appearance and fierce combat prowess was jarring yet oddly fitting.

The battle that unfolded before me was a blur of motion and violence. Stubby swords sang through the air, cleaving through chitinous limbs with sickening efficiency. I winced as alien appendages flew in all directions, green ichor spraying in arterial arcs. The Symbios' tridents found weak spots with unerring accuracy, piercing vital organs and dropping the massive insects like stones.

Most gruesome of all were the decapitations. Symbio blades flashed, and insectoid heads rolled, their compound eyes dimming as they separated from twitching bodies. The battlefield quickly became a gory tableau, painted in vivid greens and reds.

. . .

Despite the 10 minutes of visceral carnage, I couldn't help but feel a surge of pride. These Symbio-Poths, artificial as they were, fought with a determination and skill that matched any flesh-and-blood warrior. As they pressed on, vanquishing foe after foe, I knew that NELLA had created exactly the morale-crushing spectacle we needed——a spectacle that played out before the compounded eyes of the Krygian warriors.

With my TAC-Band show-and-tell presentation now history, my Symbio cohorts and I leered back at the Krygian army before us. Had it accomplished what I'd intended? I had no idea. Not one of the big bugs had taken a step backward, nor had any of them broken down into terrified sobs.

My comms crackled. "That's a tad unnerving," Sonya commented. "What are they doing... it's creepy how they're just standing there like that."

I was weary of speaking, making a movement that would jump-start an attack.

Derrota's voice filled my helmet. "Galvin, I'm assuming you want delivery of the chariot teams there in front of you?"

"They're ready?"

"Correct... and more chariots and horses are being hitched as we speak, but yes," Derrota said. "You, Captain Ryder, and Lieutenant James will have twenty rigs quansporting over... right... now."

The air crackled with energy as multiple blocky quansport flashes erupted mere feet in front of me and my Symbio cohorts. In an instant, the serene parkland transformed into a scene straight out of ancient Rome. Twenty magnificent chariots materialized, each pulled by a team of six horses with coats as white as freshly fallen snow.

The chariots were breathtaking in their authenticity—

gleaming bronze and iron, adorned with intricate engravings and fluttering crimson banners. Flags mounted on slender rods snapped in the artificial breeze, adding splashes of color to the already vibrant scene.

The horses, restless with pent-up energy, nickered and snorted, pawing at the lush grass with impatient hooves. Their nostrils flared, and I could almost feel their eagerness to charge into battle.

"To the chariots!" I bellowed, my voice carrying over the din. "Move, move, move!"

As if my words had broken some unseen spell, chaos erupted on both sides. My Symbio army surged forward, racing toward the awaiting chariots. At the same moment, the Krygian horde seemed to shake off their trance-like state, their mandibles clicking furiously as they charged en masse.

I sprinted toward the nearest chariot, my heart pounding in my ears. As I reached it, I noticed a Roman Guardsman had already leapt aboard. Without a word, he grasped the leather reins, leaving me free to focus on the approaching enemy.

The instant my feet touched the chariot's floor, the Guardsman snapped the reins hard. The team of horses responded immediately, muscles rippling beneath their shimmering coats as they launched forward with explosive speed.

Wind whipped through my hair as we accelerated, the chariot's wheels barely seeming to touch the ground. I unslung my shredder, bracing myself against the chariot's frame as I aimed at the attacking Krygians.

The weapon hummed to life in my hands, as I squeezed the trigger. A steady stream of plasma bolts erupted from the barrel, cutting a swath through the charging insects. Five of the nearest Krygians fell, their bodies tumbling in a grotesque tangle of limbs and spraying green ichor.

All around us, the battle had erupted into full-scale pandemonium. Chariots crisscrossed the field in dizzying patterns, Symbio drivers expertly maneuvering their vehicles through the chaos. Those armed with shredders, like me, laid down suppressing fire, while others closed in on the Krygians with more traditional weapons.

I watched in awe as a Symbio senator, his toga billowing behind him, stood tall in his chariot and swung a gleaming gladius. The blade connected with a Krygian's neck, neatly severing its head in a spray of alien blood.

But for every small victory, the battle exacted a toll. To my left, a chariot struck an obstacle and flipped, sending its occupants hurtling through the air. They landed amidst a group of Krygians, disappearing beneath a frenzy of slashing limbs and snapping mandibles.

I tried to listen for any word from Akari or Ryder, to gauge how their sections of the battle were progressing. But the cacophony of combat drowned out all but the most immediate sounds. The clash of metal, the screech of dying Krygians, and the thundering of hooves filled my world.

My focus narrowed to the rhythm of aim, fire, and repeat. The shredder grew hot in my hands, the barrel glowing an angry red from constant use. Beside me, the Guardsman multitasked with impressive skill, steering our careening chariot with one hand while his sword flashed in deadly arcs with the other.

The once-pristine parkland had become a nightmarish battlefield. The lush green grass was now slick with the mingled fluids of Krygian and Symbio-Poth alike. Broken chariots and dismembered bodies, both insectoid and bio-mechanical, littered the ground.

In a moment of distraction, I failed to notice a Krygian lunging from my blind spot. Pain exploded in my chest as one of its legs pierced my battle suit, the chitinous appendage embedding itself deep in my flesh.

My knees buckled, and I felt myself starting to fall. But before I could hit the floor of the chariot, a strong hand grasped my arm. The Guardsman had me, his face splitting into an exhilarated grin despite the dire situation.

"Not today, Legatus!" he shouted over the din, hauling me back to my feet.

Gritting my teeth against the pain, I raised my shredder, the pain of that simple movement blurring my vision. Ahead, a cluster of Krygians was bearing down on us, their mandibles clicking in anticipation of an easy kill.

"Big mistake," I muttered, squeezing the trigger.

The shredder roared to life, spitting death at our would-be killers. Krygian after Krygian fell, their bodies riddled with smoking holes.

As we plowed through the falling insects, I caught snippets of chatter over my comms. Ryder's voice, tense but controlled: "...flanking maneuver on the east side..." Akari, her words punctuated by the sound of weapon fire: "...need backup at sector seven..."

I wanted to respond, to coordinate our efforts, but the relentless pace of our own battle demanded every ounce of my attention. The Guardsman beside me let out a whoop of joy as he ran another Krygian through with his sword, the blade emerging gore-covered from the creature's back.

Our chariot thundered on, the horses somehow maintaining their frenzied pace despite the carnage surrounding them. We cut a swath through the Krygian ranks, my shredder never silent for more than a moment.

But for every insectoid monstrosity we felled, two more seemed to take its place. The sheer number of our foes was staggering, their chittering battle cries rising to a deafening crescendo.

A sudden impact rocked our chariot, nearly throwing me

from my feet again. I turned to see one of our wheels had been sheared off by a particularly large Krygian, its mandibles still clamped around the broken remnants.

"We're going down!" I shouted to the Guardsman, who nodded grimly in response.

As our chariot began to lose speed and stability, I made a split-second decision. "Jump!" I commanded, grabbing the Guardsman's arm.

Together, we leaped from the failing vehicle, hitting the ground in a roll that knocked the wind from my lungs. The pain from my chest wound flared anew, but I forced myself to my feet, dragging the Guardsman up with me.

We found ourselves in a momentary lull, a small clearing in the chaos of battle. All around us, the fight raged on. Chariots continued to circle, their occupants dealing death with sword and shredder alike. Symbio-Poths on foot engaged in brutal close-quarters combat with the Krygians, matching the insects' inhuman strength with skill and determination.

Chapter 47

The Guardsman stood at attention, his voice steady. "Your orders, Centurion? We stand ready to engage the enemy."

As we prepared to plunge back into the melee, a familiar voice crackled over my comms. "Uncle Galvin," Sonya's tense tone cut through the battle noise. "I've got something that might buy you some time. Can you make it to the far end of the parkland, near the central support pillar?"

I quickly oriented myself, spotting the massive column that stretched from floor to ceiling of this vast enclosed space. "This isn't a good time," I responded, my voice tight. "Best you stay off comms—"

"Just get there," came her curt reply. "And hurry."

I turned to the Guardsman. "Change of plans. We're headed for the central pillar. Watch my back?"

He nodded grimly. "As you command, Legatus."

Together, we set off through the chaos, fighting our way towards whatever Sonya had in store. The battle raged on around us, a cacophony of destruction and desperation. Symbio-Poth gladiators grappled with Krygians in brutal hand-to-hand combat, while Roman senators, their togas stained with alien ichor, fought with a ferocity that belied their dignified appearance.

We were nearly to the central pillar when a massive Krygian, easily twice the size of its brethren, loomed before us. Its compound eyes gleamed with malevolent intelligence as it sized us up.

"I'll distract it, Legatus," the Guardsman shouted, darting to the left.

I nodded, circling right. The Krygian's head swiveled between us, unsure which target to focus on. That moment of indecision was all we needed.

The Guardsman lunged, his sword flashing in the artificial sunlight. The blade bit deep into one of the Krygian's legs, eliciting a shriek of pain and rage. As the creature turned to retaliate, I raised my shredder and emptied what remained of its charge into the beast's thorax.

The combined assault was too much. With a final, ear-splitting screech, the giant Krygian collapsed, its legs twitching in its death throes.

"Nice job," I panted, offering the Guardsman a nod of grim appreciation.

He returned the nod, wiping alien gore from his blade. "And you, Legatus."

We had no time to catch our breath. The area near the central pillar was just ahead, and I could see something materializing there—more quansport flashes.

As we fought our way across the battlefield, a low rumble began to build, like distant thunder. The ground beneath our feet started to tremble, causing both Symbios and Krygians to stumble. The vibrations grew stronger, and with them came a new sound—a high, trumpet-like call that cut through the din of battle.

Then, materializing through the quansport flashes, I saw them. My breath caught in my throat.

Elephants. War elephants. So this is the secret surprise Sonya had been working on.

Even from this distance, their sheer size was staggering. Each beast stood at least fifteen feet tall at the shoulder, their massive forms silhouetted against the artificial sky. Gleaming armor plates covered their bodies, catching and reflecting the light in harsh flashes. As they moved, I could make out the glint of what looked like reinforced tusks, wickedly sharp and easily as long as a man.

Atop each elephant, I could just discern the outlines of fortified howdahs. Even from afar, I could see they bristled with activity—no doubt filled with Symbio archers and spear-throwers preparing for the onslaught. More figures clung to the elephants' flanks, though at this range they appeared as little more than specks against the beasts' enormous bulk.

A trumpet-like blast echoed across the battlefield, followed by the groan of the deck's superstructure straining under the weight as the elephants began their advance.

I watched, a mix of hope and dread churning in my gut, as the elephants lumbered forward. Their thunderous footsteps continued to send tremors through the ground. For the first time since the battle began, I saw hesitation ripple through the Krygian ranks.

"Understood," I replied, my voice hoarse. "We'll make the most of it."

The Guardsman beside me tightened his grip on his weapon. "Your orders, Legatus?"

I steeled myself, pushing down the exhaustion that threatened to overwhelm me. "We press forward. Use the elephants as cover and hit the Krygians with everything we've got. It's our only chance."

With a grim nod, we charged toward the approaching behemoths, knowing full well this could be our last stand. As we closed the distance, the true scale of the war elephants became apparent. Their armored legs resembled ancient tree trunks, each step leaving craters in the green landscape and, undoubtedly, denting the deck plating below.

The first elephant reached the Krygian line, and the effect was devastating. Its massive foot came down on a cluster of the insectoid aliens, crushing their chitinous bodies with a sickening crunch that echoed across the battlefield. The beast's armored trunk swung in a wide arc, sending more Krygians flying through the air like broken dolls.

"Let's move!" I shouted, snatching up a fallen Symbio's sword. The weight felt familiar in my hand, a grim reminder of past battles. I led our Symbio-Poth forces in a charge behind the elephants' advance. We struck the disoriented Krygian ranks like a tidal wave, exploiting the chaos sown by our new Symbio beasts.

The battle devolved into a frenzied melee. Krygians swarmed up the elephants' legs, only to be picked off by archers in the howdahs or crushed against the beasts' armor. The air filled with the screeching of dying aliens, the trumpeting of enraged elephants, and the war cries of our Symbio warriors.

I fought with a desperation I'd never known, my sword arm moving on instinct as my mind struggled to process the surreal scene around me. The blade sang through the air, finding gaps in Krygian armor, green ichor spraying with each strike. Without the Gorvian plasma coursing through my veins, there was no way I'd still be standing—my reflexes sharper, my strength enhanced, but all of it still ratcheted up against the terrifying reality of the battle. A silent thanks to Doc Viv flickered in my mind for enabling this miracle. A Krygian leapt at me, mandibles gnashing, and I ducked under its attack. My sword lashed out, catching it mid-leap. The Guardsman was there in an instant, his blade finding another weak spot between the alien's chitinous exoskeleton plates, finishing what I'd started.

"We're pushing them back!" someone shouted over the comms. I couldn't tell if it was Ryder or Akari—everything was a blur of motion and noise.

But even as we gained ground, I knew this was far from over. The Krygians were adapting, focusing their attacks on the elephants' less armored joints. One of the massive beasts trumpeted in pain as its leg buckled, and I watched in horror as it toppled, crushing friend and foe alike beneath its bulk.

"Hold the line!" I shouted, gesturing with my sword. "We can't afford to falter now!"

As the battle raged on, I couldn't shake the feeling that this —this impossible, desperate last stand—would determine not just our fate, but that of our entire species. And so we fought on, under the shadow of armored giants, against an endless tide of alien horror, my borrowed sword growing heavier with each swing.

Chapter 48

StarPoint Station
PURPLE Section

Sergeant Max Dryer

Max's heart pounded in his chest as he materialized within the oppressive darkness of StarPoint Station. The quansport had left him momentarily disoriented, but years of combat training kicked in, sharpening his senses. He blinked rapidly, willing his eyes to adjust to the gloom.

Focus, Marine.

As his vision cleared, Max took in the nightmarish landscape. The corridor stretched before them, its bulkheads pulsing with an otherworldly, organic quality. A thick, smoke-like haze hung in the air, limiting visibility and adding to the claustrophobic atmosphere. The acrid stench of alien biology assaulted his nostrils, even through his helmet's filters.

"Sound off," Max ordered, his voice tight with tension.

"Ham, ready to rock," came the immediate response.

"Hock, locked and loaded," followed closely.

"Grip, good to go," the final member of his team chimed in.

Max nodded, more to himself than his squad. They were down two valued members—Wanda, lost in the explosion that had crippled Roosevelt, and Aubrey, reassigned to hostage rescue. The absence of their skills and camaraderie weighed heavily on Max's shoulders.

Best not to dwell on it—the mission comes first.

"Alright, Marines," Max began, his voice steady despite the knot in his gut. "We're in the belly of the beast. Our job is simple—exterminate every bug we find, and destroy their eggs. No mercy, no hesitation. I'm not exaggerating when I say the future of humanity depends on us wiping these bastards out."

He paused, letting the gravity of their task sink in. "Stay alert, stay alive. Watch each other's backs, and for fuck's sake, don't let them get too close."

Grip's baritone followed, "Those mandibles will snap you in half like a twig before you can fucking blink."

Max adjusted the weight of his oversized DDT tanks, the nozzle of the sprayer already slick with condensation in the humid air.

"According to my HUD, we should hit the first hatchery in about two minutes. Lock and load, people. It's time to make these bugs wish they'd never crawled out from the rocks they came from."

"They come from under rocks?" Ham asked.

"Ham, it's just a fucking saying... like an idiom, not to be taken literally," Grip explained.

"I don't know nothing about, um, idioms... is that a kind of rock or something?" Ham asked.

Max rolled his eyes, *you gotta love a simple mind.*

They moved forward as one, years of training evident in their synchronized movements. The corridor seemed to constrict around them, the organic bulkheads pulsing with an unsettling rhythm. Tendrils of mist curled around their ankles, adding to the otherworldly atmosphere.

It's like walking through someone's nightmare, Max thought, suppressing a shudder.

As they rounded a bend, Max's HUD flared to life, proximity warnings flashing urgently. "Contact!" he barked, raising his sprayer. "Twelve o'clock, multiple hostiles!"

The air erupted with the chittering of countless Krygian warriors. The insectoid aliens poured from hidden recesses in the bulkheads, their chitinous bodies gleaming in the low light. Compound eyes fixed on the Marines with predatory intensity.

"Light 'em up!" Max roared, depressing the trigger on his sprayer.

A stream of DDT mixture burst forth, engulfing the nearest Krygian in a deadly mist. The effect was immediate and horrifying. The alien's exoskeleton began to bubble and melt, its legs thrashing in agony as it collapsed into a puddle of steaming goo.

The stench of dissolving Krygian filled the air, once more nearly overwhelming Max's helmet filters. He fought back the urge to retch, focusing instead on the next target, and the next. Around him, his team unleashed similar torrents of destruction.

Ham's voice was tight with controlled rage as he caught three Krygians in a single spray. "For Wanda," he muttered, pressing forward without pause.

Hock moved with cold efficiency, methodically dousing every alien that came within range. "We're making a dent, Sarge, but there's no end to them!"

Grip, usually the quietest of the bunch, let out a string of colorful curses as he narrowly avoided a Krygian's slashing foreleg. "These fuckers are quick! Watch your six!"

Max's mind raced as he assessed the situation. They were holding their own, but the sheer number of Krygians was staggering. For every alien they melted, two more seemed to take its place.

Christ, we can't keep this up forever. Where the hell is that hatchery?

"Form up!" Max shouted over the din of battle. "Wedge formation! We're punching through to the main chamber!"

The team responded instantly, years of drills paying off. They formed a tight triangle, with Max at the point. As one, they advanced, Kryzite/DDT sprayers unleashing a constant barrage of deadly mist.

The Krygians fell before them, their bodies dissolving into bubbling puddles that made the deck treacherously slick. Max's boots squelched through the remains, each step a grim reminder of the carnage they were inflicting.

This is necessary, he told himself, trying to quell the nausea rising in his throat. *It's us or them.*

After what felt like an eternity of combat, they burst through into a vast, cavernous space. Max's breath caught in his throat as he took in the sight before them.

The hatchery stretched as far as the eye could see, its walls lined with pulsating, organic structures. Thousands—no, millions—of eggs glowed with an eerie green light, each one containing a developing Krygian warrior.

"Sweet Jesus," Ham whispered, his voice filled with awe and revulsion.

"Stay focused," Max snapped, even as his own mind reeled at the scale of what they faced. "We've got a job to do."

They spread out, moving deeper into the hatchery. The deck here was coated in a thick, mucus-like substance that made every step treacherous. Overhead, strands of the same material hung like weeping stalactites, dripping a foul-looking liquid.

As they advanced, a mournful wailing filled the air. The

sound sent chills down Max's spine—it was the cry of Krygian who had realized their young were under threat.

They're sentient, a small voice in the back of Max's mind whispered. *They feel. They grieve.*

He shook off the thought, steeling himself for what needed to be done. "Spray everything," he ordered, his voice hoarse. "Don't leave a single egg intact."

The team moved methodically, their Kryzite/DDT sprayers coating every surface in a fine mist of death. The effects were immediate and horrifying. Eggs began to crack and shrivel, their contents dissolving before they could fully form.

Max watched as a partially developed Krygian larva emerged from a ruptured egg, its tiny mandibles working frantically as it dissolved into nothingness. He swallowed hard, fighting back the bile rising in his throat.

This is genocide, part of him screamed. *We're murdering an entire species in its cradle.*

It's necessary, another part countered. *If we don't do this, humanity is fucked.*

The internal struggle raged as Max continued his grim work. Around him, his team pressed on, their faces set in masks of grim determination. They all knew the weight of what they were doing—and the consequences if they failed.

After what felt like hours, the last of the eggs in this chamber had been neutralized. An eerie silence fell over the hatchery, broken only by the soft patter of dissolving organic matter.

Max's shoulders sagged with exhaustion and the weight of what they'd just done. He turned to his team, seeing the same mix of relief and horror in their eyes.

"Good work, Marines," he said, his voice rough. "We've dealt a major blow to the Krygian forces."

Before anyone could respond, Max's helmet comm crackled

to life. "Sergeant Dryer, this is Science Officer Derrota. Do you copy?"

"I copy, Science Officer, Derrota. Go ahead."

"We've received updated sensor data from Hardy," Derrota's voice was tight with tension. "I'm afraid I have some bad news."

Max's stomach clenched. "Let's hear it."

"Our initial estimates were... optimistic. We've detected at least ten more hatcheries of similar size scattered throughout the station."

Max felt the news hit him like a sledgehammer. He glanced at his team, their expressions reflecting the same shock and despair he felt. They had all been listening in on the open channel, absorbing the grim reality together.

"Copy that," Max managed, his mind racing. "We'll regroup and—"

His words were cut off by a bone-chilling sound—the angry hiss of approaching Krygians. Max's HUD lit up with warning indicators, showing a massive swarm of hostiles converging on their position.

"Incoming!" he shouted, raising his sprayer. But as he depressed the trigger, nothing happened. The tanks were empty.

A quick glance confirmed his worst fears—all of their fortified Kryzite/DDT tanks were depleted. They'd used every last drop to destroy the eggs.

We're surrounded and outnumbered, Max realized, a cold dread settling in his gut. *So... this is how it ends.*

"Lose your tanks, switch to shredders!" he barked, already unbuckling the straps.

The hissing grew louder, accompanied by the skittering of countless legs on the organic surfaces. The Krygians were closing in, driven by rage and the need for vengeance.

Max looked at his team—Ham, Hock, and Grip. These men

had followed him into hell itself, trusting his leadership. Now, he was about to lead them to their deaths.

Hey Wanda... he thought, a lump forming in his throat. *Looks like we'll be seeing you sooner than later.*

As the first wave of Krygians burst into view, their mandibles gnashing with fury, Max checked his shredder—full charge. If this was to be their last stand, they'd be going down fighting.

"Marines!" he roared, his voice filled with defiance. "Prepare for close-quarters combat! We fight to the last man!"

The team formed a tight circle, backs to each other, as the sea of chitinous horror closed in around them. Max's heart pounded in his ears, time seeming to slow as the Krygians prepared to strike.

This is it, he thought, squeezing his weapon's trigger. The end of the line.

As the first Krygian leapt towards him, mandibles spread wide, Max couldn't help but smile, "Let me introduce you to a whole lot of hurt you son of a bitch!"

Chapter 49

**StarPoint Station
GREEN Section**

Hardy

Hardy's metallic form looked dull and unimpressive beneath the harsh lights of StarPoint Station—the once-pristine plating now pocked and scarred by countless energy blasts. Green ichor coated his limbs, a testament to the trail of destruction he'd carved through the Krygian hordes. His five energy cannons glowed a molten orange, barrels sizzling from near-constant use over the past hour.

The ChronoBot pressed forward with the relentless momentum of a Sherman tank, each thunderous step leaving dents in the deck plating. His sensors swept the area continuously, searching for any sign of his elusive quarry. The Krygian Queen had proven frustratingly adept at slipping through his grasp, always one step ahead despite Hardy's brutal efficiency.

As he rounded yet another corner in the seemingly endless maze of corridors, Hardy's audio receptors picked up the distinctive click-hiss of approaching Krygian guards. These were no ordinary warriors—their movements were too coordinated, too precise. These were the elite, tasked with protecting their monarch at all costs.

Hardy's faceplate flickered, the digital representation of John Hardy's weathered features set in grim determination. "Alright, you oversized cockroaches," he muttered, leveling his arm-mounted cannons. "Let's dance."

The first wave hit like a tsunami of chitin and fury. Hardy's sensors registered dozens of energy signatures as the guards opened fire, their weapons far more advanced than those wielded by the common Krygian drones. Plasma bolts sizzled past, leaving scorch marks on the bulkheads and adding new pockmarks to Hardy's already battered frame.

But the ChronoBot was far from helpless. His own weapons roared to life, filling the corridor with a storm of destructive energy. Krygians fell by the score, their exoskeletons rupturing under the barrage. Yet for every insectoid form that collapsed into a twitching heap, two more seemed to take its place.

"Come on!" Hardy bellowed, his voice synthesizer straining with the volume. "Is that the best you've got?"

As if in answer, a particularly massive Krygian burst through the ranks of its fallen comrades. Its carapace gleamed with an iridescent sheen, marking it as something beyond the usual warrior caste. In its claws, it brandished a weapon that made Hardy's threat assessment protocols spike with alarm—a plasma cannon nearly as large as the alien itself.

Time seemed to slow as the weapon's muzzle flared with building energy. Hardy's processors worked in overdrive, calculating trajectories and analyzing weak points. At the last possible moment, he launched himself to the side, his massive one-thousand-pound frame crashing through a nearby bulkhead.

The plasma bolt streaked past, missing Hardy by mere inches. The ChronoBot rolled to his feet, chunks of debris clattering off his chassis. Through the newly created hole, he caught a glimpse of movement—a flash of a truly immense Krygian creature—its forest-green coloring like none other he'd come across.

The Queen.

Hardy's optical sensors zoomed in, confirming what his other systems had failed to detect. There she was, her towering form dwarfing even her largest guards. But before he could bring his weapons to bear, a wall of Krygian bodies interposed themselves between predator and prey.

"Oh no you don't," Hardy growled, charging forward. His fists became battering rams, smashing through the living barrier. Krygian limbs snapped like twigs, alien ichor spraying in all directions. But the delay had served its purpose—by the time Hardy broke through, the Queen was gone, spirited away down another branching corridor.

Frustration threatened to overwhelm Hardy's logic circuits. This game of cat and mouse had gone on far too long. He needed a new strategy, a way to anticipate the Queen's movements rather than always reacting.

As he barreled down the hallway in pursuit, Hardy's sensors worked overtime, trying to lock onto any trace of the Queen's unique bio-signature. But it was as if she had vanished into thin air. The ChronoBot's suspicions crystallized—she must be using some kind of bio-reading cloaking device to mask her presence.

"Clever girl," Hardy muttered, his voice tinged with grudging respect. "But not clever enough."

He pressed on, leaving a trail of destruction in his wake. Bulkheads crumpled under his relentless advance, and any Krygian foolish enough to stand in his way was swiftly reduced to a smear of ichor on the deck plating.

As he progressed deeper into the station, Hardy became aware of a subtle shift in his surroundings. The corridors here were wider, the overheads higher. The walls pulsed with an organic quality that made his sensors prickle with unease. He was entering the heart of the Krygian infestation.

Suddenly, his audio receptors picked up a new sound—a high-pitched keening that set his circuits on edge. It was coming from up ahead, beyond a massive set of ornate doors that looked wildly out of place in the utilitarian setting of the space station.

Hardy approached cautiously, his weapons primed. As he neared the doors, they began to open of their own accord, revealing a vast chamber beyond. The ChronoBot's optical sensors widened as he took in the sight before him.

The room was a grotesque fusion of alien biology and advanced technology. Pulsating organic matter covered every surface, interwoven with glowing conduits and humming machinery. And there, at the center of it all, stood the Krygian Queen.

She was even more imposing up close, easily twice Hardy's height. Her carapace gleamed with an otherworldly iridescence, and her compound eyes seemed to hold the wisdom and malice of eons. In one clawed appendage, she held what appeared to be a scepter of sorts—clearly the source of her cloaking ability.

"Well, well," Hardy said, his voice pitched low and dangerous. "Looks like I've crashed the royal court."

The Queen's mandibles clicked in what might have been amusement. When she spoke, her voice was a multi-toned screech that Hardy's translation software struggled to interpret.

"Metal abomination," she hissed. "You dare to challenge the might of the Krygian Empire?"

Hardy's arm cannons whirred to life. "Lady, I've taken down bigger bugs than you before breakfast." Yeah, sure that was a lie, but it sounded good.

USS Resilience

With a shriek that shook the very foundations of the chamber, the Queen raised her scepter. Energy crackled along its length, and suddenly the air was filled with a swarm of smaller, drone-like creatures. They pelted Hardy from all sides, their bodies exploding on impact and coating him in a viscous, corrosive substance.

Warning signals flashed across Hardy's HUD as the acid began to eat away at his outer plating. But the ChronoBot stood his ground, his weapons blazing. Drones fell by the dozens, but more kept coming, an endless tide of suicidal attackers.

Through the chaos, Hardy caught glimpses of the Queen retreating towards a hidden passage at the far end of the chamber. He tried to pursue, but the sea of drones held him back, their bodies forming an impenetrable wall.

"No!" Hardy roared, his frustration boiling over. He redoubled his efforts, his fists and energy cannons working in tandem to clear a path. But it was too late. By the time he reached the hidden passage, it had sealed shut, leaving no trace of its existence.

Hardy stood there, his metallic form pitted and smoking, surrounded by the twitching remains of countless Krygian drones. The Queen had slipped through his grasp once again, this time fleeing to an entirely different section of StarPoint.

The ChronoBot's faceplate flickered, displaying a rare expression of defeat. He had been so close, only to have victory snatched away at the last moment. As the battle subsided and sensory inputs faded, Hardy became acutely aware of the damage he had sustained. His self-repair systems were working overtime, and it would take time to fully recover.

With a weary sigh that sounded more human than machine, Hardy opened a comms channel. "Stephan, you copy? I need a status update."

The science officer's voice came through, tinged with static. "Hardy? What's your situation?"

"The Queen gave me the slip," Hardy replied, his tone bitter. "She's moved to another section of the station. I need new coordinates, fast."

There was a pause, filled only by the sound of rapid tapping. When Derrota spoke again, his voice was heavy with concern. "Hardy, I'm still not picking up the Queen's signature. If you're not detecting her, NELLA won't be able to either."

"I've been outsmarted by that big, ugly bug again. Unbelievable." Hardy's voice held a note of grudging respect. Failure in his mission weighed heavy, and the stakes couldn't be higher. The Krygian threat still loomed large, with their leader now 'somewhere' else within this massive space station.

As he stood there, surrounded by the carnage of battle, Hardy's thoughts turned to his fellow combatants. The Cap, XO, Max and his team—were they faring any better in their respective missions? And what happened to Aubrey? He'd stayed off the open channel for the most part.

Derrota interrupted his inner musings, "The good news, with the exception of a few stragglers, we've brought almost all of the hostages over to *Resilience*."

"Mm, that's nice," Hardy muttered, his thoughts still locked on the elusive Queen.

"Unfortunately," Derrota continued, "Petty Officer 2nd Class Aubrey Laramie is suspected to be one of the fallen. Her biosignature went dark several hours ago. Her remains have yet to be located—"

"Nah... she's alive. My sensors are fried, but I have a confirmed DNA cross-match. Her bio-health stats are barely registering."

Derrota's response took Hardy by surprise, "She's alive! Are you sure? We need to get to her. Get her into HealthBay!"

"Okay. I'm sure I'll have better luck with that than my previous mission. Quansport me into the hostage's hold area and I'll locate her. By the way, what's the situation with the other teams? Red, Purple, Yellow..."

"So... you haven't heard. You should have been monitoring the open channel, Hardy."

"Fine, I've been duly chastised. What's the scoop?"

"We'll be pulling everyone back to *Resilience*. Valiant efforts all around, but in the end there were just too many Krygians. The Symbio-Poth regiments have been decimated. Even the war elephants..."

"Wait, did you just say war elephants?"

"Not important, Hardy. Leave it to say, that the operation to take back StarPoint Station, kill the Krygians and their queen has failed. But we have saved thousands of StarPoint hostages. That will have to suffice, I'm afraid."

Hardy quickly scanned the station; the Captain, Akari James, and Wallace Ryder were alive... as the robot was now up on their respective bio-readings. But with another quick check, he discovered Max and his Purple team were no longer on the station—he located them back on *Resilience*—all were within the confines of HealthBay.

"We need you back on *Resilience* ASAP, Hardy. Please find Aubrey and bring her home. Quansporting you to the hostages' hold area now."

Chapter 50

StarPoint Station
Sub-Station Hold

Captain Galvin Quintos

I had escaped by the skin of my teeth. Visions of the battle still raged within my mind—the inevitable end was always the same. More and more Krygians had flooded into the space as if there were an endless supply of the insects—THEY JUST KEPT COMING.

My Red team, even with the help of the chariots, Symbio horses, and those magnificent war elephants... in the end, they were all brought down and torn apart with a vengeance that was both startling and sobering. I was not the last man standing... but close enough.

No. A commanding officer needs to be able to recognize defeat. I was taking cover behind the hulking remains of one of the elephants—it wouldn't be long before I'd be discovered.

I reached out to Derrota, who pleaded, "Galvin, let me quansport you to HealthBay. Your bio-readings are faltering—

you've lost a significant amount of blood from that upper chest wound. Both Akari James and Wallace Ryder are being tended to, you need to join them."

Having checked twenty minutes earlier, I already knew Pristy was still engaging with the enemy—doing her best to keep what was left of *Resilience* in one piece.

"What's the situation with Hardy and his pursuit of the Queen?" I asked, changing the subject.

"While Hardy took out a significant number of the enemy, the Queen, in the end, eluded all his efforts and, apparently, has now taken refuge in another part of the station. He also informed me that Petty Officer 2nd Class Aubrey Laramie may still be alive and asked that I quansport him into the hold area."

Hearing that Aubrey was still alive brought an overwhelming sense of relief. Like a wave crashing over me, it took everything I had to control my urge to unleash the waterworks right then and there.

"Galvin, we need everyone off that station. There's been more than enough carnage. It's time to concentrate our efforts on returning to Earth if that's even possible."

"No. Quansport me into that hold. Do it now, Stephan."

MY HELMET FILTERS WERE USELESS BY THIS POINT—the acrid stench of death and decay hit me like a sledgehammer once I materialized within StarPoint's massive substation hold. Derrota's quansport had been precise, but nothing could have prepared me for the nightmarish scene that unfolded before my eyes. The cavernous space stretched out in all directions, easily the size of four football fields arranged in a square formation. Dim, flickering emergency lights cast an eerie glow over the hellscape, revealing a tableau of horror that made my stomach churn.

Bodies littered the deck like broken dolls, their limbs twisted at unnatural angles. Most were human—station personnel and civilians alike—their faces frozen in final expressions of terror and agony. But interspersed among them lay the chitinous husks of Krygian warriors, their alien forms no less disturbing in death. The sight of so many felled insects sparked a glimmer of hope. Had Laramie managed to inflict this level of damage before being overwhelmed?

I took a tentative step forward, my boots squelching in something I didn't want to identify. The sound echoed in the vast space, seeming to amplify the deathly silence that hung over the hold. My chest wound throbbed with each movement, a constant reminder of my previous battles within the station.

Against my better judgment, I reached up and removed my helmet. The full force of the hold's putrid atmosphere assaulted my senses, nearly causing me to retch. It was a noxious cocktail of decay, alien biology, and the acrid tang of spent energy weapons. I forced myself to take shallow breaths through my mouth, fighting back the wave of nausea that threatened to overwhelm me.

Slowly, I rotated in place, straining my eyes to penetrate the hazy gloom that seemed to cling to every surface. My ears strained for any sign of life—a whimper, a groan, anything to indicate that all hope was not lost. But the hold remained stubbornly, oppressively silent.

"Hardy?" I called out, my voice sounding small and lost in the vastness. "Where the hell are you, you chrome bastard?"

For a heart-stopping moment, there was no response. Then, just as despair began to creep in, I caught sight of movement in the distance. Dark shapes shifted near a far bulkhead, barely distinguishable from the surrounding shadows. My instincts screamed at me to run, to close the distance and find answers.

But the stabbing pain in my chest forced me to adopt a quick, awkward walk instead.

As I drew closer, the shapes resolved themselves into a small group of figures. Most were hunched and cowering, undoubtedly survivors of the Krygian onslaught. But towering above them, his massive frame unmistakable even in the dim light, stood Hardy. The ChronoBot's usually pristine chrome plating was now a patchwork of scrapes, dents, and what looked disturbingly like acid burns. His faceplate, typically a vibrant blue, now flickered weakly, barely visible beneath a layer of grime and battle damage.

Hardy's head swiveled towards me as I approached, his audio sensors apparently still functional despite the beating he'd taken. "Cap!" he called out, his voice carrying a strange mix of relief and... was that sarcasm? "I'm glad you decided to drop by. We were just about to start the party without you."

I bit back a sharp retort, uncertain if the robot was truly being a smartass or if this was just his way of coping with the nightmarish situation. Instead, I focused on what mattered most. "What's the situation, Hardy? Where's Laramie?"

Before the ChronoBot could respond, a raspy voice spoke up from the huddle of survivors. "She's under that fallen girder over there. Her helmet's the only thing that kept her from being crushed outright."

My heart leapt into my throat as I followed Hardy's gesture. Sure enough, about ten meters away lay a crumpled form pinned beneath a massive steel beam. Even from this distance, I could make out the unmistakable shape of a U.S. Space Navy combat helmet. The girder was lying diagonally across her body.

"Aubrey," I breathed, shouldering my way through the group of onlookers. My legs felt like lead as I crossed the short distance, each step bringing the grim reality of the situation into sharper focus.

I dropped to my knees beside Laramie's prone form

I could now see that the beam was making contact with her helmeted head, center sternum, and left hip. After taking in the dire situation, I immediately drew my eyes back up to her helmet.

Her faceplate was cracked, a spiderweb of fissures obscuring her features. But as I leaned in closer, I could see her eyes—open and alert, tracking my movement.

"Oh... hi, Captain," she managed, her voice weak but tinged with that trademark dry humor. "I was just thinking about you. Funny how a little near-death experience brings certain people to mind."

I tried to assess her injuries, but the combination of poor lighting and the girder's position made it nearly impossible. "We're going to get this thing off of you, Aubrey. Just hold on."

Her laugh was more of a pained wheeze. "You move that girder, and I'll die, Sir. You think I'm lying here like this because it's comfortable?"

I felt my brow furrow in confusion, a cold dread settling in the pit of my stomach. I looked up at Hardy, silently pleading for an explanation. The ChronoBot's faceplate flickered, a rare display of uncertainty from the usually unflappable machine.

"Cap," Hardy began, his voice uncharacteristically somber, "my sensors are pretty fried, but from what I can tell, that girder isn't just pinning her down. It's... it's acting like a cork in a bottle. The only thing keeping her insides from becoming outsides, if you catch my drift."

The full weight of the situation crashed down on me like a collapsing bulkhead. I looked back at Aubrey, really seeing her for the first time since I'd arrived. Her face was pale, beaded with sweat despite the hold's chill. But her eyes... those eyes still held that spark of defiance I'd come to admire.

"How bad?" I asked, my voice barely above a whisper.

Aubrey managed a weak smile. "Bad enough that I can feel my organs trying to rearrange themselves. It's not just the beam... turns out Krygian claws are pretty effective can openers when it comes to combat suits."

I glanced around at the carnage surrounding us, truly taking it in for the first time. Krygian corpses littered the deck, their chitinous bodies riddled with plasma burns and limbs twisted at impossible angles. "You did all this?" I asked, a mix of awe and horror in my voice.

"Had to keep the civvies safe somehow," she replied, her words punctuated by a wet cough.

I noticed the fleck of blood that appeared on her cracked faceplate.

"Wasn't about to let those oversized cockroaches use these people as a damn buffet."

Pride swelled in my chest, tempered by a growing sense of desperation. We couldn't lose her. Not like this. Not after everything we'd been through.

"Hardy," I barked, my mind racing. "Options. Give me something we can work with."

The ChronoBot's massive frame shifted, casting long shadows across the grimy deck. "Without proper medical equipment, our choices are limited, Cap. We could try to cut around the girder, take a chunk of the deck with us. But the risk of further injury or structural collapse is high."

"No," Aubrey interrupted, her voice weaker now. "You start cutting... the reverberation might cause this whole section to come down. There are still people trapped in here, civilian engineers working on...on something. We can't risk it."

I felt my fists clench, frustration and anger bubbling up inside me. "So what, we just leave you here? Like hell we will."

The hold seemed to close in around us, the fetid air growing thicker by the second. In the distance, I could hear the chittering of Krygians. They were regrouping, no doubt preparing for another assault. We were running out of time.

"Captain," Aubrey's voice was softer now, a hint of resignation creeping in. "You need to get these people out of here. That's the mission. That's what matters."

"No," I growled, leaning in close. "The mission is to get everyone out alive. That includes you, Petty Officer. I'm not leaving anyone behind, not now, not ever."

As if in response to my declaration, a distant explosion rocked the station. Dust and debris rained down from the overhead, and the emergency lights flickered ominously. The situation was deteriorating rapidly, and I knew we were out of time.

I activated my TAC-Band comms, praying they still worked in this nightmare. "Derrota, do you copy? We need an emergency evac—now! And get a doctor on standby in HealthBay. We've got a critical situation here."

Static crackled in my ear, then Derrota's voice came through, strained but clear. "Copy that, Galvin. But our power reserves are critically low. We might only have one shot at this."

Chapter 51

"Then make it count," I snarled, my voice urgent, razor-sharp. "Lock onto my signal and prep for a wide-area quansport. Hardy will forward a detailed sensor scan of our situation—the critically injured patient, the steel girder pinning her down, the deck plates beneath her... everything."

"Um... okay..." Derrota muttered.

"I want a triage area set up in a suitable hold, medical personnel on standby, every piece of equipment at the ready. We hit the ground running, understood?"

Derrota's voice crackled with static, tension evident even through the distortion. "Galvin, that's a tall order. We'll need time to—"

"You've got ten minutes." My voice left no room for debate. "Make it happen. Captain out."

I turned my attention back to Aubrey, her eyelids fluttering like wounded butterflies as she fought to maintain consciousness. The sight of her, usually so vibrant and full of life, now teetering on the brink of oblivion, sent a spike of icy fear through my gut.

"Hold on, Petty Officer," I commanded, infusing my voice

with all the authority I could muster. "That's an order. We're getting you out of here in a few minutes."

Even as the words left my mouth, doubt gnawed at me. Did she even have a few minutes left? I pushed the thought aside, grasping her hand in mine. Her skin felt like ice, lifeless and pale. I gave it a gentle squeeze, silently willing my strength into her.

A burst of animated conversation drew my attention. Hardy stood a few meters away, engaged in what appeared to be an enthusiastic discussion with one of the hostages. Irritation flared within me, hot and sudden.

"Hey!" I barked at the ChronoBot. "Show some damn respect. We have an injured—"

"Cap!" Hardy interrupted, his tone uncharacteristically excited. "It's him!"

I shifted my gaze to the unimpressive figure beside Hardy—a slightly pudgy, balding man who looked as out of place in this nightmare as a penguin in a desert. My patience, already stretched thin, threatened to snap.

"Who are you?" I demanded, not bothering to mask the irritation in my voice.

The man shuffled nervously. "Uh... hey there. I'm Bob. Bob Hardy."

For a moment, my brain refused to process the information. Then it clicked, and despite everything, I felt a smile tugging at my lips. "Hardy's... cousin? Bob Hardy?"

Bob's face scrunched up in confusion. "Super distant cousin but, yeah, I guess. Never thought people and robots could be related... you know, like family. But the more he talks about who he was back in Boston, his brother, his parents... yeah, that's pretty much my family tree. I'm into genealogy and stuff."

I nodded, attempting to maintain a semblance of politeness while silently willing Derrota to hurry the hell up. Now that

Bob mentioned it, I could see an uncanny resemblance to the digitized 3D avatar Hardy typically projected onto his faceplate.

"Bob and most of the other maintenance workers here have been on a prolonged strike," Hardy explained, a note of pride in his synthesized voice.

My attention snapped back to Bob, a new tension coiling in my gut. "A strike?"

"Bob's a member of the Intergalactic Freight Alliance Union," Hardy clarified, oblivious to the storm brewing within me.

The words hit me like a physical blow. I felt the hairs on the back of my neck stand on end, a cold fury building in my chest. "The same IFA Union that caused that hellstorm that brought us here in the first place? That union cargo ship that just happened to jut out of their dock just in time for *USS Roosevelt* to careen into them! The same *USS Roosevelt* that— not long after that—fucking exploded?!"

I surged to my feet, furious momentum reeling me toward Bob. All my pent-up anger, my thirst for vengeance, found a target in his wide, nervous eyes.

"Uh, look," Bob stammered, shrinking back. "I'm just the station's utility foreman. Basically, a glorified plumber. I'm sorry about your ship, Sir. Honest, I'd never hurt anyone."

The fear in his voice doused my rage like a bucket of ice water. Shame washed over me, and I took a step back. "No. I'm sorry. This has nothing to do with you." Guilt gnawed at me. Here Hardy had finally made a real connection with family, and I was treating the man like a criminal.

"You say you're a plumber?" I asked, attempting to smooth over the awkward moment. "I imagine that's a lot of responsibility for a space station of this size."

Relief flooded Bob's features. "You can say that again. The

fire suppression system alone is incredibly complicated. Piping that's a virtual circulatory system spanning thousands of miles and close to a million sprinkler heads..."

His words hit me like a bolt of lightning. "Stop!" I barked, raising my palms, my mind racing with sudden possibilities.

The union worker exchanged a nervous glance with Hardy. "Did I say something wrong?"

"No, Bob," I replied, a grim smile spreading across my face. "You may have just saved... humankind."

His jaw dropped open, confusion evident in his eyes.

"Bob," I pressed, urgency coloring my voice, "where exactly is the supply tank for the station's fire suppression system?"

"Uh... that would be two decks below this one. Close to the very bottom of the station, but I still don't understand..."

I was already tapping at my TAC-Band hailing Derrota.

"Yes, Galvin... we are hurrying as quick as we can—"

"Stephan!" I cut him off, my words tumbling out in a rush. "Listen to me. You mentioned you'd made up extra quantities of the DDT/Fryzite mixture."

"Yes," he replied, confusion evident in his voice. "Way more than would be needed. You know, it's hard to judge what will be utilized—"

"Stephan, just listen," I interrupted, a savage grin spreading across my face. "I think I've found an excellent means to utilize the rest of that wonderful concoction of yours."

As the plan crystallized in my mind, I felt a surge of hope, dark and desperate. We might just have a chance to turn this nightmare around, to strike a blow against the Krygian infestation that threatened to overwhelm us all. And it all hinged on a space station's plumbing and a glorified bug spray. The universe, it seemed, had a twisted sense of humor.

Chapter 52

I stumbled onto *Resilience's* bridge, my body screaming in protest with every step. The acrid stench of burnt circuitry and ozone assaulted my nostrils, a stark reminder of the recent hell that had transpired within these bulkheads. My combat suit was a mess of gouges, punctures, and scorch marks, dried blood caked around the gaping wound in my chest. I could feel the eyes of the bridgecrew on me as I moved forward, their collective gaze a mixture of relief and concern.

Pristy was seated at the captain's mount, her fingers working a small tablet.

"What the hell? Sonya's redirecting hack's no longer working?" Grimes asked.

"Nope," Pristy said all her attention locked onto the halo.

"I know you were saving our one remaining bowler for Varapin 1, but..." Blunderton let her words trail off as she nervously watched the fast-approaching cluster of missiles up on the halo display.

Inbound Missiles! Prepare for Impact in 69 seconds.

Pristy started to rise, but I waved her back down. "Stay put, XO," I managed, my voice hoarse from smoke and exhaustion. "You've kept this ship in one piece so far. No one's better suited to see it through."

"NELLA," Pristy said, her voice loud and commanding, "lock onto the centermost Varapin missile and fire our broadside cannon. Do it now!"

BOOM!

The big cannon's recoil sent tremors throughout the ship—something the barely held-together vessel could ill afford.

A massive explosion within the void jolted me to attention. Everyone waited, no one spoke. Then NELLA's voice filled the bridge.

Incoming missiles... Nullified.

A collective sigh swept across the bridge as if an invisible weight had been lifted from the crew.

"Nice job, everyone," I said knowing my words were less than adequate for what they had all been put through as of late.

I took up a position beside Pristy, occupying the space where Hardy usually stood. The ChronoBot's absence was a palpable void, another reminder of the cost of our mission. No, the ChronoBot was still among the living but had his hands full at the moment.

My gaze swept across the cosmic graveyard, concentric rings of debris stretching beyond the horizon of space. It was impossible to tell what mangled remnants were from what.

"SitRep, XO?" I asked, forcing myself to focus on the multiple halo displays before us. Local space had become a scrapyard, the void littered with the fragmented remains of warships. Residual sparks and small explosions continued to flicker in the darkness, like dying fireflies in an endless night.

I couldn't help but stare at Pristy, awestruck by what she'd accomplished in my absence. She met my gaze, a flicker of pride mixed with exhaustion in her eyes.

"All three Krygian dreads have been destroyed," she reported, her voice clipped and professional. "Along with two of the traitorous Varapin ships." She paused, taking a deep breath before continuing. "As I'm sure you're aware, *Resilience* has sustained heavy damage. Multiple decks are still venting atmosphere, though SWM is making headway on that front."

I nodded, processing the information. "And our offensive capabilities?"

Pristy's lips tightened into a grim line. "Weapons systems are pretty much kaput. Our four Off-Worlder powerplants are currently offline. With any luck, once they've had sufficient time to cool, we can bring them back up and maneuver for a proper firing solution."

"And the remaining Varapin warship?" I asked, my eyes scanning the displays for any sign of our traitorous 'allies'.

Pristy gestured to one of the halo feeds, where a lone, heavily damaged dreadnought sat motionless against the backdrop of stars. "That's your friend Toe's command ship. It's as heavily damaged as *Resilience*."

She frowned, frustration evident in her voice. "NELLA's sensors are mostly down, and without Hardy here, we're not exactly sure if they're totally without weaponry and propulsion, or just waiting for the perfect moment to strike. We're sitting ducks, Galvin. One or two more plasma strikes, and we're done."

I turned my attention to Roisin Blunderton—her ever present bird, Lucy, perched upon her shoulder. The Lieutenant was seated next to Paxton at the dual operations station.

"Have you reached out to Captain Toe?" I asked. "Seems like a good time for a mutually beneficial parlay, no?"

Blunderton exchanged a nervous glance with Pristy before shaking her head. "I didn't think that was an option..."

Pristy spoke up, her tone sharp with irritation. "We have different ideas on how to proceed. To be frank, I wanted that ship destroyed. We attempted to trust them once. Doing so again could put the final nail in this flying coffin."

I listened, nodding slowly as I weighed the options. The tension on the bridge was palpable, every crewmember acutely aware of how precarious our situation had become.

"We need to end this with the Varapin," I said finally, my voice low but firm. "We still have the Krygians to deal with." I turned back to Blunderton. "Hop back to your comms station and hail Captain Toe."

Blunderton hesitated for a moment, then nodded, moving quickly to comply. The bridge fell into an uneasy silence as we waited, broken only by the occasional beep of malfunctioning consoles and the soft murmur of Lucy repeating, "Incoming, Incoming," over and over.

After what felt like an eternity, the primary halo display flickered to life. Captain Skrinn Toe's hideous visage filled the screen, his skeletal features as unreadable as ever. I forced a bemused smile, though I couldn't tell if the hooded ghoul was returning the expression.

"I must commend you, Captain Toe, on a courageous battle today," I began, my tone carefully neutral. "As we were—you too were—combating two enemies with multiple opposing assets."

Toe's bony jaws and exposed white teeth chattered, a sound that sent shivers down my spine. "Spare me your false flattery, Quintos," he rasped. "What do you want?"

I leaned forward, ignoring the stab of pain from my chest wound. "I want to end this, Toe. We've both taken heavy losses.

The real enemy—the Krygians—are still out there, breeding and expanding even as we speak."

"And why should I care about your insect problem?" Toe's voice dripped with disdain. "My only concern is for my people, my ship."

"Because if we don't stop them now, there won't be a galaxy left for any of us to fight over," I shot back, my patience wearing thin. "Look, you know this to be true. The Krygians having shown up in Varapin space, you have to know... that's a foreshadowing of something far worse coming down the line."

Toe's hollow-socketed eyes glowed red like two hot embers—perhaps I had piqued his interest... though it was hard to tell with his alien features. "Go on," he said, a hint of curiosity creeping into his tone. "What do you want from me, Quintos?"

"Nothing. Just the opposite, in fact. I want you to leave this quadrant of space and keep going. I'll deal with... how did you phrase it, our insect problem? Go now. I swear no harm will come to you if you leave. But stay, and we'll have to destroy your ship and crew."

"Agreed," Toe growled, his skeletal features twisting into a grimace. "But make no mistake, Quintos. This ceasefire is temporary. Our battle isn't over—it's merely postponed. Honor demands we finish this."

"I'm good with that," I said, signaling Blunderton to cut the connection.

Pristy did not look pleased—I'd big-footed myself right into the middle of her command, doing exactly what I said I wasn't going to do.

She stood, splayed a hand toward the now open captain's mount, "Sit, your throne awaits you, Marcus Junius Brutus." Turning toward Tactical, a hand came up to cover her mouth—I saw the smile she was trying so hard to hide. It made my heart skip a beat just knowing we were still alright.

The auto-hatch to the bridge slid open with a hiss, revealing a flurry of activity. Sonya burst through first, her face flushed with exertion, followed closely by Derrota, his lab coat flapping behind him. Hardy's dull, stained form conveyed the hell-storm he'd survived as he strode in, with Bob, the union maintenance worker—Hardy's cousin—bringing up the rear. The group rushed toward us, their footsteps thudding urgently across the deck.

Now only one of Sonya's arms was in a sling and she looked to be well on her way toward recovering.

Eyeing me, she shook her head. "I thought Hardy looked bad, but you, Uncle Person, you look like shit."

"Thank you, but I'm sure I look better than I feel."

I placed a hand on Derrota's shoulder. "Tell me... Laramie. Is she—"

"She's resting comfortably within the confines of a regrow pod. Her injuries were substantial, but with a little luck and no further power outages, she should make a full recovery."

"That's excellent news. Thank you, Stephan... truly, I couldn't have taken another loss."

Hardy was at Tactical 2, tapping at the board, seeming frustrated.

"Tap any harder and you'll break the thing!" Pristy scolded. "Why don't you just ask for some help, robot."

"I got it, I got it..." Hardy said.

Five halo displays sputtered to life, their flickering screens stabilizing to reveal gloomy interior feeds. The shadowy images, presumably from within StarPoint Station, cast an eerie glow across the bridge.

"What am I looking at?" I asked.

But before anyone could answer, I saw each of the feeds was anything but static empty compartments—it was as if there was a flowing ocean of green insects—thousands upon thousands of Krygians rhythmically on the move.

"There's so many of them," I said. "Far more than we'd assessed. Did we ever find the Queen?"

Nobody said anything—the answer being a definitive no.

My niece had taken a seat at the captain's mount, her eyes yet to come away from her tablet.

"Um, so what are you doing, Sonya?" I asked.

Silence stretched between us. Her lips pursed as she stared at her tablet, her posture hunched. I suppressed a sigh, recalling the unwritten rules of teenage communication—their ability to provoke frustration served as its own twisted reward.

"Your idea..." Sonya said, "the one to use all that unused DDT mixture... pure genius."

I shot a glare at the ChronoBot, but Hardy looked away as if something important had captured his attention elsewhere.

"But an idea is just an idea," Sonya continued, "someone has to make it happen, put the wheels on the cart, so to speak."

Hardy rejoined the conversation. "Bob's been a big help, his indispensable knowledge of StarPoint's fire suppression system —invaluable."

"You asked what I'm doing," Sonya said, back working her tablet, "only configuring the pressurization algorithms for the altered liquid consistency that will soon be flowing through miles and miles and miles of pipe. Oh, and putting the entire fire suppression system into a long-running test mode... since there's no real fire taking place within the station."

I looked at Derrota. "How did we get the DDT/Fryzite mixture into the supply reservoir?"

"That was a fairly simple process. I quansported it over. Dumped the entirety of what we had in reserves into the reservoir. The mixture will be somewhat more diluted than what

Max and his team had been spraying, but I'm optimistic it will suffice."

We all looked at each other.

"What are we waiting for?" I asked. "No time like the present."

The union worker nodded. "The system's ready to go. No holdup on my end."

"Thank you, Bob," Sonya said with little sincerity. "But there are more than pipes and sprinkler heads needing my attention." She looked up and found Derrota's eyes.

Sonya twirled a lock of hair with her fingers. "Stephan, you said if you had time, and there was space, you'd let me bring back some of the less damaged elephants."

Derrota shifted his weight from foot to foot. "With close to five thousand StarPoint personnel now taking up residency on the Symbio Deck, it took me a while to find an adequate storage hold. Rest assured, Sonya, three of your magnificent elephant beasts are safely secured on Deck 3."

"Thank you, Stephan. That means a lot to me." Sonya's lips curled into a smirk. "Okay then, I guess that's it." She shifted her gaze to me, shoulders rising in a nonchalant shrug. "All we need now is for our illustrious Captain to give the word. One command that'll unleash unspeakable pain, carnage, and just maybe be the first step to wiping out a whole alien race."

My mind reeled with the staggering losses of the past few days. The destruction of *USS Roosevelt*, once a proud vessel, now reduced to the battered *Resilience*. But far worse was the toll on human life. Faces flashed before my eyes—crewmembers who had become more than colleagues, more than friends. They were family. Each loss carved a new wound in my heart, a stark reminder of the brutal cost of this escalating war with the Krygian Empire.

US Marines Sergeant, Wanda Sykes

USS Resilience

Commander "Con" Cornelius Strickland
Dr. Pippa Tangerie
Engineering & Propulsion Chief, Craig Porter
Engineering Supervisor, Kaelen Rivers
Communications Officer, John Chen
Lieutenant Commander Jorkins
Crewmember Davit
Ensign Lira
Crewmember Barrow
Crewmember Lindsay Soto

Additionally, it's mentioned that there were significant casualties among the crew, including most of the 1000+ U.S. Army Rangers stationed on Deck 6 and numerous unnamed crew members across various decks.

Everyone's eyes were now locked on me—my bridgecrew, Derrota, Sonya, Hardy, and even Bob.

Sonya handed me her tablet. "You can't miss it—the big, green button that says, PRESS HERE."

I pressed the big, green button.

Pristy rose from her station and made her way to my chair, perching on the armrest. She draped an arm around my shoulder, drawing me close. A sharp twinge from my chest wound elicited a wince, but I leaned into her comforting presence, nonetheless. Additional halo displays materialized in front of us, offering a bird's-eye view of the station's innards. The projections revealed dozens of feeds, sprawling corridors, winding passageways, and the three vast battlegrounds of Red Section. Purple Section's ravaged hatchery came into focus, along with numerous other areas, each telling its own tale of destruction and desperate struggle. What was most staggering were the vast quantities of insectile Krygian bodies always on the move—never not busy.

The first of the overhead sprinkler heads was now fountaining out a steady flow of water-like liquid. Liquid we all knew was far more caustic than good old H_2O. At first, the bugs seemed more curious than bothered by the sudden rain-like dousing. I sent a quick glance toward Derrota, who returned my look with a 'wait and see' expression.

Sonya took a step forward and leaned in. "Is that steam rising from..." Her words trailed off as we all watched in horror.

The feeds flickered with nightmarish images, each one a window into hell. Krygians writhed and contorted, their exoskeletons bubbling, as insecticide ate through chitin and flesh like acid. Thousands upon thousands of alien bodies twisted in agony, mandibles clicking in silent screams. The air itself seemed to sizzle. I could almost smell the stench of dissolving insectoid matter. There was no need for words—the devastation spoke for itself.

"We don't need to see any more of this," I said.

Pristy rose, heading for her station. With a few taps on her board, every halo display dissipated like smoke in a breeze.

Crewmember Grimes broke the dreadful silence.

"Our four Off-Worlders are coming back online, Captain. Should I set a course back to Earth?"

I looked to my crew. All heads nodded in solidarity.

"Yes, Mr. Grimes, maximum speed. Put as much distance between us and StarPoint Station as you can."

We hope you have enjoyed **USS Resilience - Honor the Fallen**, ***Book 11*** *of the* **USS Hamilton Series** *by Mark Wayne McGinnis. If you enjoyed this book, PLEASE leave a review on Amazon.com—it really helps! And to be notified the moment all future books are released, please join my mailing list.*

I hate spam and will never ever share your information. Jump to this link to sign up: http://eepurl.com/bs7M9r

Discover more of Mark's exciting novels on <u>Amazon.com</u>

And stay tuned! The next book in the USS Hamilton series in in the works.

Acknowledgments

First and foremost, I am grateful to the fans of my writing and their ongoing support for all my books. I'd like to thank my wife, Kim—she's my rock and is a crucial, loving component of my publishing business. I'd like to thank my mother, Lura Genz, for being a tireless cheerleader of my writing. Others who provided fantastic support include Lura & James Fischer, Sue Parr, Charles Duell, and Stuart Church.

Check out my other available titles on the page that follows About the Author.

About the Author

Mark grew up on both coasts, first in Westchester County, New York, and then in Westlake Village, California. Mark and his wife, Kim now live in Castle Rock, Colorado... with their two dogs, Sammi and Lilly.

Mark started as a corporate marketing manager and then fell into indie-filmmaking—Producing/Directing the popular Gaia docudrama, *Openings — The Search For Harry*.

For the last fifteen years, he's been writing full-time, and with over 40 top-selling novels under his belt, he has no plans on slowing down. Thanks for being part of his community!

Also by Mark Wayne McGinnis

Scrapyard Ship Series

Scrapyard Ship (Book 1)

HAB 12 (Book 2)

Space Vengeance (Book 3)

Realms of Time (Book 4)

Craing Dominion (Book 5

The Great Space (Book 6)

Call To Battle (Book 7)

Scrapyard Ship – Uprising

Mad Powers Series

Mad Powers (Book 1)

Deadly Powers (Book 2)

Lone Star Renegades

Star Watch Series

Star Watch (Book 1)

Ricket (Book 2)

Boomer (Book 3)

Glory for Sea and Space (Book 4)

Space Chase (Book 5)

Scrapyard LEGACY (Book 6)

The Simpleton Series

The Simpleton (Book 1)

The Simpleton Quest (Book 2)

Galaxy Man

Ship Wrecked Series

Ship Wrecked (Book 1)

Ship Wrecked II (Book 2)

Ship Wrecked III (Book 3)

Boy Gone

The Expanded Anniversary Edition

Cloudwalkers

The Hidden Ship

Guardian Ship

Gun Ship

HOVER

Heroes and Zombies

The Test Pilot's Wife

The Fallen Ship

The Fallen Ship: Rise of the Gia Rebellion (Book 1)

The Fallen Ship II (Book 2)

USS Hamilton Series

USS Hamilton: Ironhold Station (Book 1)

USS Hamilton: Miasma Burn (Book 2)

USS Hamilton: Broadsides (Book 3)

USS Hamilton: USS Jefferson – Charge of the Symbios (Book 4)

USS Hamilton: Starship Oblivion – Sanctuary Outpost (Book 5)

USS Hamilton: USS Adams – No Escape (Book 6)

USS Hamilton: USS Lincoln – Mercy Kill (Book 7)

USS Hamilton: USS Franklin - When Worlds Collide (Book 8)

USS Hamilton: USS Washington - The Black Ship (Book 9)

USS Hamilton: USS IKE – Quansport Ops (Book 10)

USS Hamilton: USS Resilience – Honor the Fallen (Book 11)

ChronoBot Chronicles

Made in the USA
Middletown, DE
22 September 2024